THOUGH THE
YOUNG REDWOOD GROWS

RICHARD THOMPSON

authorHOUSE®

AuthorHouse™
1663 Liberty Drive
Bloomington, IN 47403
www.authorhouse.com
Phone: 1 (800) 839-8640

Published by AuthorHouse 03/21/2019

ISBN: 978-1-7283-0388-8 (sc)
ISBN: 978-1-7283-0387-1 (e)

PROLOGUE

Jude wipes himself after unrolling a certain length of toilet paper. For over twenty minutes, he has been in that men's lavatory. That men's lavatory which is in the *Wax On* museum that him and his university classmates are being gave a tour of. The white roll of toilet paper goes through several revolutions, as Jude periodically tears off sheets to wipe his anus. He is defecating the hickory beef jerky that he ate several minutes prior to walking inside his classroom that morning at the university he attends: The Ergonomics School of Humanity. It takes Jude five wipes of the toilet paper to completely clean himself of the defecation.

After being a wiper Jude stands up then pulls his pants and boxers up from around his ankles, before turning around to raise his leg-the shoe on Jude's right foot comes down upon the toilet stool's handle. While the toilet stool is flushing, Jude walks out of the lavatory's stall. He walks towards one of the white porcelain sinks and uses his right hand to dispense soap out of the soap dispenser above it into the palm of his left hand. With a glob of soap in his left palm, Jude makes a fist on his right hand and brings it down atop of the sink's faucet knob. A constant spray of water bursts out of the sink's faucet the same way rainwater will burst out of a cloud. Jude cups his hands and pushes them into the spray of water. Jude then lathers soap on both of his hands, and starts scrubbing them. He does so for almost a minute before he looks up at his reflection in the sink's mirror in front of him. The reflection in the mirror is looked at by Jude and he again deceives himself into judging that he's a handsome fellow.

A handsome fellow that is twenty-years old, has a black pompadour, and is Filipino. Bifocals are invariably worn by that Filipino male who judges himself, no matter what people say, to be handsome. Despite the fact that his face is covered with acne. Acne started appearing on Jude's face when he was fourteen-years old. Slathering cream on his face is what Jude has been doing almost daily for the last six years of his life, yet the skin condition marked by inflammation of skin glands and hair follices remains on his face. Only four days have passed since Jude purchased a, to him, very very old videogame console from that pawnshop he went to. He purchased it so he could hone his craft in machinery by taking it apart it apart then studying all of it's components. The videogame console he bought was a *Super Nintendo*, and that pawnbroker who sold it to him fast-talked him into buying that videogame with it. Before Jude started taking apart the *Super Nintendo*, he played *Battletoads* for a few hours. He played that videogame created by a company named *Rare*. *Rare* was the first to develop *Battletoads* which is a videogame franchise that began with the original one for the *Super Nintendo* in the year of 1991. 1991 is in the twentieth century and Jude bought that *Battletoads* videogame for the *Super Nintendo* thirteen centuries after it came out since he exists in the thirty-third. *"He subliminally insulted me,"* Jude said to himself while the videogame controller was in his hand and before he selected one of the three playable characters on *Battletoads*. Jude said that because he saw that all three of the toads are named after skin conditions: Rash, Zitz and Pimple. He debated with himself on whether he should select the green toad whose name is Rash and whose trademark is sunglasses, the orange toad whose name is Pimple and has the trademark of arm bracelets, or Zitz who is the black toad who is wearing gauntlets which are his trademark.

The videogame controller remained being held in Jude's left hand as he used the fingers on his right hand to gently rub the "craters" on his right cheek, and he was doing that while deciding on which one of the three toads to select. Jude finally decided to select the big, muscular orange toad by the name of Pimples. He used Pimples to brezze through that initial *Battletoads* videogame which was renowned for it's difficulty-Jude easily reached the last stage of that game. He reached the last stage of that game whose main villain is a mystery ruler of evil and superior commander of a space army consisting of pigs and rats-pigs and rats who are controlled by a female villain bent on galactic conquest. An erection is what Jude possessed as he looked at the villain of that game: The Dark Queen. That wasn't avoidable because many gamers who played *Battletoads* have given her considerable attention due to her sex appeal and that was particulary during the early years of videogaming when she was the first major villain in a videogame. Jude stops looking at his reflection in the mirror, leans up from over the sink, and moves his hands to-and-fro as he walks to the paper towel dispenser. He unrolls several sheets of the brown paper towels, drys his hands, crumples the sheets into a wad, and drops the little mass into one of the lavatory's trash cans. With his hands completely dry, Jude walks back to the white porcelain sink he was just standing at. He looks at his reflection one more time. He looks at the fellow with intelligent eyes deeeply sunken into a face that looks as though it has been sculpted out of chopped meat and hastily decorated with hair. Looking at his image's reflection in the mirror Jude stops doing, and he walks out of the men's lavatory. He walks out of the lavatory into the darkened hallway of the museum.

All of the hallways and interior of the building is darkened because the management of the *Wax On* museum wants it that way-it is felt that a dismal atmosphere gives a certain air to all of the wax figures. As the lavatory's door is swinging back shut, Jude traverses through the hallway to his left. About ten seconds later he approaches the entrance to another room in the museum, but he doesn't walk through it. He doesn't walk through it because blocking it's entrance is the likeness of a Caucasian male whose side profile is seen by Jude. The Caucasian male that Jude sees is in a photographer's squat, held in his hands is a camera whose strap rests around his neck, and peering through the camera in his hands at an unseen object. Time passes by as Jude stands about twenty feet away from the khaki pants wearing Caucasian photographer whose short-sleeved collared t-shirt has the staple of a muumuu-Jude politely waits for the photographer to snap the picture so that he can proceed through the door. Almost a minute passes before Jude sees that no snap is forthcoming and he starts to become mentally frustrated. Jude isn't used to mental frustration-he has spent three years as a novice in a linguistic sect called Kowtowers whose members pride themselves on their complete and utter mental control in all categories of perception, and it isn't generally known by his colleagues at The Ergonomics School of Humanity that he enlisted in it.

Regardeless of it's contents the Kowtowers believes in the unheard-of and new age language of Geminga spitta speak since it gives spiritual insight to the brain of a multi-tasker. Gibberish, medley, jabberwocky-they are each basically addresses of the e-mail maliciously sent to the universal computer owned by the zealots of Geminga spitta speak. Geminga spitta speak is a language that consists of words, and sentences, that are spoken in a half-and-half method (those who can's speak the vaporing language of Geminga spitta speak consider it to be an off-the-wall language). The linguistics of Geminga spitta speak give their students an earful of their finesse as they regurgitate and daisy-chain words in their lessons. Since he pursued to learn it, Jude was mesmerized by the babel of Geminga spitta speak, that sounded like a third-dimensional knock-off of an incomprehensible foreign language to him. Actually mastering the lingua franca has been done by a small amount of the idiomatically bilingual teachers of it in the history of that cult whose teachers are single-minded and persnickety. Having had to be in contact with the paler nuances of mastery occasionally revealed through the acoustic learning process has been done by others besides Jude. Jude himself left the order after a few years of wading through the language-attaining perfect grades had become more difficult for him and the rewards became proportionally less tangible.

Moreover, he had been quite turned off by some of the intimate practices he would have to start performing to achieve them, and had been explicitly turned off by the spinster he would have to perform them with. Still, not for a moment does he regret his acquired knowledge of cheesepairing words in his brain, the central nervous system in his skull that is composed of neurons. The other reason why he doesn't is that Jude came away from his experience there with a sturdy capacity for mental discipline, not to mention a deep and abiding distrust of all things subjective. Jude becomes tired of waiting, and he starts to near the photographer. Jude nears the photographer who he starts to see is just a wax figure when gets up close to it.

"We are not amused," Jude says, peering closely at the wax figure.

"We are not amused at the trickery." Jude stops peering at the wax figure and he strolls past it into the hagiographic room of the *Wax On* museum, and he looks at the sights he sees in it.

Lining the walls to the left and right of him are wax figures of saints and religious teachers. Saints and religious teachers whose golden-hued images are suffused by the lighting in that room which Jude just entered. Bizarrely decorated religious murals are painted on the ceiling of that hagiography room. Jude raises his eyes to the mural that dominates the ceiling of it-God, in battle fatigues, stretching out Her hand and making contact with Adam's finger.

"Caviar to the general," Jude says, staring upwards at the mural with transcendental serenity.

Jude's radiant expression ends when he lowers his eyes, and continues walking through the capacious room. Along with being lined with wax figures, art work is painted on it's walls. Jude starts walking and looks at one painted on the left side of him. He stares stony-faced now at the bizzarely decorated religious mural that dominates the left wall: an apocalyptic scene of fat-cheeked angels blowing impossibly elongated trumpets, perched on top of tanks that are in the process of rolling over sinners. Jude shakes his head from left to right, stops looking at it, and proceeds to walk through the hagiography room. Towards the door that leads out of it he walks. Upon reaching it, Jude puts his hand on the door knob's handle. The door is opened by him, and he walks through it. Ahead Jude looks and he sees his classmates gathered in a group to the left of him. Towards them Jude starts walking, as the door he just walked through starts swinging back shut.

A jarring sound is what the door makes when it closes, and all of Jude's classmates turn around. They look at him as if he's an unexpected guest-or perhaps a very large insect. As if that is what they're all looking at, Jude himself turns around and looks at the door. Jude looks at it for a second then turns back around and exhibits to them all a shrug. Every person in the tour group except for one collectively turn back around-Jude starts walking to the Black female who remains looking at him. Jude nears the Black female whose body is still partially turned around in his direction, and she sidesteps to her right when he gets closer so he can stands beside her in the tour group.

"You know, Jude, I'd always thought the Peter Principle was a myth until I met you," the Black Female says.

"What's that?"

"A myth is a traditional story serving to explain some phenomena or custom," interferes a tall albino teen standing on the other side of the Black female, who hadn't taken her eyes off of Jude since his re-entry into the tour group.

"I know that!" Jude protests.

"The Peter Principle states than an individual shall rise in the hierarchy to the level of his incompetence," says an eavesdropper standing in front of Jude. Jude turns back to the Black female and nods thoughtfully.

"Hmmm. That makes perfect sense, but I fail to see what it has to do with me."

The Black female sighs in exasperation, then turns to face the speaking *Wax On* tour guide. Jude does the same after he shakes his head with the motion of someone resigning himself for a long, long day at work.

"The wax statue that you all are looking at now is in the likeness of Annie Oakley," the woman tour director says, raising her arms oratorically towards the wax figure of a diminutive White female wearing a historically accurate dress and cowboy hat.

"Annie Oakley was an American sharpshooter who was born in the year 1860. Tiny in stature and cute as a button, Annie led the charge against any bad man that came in contact with her hometown of Diablo."

Jude looks at the wax figure of Annie Oakley, and sees long black curly hair reaching to her shoulders underneath the cowboy hat that she is wearing. The tour director continues, "As you all can see here"-she points to the weapon whose butt touches the ground as Annie is holding its shaft up with one hand-"she is holding the weapon which brought her worldwide fame. Her markmanship with a rifle-laser rifles didn't exist in her era-is why she was called Little

Sure Shot by the famous Sioux Indian chief by the name of Sitting Bull.

Annie Oakley could hit a dime in the air and a cigarette held in her husband's lips. She was fond of displaying her skill by having a playing card tossed in the air and shooting it full of holes before it fell. Annie Oakley was only five feet tall which is why she was called Little Sure Shot by sitting Bull. Her fame as a markswoman led to a contest in Cincinnati with Frank E. Butler, a noted marksman and vaudeville performer-she defeated him by one point. He fell in love with her and several years later they were married." The Black female turns to Jude.

"If you were living during the Wild West Time, would you have married such a masculine woman like Annie Oakley?" As a machinist very new to adulthood, it doesn't yet occur to Jude to lie openly-only to bend the truth a little.

"Program all the sexism out of a culture; rewrite laws and books and languages; still you cannot escape the fact that western culture has hunted for the form of woman since Plato laid about with little boys."

"You can never give a straightforward answer," the Black female says to Jude, before turning back to the *Wax On* tour guide. Jude too turns back to the tour guide and hears her say "-which is why she died in the year 1926," before she starts slowly walking away from the wax figure of Annie Oakley while motioning for the group to follow her.

"Legends have sprung up about her," the tour guide says, leading them towards the next wax figure.

"Future generations may transform her, as past generations transformed Vlad the Impaler into Count Dracula. This next wax figure"-she stops and sweeps her arm towards it- "is a movie star who acted in roles for movies which came out in the twentieth first century; to be specific, the ridiculously campy *Dracula 2000*."

Jude looks at the wax figure and he sees an apparently wet Caucasian, evidently damp is his short brown hair and apparently soaked is his black underwear and tweed plaid shirt that he is wearing half-buttoned, whose scraggly facial hair is neatly groomed; he then looks back at the tour director. While continuing to hold her arm swept at the wax figure, the woman tour director says, "This world-trekking, ATV-riding, Romanian model-dating Scotsman by the name of Gerard Butler-no relation to Annie Oakley's hubby-courted danger at every turn during his lifetime. Gerard Butler's acting career was vaulted after he auditioned for a role in the movie titled *300*; it was his first big break. Breakers are surfed by Gerard Butler whose likeness right here is taken from how he looked on the set of a big-wave surf drama he acted in. During a filming of it, Butler almost lost his life. He almost lost his life in *Chasing Mavericks* when he was caught in what surfers call a two-wave hold down. The wave forced him so deep so fast that he couldn't get back to the surface before the second one hit him-he was trapped underwater for nearly a minute. Luckily, he survived. He survived to continue portraying a real-life surf guru, at the time the movie first came out, by the name of Rick "Frosty" Hesson. Gerard Butler, while acting as "Frosty", teaches his pupil about surfing and life while training him to tackle the deadly wave known as Mavericks. Mavericks was the name of a legendarily huge northern California break, and Frosty's pupil-Jay Moriarity-was believed to be the youngest person to ride it. Jay Moriarity was a surf prodigy who paddled onto the Mavericks' and jumped to his feet while the wave's face went vertical-at the age of sixteen. A photo of him is seen on the cover of the May 1995 *Surfer* magazine -yes, I know that the photo is over thitreen centuries old-and on it he is seen posed for a spill while riding the Mavericks', affirming it's reputation as a big-wave mecca." The tour director turns to the tour group.

"Butler's performance in *Chasing Mavericks* is a tearjerker. He was one of those movie stars who became famous relatively late in life-he skyrocketed onto the A-List at the age of 37-however, he seemed ten thousand more times appreciative of it. Anybody have any questions?"

The tall albino teen raises his hand while saying, "I do," and the tour guide director acknowledges him. "What other movies besides *Dracula 2000*, *300*, and *Chasing Mavericks* did Gerard Butler act in?" the tall albino teen asks.

"He also acted in a romantic comedy titled *The Ugly Truth*," the tour guide director says. Oh, glitch! Jude thinks to himself. Turning towards Jude the tall albino teen does and he jests, "I wish I inspired the name of a movie like you did," while smiling mockingly at Jude.

"I know," Jude says complacently.

"Yet do not feel humiliated, for comparing the beauty of me to that of you is absurd as comparing the brilliance of a star with that of a luminous fungus."

The Black female works hard to keep a straight face. Jude is almost supernaturally ugly, and his bifocals only increase the effect. Turning back towards the tour guide director looking at him is what the tall teen albino does, before Jude and the Black female do the same. Taking her eyes off of him the tour guide does and she says to the group, "Are there any more questions?"

"Yes," the Black female says, raising her hand then being pointed at.

"I know the persona of many thirty-third century movie stars, but I don't know the persona of none during his day. What kind did Gerard Butler have?"

"That's a good question," the tour guide director says.

"And another one that I can answer. Gerard Butler had a persona and duality in his movies that won him a fan base which cutted genders and age groups while simultaneously earning him pretty much zero critical props. His, excuse my profanity, why-the-hell-not optimism made him utterly and lovably up for anything. He once told an interviewer a story of when him and a friend were riding motorcycles in Arkansas. Butler said that he lost his keys and had to be rescued by some Harley riding evangelists. Butler's exact words were 'I was very close to joing a Christian bike gang'."

Starting to walk away from the wax figure is what the tour director starts doing and she says, "Now if you all will follow me to our next wax figure," before the group follows behind her.

"As I said earlier in reference to Annie Oakley," the tour guide director says, nearing the wax figure.

"Legends have sprung up about her. Future generations may transform her, as past generations transformed Vlad the Impaler into Count Dracula."

Motioning towards a ghastly wax figure with her arms is what the tour director does, and Jude looks at it. Before his eyes he sees a macabre sight-a macabre sight with pasty white skin, two deep-socketed eyes which looked blackened and a mouthful of fanged teeth that look as if they belong in a shark's. Standing at an invisible turntable while scratching the invisible records on it as it's hands are crossed is the ghastly wax figure's prim, statuesque pose. Along with wearing a voluminous solid black sleeveless garment hanging from it's neck over it's shoulder's, two trickles of red blood are seen to be running down it's chin-it's chin that is part of a death-like face with a very pronounced forehead emphasizing the receding hairline it has. "Count Dracula," the tour guide director begins, "is the main character of *Dracula* which was a novel first published in 1897, and it was written by Irish author Bram Stoker. His novel is the most famous vampire story of all time. The main character in *Dracula* is this guy."-she points to the ghastly wax figure- "And he is a wicked nobleman who is said to be a vampire-a corpse that returns to life at night to suck people's blood. In the novel Count Dracula is said to reside in Transylvania, a region of Romania. Does anybody have any questions so far?" Standing not far from Jude is a White female wearing gothic clothing, and she raises her hand. "I do," the White female wearing gothic clothing says. Turning towards her the tour director does.

"Go ahead. What's your question?"

"Why do the vampires I see in movies sleep in coffins?" the White female wearing gothic clothing asks.

"Why do the vampires you see in movies sleep in coffins?" the tour director repeats, before thinking about the question.

"Sorry, but I have no clue why they sleep in coffins. I can't tell you why they are sometimes portrayed as sleeping in coffins but I can tell you why certain rebels"-the tour guide director scrutinizes the White female wearing gothic clothing-" dress in all black clothing and are named Goths.

The tour guide director takes her eyes off of the White Gothic female and stares out at the entire group.

"The real definition is entirely different. Originally a Goth was a member of a Germanic people that early in the Christian era over ran the Roman Empire. Many centuries passed after the Roman Empire crumbled, before the introduction of the famous Count Dracula-a vampire-who lived in the country of Romania. Romania is composed of the word Roman, and I may be going out on a limb by saying this but Goths"-the tour director looks at the White female wearing Gothic clothing-"such as yourself are named that because Goths impersonate Dracula and his clothing's color since it was the original Goths that conquered the Romans. They conquered the category of humankind whose race's name is found in the country of Romania. Does anyone here know what language the Romans spoke?" Jude raises his hand and the tour guide director points at him.

"They spoke the dead language of Latin. I'm also proficient in that language."

"Oh?" the tour guide director says.

"Say a phrase in Latin for us all." Jude clears his throat and says, "Vade retro Satana. That means 'Step back, Satan' in English."

"I didn't know that," the tour guide director says.

"I learn something new everyday."-she looks away from Jude- "Moving on, women accused of being witches during the century which was said to have existed was burned alive for worshiping the Devil. Witches and vampires, those who pratice vampirism are both by-products of the Devil."

"So you're saying that Goths worship the Devil also?" Jude asks.

"I'm not saying that so-called Goths do," the tour director says.

"In your words, all I'm saying is "-the tour guide director turns to the White female-"'Vade retro Santana'". Murderously, the White female wearing gothic clothing turns her head and looks at Jude. She glowers at him for a few seconds.

"You set the stage for her to say that to me," the White female wearing Gothic clothing says.

"I'm sorry," Jude says.

"I wasn't implying that you worship the Devil."

"Maybe you work for him." A low voice from somewhere in the group says contemptously, "Shit." No one else interrupts her. The tour guide director breaks their stare at each other and gets the entire group's attention by saying, "Students. May I continue? As I was saying the fictional Count Dracula of Transylvania is based on vampire legends that probably arose from hundreds of savage murders committed in the 1400's by Vlad Tepes.

Vlad Tepes was a cruel prince from a region south of Transylvania named Wallachia. In the novel, Dracula's search for new victims leads him to England. It is there in England that he pursues two young women by the name of Lucy Westenna and Mina Murray. Not too long later, Mina's fiancée and an authority on vampires both hunt Dracula. They overtake his body"-the tour guide director again sweeps her arm to the wax figure- "while it is on it's way to his castle and drive a stake through his heart. They drive it through his heart and end the count's nocturnal days. Dracula is killed by Mina's fiancée and the authority on vampires." The Black girl raises her hand and says, "I've never read the book. What's the authority on vampire's name?"

"I'm glad that you asked that," the tour guide director says, "and I was just about to tell everyone his name.

The authority on vampires who helped killed Dracula was Abraham Van Helsing. And Abraham Van Helsing has the same first name as"-the tour guide director starts walking away from the wax figure of Dracula and motions towards the students to follow her- "our next wax figure." Towards the wax figure Jude walks, and he stops upon getting ten feet away from it. The wax figure with a hairless upper lip, thick beard, and seated before him in a chair is one of the truly great men of all time. One of the truly great men of all time that happened to be the sixteenth president of the United States.

"Our next wax figure that you all are looking at," the tour guide director says, "was the sixteenth president of the United States, and his name is Abraham Lincoln.

Abraham Lincoln is one of America's finding fathers. Abraham Lincoln didn't bring glimmer and glamour to the White House as one of America's greatest and most courageous leaders-but, what he did do was something that really mattered. Before I get to that however, I'll reveal what he was as a child. Abraham Lincoln was a dirt farmer's son determined to make something of himself. He was a dirt farmer's son but that didn't stop him from becoming a lawyer. A lawyer who rose in politics-and his rise in politics was highlighted by his election campaign that led him to the White House. A woman whose first name whose name was

Mary was Lincoln's wife during his time in it. In contrast to Abraham Lincoln's parentage, Mary Todd was the daugther of wealthy southern aristocrats. That itself could have stopped the two from getting married, but it didn't. That didn't stop the two of them from getting married, and the fact that she was the daugther of slave owners also didn't. Any questions so far?" The tour guide director scans the crowd and receives no response.

"Okay," the tour guide director says, then looking back at the seated wax figure of Abraham Lincoln.

"There's a saying 'Match made in heaven', and Abraham Lincoln's marriage to Mary proves that matches really are made in heaven. Mary Todd supported her husband-Abraham Lincoln, who is sometimes referred to as the Great Emancipator-as he led the United States during the Civil War. Fought between the years of 1861 and 1865 was the Civil War which was the greatest crisis in the United States' history. It was the greatest crisis in the United States' history because the country went to war with itself. The South half of America was composed of bigoted Whites, and the North was composed of ones who weren't. Abraham Lincoln was the president of the United States during America's most destructive, and defining, conflict. Strongly opposing the servitude of others, he helped end slavery in the United States. He helped end slavery in the Unites States and helped keep the American union from splitting apart during the war." Jude raises his hand and the tour guide director points at him.

"Yes?" Jude asks, "So America had to divide itself to become one?"

"Yes," the tour guide director says.

"America had to divide itself to become one'; which is sad. But, it's not as sad as what happened to Abraham Lincoln. It happened during the same year that the Civil War ended. On the evening of April 15th, 1865 Lincoln attended a performance at Ford's Theatre in the state of Washington. A few minutes after ten o'clock, a shot rang through the crowded house. A shot rang through the crowded house because one of the best known actors of the day-John Wilkes Booth-had shot the president in the head from the rear of the presidential box. Once shooting the president Booth leapt to the stage and fell and broke his leg after catching his spur in a flag draped in front of the box. He broke his leg but that didn't stop him from limping across the stage while brandishing a dagger and crying something."-the tour guide director turns and looks at Jude- "Jude, do you know what it was that John Wilkes Booth said?" Jude pushes his bifocals up on his nose.

"Yes I do."

A few seconds passes before the tour guide director says, "Well, what did he say?" Jude looks at the tall albino teen standing by the opposite shoulder of the Black female in between them then back at the tour guide director.

"I believe he said the motto of Virginia: 'Sic semper tyrannis'."

"Correct," the tour guide director says, looking back into the group in its entirety.

"'Sic semper tyrannis is what John Wilkes Booth said while limping across the stage in Ford's Theatre, and 'Sic semper tyrannis' is a Latin phrase that means 'Thus always to tyrants'. I do not believe that America's heroic and transcendent president was a tyrant. John Wilkes

Booth did, which is why he caused Lincoln to be the first U.S. president to be assassinated. Several quotations from Abraham Lincoln"-the tour guide director looks back at the wax figure of him- "are 'He who would be no slave must be content to have no slave'. 'Those who deny freedoms to others deserve it not to themselves, and under a just God, cannot long retain it'. Another quotation from him is 'I claim not to have controlled events, but confess plainly that events have controlled me'." Turning back towards the group the tour guide director does. "Hodgenville Kentucky was Lincoln's birthplace and he was born in a log cabin there. Being born in a log cabin played a role probably in why Lincoln was said to say"-the tour director starts slowly walking away from the wax figure and she motions for the group to follow her-"'To be well prepared is important in so much of life. If I had eight hours to chop down a tree, I'd spend six sharpening my axe'."

The tour guide director stops in front of a strapping wax figure hoisting an axe that is slung over its right shoulder and held in its right hand while its left foot rests on top of a tree stump. Propped on the stooping wax figure's left thigh, the thigh on its leg connected to the foot resting on the tree stump, is its left hand. A red flannel shirt and blue jeans are the clothing on the strapping wax figure. Sweeping her arms towards the stooping wax figure the tour guide director does and she says, "This last wax figure on our tour knew a thing or two about axes. The statue that you all are looking at is none other than Paul Bunyan. Unlike Abraham Lincoln, Paul Bunyan wasn't a real person. On the contrary he was just the opposite. Paul Bunyan was a mythical hero of the lumber camps in the American northwest. He was a hero there because of what he was: A giant superlumberjack. Due to the limited room in here"-the tour guide director sweeps her surroundings with her eyes-"we had to incorrectly make Paul Bunyan's wax figure on a much smaller scale." Returning her eyes to the group the tour guide director does.

"We had to incorrectly make Paul Bunyan's wax figure on a much smaller scale, but none of the things that he did were small. The giant superlumberjack was credited with digging the St. Lawrence River and Puget Sound."

The Black female raises her hand and says, "Excuse me miss?" before being pointed to.

"Go ahead young lady," the female tour guide director says, pointing at her.

"What is Puget Sound?" the Black female asks.

"I've never heard of it." The tour guide director says, "I think the more fitting question would be 'Where is Puget Sound?'"-The tour guide director prepares herself to answer bluntly- "Puget Sound is at the arm of the north Pacific sea and it is west of Washington."

"Okay." "Excavating the Grand Canyon is another thing that Paul Bunyan is said to have done," the tour guide director says, looking at the entire group.

"Folklore has it that he was the one who created the Grand Canyon. Folklorists say that it was a mere man who hollowed out all those mountains situated near each other, and created that colossal gorge in the state of Arizona." Facing the wax figure of Paul Bunyan the tour guide director does.

"Another famous myth is Bunyan's discovery of the blue ox. We don't have a wax figure of Babe, his blue ox, and Babe is said to be 'Twice as big as all outdoors and playful as a hurricane'. There's a classic tale about Paul's pancake griddle. The tale says that it was so large that skaters had to tie sides of bacon to their shoes to grease it." Jude doesn't understand this. Food to him is fuel, nothing more.

"Were his logs big too?" calls out someone, or something, from the rear of the crowd.

"Logs like the ones Jude just dumped in the bathroom about twenty minutes ago?"

Laughter erupts from the group, and Jude looks around to see who said that but he can't find out. Once the laughter dies down and everybody turns back to the tour guide director, Jude looks at the Black female. She is looking back at him.

"I don't like class clowns," the Black female says.

"Everybody boo-boos sometimes."

"You're right," Jude says.

About ten seconds passes by while the two of them just look each other without speaking, while the tour guide director continues talking about Paul Bunyan. Out of the blue, the Black female asks Jude, "Did you buy a new motherboard?"

"No," Jude says.

"Why you didn't buy a new one?"

He raises his lifeless eyes over the Black female's head to start, "Can't scrounge up the money-folks don't wanna inshare, and I sure as hell ain't gonna deb for it myself."

"Oh," the Black female says, before turning to look at the tour guide director. Jude does the same and he catches the beginning of her next sentence.

"The stories about Paul Bunyan are a mixture of oral folklore tradition and conscious literary work. Today Paul

Bunyan essentially personifies the American genius for inventing the means of doing jobs required."

Those words are heard by the Black female who turns to look at Jude. She sees him looking at the tree stump that the superlumberjack's foot is pressing down on. She sees him looking at it with a vacant look in his eyes. His flat face holds no more expression than wood in an idol's.

CHAPTER 1

Man must work in order to live. Work has made almost everything used in living. Carried to homes and factories is coal used for heating homes and driving engines. Cutting, drilling, riveting, and made is what has to be done to steel for buildings and bridges. Grown or made, woven into cloth, sewed into clothes, and transported is what to be done for material for clothing. Harvested, transported, and processed is what has to be done for crops; the crops that come from soil that has to be plowed and seeded in order to grow food. To help do all of that work man has invented many kinds of machines. Each of them are a source of power.

The power is showed today-in the year 3217-by engines, motors, and turbines. Atomic, jet rocket, electric, diesel, gasoline, gas, steam, or water power can be used. Ran by hand are some of the machines but most of them need a large amount of power to do work. Man's only power-at the dawn of history-was his own muscles. To build pyramids for the pharoahs, Egyptian slaves spent their lives digging stones-ancient Egypt was just one of the large slaveholding nations that developed in that way. One group of men was sometimes enslaved by another group of men, and they forced them to work. It took many men a long time to move a rock or tree. It took the White man over a thousand years to learn to use the power of animals to do work. Doing heavy work such as grinding grain or pumping water out of mines was done by oxens and horses-oxens and horses also pulled wagons and plowed fields for the White man. All races of men made rafts to carry cargo.

Logs floated downstream from the power in rivers. Nature holds another kind of power. Nature is able to make fire, and fire gives off heat. About thirty-two thousand years ago, it was found out that heat can power an engine. I think it was a White man named Thomas Newcomen that invented a pratical steam engine in 1712. His steam engine wasn't too small to pump water out of coal mines. It wasn't too small to do that but it used too much fuel. Fuel that is used to make power. Power of wind was learned to be used by men. They used the power of wind to sail boats. I'm not a oarsman but I can guess how tiring rowing can be. Rowing no longer had to be done by oarsmans, and Black slaves, after the power of wind was found. Grinding grain and pumping water is what can be done by wind that turn windmills. Windmills nowadays are sort of rare, but some can still be seen in the Netherlands.

The Netherlands that is a constitutional monarchy, and often called Holland. I see a large rock ahead of me as I'm pedaling. I slow down my bike, approach the rock, and stop before picking it up. Hefty is what it is. After moving it up and down with my hand, I hurl it into the nearby bushes. A rock that size shouldn't have been laying in the middle of the trail like that. I get back on my bike, raise the kickstand, and return to pedaling. I return back to thinking about Holland. Holland's principle language is Dutch I know, and I've read that the country is crowded. That's probably why the most popular vehicle there are bicycles like this one I'm riding on. I continue pedaling through the recreational area of Toad Island. I took the short trail behind that log cabin, into a old coniferous forest that has managed to survive clear-cutting throughout the thirtieth century. Those thick arching ferns and spreading canopy of branches cast everything in a sun-spotted gloom. Ahead of me I see two Toad Island campers. They are both by their bikes that have their kickstands down, and I slow down as I approach them.

"Good morning campers," I say, stopping my bike and putting both of my feet down on the paved road.

"Good morning," the old White man says, standing up over his bike's seat as his left hand rests on the bike's handlebars. His feet are close to each other, and his right hand rests on his hip.

"I was just showing my granddaughter here"-he nods towards the little girl standing by her little bike- "what to never touch." I look at the little girl and I see that she is also wearing a bicycle helmet like her granddad. She is wearing a long, lime-green t-shirt over a Day-Glo orange t-shirt, pulled down over baggy blue shorts. The sparse sunlight, in the sun-spotted gloom, makes all of the colors so bright that I feel like shielding my eyes as I look at her.

"Hello there, little one," I say, looking at the little girl.

"That's a pretty bike you got there. Where did you get it?"

"Santa gave it to me," the little girl says.

"He gave it to me for Christmas."

"Oh, he did?" I say, smiling at her.

"Did he give you that helmet"-I glance at her helmet-"too?" The little girl says, "No. My grandpa gave it to me last week." I look at her grandpa and ask him, "What were you telling her never to touch?" The old man points to his left.

"Those right there. I told her that she should never touch those, because she can get a rash if she do."

I look at the poison ivy on the tree that he is pointing to. Out the corner of my eye I see the little girl stop looking at me and also turn towards the tree, wrapped by a crimson-flowered vine that is slowly and beautifully strangling a tree.

"You're right," I say, looking at the tree.

"Poison ivy can be harmful to touch."-I turn to the little girl- "Never touch those types of leaves, because you'll start scratching if you do." The child turns her eyes up to me, disturbingly adult eyes: She can't be no more than six-years-old. And she says: "I won't. What's your name?"

"Marshall," I say.

"Oh," the little girl says.

"Do you work here Marshall?"

"Yes," I say.

"I've worked here for about a year."

"That's a long time," the little girl says.

"What do you do here?"

The kid is an information sponge, a black hole for knowledge. She knows next to nothing about the world and anything I can tell her is a major new discovery. The little girl looks on me as a font for learning. I have three kids of my own and they think I'm the greatest guy walking this Earth. Kind of nice. Makes me want to live up to their expectations.

"Foresters like me do many things," I say, smiling at her.

"Foresters manage and protect forests and woodlands. We maintain campsites and recreation areas like this one."-I take one hand off the handlebar and sweep it into the air- "We decide which trees to cut for timber. That's just to name a few of the things."

"Oh," the little girl says.

"Do all foresters wear Toad Island shirts like the one you're wearing?"

"Yes," I say, looking down at the emblem on the left shoulder of my grey collared shirt.

"This right here"-I pinch the grey fabric around it and pull the emblem up- "is on all the shirts of all the ones that work here." The old man looks at me and chuckles.

"She's a curious little rascal ain't she?"-The old man turns to the cute schoolgirl- "Let's hurry up and get on back, Andy. I'm sure you want to do some more coloring on your new desk." The old man looks at me and says, "I had a tiny desk built for her," before the two of them raise their kickstands and ride off. I look at them as they ride off. I imagine a six-year-old with a desk. Does she have a tiny secretary? What's a six-year-old's billing rate? They can no longer be seen as they ride off into the distance, so I turn around and return to riding my own bike. Wind blows past me as I pump the pedals on my bike. I look down at my black short pants as I am then back up. Back up at the trail before me. This certain trail doesn't wrap around the whole park like that other one, but is traveled often by visitors. And it is scenic. I slow my zippy bike down, stop, and look to my right-to the tree lining. Trees are what I see of course. In front of the trees I see foilage. And greenery on top of greenery. To the untrained eye, that mass of leaves there can pass as a wax myrtle. You know that large, fragrant evergreen shrub. The wax myrtle that is found along the eastern coast of the United States. It grows as far west as Texas, but it's more common in southern New Jersey to southern Florida-I know it also grows in the West Indies. That shrubbery there is made up of leaves that are covered with brown dots. Just like the wax myrtle. Those leaves have brown dots just like the wax myrtle, but since it's full grown it doesn't have the height of one.

A wax myrtle can grow up to thirty five feet, and that mass of leaves there doesn't look to be ten feet. I also saw a wax myrtle in that store, since it also grows as an ornamental. Also grown as an ornamental like that gingko tree I bought. That woman told me that gingko trees are desirable ornaments because of their handsome foilage and their resistance to insects, so the price I paid was a bargain. She also told me that gingko trees in nature commonly attain heights of sixty to eighty feet. That's tall. It's not that tall, but still impressive. More impressive than that other thing about gingko trees she told me before selling it to me. She told me that the gingko tree is native to China and Japan and apparently escaped extinction through cultivation in temple gardens.

Apparently escaped. Her choice of words must mean something, but I don't know what. I'm glad I bought a female gingko tree, since fruit is only produced by the female trees. She told me that a plumlike structure about one inch in diameter with a large, silvery pit will grow fruit in them-I'll be eating plumlike structures soon. I hope that they're juicy. And mouthwatering. And....What's another word to describe the juiciness of fruit? Oh yeah, and succulent. The professor at that forestry college I went to for four years used the second defintion of succulent. He said, "Forestry is the science of managing forest resources for human benefit" and "Forests need much more tending to than deserts. The deserts that grow cacti and aloes-both are succulents-in their arid environments". I take my eyes off of the shrubbery, and look to my right then to my left. I then rub my right hand up and down my left arm while sitting on my bike.

The forest isn't arid like a desert, so it's kind of chilly. It's probably because of my clothing-short black pants and a short sleeved collared grey shirt and the morning hour that I'm lacking warmth. It could be either of those reasons, the fact that I'm under a canopy of tree leaves, or something else entirely. Returning to bicycling through the trail I do. Again wind starts to whip past me, and the helmet on my head, as I ride. As I am, I look to my left this time. I again see trees and greenery on top of greenery blowing by. The dark green blur continues for about half a minute, before I slow down. I slow down while continuing to look to my left. A bird air dives into the branches of a tree I'm looking at. I stop completely, and squint into the top branches of that tree. Squinting a lil harder, I see the outline of the bird that just landed in it. It's now settled into a nest I guess it built. I move closer to the tree to get a better look at the bird, while craning my neck upwards.

That bird I'm looking at looks like it's a cedar waxwing. It must be because of its plumage and because of its secondary flight feathers that have little bright red waxy-looking projections on its tips. I don't have 20/20 vision like my real Dad that is in the Air Force, but from here I can also see a band of yellow across the end of its tail. Yep, that's definitely a cedar waxwing. Let me get closer to it. As I'm sitting on it, I shuffle my bike towards the tree. While I'm still looking upwards. Whistling is what the cedar waxwing sound like its doing. Whistling since it can't sing. Only produce a soft, high-pitched whistle. I continue listening to the shrill clear sound of the cedar waxwing. Its voice is feeble and lisping. That chirping sounds nothing like the chirp of a sparrow. It sounds weaker even though waxwings are larger than them. That waxwing up there not only have red wax like drops on its wing feathers, but it's sitting in a nest that from here looks bulky.

There might be three to five pale bluish or purplish grey eggs in it. And if there are they'll be speckled with black, purple, or brown. Brown. I look down at my arm and its color. I'm a dark brown. Too dark probably, but that's alright with me. Back up at the nest I look, and I see the cedar waxwing shoot back off out of its nest. It shoots back off while flapping its feathers. Featherbedding. I'm lucky to have this position at Toad Island, because if it wasn't for featherbedding, I wouldn't have it. I'd probably still be driving trucks, or a night-shift manager at Waste-That-Little. Sure the salary I was paid off-set the hours, but I still didn't like having to work the graveyard shift. While everybody was out at night doing their thing, I was walking around in a grocery store and managing the stockers in it.

With this job, that I went to four years of college for, I can enjoy the nightlife like everyone else. I can enjoy it, and work during the day like a normal person would. There is no downsize to working a nine-to-five job. A nine-to-five job that allows me to do what I love. Driving trucks and managing others is fun, but it's nowhere near as fun as forestry. I'd rather be bicycling through a forest at ten o'clock in the morning and getting paid to do so, than sit up high in a truck any day. Driving truck's for the birds. What kind of birds? Cedar waxwings. I look at the bird until I can't see it no more-I then get completely back on the paved trail, and return to riding my bicycle. As I'm pedaling, I look down at my right clenched fist on the handlebar. I hope this wart growing on the back of my middle finger goes away soon. This hard, rough growth has been on the back of my hand too long. It's a harmless tumor on the outer layer of my skin, but I still hope that it goes away.

Warts are caused by viruses and occurs most frequently in children, so why do I have one? I'm glad that it's at least on the back of my finger, and not somewhere else. That dermatologist on tv said that warts may appear in many shapes, sizes, and places. And that they even appear on the lips or the tongue. He also said 'Although warts can arise almost anywhere on the body they are most common on the fingers, forearms, and palms'. I take my right hand off of the handlebar as I'm pedaling, and look closely at my palm. Nope. There aren't any warts there. I do the same thing with my left hand. There also aren't any warts. I bend a turn on the trail then I go back to looking at the wart on the back of the middle finger on my clenched right hand. They say warts disappear spontaneously, but in many cases must be removed. If I have to, I'll remove it by freezing it with dry ice. Hopefully that'll work. If it doesn't-if the wart's stubborn-then I'll have to get a doctor to use an electric needle on it or do surgical removal.

X-Ray treatment is also an effective method of removal. One thing I know I won't do is scratch it open. Warts have viruses-and the virus of a scratched open wart may spread by contact to another part of the body or to another person.

A person that might be superstitious. Superstitious people think that touching the skin of a toad will cause warts, but that's not true-contrary to superstition, touching the skin of a toad will not cause warts. Most warts disappear by the time a person reaches age twenty. I'm twenty-four so I shouldn't have this wart. I feel as young as twenty, as exuberant as a boy experiencing first love, as strong as a Mesklivite ox. Animals can get warts and the viruses in animal warts don't infect people, just like the warts that people have can't infect animals. The human wart virus can't infect animals.

Animals like a Mesklivite Ox. A Mesklivite Ox is an animal just like a giraffe. One of my daughter's favorite animals is a giraffe, so I know a lot about them. Giraffes are the tallest of all mammals, and the males attain about fifteen feet in total height. The top of their heads are usually at fifteen feet, and their shoulders usually reach nine feet. And they usually weigh around fifteen hundred pounds. 'Warts can even appear on the tongue', so many warts can appear on a giraffe's tongue. Many warts can appear on it since a giraffe's tongue is seventeen inches long. They use their long tongues to wrap around and pluck off the fruits on many species of trees. Their favorite tree to browse on is an acacia I think. The fruits of an acacia tree are ate by giraffes and some of those types of trees are hundreds of miles from water.

Giraffes are sometimes found hundreds of miles from water and it's very likely that they never need to drink, since their food is high in water content. Reaching down to the water bottle holder on my bike is what I do, before pulling out the plastic water bottle in it. My legs continue pumping on the bicycle pedals while I lean my neck back and squirt water into my mouth. I put the water bottle back into the holder after I squirt a stream of water into my mouth. I'm riding along the path when a sight ahead of me catches my eye. I see a frog leaping onto the trail, from the forest it emerged from, and it leaps a few feet before stopping. It stops right in the middle of the road, so I slow down then completely stop as I near it. *Oh hell no!* I start backing up on my bike as soon as I get closer to it. That brilliantly colored, emaciated-looking frog there is an arrow poison frog. It's red and black body is a dead giveaway. Those types of frogs are highly poisonous, because their skin glands secrete a powerful poison. I continue backing my bike up until I'm well over ten feet away from it. I continue looking at the black and red poison arrow frog, and it strangely just sit there.

Sits there in the middle of the road. My job is to supervise the camping and picnic areas, and protect the visitors in it. What if that little girl-Andy-run across this frog and picks it up? She would be poisoned and probably fatally poisoned. Her, her grandpa, or anybody else can run across it. One of my jobs is to make this forest safe, and that's what I'm about to do. I get off of my bike, lower the kickstand on it, and start walking to my right towards the edge of the road. I see a large rock that I pick up-both of my hands are needed and used to pick it up. With the large rock in my hand, I start wobbling towards the arrow poison frog-the arrow poison frog just sitting in the middle of the road. As I get closer to it, I raise the large rock over my head.

I prepare to squash the vile thing, and as I'm bringing the large rock down it hops away. It hops away across the road into the forest on the other side of the road. I quickly pick back up the large rock and run after it. I follow it as it goes about forty feet inside the forest and stops-it stops onto the surface of a boulder. I brush aside leaves with my shoulder as I creep to it. When I get a few feet away from it, I again raise the large rock over my head. This time, I move so very slowly as I inch towards it. My shadow finally overshadows the arrow poison frog and I mash the gas-I forcefully bring down the large rock and a geyser of blood spurts out of the arrow poison frog. I see its leg move for a few seconds, before the soft pulpy mass stops moving entirely. Smiling to myself I do, and I start walking out of the heavily forested area back to the paved trail. While I'm walking out of it, I didn't realize I ran this far into the area. Stepping on and through all types of things I do. An unknown giant lumbering through web after fragile web of biological universes is what I am, and it's alarming enough to note the enormous effect my mere passage has on the forest. Studying the deep bed of moist leaves I do as I'm walking over it. Crushing a world is done every step I take.

Covering an ax blade will be a panicky swarm of ants after I chop a log for firewood. A warm, slumbering black salamander finds himself in the middle of winter and scuttles off after I move a stump in the way. A frog jumps after I kick a rock. Rustling of leaves and the faint snap of a twig catches my attention, before I emerge back onto the paved trail. Getting back on my bike is what I do, before raising its kickstand off of the ground-I return back to riding my bicycle. If I didn't kill that poison arrow frog, it would have poisoned a camper. That's how I feel.

Savagely, the savage behavior I displayed back there is pushed to the back of my mind. It's pushed to the back of my mind, as I continue to ride my bicycle. I start whistling while I'm cycling. I whistle a song, one I hadn't played or even thought of since childhood. While I'm whistling, I look towards my left-trees blow by, and so do shrubbery. I stop pedaling after about five minutes, and stop completely. I reach down to the bike's water bottle holder and pull out the water bottle-squirts of water are squirted into my mouth. I'm not thirsty, but it's essential to stay hydrated. That's why I'm posted in the middle of the trail, squirting water from a water bottle in my mouth. A chirping sound goes into my ears as I am. I look around but it's hard to figure out where the sound is coming from, because of all the foilage.

The chirping sounds continues and it gets louder. I look to my left then to my right. It sounds like it's coming from over there. I walk towards my right, near the trees, then squint into the tree branches. I squint and move closer to them for about a minute before I see the source of the chirping: An eastern whip-poor-will. I don't know much about eastern whip-poor-wills, but I do know that those types of birds are closely related to those birds that sort of look like frogs. Those birds that are called frogmouths. I know that frogmouths are any of a family of nocturnal birds found in Australia, the Solomon Islands, the Philippines and in Southeast Asia from India through Malaysia and Indonesia. I also know that frogmouths are nine to twenty one inches long, and have large tufts of powder-down feathers on each side of their butts. They're called frogmouths because they have large, forward-looking eyes, enormous froglike mouths, hooved bills, short legs, and small feet.

Mottled grey and brown is the color of their soft plumage. Unlike a frogmouth, I don't sleep during the day-I can't sleep during the day since I have this job. A frogmouth in the Philippines, or anywhere else, during the day will be sleeping. It'll be sleeping while perched lengthwise on a limb. A brown branch is what species of frogmouths resemble after they are disturbed on the limb, because they assume an erect position with their eyes shut and their bills pointed upward. What was it they are again? Oh yeah, frogmouths are primarily insect eaters that occasionally flutter down on frogs, mice, and small birds. Birds build nests like the frogmouths do, but a frogmouth's nest is a flimsy platform of sticks laid on a horizontal tree fork. Frogmouths nest are either that or a padded mat of down feathers, lichens and cobwebs. I know what feathers are-feathers are those light horny outgrowths that form the external covering of a bird's body. And I know what cobwebs are-cobwebs are threads spun by a spider. But I don't know what lichens are. Maybe you know what they are, my unknown, would-be, nonexistent reader.

CHAPTER 2

I pull my Ford Taurus up to the corner of a quiet cul-de-sac of stone-built houses. A right turn is made into it and I pull my car up to my house in Blacksmith's End-Blacksmith's End is a very quiet and suburban neighborhood with manicured lawns at the front and lace curtains at the windows-and turn off the ignition. I get out of my car, and close the car door back. Towards my mailbox I walk under the afternoon sun. I see four pieces of mail in it before I take them out. With the mail in my hand, I start walking towards my house. As I'm walking I look across the street towards my right-at the house over there. There is a meticulously polished car parked outside and inside its owner, an ageless ever frank African-American by the the name of Sherman Barkham, the judge. I thought of myself as being jinxed when I found out that I rented a house close to a judge. I have already stayed too long in Blacksmith's End, not that anyone is looking for me. Having the skeletons like the ones I have hiding in my closet means that you can never settle down.

For openers, I was dodging the brother of a female whose child I claimed on my income tax return. No money was gave to me because the entire return was garnished-garnished because of child support money I owed. And I have even more damning skeletons than that. I step up my front porch steps, approach then open my screen door, and insert my key into the front door. I walk into my house and close the door back. Further into my spacious three bedroom house I walk, before plopping down on my sofa in the living room-in front of my sofa there is a long vulwood coffee table, and a single book is placed there; on the purple of the vulwood tabletop. I shuffle through the four pieces of mail in my hand. My baby-mama. My other baby-mama. This one is also from my baby-mama. The last piece of mail I look at is a flyer full of coupons for the Waste-That-Little grocery store. Looking at the coupons reminds me of that experience I had when I was in the first grade and I thought that that was the most embarassing moment in my life.

Working two and three jobs at the time is what my Mom did when I was a kid; she didn't want us to become statistics. She was a young, single Mother with us and she didn't want to be one raising her children on welfare. But before she started working so hard she had to be on welfare, and I remember when I was in the grocery store with her when one of my classmates got in line behind us. When it was our turn to get checked out, I wanted to disappear when my Mom pulled out all those books of food stamps to pay for the grocery bill-the entire class knew I was on food stamps by the time I got to school the next morning. Those jokes followed me all the way through elementary. I swore to do whatever it takes to stay off of welfare because of that day, which is why I've never received government assistance. I stop remembering that embarrassing day, and I put the coupon flyer down on my vulwood coffee table. Remaining in my hand are the three other pieces of mail, and they are each from my baby-mamas. I decide to read the letter from my oldest daugther's momma first, so I sit the other two envelopes down on the tabletop by the coupon flyer and book already on it. Ripping the envelope open from Roz I do, before I pull out the letter in it. I start reading it:

Marshall,

I got a letter from you today and I debated should I write you back. As you can see I've decided to. I read your letter and it brought tears of anger to my eyes. For me, all of this is deja vu because someone has once again taken advantage of my innocence and that someone is you. My appreciation for you had long ago turned into contempt. I looked at a picture of you earlier and I hate the sight of you. I hate the sight of you and the sound of your voice makes me sick to my stomach. You are the root of all evil in my eyes. You were once my Prince Charming. You was all that I had ever wanted, but the reality is, we would never be together. It is impossible for us to reconnect, after all that has happened. Things would never go back to the way they used to be. I'm tired of crying. I have no more tears left. I also have no more love for you left, and even if I do have just a lil bit of love for you the closest image I can ascribe to it is the metaphor being french-kissed by a frog, you know those green creatures with all those warts and boils on their tongues. I don't even give a fuck anymore. Once you've fucked one, you've fucked 'em all. I've accepted the fact that this is my life. As far as I'm concerned, you could be laying dead in an alley somewhere.

Roz

I finish reading the letter, but I keep it in my hand as I stare at it while shaking my head from left to right. I stop staring at it, put it down on the vulwood coffee table, and pick up the envelope from the second girl I impregnated. I hold Deidre's letter in my hand, rip open the envelope, take the letter out, and sit the envelope back down on the tabletop. Leaning forward off of the sofa is what I do as I put both of my elbows on my knees. I start reading the letter in my hand:

Marshall,

I called your house phone and cell phone several times. Since you aren't picking up neither one of them, I'm forced to write this letter. You're a bitch you know that? You're a bitch just like all those other times I've called you one. You treat me like shit, but you bow down and suck up to the White man. You're more than a bitch; you're a punk bitch. I call them like I see them. Gone ahead and admit that you're one of them house niggas. You'll pick up a lasergun and aim it at another Black man, but you'll throw that bitch down and put ya hands up when the White man comes around. You're a coward and a quitter. A real built-to-last nigga you ain't. You ain't shit when it really comes down to it. Quick with ya mouth, big bad man, tough with a lasergun. You ain't shit without it. I know your type, and I know you. You're about the only man I have ever loved. It was the night that you decided to keep your promise to me and stand by my side and be there for me that my entire life changed for the worse. My high school sweetheart promised to take care of me. You said you wouldn't let anything happen to me before getting me up out of the hood. But look at me now. Not only am I still in the hood, but you're not here for me.

Deidre

After reading Deidre's name I pick up the envelope it came in off of my vulwood coffee table, and put the letter back in it. I then put the envelope back down on the tabletop, before picking up Chamiqua's letter-the envelope her letter came in is picked up and I tear it open. The letter is pulled out, the envelope it came in is sat back on the tabletop, and I lean back on my sofa with it in my hand. I close my eyes and pinch the bridge of my nose; that is done before I open them back and sit up and start reading it:

Marshall,

Please help me. What did I do to deserve losing you? You are my everything, my reason for breathing. You don't want me anymore and you don't even want to see me, but why? Really why? Life hurts so bad, Marshall. It hurts. I know I did this to myself so I'm not looking for a pity party, and I don't want to have to go into the whole situation again, but I couldn't stop him from feasting on me since I was wearing a crotchless camisole that gave him full access. I know myself but I would have never imagined knowing another person better. Before you, I didn't love. God bless my life when She brought you into it. I probably don't deserve a seond chance, you have the choice to forgive me, after causing the crowd to go crazy? I'm no longer stripping because I really want you back. Everything about Bikini Beach turns me off. The no-class-having-ass bitches, the broke corn-ball ass niggas, my nostrils being filled with the smell of weed every night, everything, including the atmosphere. The atmosphere there is like being stuck having dinner with that dung-worshipping cartoon character Toquag as he's attempting to have a philosophically profound discussion while all he wants to talk about are the different types of dung from all across the galaxy. The very last night I worked there was like Toquaq asking me for a dung sample and telling me he'll taste mines if I taste his'. The only thing I want to taste are your lips again. Those lips that felt like orange slices in my mouth. Yours are the sexiest lips I've ever came across. And you had the most dreamy brownish-green eyes that a girl can ever imagine. I loved it when you sat between my legs while I braided your long hair and stared up at me with those damn emeralds you call eyes. I'm getting wet just thinking about how fine and cute you are. I want to be mad at you forever. But this deep-seated love I have for you outweighs every other emotion. It even outweighs the suffering Marshall, but spare me. I'm pleading with you.

Chamiqua

Crumpling up Chamiqua's letter is what I do after I finish reading it. The wad of paper is thrown down on my vulwood coffee table, before I violently lean back on the sofa then stretch out on it to lay supine. I look at the circulating ceiling fan as I'm laying down on the couch. Laying down on the couch and thinking about my failed relationships. I'm a good man who's steady and reliable, but somewhere along the line I'd missed out on the essential ingredient for managing a woman: Don't ever, ever for even a second, disregard the fact that when you associate with a woman that you're associating with a being that is generally only somewhat a complex child suffering from delusions of grandeur. Adhering to that principle I didn't do, so now here I am alone and by myself. If I forgive Chamiqua and let her come back, I won't be alone and by myself. But I forgave her cheating ass before, so the shame won't be on me since I won't let her fool me twice. My first stepdad, Yee, is really the one to blame for my problems with women. When Yee chose to make a home with her, my Mom thought she was the luckiest woman in the world. They were together for about two years after they were married. Yee left me, my lil brother, and my Mom when I was eight years old-I never knew what happened.

All of his things were gone I saw when I came home from school that day. My Mom's only reply was, "He left," when I asked her where Yee was at. I hated Yee for leaving us until I was about twelve years old. Without ever saying good-bye he did, and I wondered how he could just pick up and leave like that. Blaming myself for Yee leaving, I spent hours in my room alone. Severed and weak is how the relationship with my Mom became-it used to be closeknit and healthy. My Mom decided it would be a good idea to tell me the truth about Yee to pull me out of my sleeping funk of depression. She didn't want to wait before it became too late to even mend our own relationship. I immediately shifted my hate from Yee to my Mom when she told me that Yee didn't just up and leave, because she put him out and ordered him to never come back. Why would she do such a thing went through my head?

Disrespecting her by cursing and yelling I started doing. The full reason why she did so is what she then saw she had to do. Explaining to me that Yee had used her and us to paint an image in order to cover up who he really was. On the inside he truly desired men, while on the outside he looked like the typical husband and father. My Mom put Yee out and told him that she would expose him for who he really was if he ever came around her or her sons. The only thing that came to my mind was that how people that didn't know about Yee would always tell me how I am just like Yee, how I kind of look just like Yee and how when I grow up, I was probably going to be just like Yee-I thought of all that after finding out he was homosexual.

The last person I wanted to be like was Yee, after hearing the bomb my Mom had dropped on me. I felt I had to do everything possible to prove myself as a real man after that day, because I didn't want to be some soft-ass punk buried in a man's body like Yee. I began getting into trouble after acting out and acting hard to prove I wasn't a sissy. I hooked up with the hardest cats in school. To prove I liked girls and not men I went through girls one after another. Impregnating my three baby-mamas was just another way of proving my manhood: Control and power was had over them. Messing me up in my head in more ways than one is what Yee's lifestyle did to me, and that is why he's the one to blame for my problems with women. Air is blown out of my mouth as I sit back up on my sofa. I put my right hand to my face and slide it downward. After doing that, I lean forward and pick up the fixture that's always on my vulwood coffee table. Sherman Barkham, the judge that lives across the street, gave it to me and Chamiqua as a housewarming gift a few months ago when we first moved into this house.

At first we thought it was an off-the-wall housewarming gift, because of it's author's unrelatable tragedy, until we read the whole book together-she read it out loud that night while sitting up as the two of us were in bed. I hold *The Other Side of Suffering*, the book the judge gave me, up in front of my face. On its cover I see a picture of a white-haired Caucasian who looks to be at peace with himself, and his name is John Ramsey. John Ramsey is the author of this book I'm holding in my hand, and he's the father of that little girl who was brutally murdered thirteen centuries ago in 1996. The little girl's name was JonBenet Ramsey and her bludgeoned body with a cord wrapped around her neck was found by her Dad in the basement of their home. He found her six hours after a ransom note was found on the stairs of his home.

The ransom note said that JonBenet Ramsey had been kidnapped and all of that happened just a day after Christmas. A day after the holiday that kids love, look forward to, and find special. More special than that holiday when they get dressed up in costumes. Costumes that are worn at a preschool costume party, and a photo of JonBenet Ramsey at her preschool costume party is one of the pictures in the pages of this book in my hand. Wearing a lei, a tattered yellow skirt that resembles a grass skirt, and a flower in her hair is what the smiling JonBenet Ramsey is doing in the photo. A wave of nausea hits me while I stare at the cover of *The Other Side of Suffering*-I can't relate to the ordeal John Ramsey went through but I know his pain was tenfold. Instead of opening it, I put the book back down on the vulwood coffee table. I do that because I'm not only angry at the killer, all child-killers, but I'm also angry at myself. Angry at myself for being the next thing to a dead-beat Dad to my daughters. I feel awful. On top of feeling awful I feel angry with everything for being as it is that I get up to walk to a wall. I punch the wall and then I feel so childish that I begin to laugh. Many seconds pass before I stop laughing.

My laughter stops, before I walk towards then in my bedroom. On top of my bedroom dresser there are a few sheets of blank notebook paper, and I pick up two of them. With the two pieces of blank notebook paper in my hand, I walk back out of my bedroom. I walk out of my bedroom into the kitchen. Next to the toaster on one of my kitchen counters there is a cup with pencils and pens in it. I walk towards it, take out a pen, then walk towards the dining area; sitting down at the dining table I do after getting to it. The two pieces of blank notebook paper is sat on the tabletop in front of me. Biting down on the butt of the pen is what I do while deciding how I should start what I'm about to write. A decision is made and I start writing. I begin the letter:

Darkling,

Confusedly is how I look at the word I just wrote because I feel that it isn't spelled right. A few seconds pass before it dawns on me. I misspelled Darling, and while penmanship might be somewhat out of my control, I'll accept damnation before I'll accept less than excellence in the things I can control. Shuffling the blank piece of notebook paper on top of this paper with Darkling wrote on it I do, before I start lowering my pen to it. Right before I start writing the first word on it, my house phone begins ringing. I get up, walk towards my kitchen, hear my house phone ring a second time, and pick it up right after it does. I look at the caller ID on my house phone receiver before answering.

"Fuck you calling my house for, nigga?"

"Just chill, Marshall," the voice says.

"Were you expecting someone else?"

"No," I smile.

"I'm not expecting nobody, but you gonna have to hurry up, 'cause I'm writing a letter."

"Damn it's like that?"

"Yeah," I say.

"What do you want?" "You already know how I get down," the voice says.

"Yo, let's go to Sanskirt Hospital and see that White ho that's up there."

"How does she look Chester?" I ask.

"She's a dime piece," Chester says.

"A dime piece that's just a little skinny." I ask, "How skinny?" Chester pauses before answering.

"Whitney Houston skinny. She's Whitney Houston skinny, but she's a freak. You want to see the freak don't you?"

"Yeah, come on, let's do the damn thing," I debut, feeling nothing but open-mindedness.

CHAPTER 3

Nearing Sanskirt Hospital, I have no problem finding a parking space. After I open my door, I step out of my grey Ford Taurus. Chester begins to also get out of it just as I'm closing my door. Chester rises out of my car, looks at me, and says, "Smelt like he had a skunk in a headlock," then grins. He grins at me, silver teeth like the grill of a '57 Chevy. It never ceases to amaze me that someone would do something like that to himself on purpose-on the other hand, I've seen some piercings and other body modifications that make Chester's teeth look like tattooed biceps. His upper teeth that he always cover with tinfoil makes him... memorable.

"I know I'm not funky," I say, raising my arm to sniff it.

Chester closes his door, sits his hat and both of his elbows on the roof of my car, and pats down the grey do-rag on his head; that do-rag which covers his short unkempt hair but not his sideburn tufts.

"They did say something about a heat wave on tv," Chester says, before he stops patting the do-rag to look at me.

"You shouldn't have worn that long-sleeved black shirt."

We stare at each other over the top of my car. Chester is tall. I'm five feet ten inches and he has me by a few inches.

But then, he may well weigh less than 150 pounds. Chester stands perfectly erect, his rigid posture and skinny body makes him look like one of the outer limbs of an old oak tree. He has brown eyes as focused and intense as sapphire lasers. If his eyes were lasers, I'd have been fried and grilled. After a moment of silence, I change the subject by saying, "Let's go."

Chester put backs on his hat and follows me into Sanskirt Hospital. Chester, meanwhile, walks as a zombie must walk. X-Ray Treatment is connected to the main building of Sanskirt Hospital. I grasp the brass handle of the massive front door, open it, and Chester follows me into the lobby. Stepping into the waiting room with its plush carpet and tapestry-upholstered chairs, we are treated to a spectacle neither of us had been prepared to see.

"I am not going to be put off!" shouts an old woman with a lot of make-up on her face. She looks to be a woman in her fifties or sixties.

"Mrs. Winegardner," says the startled receptionist.

"Please!" The receptionist is cowering behind her desk chair.

"Don't Mrs. Winegardner me!" the old woman shouts.

"This is the third time I've come in here for my records! I want them now!"

I see the cosmeticized bad-tempered old woman's hand shoot out and sweep the top of the receptionist's desk clean. Pens, papers, picture frames, and coffee mugs crash to the floor along with the jolting shatter of glass and pottery. I wince at the sound of breaking glass. Stunned by the outburst, the dozen or so patients in the waiting room freeze in their chairs. Afraid to acknowledge the scene being carried out before their eyes is done by some of them, because their eyes are trained on the magazine before them. My initial response to the situation is to don't get involved. When I see Mrs. Winegardner make a move around the desk, I fear she's about to attack the poor receptionist. I shoot forward and catch Mrs. Winegardner from behind, with speed, as I'm gripping her waist. Hoping to sound commanding and at the same time soothing I say, "Calm down."

The gray-haired woman far advanced in years twists around-as if she was expecting such interference-and swings her sizable Burberry purse in a wide arc. It hits me on the side of my face, splitting my lip. The blow does not dislodge my grip, so Mrs. Winegardner cocks her arm for yet another swing of the purse. I'm aware of the second blow in the making which is why I let go of her wrist and smother her arms in a bear hug. She hits me again, but this time with a clenched fist before I can get a good grip. I'm surprised by the blow and say, "Ahhh!" Mrs. Winegardner is pushed away.

Fleeing to the other side of the room is done by the woman that had been sitting in the area. I eye the old woman whose features are covered with make-up suspiciously, while massaging my shoulder that she punched. Mrs. Winegardner looks at me and she snarls, "Get out of my way. This doesn't involve you."

"It does now," I snap.

The door to the outside bursts open as two doctors dash in. A uniformed guard is behind them, and he has an X-Ray Treatment patch on his sleeve. All three of them go directly to Mrs. Winegardner. The shorter of the two doctors says, "Heloise, what on earth has gotten into you?" in a soothing voice.

"This is no way to behave, no matter how you may be feeling."

"I want my records," Mrs. Winegardner says. "I get the runaround everytime I come in here. I want my records. They are mine."

"No, they are not," the shorter doctor calmly corrects.

"They are the X-Ray Treatment's records. We know that machinable treatment can be stressful, and we even know that on occasion patients displace their frustrations on the doctors and the technicians who are trying to help them. We can understand if you are unhappy. We've even told you that if you want to go elsewhere, we will be happy to forward your records to your new physician. That's our policy. If your physician wants to give you the records, that's his decision. The sanctity of our records has always been one of our prized attributes."

"I can hire a lawyer who knows my rights," Mrs. Winegardner says.

"Even lawyers can occassionally be mistaken," the shorter doctor says with a smile. The taller doctor nods in agreement.

"You are welcome to view your records. Why don't you come with me and we'll let you read over the whole thing. Maybe that will make you feel better."

Tears begin to stream down Mrs. Winegardner's face and she says, "Why wasn't that oppurtunity offered to me originally? I told the receptionist I had serious questions about my condition, the first time I came here about my records. Suggesting I would be allowed to read my records was never done."

The shorter doctor says, "It was an oversight. I apologize for my staff if such an alternative wasn't discussed. We'll send around a memo to avoid future problems. Meanwhile, we will take you upstairs and let you read everything. Please."

Holding out his hand is done by the doctor. While covering her eyes, Mrs. Winegardner allows herself to be led from the room by the other doctor and the guard. The shorter of the two doctors turns to the people in the room. "The facility would like to apologize for the little incident," he says as he straightens his long white coat. He turns to the receptionist, says something to her, then walks towards me.

"I'm terribly sorry," the doctor says as he eyes my cut. It's still bleeding, but it has slowed down a bit.

"I'm okay," I say, rubbing my shoulder.

"It's not too bad."

"You might need a stitch, or a butterfly," the doctor says, tipping my head back to get a better view of my lip.

"Come on, I'll take you." I pull away from him and say, "I'm okay."-I turn to Chester- "Come on."

I motion my hand to the door leading outside, and start walking to it. After opening the door leading outside and walking out of it, I walk with Chester into the overhead walkway connecting X-Ray Treatment to the main building of Sanskirt Hospital. Chester takes out his cell phone and says, "I'm finna call this ho," as the door shuts behind him. I look at Chester as he's looking down, him and I are both walking slowly through the walkway, at his cell phone and dialing a number on it.

"What's her name again?" I ask, walking besides him. Chester briefly looks up at me and says, "Allison," before looking back down. Chester and I walk through the overhead walkway for about ten seconds before Chester holds the cell phone to his ear. More seconds pass as he walks while waiting for Allison to pick up.

"We here," Chester says into his cell phone, looking at me. I hear murmuring come out of Chester's cell phone. Chester takes his eyes off of me.

"What floor are you on?"-a few seconds pass- "Okay. Me and Marshall are about to get on the elevator now." Pressing the END button on his cell phone, putting it back into his pocket, then turning to me is what I see Chester do.

"What floor did she say she was on?" I ask Chester.

"The second floor." Before pressing the UP button on it, Chester leads me to the elevator. The elevator door opens up, Chester and I step into it, and the door closes behind us. The elevator arrives on the second floor and we step out of it. We walk out into a glass-enclosed walkway, as Chester takes out his cell phone again. Chester dials her number again.

"We're on the second floor Allison."-seconds pass and he peers at the directory on the side of the elevator's door- "The arrow pointing to my right says rooms 501-590 and the other one-" I see Chester stop talking, and he listens for a second or two before hanging up. Chester puts the cellphone in his pocket and looks at me.

"She said she's standing outside room 519-her Mom's room-and she's about to walk out here."

Nodding at him is what I do, before he and I start to pace up and down the glass-enclosed walkway. Our pacing ends after about a minute, when a shout is heard behind the both of our backs.

"Chester!" Chester and I turn around and I see an approaching White girl in her early teens. A skinny, rail-thin, coltish teenage White girl that is wearing glasses. She stops in front of me and Chester.

"Allison, hello," Chester says shakily. Allison directs all of her attention to Chester. "I take it you're Chester."

"That's me," Chester says. "And this"-Chester jerks his thumb towards me- "is Marshall." Allison looks at me and pushes her glasses higher on her nose.

"Marshal? As in fire marshal?"

"Yeah," I say.

"But there's two L's at the end instead of one. You're a skinny girl. Don't you know you gotta eat?" Chester adds, "And not just cotton candy." Towards Chester Allison turns and she says, "I eat more than just cotton candy; besides, I don't like cotton candy." "What do you like?" Chester asks, smirking. She looks at both of us with fond exasperation.

"Oh, you two guys." I'm looking at Allison and she has one of those rich-monkey-Chelsea faces, but the first thing I noticed about her were her eyes. Eyes so huge there isn't hardly room for anything else on her face. Since I'm falling into them I feel that I'll be staring all the way around the universe at the short hairs on the nape of my neck if they were a millimeter deeper. Besides having magnified eyes, she is tall. She is tall, tall and skinny and still-growing gawky.

"You've got some height on you, girl," I say to Allison.

"How tall are you?" Allison says, "Tall enough to wrap my legs around a guy's back and let him pummel his dick into me *all night long.*" Chester and I glance at each other. Chester turns to Allison and while smirking says, "Never play leapfrog with a unicorn." Allison gives no sign of having noticed the exchange and shakes her head like a proud young filly shaking her mane.

"God, I love it when you talk polysyllabic."

"Polysyllabic?" Chester asks.

"What does that mean?"

"Look, you guys," Allsion says, ignoring Chester's question while turning to look at me with her right eye. I wonder if she bought her glasses from a street doctor because the left lens is far too thick. Her left eye bulges behind her glasses.

"What are you two doing tonight? 'Cause my sister's friend is having a party."

"Nothing," Chester says, looking at me then back at her.

"That's good," Allison says.

"Do y'all want to come to it?" Chester and I say, "Yeah," together.

"Okay," Allison says.

"I wish I can go with y'all boys," Warren says from the backseat of my car. Driving down Chief Street is what I'm doing at this early night hour. It is now 9:32 p.m., and about three hours have passed Chester and I left Sanskirt Hospital. We hit it after we talked to Allison for about twenty minutes after she invited us to a party. A party that is being held at a trailer home inside of a trailer park which she gave us the address to. Before she gave us the address to it, Allison told us that the party'll start popping off at 10:30. The name of the city I live in Eddy and Eddy is on the other side of town from where Chester lives.

So after leaving Sanskirt Hospital I had to drive many miles to a bridge then cross it to take Chester back home. After I got to Chester's aunt house, I parked my car in front of the house. Chester's cell phone rang around five minutes after I put the gear into park. Chester looked at his ringing cell phone, answered it, and said, "What up nigga," as I looked at him. A few seconds passed before I heard him say, "I'm chillin' with Marshall in his car in front of my aunt's house."

Seconds after saying that Chester turned to me and said, "Warren wants us to come scoop him up." My house is on the other side of town from where Chester and Warren live, and Warren's house was drove to after I started my car back up. It took less than fifteen minutes to drive to it, since Warren's Mom house is in a neighborhood close to Chester's aunt house. I drove onto the highway from her house, traveled on it for a few minutes, and made a right onto Quartz Road. We drove to Warren's Mom house on Quartz Road, Chester called him when I parked outside of it, and Warren walked outside then got in my car. It was only 8:02 p.m. at that time, but I still drove to that trailer park so I could know where it's at for when the party actually start. With Warren and Chester inside my car, I drove inside that trailer park to find the trailer home. I found it, and once finding it I drove back out of it-it was 8:34 p.m. at that time. Just like now, in the backseat Warren was while I was driving back across the Hart Bridge to their side of town-the county jail was seen on the left as I was driving off of it. Warren said from his backseat, "That's where all the hardheads are," while all three of us was looking at the passing high-rise building.

"I understand why muthafuckas lose it in there," I said in response to Warren's comment.

"Time ain't no easy thing to do," Warren then said, "especially in there, nothin' to do but think. Think about shit you don't wanna think about." To no one in particular Chester said, "Caged like a fuckin' animal." About ten seconds of silence passes before Warren says it again.

"Damn, I wish I can go with y'all boys." A few seconds after I passed the county jail Warren's Mom called his cell phone and said that she need him home by ten because she's going out to the club.

"There's nobody else that can watch the lil nigga?" Chester asks Warren, slightly turning his neck to look back at him.

"Naw," Warren says.

"She said that I need to watch him." Chester turns all the way around back in his front seat, and we travel in silence for a while. Still driving down Chief Street I am when a red traffic light stops my car. I'm stopped at the red light when Warren says, "Marshall, you wanna go to the grocery store before you drop me off?"

"Your Mom wants you to pick up groceries too?" I ask Warren, looking at him through my rearview mirror.

"Naw," Warren says. "We can probably get some digits in it. We can walk around it until we do. You game?"

"I'm game," I say, just as the light turns green.

"Which one?" I ask while my car is accelerating, "The Waste-That-Little up ahead on our left?"

"Yeah," Warren says. "The Waste-That-Little coming up."

Only a minute passes before I enter the parking lot of Waste-That-Little on this Tuesday night at 9:36 p.m. I don't have a problem with grocery stores but my first baby-mama, Roz, did. "Grocery stores are nothing but a bunch of bratty-ass kids begging their parents for candy, sugar infested juices, or salty foods," is what Roz told me that day after I asked her why she hate them. A parking space is pulled into, I cut off my car, and all three of us get out of it. We start walking towards Waste-That-Little and as we are I look at Warren. He is an African-American just like Chester and I, and his body frame is somewhere between average and muscular. His physique is kind of hidden by the black hooded pullover with white letters on it that he's wearing, and the hooded pullover he's wearing is the same color as his black pants. A white snapback hat rests on his head, and it's turned backwards. As he begins to open his mouth to talk to Chester, I see Warren's gold teeth gleam.

"You think you can get one tonight, Murk?" Warren asks Chester, smiling. It's been a few weeks since the first I've heard Warren call Chester Murk, and I asked why he did right after the first time I heard him say that. Warren told me that he call him that because he saw Chester beat a nigga's ass at a block party that he went to.

"Yeah," Chester says. Warren turns to me.

"You believe that?" I take my eyes off of Warren and look at Chester for a few long seconds before answering. I finally say, "Hell no," and Warren chuckles. He continues chuckling as we near the sliding front doors of Waste-That-Little, and they slide open when I step on the doormat in front of them. Into the brightly lit grocery store we all walk-ahead of me I see many checkout lanes, but only one of them are occupied by a cashier. That's due to the late night hour. Going through one of the empty check out lanes is what I do as Chester and Warren follow me. They follow me as I pass an easel that has writing on it:

Special's this week at your Waste-That-Little Supermarket!

Okinawa Squash, reg $0.89	$0.75!
Penguin Eggs (low on DDT, PCB) reg $6.35	doz $6.05!
Pacific Potatoes (unwashed) reg $0.89	lb. $0.69!
Butter from sunny New Zealand reg $1.35	qrt. $1.15!

You too can afford at Waste-That-Little!

I take my eyes off of the easel, continue walking further into the grocery store, and look at Warren. "It's dead as a bitch in here," Warren says, looking at me then over at the meat section to our far left.

"Let's go over there." Warren walks past me, and Chester and I follow him as he walks to the meat section. As we're nearing the meat section, I see the back of a lone Black female with sepia skin looking down at a package of meat held in her right hand while her left hand rests on the handle of a shopping cart. Warren turns to us and says, "Let me holla at her," before he starts walking towards the Black female. Chester and I look at him as he is. Instead of directly approaching her, Warren walks to a section of the freezer-shelfed meats that are about ten feet away from her. I see Warren pick up a meat package, start sniffing it, then put it back down. His front is believable because the meat looks less than kosher everytime I shop for it, and some of the past chickens I bought reeked with salmonella. I always sniff meat before buying it because I don't want to get home, rip off the plastic, and fall out from the stench.

About a minute passes before Warren makes it to the side of the Black female. I look at Warren as he starts mackin' to her. Over a minute passes while he is, so I think that he got him one. Wrong is what I see I am when the Black female walks away not too long later. My thinking is that because I didn't see her give Warren her number before walking away; he starts walking back to us after she does. Chester moves closer to Warren as he nears us. "What happened?"

"That ho must be a dyke," Warren says caddishly.

"Why you say that?" Chester asks. Warren says, "I asked her 'Is there something wrong with the meat?' and she said 'Yes, the hell there is something wrong with the meat'."

When I take over, we start walking down the pasta aisle. Up ahead I see the back of a thin light-skinned Black man that looks to be in his forties, and he's slowly pushing a shopping cart. In front of him there's a kid that's blocking his way which is why he's slowly approaching him. Chester, Warren, and me all look at the middle-aged Black man as he jerks his cart towards the kid but he doesn't budge-the kid just glares at the man and rolls his eyes. I glance at his Mom and see that she's picking out a box of elbow macaroni. Chester and Warren follow behind me as I slowly near the back of the thin light-skinned Black man. I get near enough to him that I can hear him speak to the Mother of the child. "Ahem, could you tell your kid to move the hell out of my way," the Black man lashes at her. The Black woman turns her head to him and scoffs like she can't believe he'd actually said that.

I see the Black man's grip on his shopping cart tighten and he says, "Are you going to move him or I should I knock his ass over with my cart?" The Black woman grabs her son by the shoulders and pulls him aside.

"Move over here, Daniel."-The Black woman leers at the man- "You don't have to be rude, sir. He's just a kid."

"Life's a bitch and then you die," the Black man responds.

"Want more do you want, heifer?" Scoffing is done by the Black woman with a pastel dress on, and she grabs the hand of her son that is wearing a Teletubbies tee then hauls ass away from us in the other direction with her kid in tow. So we can walk past him, we begin to get even nearer to the Black man. He turns around and looks at us.

"What do people *do* in these places?" the avuncular-looking Black man asks, and he answers himself angrily, "They live." Warren chuckles.

"They live? You're drunk as fuck, unc." After Warren says that, I try to smell a whiff of alcohol in the air; no alcohol is smelled by me. The avuncular-looking Black man turns completely to Warren. "Yes, that's true. Normally when I commit necrophilia-" "Necrowhat?" Warren interrupts. "Necrophilia," the avuncular-looking Black man says.

"You don't know what that is?"

"No," Warren says.

"I'll let you find out on your own," the avuncular-looking Black man says, in his lugbrious tone. He extends his hand out to Warren.

"My name's Terry. And you are?"

"Warren," Warren says, extending his hand. Warren and Terry shake hands, before Terry extends his hand out to me.

"Marshall," I say, shaking Terry's hand. Our handshake is broken off by him, and the last person's hand he shakes is Chester's.

"Chester," Chester says, also shaking Terry's hand. The two of them stop shaking hands and Terry backs up. While looking at us Terry says, "Well, I'ma get back to what I was doing," before turning around to start pushing his shopping cart. Warren's cell phone rings as we are watching Terry walk away. I turn to Warren and look at the Black man around my age wearing a white snapback hat turned backwards on his head covered with hair that is braided-the two fat braids hanging from each side of his head droop down like bangs. Warren looks at his cell phone, answers it, and says, "I'm on my way right now," before hanging up. I look at Warren and ask, "That was your Mom?"

"Yeah," Warren says.

"That was Mom dukes."

I look at Chester, motion my hand towards Waste-That-Little's front doors, and he and Warren follow behind me as I start walking towards the doors. We walk out of Waste-That-Little into the night air, get into my car, and I start it. Fifteen minutes later, Chester and I look at Warren's back as he walks up the sidewalk leading to his Mom's house.

"Call her and tell her we're outside," I say with know-how to Chester. Chester takes out his cell phone and starts dialing. I hear the line ring four times before someone finally picks up. Loud music coming from the background is what I hear coming out of Chester's cell phone. It sounds like a party. Chester says, "Allison, we're outside-okay," before hanging up. Chester opens his car door, gets out, and I do the same.

My car is parked in the street up against a curb, so when Chester and I get out we start walking up the sidewalk leading up to the trailer home. As we are nearing the trailer's home front door steps, I look at the carport we are approaching. Underneath it there's a funereal grey truck that has on it a bumper sticker I read: 'The Redneck Doesn't

Fall Far From The Tree'. When the trailer home's door on my right begins to open, I take my eyes off of the funereal grey truck. "Chester!" I see Allison and a splash of dim light spill out of the front door into the dark night. Chester and I walk up and go through the front door smilingly held open for us, while looking at Allison. We walk together into the trailer home. In the dimly lit frontroom I see a recliner, tattered couch, and loveseat that has seen much better days, a scratched-up coffee table, and a new nineteen inch tv sitting on top of the original box by the window we passed walking outside. The air-conditioning unit in the window isn't efficiently working so it's hot in here-I immediately start sweating. As I am, music continues blaring out of the boombox I see on the scratched coffee table. Sitting on the loveseat by herself is a teenaged White girl, and I nod a "What up" at her.

The kitchen of this trailer home is seen way in the back from where I'm standing at, because this frontroom we're in is one big room that combines both of them. The back of a grown White woman with red hair is what I see standing at the sink in the kitchen, and I look at her then again at the girl sitting by herself on the loveseat before turning around to Allison as she's closing the front door.

"What kind of party is this?" I ask Allison, over the music. "All I see is three people." Allison shrugs.

"It's a school night. I want you to meet my sister's friend."- Allison turns her head towards the kitchen- "Frieda!" As she calls out the woman's name, I turn towards that woman in the kitchen. I see the woman turn around from the sink then walk towards us. As she is walking towards us I start to clearly see her. The red-haired White woman I see is wearing plastic thong sandals, a shortie nightgown and a mustard blazer. I look at her and I'm immediately lost, as I was the first time I saw Allison, in her creamy jade green eyes-eyes like ice, that I hope isn't an indicator that her personality is cold and distant. Her red hair is fixed in a bun, making her high cheekbones and prominent chin have an austere air. She smiles at me as she stops, and the way her lips press tightly against her teeth convinces me that she's a veritable heart stopper when her hair is down her shoulders. Frieda looks at me.

"Lonely Hearts Club. Join now. Misery loves company."

"Do you take masochists?" I ask, smiling.

"Two for one if you join with a sadist," Frieda says.

"By the way, I'm Frieda." I look Frieda up and down, admiring her curves.

"Do you want to take shots of Black Jack?" Frieda asks, and manages a ghastly let's-party smile. I nod. Wordlessly Frieda grabs my hand and leads me to the tattered couch. We both sit down on it and in front of it is the scratched-up coffee table with several things on it including a bottle of Black Jack. Frieda picks up the bottle, turns to me to say, "Let me get you a cup," and she gets up as music from the boombox continues playing.

While Frieda is walking past me to the kitchen I look over at the teenaged White girl sitting by herself on the loveseat. She smiles at me and I smile back. About half a minute later, Frieda returns. I take the cup she hands me, and hold out my cup as she pours the brown liquid in it. After filling mines, she then fills her own cup. We sit for a moment in silence, while I drink two cups of Black Jack as she downs three. When Frieda gets very drunk, although the party has been underway for only an hour, she starts talking about things. About the cost of hospitalization insurance; about her older sister who birthed two children in New York, and the one who was arrested for showing his dick to some little kids on a playground; about flowers she had tried to grow in a window-box at her old apartment, that wilted and drooped their leaves after a week; about the beggar she found wheezing against a wall; about the rain that melted her panty hoses and stockings. I've experienced acid rain before.

Acid rain ruined one of my Toad Island uniforms. I take my eyes off of Frieda as she's talking about acid rain, look at the White girl sitting by herself on the loveseat, then behind me towards the kitchen where I saw Allison and Chester get up to go to about ten minutes ago. I see Chester sitting down on one of the kitchen chairs he pulled all the way out, and Allison is sitting on his lap as her flat ass is gyrating on it-her back is facing Chester's face as she is giving him a lap dance. Back towards Frieda I turn and I ask, "Do you have any kids?"

"Yes. I have one." Frieda's smile isn't so attractive this time. "I have a son."

"A son." I repeat.

"From the same guy?"

"Yes," Frieda says.

"We used to be married."

I ask, "Why aren't two married anymore?" An irritated look appears on Frieda's face and she says, "Curious, aren't we?" I smile at her. "Girls with red hair are pretty and yet so fiery." Frieda remains looking at me irritatingly for a few seconds then smiles.

"Me and my ex-husband aren't together anymore for many reasons. We were at loggerheads during our first couple months of marriage, so I knew then that it wasn't going to work out. It really stopped working after what he did that night."

"What did he do?" I ask, holding my cup. Frieda looks at the White girl sitting by herself on the loveseat while looking down at the cup in her hand. She looks at her for a few seconds then back at me.

"You really want to know?" Frieda asks, picking up the bottle of Black Jack.

"If I didn't, I wouldn't be asking," I say.

"One night he got hammered on Black Jack and Xanax, and used a three-inch wood bit to drill a perfect hole in each of his palms," Frieda says, gesturing to me with the bottle of Black Jack. "Now he's one of the stars of a Christian pilgrim tour, and he's the only member of it that is a carpenter just like Jesus. I've seen him assiduously picking at the circular wounds in his hands to keep them authentically unscabbed and bloody. There's a rumor going around that he's planning to drill his feet soon."

Frieda stops, pours more Black Jack into her cup, and I hold my cup out to her to refill; she refills it then sits the bottle of Black Jack down on the scratched-up coffee table. While the music is playing, we both return to drinking in silence for a while. By now Frieda has gotten bored. She gets up, walks to then down the hallway, comes back and sits down, and pulls out a thick, long joint rolled with a white substance. She lights it, takes a single inhalation of the roasting cat-pee smelling smoke, and her eyes immediately bug out like her brain is on fire. Frieda turns and fixes me with a look of utter contempt, but when I reach for the joint, she hands it over willingly enough.

"In the Garden of Eden there was a Tree," Frieda says, passing me the joint. Tendrils of green smoke drifts from both ends.

"The Tree of Good and Evil. You ever heard of it?"

"Yeah. It's in the Bible," I say, taking the joint. Frieda says, "That's right. And on the tree was an Apple." I say, "Alright," before taking a puff so small it's actually a sip. I fear that if I take a deep lungful my head will explode off my neck and fly around this frontroom like a rocket, shooting fiery exhaust from its stump.

Frieda remains looking at me. "The flesh of that Apple is Truth, and the skin of that Apple is *wet*." I blow out smoke then turn to Frieda and say, "This is *wet*?" while handing it back to her.

"Yes," Frieda says, taking the *wet*. While burning, *wet* smells like three-day-old piss in an uncovered thunderjug. After my first tentative puff of it the blood vessels in my neck swell to throbbing cables, my heart spikes, and my balls crawl in an adolescent way. Frieda takes another toke of the *wet*, before she tries to hand it back to me.

"No more," I say, shaking my hand and head. Frieda shrugs and leans over me to pass the *wet* to the White girl sitting on the loveseat by herself; her breasts brushes me as she does. The girl takes the *wet*, and Frieda returns to sitting up erect on the couch. Abruptly Frieda croaks, "Allison took to *wet*-weed doused in embalming fluid-like a frog on flies."

"She did?" I say.

"Yes," Frieda says.

"My husband did too."

"Was that his truck I saw outside earlier?" I ask.

"The grey truck with that bumper sticker that says 'The Redneck Doesn't Fall Far From The Tree'?"

"No," Frieda says. "It's mines." Minutes pass by as I watch Frieda and the other White girl take tokes of the *wet*. Unbeknown to me Frieda's son has been looking at us from the hallway for the last several minutes, and I notice him for the first time after he steps from the shadows of himself into the light-he is drawn out and curious about the music and laughter he hears at an adult party. The shy child's unacknowledged act of will causes me to turn to Frieda. I look at Frieda and say, "Is that your son?" before pointing to the lil boy. Frieda looks to where I'm pointing at.

"Joey! How long have you been standing there? Come over here." I look at Joey as he dashes towards us, and Frieda slides away from me so the lil kid can squeeze in between the two of us on the couch.

"Shouldn't you be sleep?" Frieda asks Joey, looking down at him.

"I couldn't sleep," Joey says in a voice that has a good ways to go before it would even consider changing. As he is saying that, the teenaged White girl sitting on the loveseat passes the embalming fluid soaked marijuana rolled in paper back to Frieda.

"Well," Frieda says, taking the drug, "I have something to help you with that." Frieda passes the *wet* rolled in paper to Joey. Joey takes it and sucks in a particularly deep lungful. How old is this kid? He can't be no more than seven-years-old. When I first saw Joey, he looked like a depraved child. Now I know why. He has gotten an early start on only God knows how many adult vices and sins. Coughing once is what Joey does, before handing the drug back to his Mom. Frieda takes it and she leans to hand it to the White girl.

While the White girl is taking a toke, Frieda looks to her right down at her son. Frieda asks, "Do you feel like you can move mountains in a wheelbarrow yet?" Joey nods solemnly. For over five minutes I look at Frieda, the teenaged White girl, and Joey pass the *wet* rolled in paper back and forth- besides being mind boggling, the view I see is bizarre. The last toke of the drug is handed to Frieda, and the red-haired woman in her middle thirties puffs until it is nothing but a nub that burns her fingers. At which point she sobers, almost like magic, because it is time for the party to break up, and says, "Okay Joey. You should be able to go to sleep now."- Frieda turns to me- "Thank you for listening to my drunken babbling earlier. Unless I get someone to take me seriously every now and then I think it must really all be a dream."

I look at Frieda stand up off the couch and grab Joey's hand. She starts leading Joey back to his room, before she turns around-I imagine how her figure looks under her shorty nightgown and mustard blazer-and says to me on the threshold, "I'd like you to stay so we can make love. But it'll have to be next time. I have another week to go before it's safe." A nod is my response, before Frieda goes back to walking to Joey's room. I turn to look at the White girl sitting on the loveseat, she's now laid out on the couch sleep or passed-out one. I take my eyes off of her and I look towards the kitchen table. I now see Allison's back as she straddles Chester's lap, she switched positions, while moving in rhythm to the music.

"Chester!" I shout, so I can be heard over the music. Chester head pops to the side of Allison so he can look at me. I wave my hand at him towards me in a

"Let's go" gesture, and I see Chester say something to Allison before getting up. They hold hands while standing up in front of each other while talking, and they kiss for a while before Chester starts walking towards me. He walks towards me and I turn towards the front door. We walk out of the trailer home together into the dusk of the night, and Chester closes its door back.

CHAPTER 4

Quiet is the inside of my car as I drive out of the trailer park-Chester is slumped back in the passenger seat next to me with his eyes closed facing the ceiling. He's beginning to go to sleep, or resting his eyes. Which I don't know, and I don't care. I drive slowly over several speed bumps before nearing the exit/entrance of the trailer park. A traffic light is placed at the front of it, and the light stops me from proceeding out onto the main street which the moonlight shines on-close to two o'clock was the time the party we just left finally ended.

While stopped at the traffic light, I stare ahead out at the street. Traffic is thin during this time of night because I see less than five cars, with their high-beams on, pass by before the traffic-light turns green. I pull out to the street while curving to my left. About twenty five minutes is how long it'll take me to get to Chester's house, and I start brooding on what I saw earlier as I begin the drive to it. I abruptly made the transition from adolescent to adult, but that kid-Joey-is doing more than that. He's being corrupted, and I don't like that. That what I saw was mind-boggling and bizarre. It was that but what I felt while watching Joey is...indescribable. This feeling is indescribable, like having a thing clutching at my stomach and leaping into my chest. I thought I've seen it all in my twenty-four years; I was wrong. My blood boils as I briefly close my eyes and envision that lil White boy again taking puffs of that *wet*. I envision that view in my head and try to think why Frieda would allow him to smoke, but I can't think straight. I turn on my windshield wipers when a light, steady rain begins to fall. The windshield wipers begin to wipe my front windshield, and I turn to look at Chester. Chester's grey do-rag covered head underneath a black hat leans backward on the seat's headrest as he's sleeping, and snoring as his mouth is gaping open. His mouth is gaping open so I can clearly see his tin-foiled covered upper teeth. I stop looking at Chester and focus back on the now rain-slicked street ahead of me. Twenty minutes later, I pull my car in front of Chester's aunt house. The ignition is turned off, and Chester wakes up as soon as it is. Chester sits all the way up, looks at his aunt's house and says, "Alright whodie," while beginning to turn to his door to open it. I hold my hand out to Chester.

"Hold up. Let me rap to you a bit." Chester stops and turns to me.

"About what?" I steel myself, lift my head with a slight, nearly audible moan, and stare unblinking into his eyes.

"Chester, I'm speaking to you not as a parent, but one that would like to continue being your dawg. Child Welfare should take that kid away from Frieda before she kills him." Chester gives me a look that I associate with the discovery of a dead bug in one's meal.

"What do you mean," Chester demands dangerously, "Child Welfare should take that kid away from Frieda?" I say, "Nigga, don't ask questions."

"Okay," Chester says slowly, like he's dragging the river for a body.

"I won't ask questions. I'll just spit facts. If you put Child Welfare on Frieda, Allison'll be convinced you aren't a thug. You'll probably cease to exist. Hell, we'll all probably cease to exist."

"What the fuck's that supposed to mean?" I say.

"And why would I care what she think?"

"That's just it!" I don't know!" Chester says. He appears extremely agitated, as if his programming is directing him to pursue several paths at once. We stare at each other without talking for a while. The silence in my car is nearly absolute, like the silence of deep space. I turn away from Chester and look to my left out my rolled-up tinted window. Mechanically, tonelessly, I begin, "I ain't never been a snake or slimy-type dude," while looking out my window. "But that was some sheisty shit I saw at that house. I feel like I have to do something."

"You never miss an opportunity, do you?" Chester says without feeling. I turn to Chester.

"Doesn't look like I've so much time that I can afford to let the slightest one slip by."

"I'll spell it out for you," Chester says, as harsh as mineral acid.

"If you contact Child Welfare, you'll be labeled a snitch." Talking to Chester is a little like talking to a minister; I feel a sense of distance, an intangible barrier. But right now it has to be breached.

"By who?" I ask confrontationally.

"By me, nigga!" Chester shouts.

51

I take my hand off of the steering wheel, and take a swing at Chester. My fist connects to his jaw, and we start tussling in my car's interior. Almost a minute passes by as we are. Anyone walking by my grey Ford Taurus at that time will see a moving, shaking, and bouncing car. Chester's hat falls off during the beginning of our fight, and the only thing on his head now is the grey do-rag. The grey do-rag covering his nappy hair, but not his sideburn tufts. Our fight comes to a standstill, when we lock-up with each other. I say into Chester's ear, "Let me go, and I'll let you go," while we are both heavily breathing. Loosening his grip is what Chester does, before I loosen mines. After he does, I shove him off of me. Chester and I glare at each other for a few seconds-we sit for a moment in the quietness of my car as we are. The rain that started earlier is now pouring and a lightning bolt comes down so close that it makes an audible hissing before it hits. The resultant thunder shakes my car like an explosion. Right after the lightning strikes Chester pleads, "Marshall, you gotta think about what you're saying. That shit you're talking ain't right. You can't go out like that."

"I ain't trying to hear that shit," I say.

"And I definitely ain't gonna pretend I never saw anything. Because if I do...."

"Don't tell me no scars are gonna be with you," Chester says.

"Fuck them rap lyrics. Talk to me like a brother. This ain't no fantasy shit. Nigga, this shit is real!"

"Real enough to ignore corruption?" I ask Chester, misfiring.

"You know the consequences of the game," Chester says, getting heated all over again.

"I don't know why niggas can't take the bitter with the sweet. The game is what it is. If you knew the rules, you just gotta play by them." Chester bangs his fist on the dashboard to add emphasis to his words, plus him saying the game has me pissed. For someone else of instead of himself is how he sounds like he's talking.

"Nigga, telling what I saw earlier isn't breaking a rule of the game," I say.

"You got life fucked up," Chester says, looking out his window.

"Droppin' a dime is droppin' a dime, anyway it goes. If you do what you're plannin' on doing, I won't wreck your credibility. But niggas in the hood would look at you as a snitch and that would open up the doors for the wolves to strike."

I look out my front window then back at him and say, "That's a chance I'm willing to take," while my left hand rests on the steering wheel. Chester turns to me and says, "You win." He looks at me as if winning is the most dangerous thing I could have done.

"You have kids, and I don't. I can't judge you for being paternal. It's two thirty in the morning nigga"-Chester puts his hand on the doorknob- "so I'll holla at you later."

I look at Chester as he opens his car door, quickly jump out and close his car door back even quicker, then dash towards his aunt's house since it's raining. His aunt's front gate is opened, and he dashes to the house's patio. I see Chester standing at the door, before the front porch light comes on and seconds later he goes into the house. After he does, I turn my car back on and pull off. Out through Chester's neighborhood I drive, before driving past

Waste-That-Little. Gliding through the streets is what I start doing and my windshield wipers are moving back and forth since it's raining.

Chester expects me to just chalk up the fact that each parent raises their child differently, but I can't do that. I can't. There was a time in my life when I hated even hearing about someone ratted on a person. I've been in courtrooms as a spectator watching a *snitch* on the stand testifying against one of my dawgs and I wanted to walk up to the person while they testified and slit their throats.

A person that thought they seen it all but hasn't seen shit. There are disturbed people in this world and Frieda is one of them. I'll backhand the shit out of Chamiqua, Deidre, or Roz if any one of them ever give drugs, or alcohol, to our daugthers together. I can take my medicine like a man but I wouldn't be surprised if anyone in my position would start having second thoughts about being a snitch. I'm starting to question myself, is this worth it? Why am I doing this? I'm even starting to beat myself up mentally. I'm supposed to follow the rules of the street; I can't believe I've become what I was against. That's why I'm rationalizing with myself that the reason I'm going to snitch is because of paternal instincts. Sometimes I wish I could start all over again. Would I do things differently if I had the chance to start all over? Probably not. The only thing I would have done different is not going to that party I left about an hour ago. I should have stayed home.

Stayed my ass home and finished writing that letter I started. If I would have stayed home, I would have never seen that. The last time I saw a lil kid do things he wasn't supposed to be doing was on that tv show. That man's flashback showed him doing all types of wrong things when he was a kid. He said, before that flashback, that his Mom was tolerable during his teenage years before she got religious. Before she did he said that she allowed him to go bass fishing with cherry bombs, play football without a helmet, shoot his laser .22 inside the city limits, smoke cigarettes, bother the girls and skip school at least twice a week. I turn to my left and glance at Mauve's Diner, before my car speeds past it.

My car continues traveling down the dead street during this late night hour. Seconds after passing Mauve's Diner, I look to my right. I see a street opening with two rows of houses on each side of that street which is a dead-end. I know it is because I drove down it before, when Chester took me to that house down there. The Christmas that just passed is when he did, and we went there around ten p.m. on a Christmas night. Before we did, Chester called me at my house while I was sleeping-Chamiqua and I had just broke up about two weeks earlier, and she left with her two boys and my daughter. Chester asked me over the phone when he called if I want to go to the movies with that girl he know and her friend.

Of course I agreed, and about three hours later I picked up Chester. I picked Chester up before he directed me to that house on that dead-end street I just passed, and that young Black girl that agreed to the double-date stayed there. Chester called her on his cell phone as we were sitting outside of her house on that Christmas night, and about a minute later we started walking up the sidewalk to her house. She greeted us at the screen door, held it open for us, and we sat on that couch her parents had sitting under the veranda we sat in. We waited for her in the veranda, as she finished getting ready. About ten minutes she came back out, and that young ho told us that she talked to her cousin earlier that day. It was kind of surprising when she said her cousin's name, because her cousin a famous comedian named after the county I live in. The word 'Lil' is in front of his stage name, along with him being named after the county I live in.

We all got in my grey Ford Taurus on that Christmas night and the cousin of that famous comedian gave me the direction's to her friend's house. From her backseat, she told me where I needed to drive to get there. I drove off of Chief Street into that trailer park which is where her friend stayed. Her Black friend walked out of that trailer home, got into my car, and all four of us went to the movies that night.

When we got to the movie theater, those two hos paid for their own tickets. Their own tickets to see a movie we all decide to see on that Christmas night. I've seen many Christmas movies before, but I've never seen that ancient one. That ancient one titled *Miracle On 34 Street*, or that other ancient one titled *Holiday Inn*. Both of those Christmas movies came out milleniums ago, but I did see the remake of that other ancient Christmas movie titled *It's A Wonderful Life*. That movie critic said that the original began with a man wanting to kill himself, but concluded with the usual nauseating sop of a Hollywood ending. I don't know what a Hollywood ending is-maybe it's a comedy having dramatic moments; I could be wrong. I could be wrong on what a Hollywood ending is, but I know I'm not wrong on what I know about Hollywood.

Hollywood is a district in the city of Los Angeles in California, and it's basically considered as the motion picture capital of the world. From about Hyperion Avenue on the east to about Crescent Heights Boulevard on the west is where Hollywood extends, and it also extends from Mulholland Drive on the north to Melrose Avenue on the south to Griffith Park. The number of people that live in Hollywood is about 300,000. Concerts, symphony programs, and Easter services are seen in that open-air theater called the Hollywood Bowl and those events are seen often at it. Set in the sidewalks along Hollywood Boulevard and Vine Street in Hollywood are over 2,000 bronze stars on the popular Walks of Fame-the name of a different Hollywood celebrity is on each star.

A landmark built in the hills above the Hollywood District is the huge Hollywood sign, and it was restored in 1978. The height of each letter on the sign is 45 feet. A section of Hollywood is called Sunset Boulevard and it has many restaurants, gift shops, theatrical agencies, and nightclubs. Sunset Boulevard is called The Strip, and that section of Hollywood was incorporated in 1984 as the city of West Hollywood. What was the name of that company again? Oh yeah, the Nestor Film Company. The Nestor Film Company built the first motion-picture studio in Hollywood in 1911. Since it lays in an area with a vast variety of natural scenery, Hollywood became a center of the motion picture industry-almost every kind of scenic background is available to moviemakers and those scenic backgrounds are within 200 miles of Hollywood.

Resulting in the building of a huge sound stage is what the production of sounds film in Hollywood did, and the production of them started in the late 1920's before many of them were used to start making television films. About five minutes has elapsed since I passed Mauve's Diner, so I'm now traveling on this highway that'll lead me to my house. My car zooms on the highway while I use my left hand to hold the steering wheel, as I use the fingers on my right hand to fiddle with the tip of one of my braids. My braided hair reaches to the back of my neck and it's been a few days since it's been rebraided. As I'm playing with my braid tip, I see a brief flash of light. After that is the lighting, and the thunder, and after a long time only the rain is left, pouring down straight and heavy like it's tipped out of a bucket. I look to my left at the passing woodland. I hope this torrent of rain isn't harmful to the woods.

When Frieda started talking about rain at her party, she reminded me of acid rain. Acid rain ruined one of my Toad Island uniforms that day it started raining while I was working, and I don't like acid rain. I don't like rain that's polluted by sulfuric acid and nitric acid because acid rain ruined my uniform and it harms thousands of lakes, rivers, and streams worldwide, killing fish and other wildlife-bridges, statues, and buildings are also damaged by it. That acid rain that damaged Toad Island was high in concentration, because forests and soil are only damaged by the kinds that have high concentration. When water in the air reacts with certain chemical compounds, acid rain forms.

Most of those compounds come mainly from the burning of oil, coal, and gasoline-many cars, factories, and power plants burn those fuels for energy. I think it was about the 1950's when the problem of acid rain started growing in rural areas-the use of taller smokestacks in urban areas enabled winds to transport pollutants further from their sources. I continue nearing my side of town, and twenty minutes later I pull into my neighborhood around three a.m. on this Wednesday morning-it's still raining cats and dogs as I near the corner of my house. I pull onto my driveway and stare at my house for a moment. For a few months I've lived in this house that's in a cul-de-sac in suburban Blacksmith's End. *Soft contemporary* is what realtors call my house, and they use that term to describe houses without style. These houses are so identical in Blacksmith's End that never knowing the difference until the alarm goes off would be done by a Blacksmith's End homeowner if they walk into a neighbor's house after coming home to this neighborhood from a night of barhopping. Even being cookie-cutter, it's a nice place, because a roof's over my head that's not gonna get wet; since I'm now pressing the garage door opener on my key chain.

CHAPTER 5

By making a superhuman effort, I've managed to drag myself out of bed and show up here at work. I'm still kind of tired from the party I went to last night. Well, not actually last night but earlier this morning. It's 7:52 a.m. and I've been on the clock now for twenty two minutes. After punching the time clock, my boss told me that he wants me to start planting the seedlings. That's why I'm now walking on this barren woodland with a backpack on. This backpack I have on is riddled with dozens of slots that vertically holds the six inch tall trees, seedlings, which are adhered into them-six inch tall trees are also adhered into slots in this bulky belt placed around my waist. I put on both of these contraptions before I left out of the office less than thirty minutes ago, and I also grabbed a planting gun before I walked out of it. Right now, I'm planting a pine seedling into this planting gun. This planting gun that digs a hole, inserts a seedling, and pats down the soil in one operation.

While I'm beginning to plant the second tree, I start thinking about the dream I had a few hours ago. I had a dream about my baby-mamas in the three, four hours I was sleep. My dream started off in a courtroom and I was on the stand. I was on the stand while instead of there being twelve people in the jury box, there were only three. Those three people were all female, and they were my baby-mamas. I remember looking at the judge and he looked just like Sherman Barkham, and Sherman Barkham asked the jury, "How do you find the defendant?" Roz spoke first and she said, "Guilty," before I dropped my head. Deidre was second, and just as she started to open her mouth I looked up. When she said, "Guilty," I began to feel light-headed. While my head was spinning, I looked at Chamiqua. She was fighting I saw to not look at me before she gave her verdict to the judge while also standing up.

During the duration of the trial I had in my sleep, I pleaded with them. I pleaded with my baby mamas-the jury-not to take my kids away from me. But they ordered me out of their lives anyway, and after leaving the courtroom I was escorted by two stone-faced jailers through a series of corridors and elevators that was on the surface of things impossible to differentiate from the path my baby-mamas guided me over earlier. In spite of that, that time there was a sinister purposefulness to the direction, that always seemed to be going down. It went down for a long time. My yielding acceptance concerning them giving me enough rope to hang enough myself vanished, only now I'm aware of the doom they've given me. At a certain point in our journey, at an elevator that looked no different from the previous one, or the one before that, my escorts began to blindfold me. While I was also wondering if there was any significance why the temperature steadily went up as the elevator went down, I asked my escorts a question.

While being blindfolded I asked them, "Is this really necessary?" One of them gave an amused snort, and the other contemptuously snorted. Right after he did, I woke up from my dream. Through the tube the six inch tree travels, before I hear the sound indicating that it's planted. The tree becomes lodged in the soil-I raise my arm that doesn't hold the planting gun, and wipe the sweat off of my forehead with the back of my left arm. I do that because this early morning sun is hot enough to suggest what it's noontime power would be. The sun continues beaming down on me as I start walking. My boots crunches on a dense mat of dry pine needles as I walk. Tall, scraggly fir, rough-barked conifers and fragrant pine grows all around me. Low and bushlike is the rectangular-leafed fare trees that grow in a grey-green profusion. The color of deadly emeralds, the color of life is green-there's so much green I see. There are no birds or insects in this area I see, so the forest is quiet. Whistling as I walk, I notice all of that without pausing. If I didn't have this planting gun, planting trees would be hard. But my job isn't since I have this machine for planting seeds in my hand. This area is kind of clear, but here and there are a few rotted trees-to get a bit of relief from the hot blazing sun, I turn and walk towards a forested wall. I near it then walk underneath it's shady canopy.

While underneath the shady canopy, I look down at yet another rotting tree that's horizontal. On it I see bromeliads, and the glorious bromeliads that has covered the fallen tree are dying. They're dying because none of them have set seed. I feel saddened by this sight of whatever pollinator it is that fertilizes these plants can't find them so close to the ground. I continue looking at the fallen tree, as I walk the length of it. I near the top of the tree, stop, and scrutinize what I see. Also covered with bromeliads are the upper branches of this downed tree. These doomed bromeliads couldn't survive since this tree's fall had carried them into an area that is too dark and too moist-the upper bromeliads knew their time was almost up so they bloomed in a last brilliant rush to procreate before they died. I hope that Chester and Warren have kids before they die; I really do. They're also in a dark place, too dark place like me but I already have kids. I wanted my name to be carried on if I died, so that's why I had kids-I wanted immortality, and I got it. I have that, but they don't. As far as I know, they don't. Neither one of them has told me that they have a child, or gotten a girl pregnant. Chester's too cautious to have kids. I remember one of the first times I picked him up. He was staying with his uncle then, inside of an apartment. I perked up after Chester walked out of his uncle's apartment, opened my car door, and stepped into my car. I perked up because inside of my car, he turned to me from his passenger seat and pulled out a roll of condoms that unfurled from his hand like a tongue.

Now that I think about it, Chester is one-of-a-kind. He's a one-of-a-kind dawg that hooked me up with all types of girls. Girls who were fat, short, skinny, tall. That party line he always call lets him meet all kinds of girls, but none of them can do nothing for me. I'm a grown man with three kids. Three little girls. I need a girl that's motherly and housewifely; not one that's loose and young-minded. Most of the girls he met on there are that. It won't be too long before Allison busts it wide open for Chester. The Thursday that just passed is the last time I made Chamiqua bust it wide open for me-that was six days ago. I remember she came home from work in the wee morning hours of that Thursday morning, crawled into bed, and asked me if I was woke. I turned to her, told her 'Yeah', and she turned her back to me then scooched closer so we could start snuggling. We were both partially clothed at the time, and Chamiqua started many conversation topics while we were cuddling. She talked about her day at work, past relationships, our friends and family, sex, the future. She talked about anything. When she started talking about movies, I told her about an action movie I rented from Whitetelephone Films. It was about a fugitive that was running away from a bounty hunter, and the fugitive led the bounty hunter into this forest. The chase continues in the forest, before the bounty hunter loses track of the fugitive-he managed to shake his pursuer.

Throughout the movie, that fugitive comes up with various ways to kill his pursuer. Some of the methods I saw were brand-new. The fugitive was wanted by some government agency, and he wasn't just a regular criminal that jumped bail. I don't remember the name of that man or that organization he worked for. I liked the setting of that movie, it gave the two main characters of it an arboreal persona. Traps are what that bounty hunter set for that fugitive, but he didn't succumb to any of them. Explaining all of that to Chamiqua was real fireside. I liked that scene in the morning when the fugitive dropped a moose. That animal was dumb to waltz right up to the killer. That was a far-cry from what I expected. If he was real and ever stepped on my toes, I'd have to kill him. I'd kill him because I know he'll do the same thing to me if he had the chance. What did I have for dinner that night I told Chamiqua about that movie? I think I had meat loaf.

Meat loaf with ketchup on it. The size of that piece I had was big too. Cutting and eating the meat loaf with a fork is what I did that night. Relatable was that scene in the movie when the bounty hunter was chasing that fugitive. Both of them ran through the cathedral-like forest. That fugitive's legs were longer than the bounty hunters, but the bounty hunter ran swiftly-both of their legs scampered like those of children in some wild game that would end only when they dropped exhausted. I also told Chamiqua how that movie ended. That movie I rented from Whitetelephone Films ended as the fugitive was dying. He got what was coming to him after he stepped on that trap that hung him upside down. That bounty hunter didn't set that trap for the fugitive, because he was surprised when he found the fugitive suspended naked from his feet from the branches of a tree. Crawling below him was the sated leeches that fed and dropped away from him, while runnels of blood crisscrossed his body. That was a gruesome scene, because he lost so much blood and flesh but still remained conscious.

While watching it I asked myself a question: Did the ones that did that to him know that suspending someone upside-down prevents them from fainting? Did they know that he would probably lose half his flesh before he died? That bounty hunter looked at the fugitive as a leech fell from him, and that falling leech set the fugitive into a slow turn. The fugitive looked pathetic when he looked at the bounty hunter with his remaining eye. It was pathetic that he whispered that bounty hunter's name, and the bounty hunter heard such pleading in his name that he almost showed mercy. That's when he aimed the lasergun at the fugitive's head for a long moment before slinging it away.

After slinging it away, he walked off. He walked off just like I'm walking off from this fallen tree-I stay under the shady canopy as I'm walking from it. I stroke each tree wonderingly as I pass. "You're a strange man, strange and at times infuriating, but a sweet guy just the same," is what Roz said to me that day. She called me strange before saying, "You and your everlasting trees! How in the world can a grown man get so wrapped up in trees? Other people could develop a empathy for animals, for birds, for flowers, but with you it's trees."

Roz said all of that to me after I told her why I was going to the forestry college. It's true that I live for trees. I love them and seem to understand them but unlike what Roz said there aren't times when it seems I even talk with them. When I place my hand on the bark of a coast redwood, I stop walking. This tree in front of me is a coast redwood I know, and a coast redwood doesn't differ much from a Sierra redwood. The sequoia is referred to as a Sierra redwood or big tree, because the sequoia is a tree that ranks among the largest and oldest living things on Earth. Sequoias grew over most of the Northern Hemisphere millions of years ago.

The western slopes of the Sierra Nevada mountains of California, at elevations from 5,000 to 8,000 feet, is now where sequoias only grow and they only do that in about 70 groves there. A Cherokee Indian leader that invented a written alphabet for his tribe inspired the name for that tree, because the Cherokee Indian's name was Sequoyah. While my hand is on its bark, I look up the length of the coast redwood. Coast redwoods are tall, and they're taller than most sequoias, because sequoias don't grow as tall as coast redwoods. They don't grow as tall as coast redwoods but sequoia trunks are much larger than coast redwood trunks. About a 100 feet around at the base is the diameter of several sequoia trunks-39 feet, 39 whole feet, is the diameter of the widest sequoia trunk. The widest sequoia trunk belongs to a sequoia called the General Giant, and the world's largest tree in volume of wood is the General Sherman tree. I've seen a picture of the General Sherman tree and that's one enormous tree. That man looked like an ant while standing in front of the sequoia. That sequoia that's the world largest tree according to the volume of its wood. That giant sequoia ranks as one of the oldest living things on Earth.

Exceeding 2,000 years of age is what many giant sequoias do-sequoias were cut down in the past. They were cut down until a law was passed that protected sequoias from being cut down, and that law passed after one of the oldest and largest of them was chopped down. The people that counted that fallen sequoias growth rings determined that it dated back to 1305 B.C.; that sequoia would exceed 3,300 years of age if still living today. Extremely durable are the giant sequoias. Disease, insect attack, or old age aren't the killers of that tree, because no sequoia has been known to die from them. Fire doesn't injure sequoias because their thick bark protects them from injury by it. They can't be injured by fire but they are injured by the effects of a rainstorm, since lightning has destroyed the tips of most of the largest sequoias. I lower my eyes from the top of the coast redwood tree, take my hand off of its bark, and continue walking. Under the shady canopy of tree branches I keep walking, because I'm in no rush to go back out onto the barren area of this forest that's shadeless; I'm enjoying the coolness. To walk further into the forest, I turn to my right then push aside some leaves. I step into a dense area of the forest, and see the sun slanting down through the early morning mist in thick golden bars.

Deeper into the area I walk. I approach an extracurricular job I did months ago-the willow tress bow towards the man-made, rock-lined brook as though paying homage to the waterfowl that swim there. The brook is made too, and I stand over it. I look down at my reflection in the brook, and see some kind of charcoaled raisin-colored beast, wearing a Toad Island issued long black pants, long-sleeved grey Toad Island collared shirt, and a Toad Island hat with braids sticking out from under it, staring back at me from the water. After looking at my reflection, I walk along the brook's length. Sounds of the forest are what I hear as I'm walking along the brook, with a planting gun in my hand and a backpack with six inch tall trees adhered into its holes on it. I approach a flock of waterfowls that fly away as I near them; a flock of white birds was disturbed by me once.

A variant of albino hawks is what they must have been because their beaks were too pronounced and formidable, and their claws were too large for me to think that they were anything other than albino hawks. Like ghosts propelling themselves from graves is how the albino hawks looked, and there were nearly fifty of them that rose from concealment-I remember hearing the flapping of their wings that were stirring the air with their determination to disappear overhead as quickly as possible. They succeeded in doing so. No more than five seconds before the air had settled as if they had never existed, and the only thing that remained was the excited beating of my heart. They say that birds of a feather flock together, so me associating with people like Chester and Warren makes me-Boom! Tha plane up there just went supersonic.The last time I heard a plane go supersonic directly over my head was when I was sixteen. I was walking in the woods, like I am now, when that plane made a booming noise in my sixteen-year-old ears. I look at the plane fly away and get smaller and smaller. Until I can't see it no more, I look at it. Like I was saying before that plane stopped me. Birds of a feather flock together, so me associating with people like Chester and Warren makes me-I was going to say also fast, but that plane just gave me a new word. Birds of a feather flock together, so me associating with people like Chester and Warren makes me...transsonic. Yeah, transsonic. I'm moving fast just like them but even faster, so I'm relating to speeds about 741 miles per hour, and the definition of transsonic is that. I stop looking at the sky, and resume to walking in the forest. I see no more waterfowls, and the only sign of life is a mosquito.

A shiny mosquito that seems to be in love with my belt. I take a swipe at the shiny mosquito, and it starts flying away. Once the mosquito flies away, I turn around and start walking back the way I came. The leaves I pushed aside earlier are made to, and I push them aside and walk out of the dense area of the forest. Towards the barren area of this forest I walk. A tree of sweat is growing on the back of my shirt, but I still walk out into the sun. The sun starts beaming on me-I decide to collect myself before I return back to planting seeds. An old mossy stump is walked to by me.

After making it to the stump I shrug out of my tree backpack, sit it on the ground, unclasp the tree belt from around my waist, sit it on the ground, then look at the old mossy stump. I half-sit, half-fall onto the old mossy stump. From my sitting position, I stretch out just my left leg. Rubbing it is what I start doing, as I'm thinking about what I saw last night. The rub ends and I lean forward then put my forehead in the palms of both of my hands. Two minutes later, I decide that I can't have what might happen to Joey on my conscience. I sit up, take my cell phone out of my pocket, and look at its screen before scrolling through the menus.

Before I got into my bed earlier this morning, I looked through the Yellow Pages and found the number to Child Welfare. I programmed the number into my cell phone then went to sleep. I find the Child Welfare number I programmed into my cell phone last night, and I move the bar down it to press DIAL. I put the cell phone to my ear, and hear three rings before a voice answers. "Child Welfare. Main Desk." I hesitate.

"Uh, yeah, I want to make a complaint."

"What kind of complaint sir?" the voice asks. I say, "A complaint about something I saw last night."

"Okay," the voice says.

"We have many departments that may assist you. Which one do you need to be connected to?"

"Which one?" I say.

"This is my first time calling Child Welfare. I don't know what department I need to talk to." The woman's voice says," You can talk to a social worker in supplement care services, supportive care services, or substitute care services. What is the nature of your complaint sir?" I say, "I saw a Mother letting her kid do something that he wasn't supposed to be doing. Last night."

"Exposure to immoral conditions," the voice says.

"You need to talk to one of the social workers in the supportive care department. Hold on while I transfer you to it."

"Alright." Elevator music is heard while wait for the transferal. A social worker answers.

"Supportive care services. Mrs. Rayfield speaking." I brace myself before speaking.

"Yeah, I want to make a complaint. A complaint about something I saw last night."

"Did what you see involve a child?" Mrs. Rayfield asks.

"Yes," I say.

"I saw the child exposed to an immoral condition."

"What kind of immoral condition?" Mrs. Rayfield asks. I clear my throat.

"Drugs. Last night, I went to a party and while I was sitting on the couch with his Mom that kid walked out of the frontroom where we was at. He came out, sat in between the two of us, and his Mom passed him the joint."

"Are you sure it was a joint?" Mrs. Rayfield asks.

"Not a cigarette or any other type of paraphenalia that may resemble it?"

"I'm telling you it was a joint," I say.

"I took a puff of the *wet* before he came out and took a puff of it." Seconds pass before Mrs. Rayfield speaks again. "So the child's Mother is a pothead?" I say, "Marijuana wasn't the only drug in that paper, embalming fluid was too, but that's beside the point."

"No it's not sir," Mrs. Rayfield says.

"I need to know what type of woman this Mother is before we go even further."

"I don't really know," I say.

71

"I just met her last night. But she didn't seem like a party girl, if that's what you mean, or a clubber."

"That's not enough to go on," Mrs. Rayfield says.

"From the amount of time that you did you know her, what kind of temperament did she have?" I say, "Quiet. Hardworking."-I decide to start pouring charm on Mrs. Rayfield- "And she really seemed to care about people. Maybe she should have been a social worker."

"In my experience, the world of social work is hardly staffed by caring people," Mrs. Rayfield says, in a tone that is expressionless probably like her face was while saying that.

"Well-meaning, but that is a different thing in my mind. The allegation that you just made against this Mother is very serious."

"Serious enough to look into?" I ask. "Yes," Mrs. Rayfield says.

"I will go to the family's home. I will confront the parents with the communities concern and try to learn about the quality of the child care they do or could provide. If I determine that your complaint is valid, I will offer to help the family through counseling and other aids to improve their parental functioning in order to prevent the possible loss of their child's custody."

"You mean her child's custody," I say. "Joey's in a single parent home."

"Thank you for clarifying that, Mr-," Mrs. Rayfield says.

"Powers. Marshall Powers," I say.

"Thank you for clarifying that, Mr. Powers," Mrs. Rayfield says.

"Now if you would, what's the address of the home I need to visit?" I sense that Mrs. Rayfield is writing down

Frieda's address as I give it to her and she says, "Okay. I'll carry this out," before her and I hang up with each other. I take my cell phone from my ear, lower it to around my waist, then look down at it. I look at it for a few long seconds, before taking a deep breath then exhaling forcefully.

A few names are scrolled through on my phone; after the bar highlights Chester's name, I press the DIAL button. I raise my cell phone back to my ear, and I hear ringing. Two rings. Three rings. Chester's answering machine comes on after the fourth ring. I hang up as the answering machine begins instead of leaving a message. My cell phone is pulled away from my ear, and I look at the time on its small screen. 9:02 a.m. That nigga's probably still sleep since it's nine o'clock in the morning. He's probably still sleep, but I have to tell him I stuck to my guns and did what I said I was gonna do. I dial Chester's number again, and he answers on the third ring. "What up whodie," Chester answers sleepily.

"What up Chester," I say, rubbing my stretched-out left leg while sitting on the old mossy stump.

"Were you sleep?"

"Fuck yeah," Chester says groggily. I say, "Oh. Well I'm not gonna hold you up. I just called to tell you that that ho with red hair will be getting a visit from a Mrs. Rayfield from Child Welfare; I just got off of the phone with her."

"You did?!" Chester exclaims, sounding as if he just jumped up.

"Yeah," I say.

"You know I was; I told you earlier this morning that I was gonna call." Chester says, "I know, but I thought you would have come to your senses. Or at least change your mind."

"God never changes Her mind," I say."

Oh, so you're God now?" Chester asks.

"No. I didn't say that," I say.

"All I said was 'God never changes Her mind.'"

"Neither does a judge at a family court," Chester says.

"I'm telling you, if that kid is took from Frieda, there'll be Hell to pay." I stand up.

"From who?"

"Not from me," Chester says.

"I'm behind you 100%. But I can't say the same for the rest of our clique."

"Who the fuck are they to judge me anyway?" I say, staring ahead at a thick stand of the forest.

"Nothing more than a bunch of leeches that always have their hands out when things are going good, but when shit hits the fan-"

As I'm looking at the thick stand of the forest, I see a dark form flitting between the trees. Because of the distance it's hard to judge its size but the form is certain: It's a man. I say, "Hold on," to Chester and start walking nearer to the thick stand of the forest to get a better look; the shadow instantly pops out and what I see is strange: A humanlike log stares at me then waves. I hold my breath as it waves at me. The humanlike log stops waving at me, turns around, and darts back into the thick forest stand.

"Chester, I'll call you back," I say, right before hanging up. As I'm putting my cell phone into my pocket, I take off after the humanlike log. I approach the thick forest stand, brush aside a frond, then start running deeper into the forest after the running humanlike log that looks back at me while I pursue it. About a minute after the pursuit started, the humanlike log slows down. It slows down, so I can clearly see the strange looking thing. The form looks human, but it's not; I've seen a tin robot before and this thing I'm chasing is like that, but instead of having a silver body it has a light brown body whose head and torso appears to be a log. Its appendages also look to be logs, and I'm frightened at its strange appearance. I start closing the distance between the two of us since it is now trotting-the frightening thing about that is it's slow, deliberate movement, its sense of power, its seeming confidence that nothing could prevent it from doing what it is doing. The humanlike log leads me into a wood clearing of the forest, and a log cabin comes into view-it trots to then up its front steps, pushes open the door, steps inside, and leaves the door open. I slow down as I near the front steps of the log cabin. The open front door entrance is stared at for a few seconds. Deciding to go in I do, and I slowly walk up the front steps then towards the open front door.

CHAPTER 6

I near the open wood-framed door until I'm at its entrance, stop, and peer inside the log cabin's interior. No life is seen-I see that it's safe for me to go in. This log cabin I walk into looks like something out of a taxidermist's wet dream. I say that because the walls are covered with trophies. The trophies are stuffed birds and fish and small animals, and the heads of larger animals-lions and bears. Taxidermy of rats and dogs and barn animals I've never seen before, but now I have. Teeming with dead animals this place is. I take my eyes off of the animal heads, and look forward at a bar of real maple. I walk towards the bar of real maple, slide open it's back cabinet, and find a dozen bottles of Black Jack. After unstopping one, I pick up the biggest tumbler I can find. About ten seconds later, I begin perusing this log cabin. I near then walk along the wall's length while looking at the animal heads, take a sip from my tumbler, then walk towards a door leading into another room. I put my hand on the door knob, turn it, and walk through.

Rustic and large is the interior of the room I enter. It has no walls aside from the exterior; the built-on bathroom is the size of a closet. Preserved in a way that I can't fathom is the hunting memorabilia, elk and deer heads, I see mounted on the wall; the hunting memorabilia is mounted on the wall besides a rainbow trout. I turn my eyes and see a historical-saloon painting of a bare-breasted woman with flowing red hair and a ribbon of flimsy gauze wrapped around her pubic area-the painting I see is hanging above an earth-tone sofa. I turn my eyes again, and I see stuffed ducks and geese suspended in time on the deep windowsills. My eyes are took off of them, and my gaze travels the room. I see that's it's also a living room, bedroom, and kitchen blended into one common place, before walking towards the door on the other end. As I'm walking, I pass a .30-.30 laser rifle hanging on pegs against the wall. The door is made to, I put my hand on its knob, and I turn the door knob. I walk through the door and- "You're late," a voice further in the room ahead of me says. I look up and see a young man with skin color different from mines, before he cocks his arm back-and hurls the deadly weapon in his hand at me with all of his strength! I stare astonished as the deadly spear point hurtles towards me, zoom right past my left-hand side, and impacts squarely into the wood of the door I just walked through. Looking at the buried barbed tip of the spear I do, before looking back at its thrower.

I shout at the thrower, "What the fuck you did that for!?!" while still holding the tumbler of Black Jack. From where I'm standing at I see a man that looks younger than me and has a head full of puffy black hair, and has on glasses-I also see that the man has a bad case of acne. The thrower with perennial acne answers in a pompous voice. "To teach you respect for your armor, Marshall. Years of repairing mounting assemblies, immense carburetors, herculean alternators, Brobdingnagian generators, prodigious combination screws, and monstrous pumps has gave me the needed knowledge to make it."

"Make what?" I ask.

"This is Sequoia," he says while looking at me, not taking his eyes off of me while sweeping his arm to his left at the humanlike log standing perfectly erect on the side of him.

"Sequoia," I say the word as if testing it, turning it over like a circuit board of unfamiliar make to look at all sides. I stop looking at the strange machinery and say, "You didn't answer my question," to the thrower while looking at him.

"What did you do that for?"

"What did I do that for?" he says.

"First, let me introduce myself. My name is Jude."-he pauses then continues- "I threw that spear at you for two reasons. The first one, you're an automaton-I've been watching you for a while now and the second one, Sequoia's armor is powerful enough to stop many weapons, such as that crude spear."

Jude turns towards the jagged weapon buried in the wooden door. Partially turning to my left to grab the spear with my free hand I do, after switching to my left hand the tumbler of Black Jack, while narrowing my eyes in rage as I'm looking at Jude. With it in my hand, I have a good mind to take the triple-pronged spear and attack the squirrely man.

"But don't think its armor is invincible," Jude says. He takes something out of his back pocket and holds up a small black box. Jude presses the single red button on it. I see Sequoia's chest open up, the wooden looking panels folding to either side. Jude walks to a nearby table, picks up a thing that looks like a circuit board and holds it up to me.

"A motherboard," Jude says, smiling.

"I debbed for it myself."

Jude walks back to Sequoia. I see him slide the small black box back in his back pocket, and plug the motherboard into the chest plate innards of the robot. The robot's light-brown boxy body shudders awake. Jude touches Sequoia's chest innards, pulls out a lasergun, then with one hand pulls back out the small black box. He presses the red button again and Sequoia's wooden looking chest panels closes. They close back, while both of Sequoia's glowing eye-view lens wobbles. I hear machinery hum-soft, electrical.

"As I was saying," Jude says to me, while pointing the lasergun at Sequoia.

"But don't think its armor is invincible." Jude turns to Sequoia and motions to a chair pressed up against the log cabin's wall.

"Go sit over there," Jude says, pointing to it. Sequoia looks at the chair as if it's a bear trap. Jude looks at me, nervously giggles, and says, "Jerry-built crap." Jude turns back to Sequoia while holding the lasergun at it.

"It's jerry-built crap, because it didn't follow my order which I programmed it to do. It sees that I'm pointing a lasergun at it. A lasergun that can dent its armor. Sequoia is automated. I've invented an idiot-child version of myself, programmed it with a sixteen-million branch decision tree-more than enough to simulate sentience. It followed my order to lead you here, but it didn't follow my order to sit down."

"Maybe because it knows you were going to blast it," I offer.

"I was," Jude says. "I was going to blast it in its chest just so you can see the minimal amount of damage that would be done to its armor."

"Why do you want me to see that?" I ask, walking closer to them while holding the tumbler of Black Jack. Jude turns to me.

"I've created this suit of armor just for you. You're the prototype for Seqouia. This high-tech protective covering will transform you into the invincible Sequoia."

"I'll pass," I say. Jude offhandedly looks at me. "We have a certain job to do here. We didn't particularly ask for it, it just happened this way, but we're stuck with it and we're going to do it, in spite of what your piddling little farm-boy conscience may feel about it."

"Piddling little farm-boy conscience?" I say.

"I'm the last person you want to rank on Forrest Gump. I said I'll pass-plus, I don't understand machinery."

"You can learn," Jude says.

"I don't want to learn," I say.

"And it just dawned on me. I know where I've seen you seen before. On the news. You're that Filipino boy that was kicked out of the Ergonomics School of Humanity. I remember what one of those teachers said about you. He said that although you showed linguistic aptitude, you wouldn't know a crescent wrench from a peasant wrench. I know that mechanical aptitude is a talent one is born with. You weren't."-I smile at Jude- "Your knowledge of ergonomics is what you learned watching television commercials for bran flakes. That means you didn't put *Sequoia* together."

"The hell I didn't," Jude says indignantly.

"Well, maybe you did. But you certainly didn't design it. And whoever did made it simple enough for a science-illiterate like you to manipulate. If you can run it, so can I, but I don't want to." Stunned is how Jude looks at me, before I turn around and walk out the door.

Since it's the end of the work day, I'm on my way home from Toad Island. About twenty minutes has passed since I left it. The atavistic orienteering that I had earlier this morning at the beginning of the work day still goes through my mind, but it disappears after I pull my Ford Taurus onto my house's driveway. I park my car outside underneath the sunny afternoon sky, instead of pulling into my car garage, then turn off my car. I get out, check my mailbox, see that nothing is in it, then walk towards my front door. Walking in my house I do, before closing the door back. After closing the door, I walk towards my sofa. Flopping down onto the couch I do. While I'm laying down on it I pick up *The Other Side of Suffering* off of my coffee table. I start leafing through its pages.

While I'm leafing through the book's pages, my front doorbell rings. I close the book, get up off of my couch, and walk towards my front door. The front door is made to, and I peek through its peephole. On the other side of it I see two little girls-one Black and one White-with uniforms on and their uniforms are identical to those worn by girl scouts. Standing behind the two little girls is an attractive Black woman with straight black hair, and she looks like she's around my age. I stop looking through the peephole, put my hand on the doorknob, and begin to open my front door. I open my front door and the two little girls say, "Would you like to buy some Girl Scout cookies?" in unison to me. I continue looking down at them and smile.

"What kind of cookies are they?"

"Gingerbread, peanut butter, chocolate macaroons," the little White girl says, looking up at me with an innocent look on her face. I look up at the attractive Black woman while still smiling.

"I like sugar."

"A lot of people do," the attractive Black woman says, smiling.

"You're right," I say. Before looking back down at the little White girl.

"I've seen you before. Your name's Andy right?"

"Yes," Andy says, shaking her head up and down. I turn to the little Black girl.

"What's your name?" The little Black girl looks up at the attractive Black woman and says, "My Mom told me to never tell my name to strangers."

"Oh, she did?" I say, looking at the attractive Black woman.

"Your Mom's a smart woman. A smart woman"-I look at the attractive Black woman's hands- "that doesn't have a ring on her finger."

"I'm not married," the attractive Black woman says.

"I'm married to my work."

"What do you do?" I ask.

"Besides this?" the attractive Black woman says.

"Besides being a Mother scout, I'm a first grade teacher at Eddy Elementary School." I ask, "A first grade teacher at Eddy Elementary school that's single?"

"Yes," the attractive Black woman says.

"My name's Judika. And you are?" I say, "Marshall," then nod at the little Black girl.

"And she's?" Judika looks down at the little Black girl whose shoulders she's touching.

"My daughther," Judika says, as though she is made of pure gold. "Her name is Anyanwu."-Anyanwu looks up at her Mom whose hands are still on her and Andy's shoulders- "You and Andy been girl scouts for how long now?" Anyanwu remains looking at Judika with her smile of innocence. "Today's our one year anniversary." That's an accomplishment," I say. Anyanwu looks at me and says, "So are you gonna buy some girl scout cookies?" I take my eyes off of Anyanwu and look at Judika.

"I will...if your Mom gives me a reason to. I'll buy a hundred dollars worth of cookies...if she comes back and braid my hair tonight."-I hold my hand out to Judika to shake- "Deal?" Judika looks at my hand for many long seconds before saying, "Deal," then sticking her hand out for us to shake. A few hours later, Judika returns to my house by herself. With no shirt on I stand back and let her in, after she rang the doorbell, and stare at her womanly curves as she walks further into my house. The front door is closed back, and I turn to Judika. "I see you already started without me," Judika says, looking at my half-and-half braided hair. I pat the side of my head that's an afro and say, "I just finished pulling this side out, and I was about to pull the other side out before I heard the doorbell."-I smile at Judika- "I want to help you as much as I can."

"That's considerate of you," Judika says. I motion to my couch, follow behind Judika as she walks to it, and look at her when she sits down. She opens her legs when she sits down on the couch, and I sit down on the floor in between them. She immediately starts pulling at my hair on the braided side. My scalp tingles at the tightness, and more than once I jump as Judika pulls too sharply at a tangle. While Judika is pulling out my last braid I say, "Hey, do you think I have too much hair on my chest," while plucking one of my chest hairs. "Have you always had that much chest hair?" Judika asks, pulling at the hair on my head. "I would assume that a less hirsute pectoral region would be more pleasing," I say, pulling up another chest hair.

"My ex-boyfriend-Anyanwu's Daddy-had a hairy chest," Judika says.

"Why the two of you don't talk anymore?" I ask, looking up at Judika. Judika says, "Living in the same house with that fool had a strange effect on me. 'Mornin', frog eyes' was how he often greeted me, just because I have big eyes. He really hurt my feeling when he said 'Is it just my imagination, or are you uglier than you were yesterday?'" I'm looking at Judika and I can see that Anyanwu's Dad did affect her. As good looking as she is, that man had the poor girl believing she's ugly. A sad expression is on Judika's face so I ask her a question.

"Not going to cry are you?" "Nope," Judika says. "I'm trying to forget how to do that." I turn around and all Judika sees is the back of my head.

"It's easy. I forgot how to a long time ago." Judika sniffles and says, "I'm not much a cryer anyway."-Judika tries to chuckle- "Watching *Judge Judy* is more my speed." We sit in silence for a while before all of my braids are pulled out. After they are, Judika's fingers begins twining in a braid-her face is close enough that I can feel her breath. While she begins braiding my hair, I pick up my stereo remote off of the coffee table in front of us. I hit the stereo, to hear the sound of *Guy's "Let's Chill"* through the speakers. While the two of us are listening to *Guy*, about half a hour passes while Judika is braiding my hair. Judika finishes braiding it, leans over me, and picks up the mirror I placed on my coffee table earlier. At last she holds out the mirror for me to see. I look at the image of my Black raisin-colored face, and my hair that is now tightly braided. I look at my face, smile, then turn my neck to face Judika.

"You did a good job," I say, smiling.

"I know," Judika says, getting up. I lean forward so Judika can stand up. She stands up, holds out her hand to me, and I grab it before she pulls me up.

"Walk me to the door?" Judika asks.

"You don't have to leave yet," I say.

"Yes I do," Judika says, turning to the door. I follow behind Judika as she walks to the door. After getting to it, she turns around, gives me a hug, and reaches into her jeans pocket. Judika pulls out a small piece of paper, hands it to me, then with her left hand caricatures holding a phone's receiver to her ear.

"Call me," Judika says, before turning to the door to open it. I look at Judika as she opens my front door. She walks through it-then closes it back. Soon as the door closes, my phone rings. I walk to it, look at the caller ID, and answer it.

"What up Warren," I answer. Twenty minutes later, I'm driving to the side of town where Warren stays.

"Do you know what these kids said to me? And yes, I said kids...these niggas are actually kids to me." I look up at the rear-view mirror of my moving car so I can see Warren's cousin in the backseat, and Warren's cousin continues his story.

"Those kids told me they're getting money here now! Where I'm from, I'm looking at those niggas like; they must be crazy to talk to me like that. They actually looked me in the face and said that shit like I'm a cold sucker. I had my hands in my hoody and both hands on the lasergun, so I hit him first....Zap, then his man zap-zap. Get money with the Devil now nigga!" Warren, in the front passenger seat, chuckles. I take my eyes off of Warren's cousin, as we approach the end of the street. I stop at the sign, look both ways, then make a right turn. 10:03 p.m. is the time I see it is on my car radio, as we start moving down the road during this Thursday night-no headlights from any other cars are seen, so the absence of them makes this road very dark. I ease my Taurus down the block.

"You said she usually be somewhere around here?" I ask Warren's cousin, looking in my rear-view mirror. Warren's cousin says, "Yeah, I know that that bitch is usually around here. Just keep driving. We'll see her trickin' ass on this road any minute now."

As if on cue, I see two bassas huddled together on a street corner.

"There she is," Warren's cousin says. I pull up to the curb next to them, see that one is female and the other male, and the female futiley squints into my car that she can't see into since the windows are tinted on my grey Ford Taurus. Warren's cousin lowers my back power window. The Black female bassa dressed provocatively approaches the window and Warren's cousin begins talking to her.

"What's happening baby girl?" How's my girl doing there? Does she needs more pampers or formula?" Let me take a second to explain what Warren's cousin is talking about. Another word for cocaine is girl. How much does she have left is what Warren's cousin is asking the bassa. He asked her if she needs cocaine by asking 'Does she need more pampers?' Heroin is the formula he's referring to.

"I need some more formula," the Black female bassa says, "I ran-" The Black female bassa is interrupted by the sudden appearance of a person that emerges out of some nearby bushes and approaches her companion, before she stops talking and looks at them. I lower Warren's power window so I can clearly see the person. The person that emerges out of the nearby bushes is a short guy with a little size on him, like he used to work out. He's wearing a green jacket, dirty brown jeans, a hat turned to the side of his head, and holding a bottle of Old E in his hand. Warren turns around in his seat and looks out his cousin's window before asking the Black female bassa a question.

"Who's that? I've never seen his bassin' ass before." While looking at her companion talking to the person wearing a green jacket she says, "That's Aries. Some shit's about to go down, because Slim was just telling me about how he's been ducking Aries for a few days now." I look closely at the two males and can overhear their conversation that is clearly heard in the quietness of the night.

"Man, let me get some of that raw so I can get a fresh one up in me," Aries says.

"I'm telling you Aries," Slim says, pleading, "I don't have none."

"Nigga, get a fresh one ready for me," Aries says.

"I can't do that," Slim says. Before he sees it coming, Aries brings the bottle of Old E down hard on top of Slim's head. As Slim is laid out on the ground, Aries looks towards us and yells out, "That's right, that's right I freshened him right on up!" before he starts dipping down the block. Warren's cousin lowers his window even more to the still shocked bassa, "Are you gonna get in or what? I have formula for you." He opens his door and slides away from her so she can get in. The Black female bassa takes one more look at Slim's sprawled-out body on the grass, climbs into my car, closes the door back, and I pull off.

"Drive all the way to the end of this street," the Black female bassa says, "then make a left." I do as she says, and after making a left I see that it's a dead end street. At the end of the dark dead end street, I turn off my car. The only light in it comes from the overhead street light we are parked under. Since my car is turned off, there is absolutely no sound-the sudden silence makes the cramp and dismal car interior seem even smaller. The sound of moving plastic goes into my ears, and I look into my rear-view mirror towards the backseat. I see Warren's cousin hand the Black female bassa a bag of heroin. The dope fiend examines the bag of heroin, holding it up and thumbing it in an attempt to make all of the contents fall to the bottom. Seconds pass, before she looks up at the rearview mirror at me.

"What's wrong with him?" the Black female bassa asks Warren's cousin, looking at me. Warren's cousin says, "What do you mean 'What's wrong with him?'".

"He's sitting all stiff," the Black female bassa says, "like he's scared." I turn around and say, "I'm not stiff," before I look at Warren. Warren stops looking at me and he too turns around to look at the Black female bassa. "Shut up bitch and make my cousin's dick stiff." Seconds pass, before the Black female bassa lights up her crackpipe in my car. She smokes the heroin, finishes, and gives Warren cousin's his payment after doing so. She starts sucking Warren's cousin dick in my car-slurping sounds goes into my ears as she does.

After Warren's cousin and the Black female bassa finish what they're doing, I start my car back up; back to the street corner where the Black female bassa was standing at I drive. She's dropped off, and I start driving to Warren's Mom house. He'll be dropped off first since he stays closer. I make it to Warren's Mom house, stop in front of it, and Warren opens his car door. Warren climbs out of my car, turns around to look at me, and says, "Be easy Marshall," as his cousin climbs out of the backseat. "Alright cuz," Warren's cousin says to Warren, grasping Warren's hand then shoulder clapping him. Warren's cousin sits in the front passenger seat, closes the door, lowers the window, and he and I both look at Warren as he walks towards then into his Mom's house. Next, I drive to Warren's cousin house; I arrive there about ten minutes later. I stop in front of Warren's cousin house, he gets out, closes his door back, before I start driving myself home. 1:13 a.m. is the time it is when I make it home.

Between four and five hours of sleep was had after I made it home earlier this morning, so I'm not tired. It is now 8:17 a.m., I'm at work, and I'm again doing what I was told to do two days earlier-supervise the camping area. I'm supervising the camping area and campers, but I'm not riding a bicycle this time. All I'm doing is walking through this section of Toad Island called 34 Stony Hillock, while the early morning sun shines on me. A boulder sits on top of an artificial slope in 34 Stony Hillock. The boulder never changed for the billions of years it circled the sun-the boulder was once part of an asteroid. Etching its surface is done by the moss I see on it because of the moss' fragile acid, and the moss beards it face. I see inside of its pores autumn rain, and rain was frozen in it last winter.

Zigzagging down its front is a hairline crack-a hairline crack that looks like it's avoiding the splotches of eagle shit. I stop looking at the boulder and walk past it, shield my eyes as I'm looking up at the sun, and bring my head back down while walking on a treeless plain in Toad Island. As soon as I bring my head down, I see a grizzly bear. A fully grown grizzly bear! It's a fully grown female, a good six hundred pounds. And she's looking directly at me! Three tentative backward steps are what I take, and my equilibrium is so bad on the fourth backwards step during my dervish act my heel slides on the slick ground. I flail for a moment, recover my balance, but after recovering I see that the harm is done.

As she is hissing her intentions, the grizzly bear stops plodding and begins bounding at me. My body becomes a blur when I turn and run, while the grizzly bear roars in pursuit. In less than two bounds she's halved the distance between us, and her jaws are wide in readiness- *"Get Down!"* I throw a glance back in the direction of the voice and there, thank God, is Jude, laser rifle raised in his hands. *"Marshall!"* Jude yells. *"Get your fucking head down!"* The message is got, and I fling myself to the grassy ground-only a body length from my heels is the distance between the grizzly bear and I. Jude fires, hits the animals' shoulder, and that checks her before she can catch up with me. An agonized roar bellows out of the grizzly bear as it rises-blood stains the grizzly bear's fur.

Joey is hunched over his desk, idly making doodles on a sheet of construction paper. He is drawing a fire truck. The absurd scribbles have little resemblance to a fire truck, to an adult-to Joey it is a three dimensional fire truck. Children think differently and see differently. Give children pencil and paper, and they will draw something which looks different to them than to an adult. Joey decides that his drawing is finished, and he gazes in awe at his own creation. He gazes in awe at his own creation, while sitting at his desk in a classroom at Eddy Elementary School. It is 2:50 p.m., so the bell signaling the end of the school day will be ringing in ten minutes for the child.

The child whose Mother made the mistake of giving a child a narcotic to smoke, and she did that in front of Marshall Powers. Joey's Mother will forever regret that what she did, because setting into motion Frieda's and Joey's seperation from each other will be done by caseworking. Caseworking by a caseworker by the name of Mrs. Rayfield. Unbeknown to Joey, Mrs. Rayfield is sitting in her vehicle parked outside of Eddy Elementary School. She is waiting for the final school bell to ring, so she can approach Joey and ask him a few questions. A few questions that might lead to Joey being one of the millions of children protected from abusement, neglect, or abandonment; about 1,500,000 such children were reported as being that thirteen centuries ago in the year of 1983-unfortunately, the actual numbers of such cases are considerably greater than the numbers reported.

About seven percent of the total number of such cases reported in 1983 was the percentage of reported abandoned children, almost forty six percent was the percentage of neglected children in 1983, and the category that Joey falls into was about twenty eight percent in 1983-twenty eight percent of the protected children in 1983 were abused. The remaining percent of reported child cases were a combination of causes. 3:00 p.m. strikes on the wall clock in Joey's classroom, and the final school bell rings. Nearly all of Joey's classmates jump up from their desks, run to their cubbyholes, and unhook their backpacks from off of the cubbyholes' hook. Doing those same things are done by Joey and he puts on his backpack, before beginning to dash past his teacher. His teacher who's a young Black woman named Judika.

"Joey wait!" Judika says, looking down at the seven-year-old. Joey stops and looks at Judika.

"Don't forget to do your homework," Judika says, "and be safe while walking home."

"I will," Joey says, before running out of his classroom. Outside, Mrs. Rayfield begins climbing out of her forest-green Suburban Outback as she sees students begin streaming out of Eddy Elementary School. The Black female in her middle thirties gets completely out of her vehicle; she turns and close the door back after she does, before pursing her lips while using her electronic key lock to lock her vehicle. She locks it then starts walking across the street towards the school. Mrs. Rayfield's long black hair is pulled back into a ponytail, and it bounces a bit as she walks towards Eddy Elementary School in her Armani plum-colored skirt suit. The street is crossed completely by her and she nears the entrance of that school while many rambunctious children flow past her. She makes it to the school's front entrance- Mrs. Rayfield stops and scans the faces of the many children walking by her. Less than a minute later, she spots Joey.

"Joey!" Mrs. Rayfield shouts to get his attention. Joey stops and warily looks at Mrs. Rayfield. He remains looking at the Black woman cautiously, while being approached by her. Standing near the front office of his school they both are, so Mrs. Rayfield feels that what she's about to do shouldn't scare Joey too much. Mrs. Rayfield stops in front of Joey and kneels down. "You don't know me Joey but my name's Mrs. Rayfield."

"Mrs. Rayfield?" Joey repeats.

"Yes," Mrs. Rayfield says, smiling.

"I just want to ask you a few questions."

"Why do you want to do that?" Joey asks, with a puzzled look on his face.

"To help you," Mrs. Rayfield says. "I want to help you if you need my help. Okay?" Joey looks at Mrs. Rayfield for a few seconds before answering.

"Okay." Mrs. Rayfield smiles even wider to put the child at ease.

"First," Mrs. Rayfield says, "what's your Mom's name?" Joey says, "I just call her Mom, but I've heard other adults call her Frieda." "Frieda," Mrs. Rayfield repeats. "How does Frieda look?"

"Byooful."

"Of course," Mrs. Rayfield says. "Aren't all Mothers? But give me some details. Her hair, for instance. Blond?" Joey shakes his head from left to right.

"Red straight." Soon as those words leave his lips, turning a hallway corner is done by Judika. Judika looks at Mrs. Rayfield squatting in front of her student, and she is looking at the two of them from a distance. She sees Mrs. Rayfield holding Joey's hand, smiling and talking to him. Her face is very animated, while Joey is laughing. Judika watches them for a while, before she approaches Mrs. Rayfield. While walking towards Mrs. Rayfield Judika says, "Excuse me ma'am." Mrs. Rayfield looks at Judika. Judika asks, "What are you discussing with my student?"

I spread the dendriform armor on my bed in front of me. Earlier today at work, after Jude saved me from being mauled by that grizzly bear, I spent over two hours in that log cabin talking to him. While talking to him, I thanked him for saving my life. I told him, "Since you saved my life, I'll sponsor Sequoia. After I did Jude smiled, and said, "You're no longer lost forever in this hellridden forest," and began explaining to me how to use Sequoia's binary programming language before showing me how to don it. It's 5:07 p.m. and less than an hour has passed since I left Toad Island with Sequoia in my trunk, came home, carried the machine into my house, and dropped its pieces on my bed. I'm now studying its pieces carefully, and I begin assembling the dendriform outfit, putting on the components one at a time- and enjoying every minute of it. Stiff and sturdy are the foot blocks that appears to be wooden which I put on first.

After the foot blocks that appears wooden I put on the greaves that appears wooden, then the shin armor that appears wooden, then the leg plates that appears wooden, then the torso that appears to be wooden, then the arm plates that appear to be wooden, and finally I slip my hand into the inner lining of the gauntlet-sized steel metal orbs that serves as Seqouia's hands; both of the steel marble orbs bite into my wrists, so they're on snugly. Already I look like I have been transplanted into the trunk of a sequoia-already I feel like a fighting machine encased in an impenetrable shell. I look at the last piece of Seqouia on my bed, and the log-looking helmet has only two features on it: Two deep sunken red orbs that serve as the eyes and a slender short twig that serves as its nose. Putting on the helmet with these steel orbs on would be cumbersome, so I take them off. After taking them off I pick up the helmet. I stare deeply into it-I see on its inside walls wires, circuits, old-fashioned transistors, and newfangled batteries with transparent shells that let me the see the blue and yellow liquids inside.

The materials in it are very streamlined, this helmet is very clean, but I can't help feeling that it has been put together with a prayer and a wing. Probably to be more accurate, a curse and a tentacle. I start raising the helmet. Put it on and then....*Oneness!* This suit is like a tree, I think. I can feel within it the same aliveness that I find in any tree. And that, is ridiculous, because this machine isn't a tree. But the thought persists: This thing inside of which I have been thrust is similar to a tree. I walk into my bathroom, turn on its lightswitch, and look at my image in the bathroom's wide tall lengthy mirror. For over a minute, I look at myself. I stand totally encased, completely encased-I can feel the machinery attached to my body. Now I'm somebody instead of someone to be reckoned with: Sequoia. While I'm staring at myself in the bathroom mirror, my house phone starts ringing. I turn off my bathroom light as I'm walking out of the bathroom, take off both steel marble orbs on my hands before tossing them on my bed, do the same with the helmet, walk into my kitchen, pick up my cordless house phone, and look down at the caller ID. I see that it's Judika, and I press the Answer button just as it starts ringing again.

"Come over here and give me some of your brown sugar," I answer.

"You know I'm a diabetic for your love."

"I've never heard that one before," Judika says.

"Marshall, I'm upset."

"Upset," I say.

"Why?" Judika says, "I'm upset because I found out about two hours ago that one of my students might be taken from his Mother. I'm a Mother myself, so I know how it'll be not only for me but Anyanwu also if she and I were ever to be separated. Separated like my student and his Mom is going to be."

"Why are they going to be separated?" I ask, standing in my kitchen wearing Sequoia from the neck down. "That social worker said something about immoral conditions," Judika says. "And it'll be easy to prove because of the vacuous look in Joey's eyes." Judika's last two words startle me.

"You said Joey?"

"Yeah," Judika says.

"He's one of the students in my class and-"

"What was the name of the social worker you talked to?" I ask, interrupting her.

"Mrs. Rayfield," Judika says. Right after she does my house phone beeps, I look at who's calling me, and I say, "Hold on Judika," before switching to the other line.

"Chester, you've just put an end to the awkwardness," I say, "Hold on." I switch back to Judika and say, "Judika that's someone important, so I'll call you back."

"Alright," Judika says, before hanging up. Chester and I are reconnected.

"What up?" I say. "You should have come with us last night. You missed a bassa knock another one out cold."

"I heard," Chester says, "Warren told me what went down. You wanna go this party at Blue Swallow motel tonight?"

Stars twinkle in the night sky above my grey Ford Taurus as I pull into the Blue Swallow Motel's premises. Chester is seated beside me in the passenger seat, and Warren is sitting in the backseat. I find a parking space, and we all get out before starting to walk to room 514. Chester takes the lead, Warren and I follow behind him, and we both remain standing behind him when he makes it to room 514. Chester rings the doorbell, waits for a few seconds, then rings it again.

Not too long after the doorbell rings a second time, the motel room door is opened-opened by a Black female that appears to be in her late twenties and has red curly weave in her hair.

"Chester!" the Black female says. "Come in!" Chester, Warren, and me all walk into the motel room that appears to be extra small because of the number of bodies in it-there are two double mattresses in it and there are three Black males sitting on that one and two Black females sitting on the other one; a light-skinned Black female is sitting on a chair pressed up against the wall just like that other one that is pressed up against the wall and that one's sat on by a Black male that appears to be around twenty. We all walk further in the room and the music from the speakers blast into my ear.

> *It's eastside in this bitch*
> *Wish a nigga wood like a tree in this bitch*
> *If a leaf fall put some weed in that bitch*
> *That's my m.o., add a b to that shit*

Chester walks to the light-skinned female that is sitting on the chair pressed up against the wall and starts talking to her; Warren approaches one of the girls sitting on one of the double mattress beds and starts conversating with her; and I stand silent as my back is pressed up against the wall while eyeing the Black girl that opened the door for us. For a few minutes, I stand up with my back pressed up against the wall as Chester and Warren socialize. I finally decide to leave, approach Chester, lean down to tell him over the music I'm about to go, then approach Warren. I stop in front of him, and hold out my fist for him to bump; Warren just looks down at it then back up at me.

"You about to go?"

Warren asks over the music, before I shake my head up and down while still holding out my fist for him to bump. Warren says, "Be easy Marshall," and bumps my fist before I turn to leave. I walk out of the small motel room filled with Black youths, make it to my car under the moonlit sky, get in it, before starting to drive out of Blue Swallow Motel premises. Just as I stop at the stop sign at Blue Swallow Motel's entrance/exit, a police car pulls up behind me; it's blue and white lights pop into view behind me while I hear the familiar whoop. I slam my gear into park, slump backwards in my driver's seat, play with the tip of one of my braids, and look out of my front window irritably while I wait for the police to come to my driver's window. When I see a police officer begin walking to my car, I lower my power window.

"What's the problem officer?" I ask the police officer as he stands at my window.

"Step out of your car so we can search it," the police officer says, smiling.

"Don't you need a search warrant first before you tell me to do that?" I ask.

"Not when I have probable cause," the police officer says, still smiling.

"Many people have been busted with drugs in their cars while driving out of here tonight." I begin to protest again, decide not to, and go ahead and get out since I know I don't have anything illegal in my car. The police officer says, "Stand over here," while backing up to the place where he wants me to stand. As him and I are standing off to the side, his partner searches my car. To keep me from watching his partner and breaking out into a run, the police officer standing by me starts making small-talk.

"What side of town do you stay on?" the police officer asks me.

"I stay in Eddy," I say dryly.

"Eddy," the police officer repeats. "I heard that the houses over there are cheap. What brings you all the way from Eddy to a motel on this side of town?" Piratical is the smile I show him.

"I was gonna check out a room for the night-I didn't feel like sleeping in my own bed; but I changed my mind soon as I parked."

Lying to the cops is done by people all the time. The guilty and bad guys aren't the only ones that do. An equal opportunity activity is lying. Lying is done by innocent people. Lying is done by Mothers of small children. Lying is done by paper-pushers. Lying is done by grandmas. The cops are lied to by everyone. Embedded in the human genetic code is what it seems to be. The cop knows I'm lying. I have no doubt he knows, but he can't prove that I am.

"A wise ass huh?" the police officer says.

"Well, we'll see how much of a wise ass you are when we find what you don't want us to find in your vehicle." His gaze breaks from me and we both look at my car. His partner diligently searches the interior, uses the lever on the inside of my car to pop my trunk, then walks to it. I don't know what's going on back at that motel room as his partner begins raising my trunk....Chester says to the young Black female before walking away, "I'll be back," and he starts walking towards the bathroom in that Blue Swallow Motel room. As he is walking to it, Warren looks at him.

"Murk! Throw this away for me," Warren says over the music, before lobbing his empty beer bottle at Chester. Chester catches it, turns back around, and continues walking to the bathroom. There are two single mattresses in that motel room, and Warren is sitting on the closest one to the door with his back facing it while he's talking to one of the three young Black females sitting on the other one.

"My bad," Warren says. "Continue what you was saying."

The Black female says, "Like I was saying Treetop walked up to Aries and said 'You stupid mu'fucka, why would you steal from me, huh?'"-she hears the doorbell ring and see her friend get up and answer the door before she continues-"Treetop slapped dude upside his head, like he was some young schoolboy getting popped by his Mama for not cleaning up his room." Warren chuckles and he begins to say something to that young Black female before she stares past his shoulder and mutters, "Speak of the Devil." Warren turns around and he sees a very bony Black male who appears to be in his early twenties: Treetop.

Treetop smiles as he walks into the party, gazes at all in it, then near one of the Black males sitting on the single mattress. He nears him and they slap their hands together, right before Treetop looks at Warren. No emotion is on Treetop's face as he look at Warren; their eyes lock into one another's.

"What they do fool?" Warren asks. Treetop says, "I'm fine as rain," then walks away from Warren to the small cooler to get a beer. *That's odd*, Warren thinks to himself; he thinks that because he knows some people say right as rain and some people say fine as paint, but none, as far as he knew, said fine *as* rain. To him it probably means nothing, but- Treetop socializes with the Black youths while drinking the beer in his hand, and that Black male with a too-tall construction body takes a cigarette pack out of his back pocket. Treetop puts a cigarette in his mouth, and it dangles from his lips while he holds the beer bottle in his hand. With his free hand, he takes a lighter out of his pocket. He is just about to light the cigarette tip when the young Black female with red curly weave stops him with a wave of her hand.

"I don't think so nigga," the Black female says.

"I debbed for this room and I can't take the smell of smoke, so take that shit outside."

Treetop looks at her with an irascible expression on his face, but he does as he's told. Warren gets up after he walks out, start walking towards the bathroom, and while walking towards it looks down at the seat of one of the now empty chairs pressed up against the wall. He takes his eyes off of the empty chair and besides it he sees sitting down on the other chair a Black light-skinned female and she has been sitting there ever since Marshall left. Warren makes eye contact with her, flashes his gold teeth at her in a smile, and an idea comes into his mind. His idea consists of him making a drug sale to that Black female by taking the sandwich bag with an eight ball in it out of his pocket, sitting it on the empty seat of the chair next to her, then telling her to watch it for him while he use the bathroom.

Warren know it's nowhere near a subtle approach, but it's the only approach that he can quickly think of. Warren takes the dope out of his pocket, sits it on the seat, then looks at the Black female.

"Watch that for me while I use the bathroom," Warren says, pointing down at the eightball. The Black female just shakes her head up and down, before Warren walks away towards the bathroom.

"You still in there Murk?" Warren asks, facing the bathroom door. Warren hears Chester say, "Yeah. I'm still shitting," before he turns around to walk back out into the party. As he's nearing the end of the hallway leading back out into the front, Warren sees Treetop. He sees Treetop's very bony and over six-foot frame standing near the empty chair he placed his dope on, as he's looking down at the seated Black female while talking to her. Warren walks back out into the party, and Treetop doesn't look at him as Warren stands near him and the seated Black female.

"I need mine," says Treetop, his eyes wide open as he rubs his hands together, thinking that in a minute he would be high as Mars.

"I'm serious," the Black female says.

"That's not mines."-she looks past Treetop, sees Warren, and begins pointing at him-"That's his'." Treetop looks behind him, sees Warren, and says, "Oh." Treetop begins to walk away from them, but quickly swings back around and sits on the edge of the empty seat. Treetop looks at the Black female while partially sitting down.

"Easter isn't the only day that I eat chocolate bunnies." Treetop looks down at the sandwich bag with the eight ball of coke in it. He glances at Warren and says, "Move that shit out my way." Warren looks at Treetop with a live-wire look on his face before saying, "It's fine where it is."

Treetop jumps up and stands stockstill in front of Warren. Only seconds pass before everybody in that small motel room has all of their attention on the stare-down, and the Black female with red curly weave cuts off the stereo. "I said move that shit out my way," Treetop says to Warren, through clenched teeth. "And I said it's fine where it is," Warren says tightly, staring up at Treetop as though he is looking down on a small child.

"Are you saying you won't do it?!" Treetop shrieks.

"Is that what you're saying?!" The silence in the motel room bristles like a cactus.

"I'll die before I let a nobody nigga like you disrespect me," Warren answers.

Treetop snatches his lasergun out of his pants' waistband and becomes amazed at how steady his hand is as he levels it at Warren's chest. "You must want me to zap you dead, right here." Warren stares at Treetop an eternal second longer.

"You ain't gonna do shit...you're sweet as bear meat."

As those words leave Warren's mouth, Chester flushes the toilet then begins walking out of the bathroom. He begins walking down the hallway, and while he is he sees Warren's side profile looking at a person he can't see. It all happens too fast for him to intervene. Chester sees a flash of light emerge then strike Warren's chest; he then sees Warren flail backwards before his body crashes into the wall behind him. Chester sees Treetop appear, walk towards Warren's fallen body, then stand over it with a lasergun in his hand. Chester rapidly backs up, bumps into the closed bathroom door, and turns around before opening it then rushing back into the bathroom....I look at the police officer as he looks into my trunk. A mystified look appears on his face when he sees Sequoia's parts, shuffles them around, then look at us.

"Prescott," the police officer says, before waving him over.

"You may want to take a look at this."

The poilce officer whose name I now know is Prescott looks at me and says, "Walk in front of me to over there," before we both walk towards my trunk. We make it to it, and Prescott also looks at Sequoia's pieces; he looks at them then at me.

"What is that?" Prescott asks.

"A Halloween costume," I say.

"What? It's illegal to have a Halloween costume?"

"Maybe," Prescott says. "Halloween is four days away but why do you have it in your trunk? Have you committed a crime while wearing it?" I shrug.

Prescott looks at his partner to say, "Did you find anything else?" before his partner shakes his head from left to right. Prescott turns to me.

"Leave."

The two police officers walk back to their squad car, it's red and blue lights are still flashing on me, while I walk to the front of my car. I get into my car, turn it back on, and begin pulling off. While I'm driving, I take out my cell phone and dial Chester's number. Chester answers on the first ring.

"Marshall!" I begin rattling off, "Chester you and Warren be clean when you two leave that party because the police are hiding at the motel's entrance with their lights turned off-" "Someone just zapped Warren!" Chester blurts.

"Someone just zapped Warren?" I ask.

"Who?" "Chester says, "I don't know the nigga name, but he's still here! I was just walking out the bathroom-I went into it after you left, and was in it for a while-when I saw him zap Warren! I think Warren's dead!" I lower my eyelids.

"Where are you now?"

"In the bathroom!" Chester says. "I backed up and closed myself in it!" While making an illegal U-Turn in the middle of the street I say, "Stay there," and I hang up my cell phone. I floor the gas pedal, slow down as I near then enter Blue Swallow Motel entrance I just left, drive to the same parking spot I was in earlier, turn off my car, then get out. It begins to rain lightly as I walk to my trunk. I pop my trunk, and it doesn't take me long to don Sequoia.

As Seqouia, I run to room 514. Just as I'm about to open the door, a twenty-something looking Black man with a too-tall construction body flings open from the inside room 514's door. He raises his lasergun to my torso and squeezes blast after blast into it-each blast pushes me backwards. It's somewhere around the tenth laser blast that he sprints into the other direction off into the night. I stagger and lurch for a few seconds, before I collapse to the ground....Upon opening my eyes I see peering down on me the ugliest face I've ever encountered throughout my entire life.

"Jude!" I croak.

"It's about time you woke up, you sorry excuse for a soldier," Jude says unsympathetically.

"What happened?" I sluggishly say.

"And"-I look around and see that I'm in the log cabin and laying on the earth-tone sofa- "how did I get here?" Jude says, "Last night you lost a fight in a rather spectacular manner-you can blame the rainwater for that; that rainwater which got into Seqouia's circuitry and was responsible for the electricity that was conducted through it after it came in contact with laser blasts which triggered the sizzling sensation you felt." I hold up my right hand to look at one of my fingers on it that twitches continually and jerks rhythmically. I turn my hand over and see that the flesh on the back of my hand crawls in an inhuman fashion-I try not to seem disturbed by the phenomenon. Turning back to Jude I do.

"You didn't tell me how I got here"-I turn and look out the nearby window and see that it's morning- "this morning." Jude says, "You didn't get here this morning. Well, actually you did-but it was night when I first brought you here. Sequoia has a sort of GPS chip in it-I always know where it is-now I just so happened to be spying on you minutes after you were repeatedly zapped. I carried you to my car and brought you here to this cabin. You've been laying down since about two o'clock this morning." I stop looking at Jude, throw my head back on the sofa's pillow, fling my right arm across my face, and tightly shut my eyes.

"That nigga tried to kill me," I say, looking at the back of my closed eyelids.

"Someone did," Jude says.

"Nine dents from a lasergun were in Sequoia's torso that I just replaced." "Warren can't be replaced," I say, still holding my left arm over my face.

"Who's that?" Jude asks.

I open my eyes, take my arm from across my face, and sit up as I look at Jude. I say, "My dawg that was killed last night in that motel room you found me by. That nigga zapped Warren after I left that party me, him, and another person went to. I left early, leaving Warren and Chester there. I called Chester's cell phone as I was driving away from Blue Swallow Motel and he told me that nigga zapped Warren.

I drove back there, put on Seqouia; thinking I'd be laserproof, and that tall nigga was running out of the motel room just as I was about to open the door. He killed Warren so I'm going to kill him; after I find him, I'm gonna show that fucker what bad guys do after they turn good." Jude gulps, looks at me with vicissitude on his face, and says, "Still Marshall, don't you think that there is a better way to persuade him to your position than by suggesting that he, um, take up pederasty with a saguaro cactus?"

I near the driveway of my house that I've been from for almost twenty four hours-I left from it yesterday, Friday afternoon, at around six o'clock so I could buy some new gear from the mall before driving to Chester's side of town-because this radio's display shows 5:22 p.m. on this cloudy sunless Saturday afternoon. As I'm pulling onto the driveway, I press a button on my garage door opener and the garage door begins rising. Without having to stop and wait for it to open I fluidly drive into the car garage. The car garage is entered, I pull up as far as I can, close the garage door back with the push of a button, then turn off my car's ignition. I get out of my car-a single light bulb is shining because it comes on whenever the garage door is opened, and it stays on for a period of time before automatically going off-and walk into my house. The cloudy and sunless sky outside makes the interior of my house almost dark as it is when it's nighttime, so I reach up to my dining room's ceiling fan cord to turn on its lightbulbs.

Light materializes, and I walk to my house phone-I haven't been able to answer it for nearly a day so there might be a handful of messages on it; I pick it up and see that there is. With the phone in my hand, I walk to my couch. I sit down on the couch then lean forward and look down at the phone for a while, before I drop my head.

"Warren," I say, while my eyes are closed. I open my eyes, raise my head, lean all the way back on my couch, stretch out on it, sit the phone on the purple vulwood coffee table in front of me, throw up my right arm across my face, then fall into a deep sleep.

Ring! I'm woke up by my house phone ringing. I pick up my house phone off of my coffee table, then down at the phone's caller ID screen, and begin raising it to my ear while looking at the time on my wall clock. I saw that it's Allison calling me, and she's calling me at 10:07 p.m.-I've been sleep for about four hours on my couch. My house phone rings a second time while it's in my hand, and it begins ringing a third time right before I answer it. I answer, "What up Allison. You know it's ten o'clock at night right?"

"I know what time it is," Allison retorts. "Didn't you get any of my messages? I called you a few times yesterday, and a million times earlier today; I left messages."

I say, "I got them. I left my house about five o'clock yesterday afternoon and I didn't make it back here until a few hours ago."

"Why didn't you call me back after you saw I left messages?" Allison asks.

I say, "I was tired, and I still am; I fell asleep as soon as I got home and you just woke me up out of my sleep."

"Oh," Allison says.

"Well I've been trying since yesterday to get in contact with Chester too, but he's not picking up his cell phone. I can't get into contact with him so you'll have to answer for him"-Allison's tone turns low and accusatory- "Did he have anything to do with Frieda's son being took from her yesterday afternoon?" I sit up.

"Joey was took from her?"

"Yeah," Allison says.

"So did he?"

"No," I say.

"What about you?" Allison asks.

"What about me?" I ask.

Allison asks, "Did you have anything to do with Frieda's son being took from her?"

"Hell no," I say.

"Are you lying?" Allison asks.

I say, "Don't ask me no stupid shit like that." "DON'T ASK YOU NO SHIT LIKE THAT!? MOTHERFUCKER…" I hold the phone away from my ear as a string of expletives sizzles over the line. Once I hear Allison revert to a more normal pitch, I put the phone back to my ear.

"Allison, listen," I say. "If the social services people even think that a child is being abused, they'll remove the kid until they investigate."

"I didn't tell you that social services took Joey," Allison says suspiciously. I hit myself in the forehead with my right hand palm, while holding with my left hand the phone that is pressed to my ear.

"I assumed that they did. This is the 33rd century. Kids aren't kidnapped anymore. At that party we went to a few days ago, Frieda told me that her and her husband are separated-the only way that Joey could have been took was if his Dad wanted his son or if social services took him. I highly doubt that you'll be calling me if Joey was with his Dad."

"I wouldn't be," Allison says.

"So you're saying you nothing to do with Child Welfare taking Joey?"

"Yes," I say. "That's messed up that they took Frieda's son away from her, but I had absolutely nothing to do with that. I was sleeping before you called so let me get back to doing that."

"Yeah," Allison says, before hanging up. I also hang up, put the cell phone on the coffee table, then lay back down before going into a deep sleep. The next morning, I wake up to the sound of my house phone ringing. The caller ID is looked at, and I answer it. I answer, "You know who the nigga is yet?" to Chester.

"No," Chester says.

"Then why are you calling me?" I ask.

Chester says, "Me and Keith are going to Queen's Tick Market to get some t-shirts made for Warren. Wanna come?"

"Yeah," I say.

"Alright," Chester says.

"Come get me first before you get Keith at his house."

"Alright," I say.

"And Marshall?" Chester says.

"Yeah," I ask.

"Bring your fire."

Bafflement appears on Chester and I's faces on this sunny Sunday afternoon as I pull up to Keith's house, because standing in the fenced-in front yard is Keith's Mom that is holding Keith back while he appears to be trying to attack that old Black man that I know is his step-dad. I stop my car in the street up against the sidewalk curb in front of Keith's house, there aren't any other cars parked there, and Chester jumps out when I completely park. I expect for the white hat that he's wearing above his grey do-rag to fly off since he moves so fast out of my car before flinging open the front gate. Turning off my car I do, and after doing that I get out of my car. I get out, then sit both of my elbows on my car roof ceiling. Looking at the peculiar scene I first saw when pulling up to Keith's house I start doing, while my elbows are propped on the roof. Seeing Keith frantically move from

111

the left to the right while trying to get around his Mom is done by my eyes. Also done by my eyes is seeing Keith's Mom turn around, see Chester slowly approaching them, then back up a bit after Chester tries to restrain Keith too by putting his hands out in front of him; I hear Chester's voice. "What you doing Keith?!" Chester shouts, stooping down while both palms face him. "What it look like!?" Keith retorts, trying his best to get past his Mom and Chester to get to the old Black man.

"I'm about to beat this nigga's ass!"

"You ain't gonna beat shit," the old Black man standing on the porch says. With the palms of her hands still facing Keith, Keith's Mom turns to look at the old Black man.

"Be quiet Clarence," Keith's Mom says, before turning back to Keith. At the top of his lungs Keith shrills, "Nigga you don't wanna see me! I'm telling you, you don't wanna see me!" Keith stops, both restrainers back up a bit while lowering their arms slighty, Keith springs towards Clarence, before he is again blocked. Keith points at Clarence and says, "I'ma knock your block off!" then tries to get around his Mom and best friend.

"Come try knocking it off youngblood!" Clarence says, getting hyped-up himself.

"I want you to! This'll be the last block you try to knock off, after I get done with you!" Keith's Mom turns to Clarence again.

"Clarence be quiet! You're not helping the situation!"- Keith's Mom turns back to Keith- "Baby calm down. I'ma tell you like I told you over the phone: 'He wasn't talking about you'. He wasn't referring to you when he said 'That nigga ain't shit'. You gotta believe me. You know I usually talk on the phone in the frontroom where the tv's at; we were sitting down in it watching tv when you called and heard him say that about"-Keith's Mom turns to Clarence- "what was his name?" Clarence huffs.

"You ain't gotta explain nuthin' to him." Keith's Mom blows out of her mouth and turns back to Keith.

"Anyway; you overheard Clarence say that about that man on the tv while I was talking to you. Believe me Keith, he wasn't talking about you."

Keith stops trying to juke past Chester and his Mom, glowers at his step-dad for a few long seconds, looks at his Mom, then starts walking to the fence. Keith opens it, walks out of his Mom's front yard, and without looking at me walks towards my car-the back right door is opened by him. As he is opening it, Chester starts walking back to my car. After both of them sit down, I start my car and pull off.

CHAPTER 7

I pull my car into Queen's Tick Market parking lot. Full of cars is the parking lot, but I don't have a problem finding a parking space; one is pulled into seconds after the parking lot is entered. Chester, me and Keith all get out of my car. I close my door, then turn to my right to look at Keith. Him and Chester resemble each other, they are both thin and have upper silver teeth but Keith has a whole mouth full of silvers that are real, even though Keith is shorter and has a bit more weight on him than Chester-short black dickies pants, a red basketball jersey, and red shoes is what Keith is wearing.

On top of his head is a snugly tied wave cap-the back of it extends down near to the top of his back-and the snugly tied red wave cap on his head almost hides his hair that is braided but his braids aren't neatly done like mines. I say almost because even though his hair is braided it is still disheveled and looks unkempt, his braids are like Chester's hair that isn't long like ours, since seen coming out the side of his snugly tied wave cap are sideburn tufts; sideburn tufts like the ones Chester have. I take my eyes off of Keith, and look at Chester-I'm still able to see that image of how he looked about ten minutes ago: Chester had his hands raised like a referee sending fighters back into their corners. Satin is what the fabric of those clothes that Chester is wearing appears to be.

Black is the color of those long pants that Chester is wearing, black is the color of the short sleeved shirt with white bordering around the collar that he is also wearing, and the short red pants both appear to be soft and satin. I continue looking at Chester, while he walks around from the passenger side door. He walks from around it and stands by Keith. Chester looks like a forty-niner besides Keith and a painfully skinny man that looks like he could have been one of the slaves forced into building the pyramids of Egypt. Taking my eyes off of Chester and Keith I do, before all three of us walk into Queen's Tick Market. In front of my eyes I see a bustling sales floor full of people, and the many stores of Queen's Tick Market are separated by seemingly carpeted partitions. As we are walking to our destination I turn to Keith and say, "Let me see that picture of Warren."

"Alright," Keith says, taking it out of his pocket.

Warren's picture is held out to me, I take it, and look down at while walking. I continue doing so, as all three of us approach the Airbrush Store in Queen's Tick Market. We all walk into it, look at the foreign-looking employee of it standing to the very back behind a glass display case that the cash register sits on, and Keith walks in front of me to talk to the foreign-looking employee that is looking at us. Before he talks to the foreign-looking employee Keith turns to me, holds out his hand for me to give him the picture of Warren, I hand it over to him, and Keith takes it then turns to him.

"I want to have my friend's picture put on a shirt," Keith says, holding up the picture to him.

"No problemo," the foreign-looking employee says, looking at the picture then back at Keith.

"On what size, color and quantity of t-shirts would you like to put it on?" Keith shrugs too then tells him the size, color, and quantity wrote of the t-shirts, and after doing that he tells him Warren's date of birth. The foreign-looking employee says, "January 18ᵗʰ, 3197," while writing down the date. "And"-he looks up at Keith- "what was the date he died?" Keith looks at me then Chester both as a defeatist would do. Keith turns back to the foreign-looking employee and says, "May 23ʳᵈ, 3217-two days ago." The foreign-looking employee looks down at the piece of paper and starts writing down the date. "I'm sorry to hear that."-he finishes, does a calculation with his fingers, then looks at Keith- "Your friend died at the young age of 20 last Friday; and I too almost died last Friday night."

"Why you say that?" Keith asks.

The foreign-looking employee looks down at the counter and says, "I'd rather not say." Keith shouts, "Now I know where I've seen you before!" before I see his face suddenly grow strained and livid, as though ten years has passed. "You were on the news and Gail said your name. It's"-he snaps his fingers in frustration- "you're the Uruguyan that was beat up and claimed it was by off-duty policemen!" The Uruguyan says, "Yes, unfortunately that is me."

"I tell you what," Keith says.

"Don't charge me for the shirts and I'll kill both those cops that jumped you."-he holds out his hands to the Uruguyan- "Deal?" The Uruguyan just looks at Keith's outstretched hand then eyes him suspiciously.

"You sure you're not the poe-poe?" Keith says, "The poe-poe?" "Yeah, the police. Five-O," the Uruguyan says.

"No, I'm not the fuckin police but I fucked a few of them," Keith says, looking at the Uruguyan's hand.

"You did?" the Uruguyan asks. Keith says, "Yeah, and you just rubbed me the wrong way with that question you asked."-disgust appears on his face- "Am I the fuckin police? When will the shirts be ready?" The Uruguyan says, "In three days. Today is Sunday, so you can pick them up on Wednesday; anytime on Wednesday before we close."

"Do I deb now or later?" Keith asks.

The Uruguyan smiles at Keith and his smile grows wider like he's about to reveal a secret. "A cryptic question such as that deserves a straightforward answer; you deb later-you deb for the t-shirts on delivery; instead of up-front."

"That'll work," Keith says, before turning to Chester and I. Keith says, "Ya'll ready to bounce?" and before I or Chester could respond he starts walking out of the Airbrush Store. All three of us walk out of the Airbrush Store together. Keith walks in the middle of Chester and I as we start walking throughout Queen's Tick Market, and Chester looks at Keith while we are.

"Was that shit true what you said back there?" Chester asks.

"About fuckin' the police?" Keith snickers.

"Yeah, it's true. Both times happened when I borrowed my Mom's car and was pulled over for speeding in it. I didn't want a ticket to come to her house if it wasn't paid or even risk her finding out if I paid it so I did what I had to do, and fucked both police officers in the back of their squad cars to get off scot-free."

I believe what Keith just said: He made those statements in a casual sounding voice, just like somebody mentioning it had been raining yesterday. Keith turns to me; he is smiling-even his tone of voice smiles-as he says, "Feel me?" I show Keith my scimtar grin. "With kid gloves on."

Keith continues looking at me, while walking, but doesn't respond. Despite the easy way he carries himself, Keith conveys a tensed, coiled quality, like his physical relaxation is a part of what makes him dangerous. He doesn't respond before he stares past my shoulder then nods towards what he sees. "Let's swing in there." I turn to my right and see an open-air store enclosed by seemingly carpeted partitions, then turn back to Keith; Keith takes the lead towards it before Chester and I begin walking behind him. We all walk into the clothing store, and walk to one of the racks in it. He flips through some shirts hanging on hangers, reaches the end, goes to another rack, and starts flipping through the clothing on it.

The difference between the rack he's standing at now and the one he just left is that the one he's at now only has on it name-brand boxers. I watch Keith remove a pair of boxers then show them to me. "A boxer man." I say that to Keith as he uses his thumb and forefinger to extend the boxers; Keith clips the boxers back on its hanger then begins walking to yet another rack. The next rack he goes to also has shirts on it. Keith flips through the shirts, and one of them catches his eye. Like he did with the boxers, Keith holds the shirt out in front of him-it is a solid black t-shirt whose front is almost covered completely by the image of silver paper currency and the image is sort of like a sticker on the t-shirt. Keith takes the t-shirt to the front counter, pays for it, then slings it across his shoulder as all three of us walk out of the clothing store. While we are walking further away from it Chester turns to Keith and says, "That nigga that killed Warren will be on one of those"-Chester nods at the t-shirt Keith is holding out in front of him while walking- "soon." Keith scowls at Chester.

"We don't know enough about him yet to have mighty whitey zipping up his bodybag."

"I know," Chester says.

Keith says, "If you know then why did you-"-he looks past me, stops, then gestures to what he sees- "I'm about to make a cd. You two wanna be features?"

"I don't," Chester says to Keith, before turning to me.

"What about you?" Chester stands silent and still and as tall as a tree as he stares into my eyes.

"I've never heard Keith rap," I say, before turning to Keith.

"I'll stand with you in the booth." Keith claps his hands together like a little boy delighted to give his friend a birthday gift.

"That's what I wanted to hear." All three of us start walking towards the make-shift studio, other Queen's Tick Market shoppers are walked past by us, and Keith approaches a Black employee of it once he get into it-the Black employee looks to be in his late thirties, is wearing glasses, and has a baby-afro.

"What'll it be today Keith?" the Black employee asks, looking at him.

Keith says, "Just one track this time." The Black employee looks past Keith's shoulder at me and Chester.

"They're with you?"

"Yeah." I look at the Black employee and say, "I've never been here before. How does this business work? And what do you charge?" The Black employee says, "Timber Studios enables customers to record their voices onto a cd-r while in our make-shift booth"-he nods towards the booth in the corner- "that they'll be in as a beat is playing. The played beat will be one of the ones they selected prior to going into our make-shift booth. As for your other question, we charge ten dollars per track. So if you want to record one song on your cd-r, your charged amount will be ten dollars. Twenty dollars for two songs. Thirty dollars for three songs and so on and so on. Does that answer both of your questions?"

"Yes," I say.

The Black employee turns to Keith to say, "So how many beats you said you want?" then picks up a folder off the desk's surface in front of him and starts handing it to Keith.

"Just one," Keith says. Keith takes the folder, opens it, and flips through its pages. About a minute later, he starts handing it back to the Black employee while pointing to the beat he chose.

"I want that one," Keith says, handing him the folder. The Black employee looks at the beat Keith chose, as he's taking the folder." Alright," the Black employee says. "You've been here before, so you know what to do."-he gestures towards the booth- "I'll have the beat started ten to twenty seconds after asking if you're ready." Keith looks at me, and jerks his head towards the booth. I look at Chester, he's now sitting down on one of the chairs pressed up against the wall, then back at Keith; Keith leads me into the booth as him and I start walking into it.

We both walk into the dimly lit studio booth that's padded, before Keith closes its door. A microphone dangles from its ceiling in the middle of the studio booth, and we walk to it. Keith walks to then grabs the microphone, looks at me, and smiles; his silver teeth gleams at me. I hear crackling then the Black employee's voice from overhead.

"You ready Keith?"

While still looking at me Keith says into the microphone, "Yeah." A few seconds pass, before the beat starts. Once it does, Keith starts swaying to the beat. Keith takes his eyes off of me, looks forward, and starts machine-gunning words into the microphone.

"I gotta plan, I say I gotta plan/ I'm gonna take my Momma out the ghetto and put Her in another land/ I stay around niggas that scheme bad, talk bad, drink bad, and dope bad/ They love trouble in small places when you make them mad"-Keith pounds his fist into his open palm for emphasis- "I ain't the realest nigga out in these streets but I'm realer than you/ Get the fuck out my face before I blast a hole the size of Old Nebraska into you/ Oh, yeah, and thank you for your energy and time/ I don't know why I said that nigga whose teeth don't blind"-Keith turns to me and smiles- "I feel that my Mom's cheated me out of my childhood/ Let me hear what you gotta say Marshall, and it better not be about wood." Keith takes a step back from the microphone while smiling at me and while the beat's playing. I wave my hand back and forth at Keith, but he walks towards me. He drapes his arm over my neck, pulls me towards the microphone, then backs away. I look at Keith and say, "I'll pass," over the beat that's playing. "Go on," Keith says, gesturing to the microphone. "Just say the first thing that comes to your mind." I look at Keith for a few long seconds, then turn around to the microphone. I brace myself, like a person squaring their shoulders and hurling themselves into a fierce rainstorm. I drop down into a fighting pose, lowering my eyes and circling with both hands. Like lighting, I shoot out a right, then a left, the air whistles around me as I dance lightly, ducking and weaving, throwing punches.

"I was born to box, that's my trade/ You don't know why they call me Wonwill so let me aid/ If my right one don't get you, then my left one will/ Left or right, nigga, either one can put you on your ass, and that's real"-I turn to Keith while continuing to shadowbox and spar an invisible opponent- "My brief career as a school yard fighter made who I am/ I went to middle school in Miami, not Birmingham/ I got on that nigga's ass after I got to my feet/ Right outside the cafeteria is where I showed him shit ain't sweet/ It takes a certain type of person to hate, then revel in the proximity of hatred/ Warren died young, and I remember what he said/ The movie was about the police staking out this drug dealer that always kept cool before he won/ Warren's exact words were 'Though a watched pot never boils, neither does a unheated one"-I wave my hand back and forth as if erasing the thought from a chalkboard- "This booth has that three in the morning feel that even windowless rooms get at night/ Keith told me to say the first thing that comes to my mind and I fight/ Wonwill, see?"

It's now Monday afternoon, a day has passed since Chester, me, and Keith went to Queen's Tick Market, and I have just got off work. I pull up to my house, and about five minutes passes before I get completely inside it. After getting inside my house, I kick off my shoes and lay down on my sofa. Reaching over to the vulwood coffee table I do, so I can pick up *The Other Side Of Suffering* on it. I look at the book's cover, open it, then start flipping through its pages. The page I read tells how JonBenet Ramsey's Dad, John Ramsey, feels about child pageants. John Ramsey wrote that it never occurred to his wife, his wife's name was Patsy, that they might be putting their daughter in harm's way-putting her in harm's way by allowing her to be in those child beauty pageants. *Would our child still be alive if she had not been in those pageants? Was the killer there all the time?*

Those are the questions that John Ramsey asks himself in this book I'm holding in my hand and John Ramsey asked them after his daughter was murdered. Patsy and him searched their souls asking if they did the wrong thing by allowing her to perform onstage in public. While I'm laying down and holding the book in my hand, the house phone rings. I close *The Other Side Of Suffering*, get up off my sofa, walk towards my house phone, and look at the caller ID before picking it up as it rings a second time.

"Hey Marshall," Judika says. "What were you doing?" I walk towards my dining room table and sit down on one of its chairs.

"Nothing really. Just laying down, flipping through the pages of this book."

"Oh," Judika says.

"Me? I just got home from work." I say, "Don't elementary schools let out at three?"-I look at my wall clock and see that it's 5:17 p.m.- "It's five-seventeen now. What have you been doing since your students left?" Judika sighs.

"Grading papers, doing odds and ends in the classroom."

"The life of a teacher," I say.

"Your job isn't stressful I hope."

"It is at times," Judika says.

"Being a teacher is sometimes stressful and demanding. But the reward I'm gonna get for being one outweighs the cons."

"And what is that?" I say.

"The reward I'm gonna get?" Judika asks. I say, "Yeah." A few seconds passes before Judika answers, "Admittance into Heaven for what I've done on Earth." My chair's plastic crinkles underneath me as I switch positions on it while clearing my throat. I decide to change the subject and say, "What's the last movie you saw Judika?"

"The last movie I saw?" Judika says.

"Yeah," I say.

Judika says, "The last movie I saw was *Jury Duty*."

"What was it about?" I ask.

"It was about a half-wit that talked in corny surfer slang," Judika says.

"I watched that movie last night after I put Anyanwu to bed, and it's an ancient flick-it came out in the year 1995."

"1995?" I say.

"What made you watch a movie thirteen centuries old?" Judika says, "Curiousity, I guess. I watched *Jury Duty* last night while I was making the outline for this week's lessons. In it, the star is romanced by a female actor whose real name was Tia Carrere, and after watching *Jury Duty,* I went onto my computer to find out more about her. Tia Carrere's biography said that she was born in Hawaii and that her acting career started when she was discovered in a Waikiki grocery store. Another thing I read about her was: 'She was a totally excellent mix of Filipino, Spanish and Chinese." I say, "So she was Chinese like that 23 year old fucker that shot up Virginia Tech on April 17th, 2007?"

"Yeah," Judika says, in a somber tone.

"That was an awful day for us. I first read about the United States second worst mass shooting when I was young, and I hope-no, I pray-that a day like that never happens again anywhere. I'm a teacher myself, but I can't relate to the feeling that must have been had by the teachers of those 32 people that-I know it but I'm not gonna say that monster's name-that monster killed." I smile viciously.

"Thirty three people died on that day-thirty three souls left their bodies-and I'm one hundred percent sure of where those souls went. That 23 year old killer's soul has been engulfed in white-hot flames for over 13 centuries now. What would you have done if you were one of the teachers at Virginia Tech University on April 16th, 2007 and one of your students was killed?" Judika is silent for a while.

Judika finally says, "I would have focused on what good could come from unimaginable evil. Blacksburg, Virginia held-hold on for a minute." I hear Judika's voice talking to a person in the background, and she returns about thirty seconds after she told me to hold on.

Judika says, "Sorry for the interruption, Marshall. That was Anyanwu. She's been bugging me ever since we came home."

"Bugging you about what?" I ask. Judika says, "Yesterday I told her I'd take her to go get some ice cream today, and she's been revved up to go since we've came home."

"I'll take her," I blurt out.

"No, no," Judika says.

"I told her I'd take her."

"Come on Judika," I say.

"Let me take her before I go to the gym tonight; I don't mind. Plus-it'll give Anyanwu and I a chance to bond together."

"You really want to take her?" Judika says.

"Yeah," I say.

"Okay," Judika says.

"I'll tell Anyanwu. What time will you be able to take her?"

"Right now," I say.

"I remember where you stay, so finding your house won't be a problem. Tell her to get ready because I'll be picking her up in about fifteen minutes."

"Alright," Judika says.

CHAPTER 8

"Hey Marshall, what do you know about court-martials?"

"The correct plural is court-martial."

Anyanwu and I are sitting down on one of the picnic tables outside of the Ice Cream Parlor we just walked out of; taking licks of our ice cream cones I just bought for the two of us. Anyanwu bounded out of my car, after I parked in front of her Mom's house and called Judika's house phone from my cell phone. I smiled as the six-year-old Black girl wearing a pink dress, white cardigan, and pink slippers neared my car then got in.

Anyanwu takes another lick of her double scoop butterscotch praline ice cream then says, "Don't be a pain. Come on, how do they work?" I lick my ice cream, two scoops of rum raisin ice cream are in my cone, while looking at the cute six-year-old...Anyanwu looks as if she belongs in a Walt Disney Parade. She glows like a real fairy tale princess wearing Cinderella's gown.

"Why the sudden interest?" I ask, swallowing the rum raisin ice cream. Anyanwu says, "I was playing double dutch with Andy today at school, and right after we finished jumping rope, she told me she heard her Mom and Dad arguing about his court-martial."

"Oh," I say.

"Well a general court-martial is a board consisting o-" Boom! My last word is drowned out by a sudden thudding noise from the sky, as though a giant clapped hands over a mosquito. Anyanwu and I wince. I look up at the sky and say, "Oh, a filthy sonic boom," while looking at a passing airplane in the sunny cloudless sky. My eyes follow the plane as it gets further and further away from us, and after it can no longer be seen I turn back to Anyanwu. Cross-eyed is what I see she is while looking at and licking her butterscotch and praline ice cream. Anyanwu stops licking her ice cream and looks at me.

"Like I was about to say before being interrupted," I say.

"A general court-martial is a board consisting of a varying number of officers, depending on what's available under wartime conditions. There's no jury. The senior officer is president of the court. There's a prosecutor, usually an officer from the JAG corps."

'JAG?"

"Judge Advocate General. And there's a defense attorney. In an emergency, though, any officer can be appointed to defend or prosecute. When the arguments are over, the board votes guilty or not guilty. Majority decides. In case of a tie, the president casts the deciding vote. They can drag on for weeks, but I've heard of courts that lasted only a few minutes-they lasted only a few minutes because they were held during battles and sieges. A general court can order any punishment, including execution."

"Ah," Anyanwu says, as if the mystery of the universe has just been revealed to her.

"So"-Anyanwu rolls her tongue over the ice cream-"court-martials kill people?" I say, "Sometimes," then decide to change a ghoulish subject.

"What time did you go to sleep last night?"

"I'm not so sure," Anyanwu says.

"Mom tucked me in at eight, but after she left, I got up and got my coloring book. I colored until I fell asleep."

"Good girls don't do things like that," I say to Anyanwu.

"I'm still a good girl," Anyanwu says. I say, "How would you know? You stayed up past your bedtime. What kind of parent would I be if-" "N-my parent!" I frown at Anyanwu.

"That stings me more than I imagined it could. Don't even know why I referred to myself as your parent." The sting must really show on my face, because Anyanwu adds: "Judika is my only parent." I look at Anyanwu mournfully for a few long seconds before replying.

"I might be slipping into a position I don't particulary care for," I start to say, "but you're allowed more than one parent, Anyanwu."

"I am?" the child demands, ice cream dripping down her chin. I hesitate before answering; you don't tell other people what's good and what's bad for their kids. And it's kind of a constructive action.

"Yeah," I finally say. "I see you're almost finished."-I point to her ice cream cone that she just bit into- "You like butterscotch praline ice cream don't you?" Anyanwu finishes crunching, swallows, and says, "Yeah. It's my favorite. Can I get another one Marshall?"

"You really shouldn't get another one," I say.

"I don't want to spoil your appetite for the dinner I'm sure Judika's making for you." I expect Anyanwu to beg for another cone but she says, "You're right, Marshall, I didn't know." I look at the cute six-year-old Black girl that has a never-fading smile and a deep-seated belief that my words are Gospel Truth. The last thing I expected Anyanwu to say was, 'You're right, Marshall, I didn't know'. Anyanwu's faith is almost frightening. I'll have to stay worthy. I'll also have to disillusion her, gently. I'll think about how while I'm sweating in the gym. That's where I'm headed after I take Anyanwu home.

The sun is setting on this Monday late afternoon that's about to turn into night, as I'm pulling into Silver's Gym parking lot-about ten minutes have passed since I've dropped Anyanwu off at her house. I see an open parking space, pull into it, turn off my car, then get out. After pushing a button on my car's key chain device to beep the locks shut, I turn to Silver's Gym. Towards it I start walking. I smooth down the front of my black underarmor muscle shirt that shows my biceps, I'm also wearing black and silver sneakers along with black gym shorts that have silver stripes going down the side, right before I open the front door leading into Silver's Gym. A vestibule whose right side, the left side is a wall, consists of glass spanning from the floor to the ceiling is what I walk through.

The vestibule is walked through, before I near then open the second door leading into Silver's Gym. Now I'm in the front lobby of it where there's a front desk, a big-screen tv, and three long sofas situated near it in a way that sitters on them can watch the screen. Passing through the lobby I do, before walking down a hallway to the weight room where the barbells are. I step into the weight room. *I got the power! Snap's* song *'I Got The Power'* is playing from the speakers in each corner of the spacious weight room, and I know the name of that song and who made it because I wanted to find out what it was I was listening to every time I come to Silver's Gym and Silver's Gym plays it at least twice every hour it seems to amp up the exercise.

A bodybuilder's anthem is what the song *'I Got The Power'* by *Snap* is to me. I stand at the edge of the action in the spacious weight room for a moment, scanning the crowd, secretly awestruck by the female bodies. It's amazing to think what an ordinary human can become through well-applied obsessive behavior and, in some cases, the miracles of modern chemistry. Along with looking at the buff female bodies, I look at the males. Every third guy in the weight room is built like The Incredible Hulk. I spot a White guy sitting on a bench. He's wearing a black t-shirt with the sleeves cut off to accommodate upper arms as thick as Virginia hams, and the muscles on him are so perfectly defined that he can be used as a line model for a human anatomy class. I see him stretching while curling a barbell.

Taking my eyes off of him I do, and I look at another White guy. The White guy I'm now looking at isn't curling a barbell; he's bench-pressing a barbell. I see him straining beneath a barbell loaded with iron plates the size of truck wheels, and in the face, squawking. The White guy finally raises the bar then locks his arms. He racks the barbell and sits up, grunting, sweat running down his face like rainwater. "Yeah!!!" I take my eyes off of him and rest them on a buffed, ponytailed woman that looks Swedish. The Swedish looking woman is on one of those simulated cross-country-ski machines, and her legs are swinging through the air. Swinging crisscross through the air are her legs that look like scissors. Right next to the cross-country ski machine there's a stationary bike. One of those stationary bikes that exercisers pedal during those endless aerobic trips to nowhere.

If I was a philosophical type person, I'd know exactly why life's like one of those stationary bikes. I'm not, so all I know is that life is like one of those stationary bikes and that's it. I can't go into into detail as to why. My gaze continues traveling through the weight room. This weight room has the ambience of a machine shop, and the stench of people with too much testerone is enough to make a normal person's eyes water. This place really does stink. It smells like...wood pussy. Wood pussy is a colloquial word for a skunk, and this weight room smells just like that-it smells like a skunk. All of these sweating bodies is making it smell like wood pussy. I haven't had any type of pussy for a while. It's obviously been years since I've had Roz's pussy, and that's because we broke up less than a year after my first daughter was born. I haven't had Deidre's pussy in a lil over a year. Chamiqua and I broke up less than a month ago, so it's only been a week since she gave me her pussy. Her pussy that a nigga ate when she wore a crotchless camisole at work. I don't like that shit. It's bad enough that she continued stripping after our daughter was born, but letting a nigga do that to her crossed the line. I kicked her ass out as soon as I found out. I stop scanning the entire weight room in front of me, and begin to walk further into it. Through the action I walk.

Passing bodies in motion I do, before nearing a see-through door leading into another section of the gym. I open the door, walk through it, look at the boxing ring in the room, then start walking to an area near it. The area walked to is where I always begin my routine when I come to Silver's Gym. I'm standing inside of a big, bare room with a wooden floor, rolled mats against the wall, some gymnastic equipment, weights, a few Nautilus machines and mirrors on one wall, with the things I need.

Everything that I need is right here in front of me: A medicine ball, a jump rope, a sitting weight bench, a small barbell with 35 pounds on each end, and a punching bag. I look down at the medicine ball and while looking at it I use two fingers to pinch a tip of one of my braids-playing with my braid is what I do before I stop, bend down to pick up the medicine ball, then hold it up in front of me. Doing two sets of shoulder rotations with the medicine ball is the first exercise in my routine, and ten repetitions is done in each set. I start doing shoulder rotations with the medicine ball, finish the first set, take a deep breath, then begin the second one.

After finishing the second set, I put the medicine ball back down on the ground. In between each exercise I do a set of 20 push-ups, so I drop down then start doing them after the medicine ball is put down. The set of push-ups are finished, I pick up the jump rope, and start doing the first of two rounds with it-two three minute rounds of jumping rope is what I do. I finish the first three minute round of jumping rope, take a deep breath, then begin the second round. The jump rope is dropped to the ground after I finish, and after dropping it I drop down to the ground to start doing 20 push-ups. After doing 20 push-ups I walk to the sitting weight bench, pick up the small barbell on the ground by my feet, and start doing the first set of two preacher curls.

The first set is finished, I set the 70 pound barbell down on the ground, take a deep breath, then pick it up and start doing the second set. Ten repetitions of preacher curls is what I do again in the second set. Once finishing, I sit the barbell down on the ground. Towards the ground I drop to start doing twenty push-ups. The push-ups are finished and I get up then walk towards the punching bag. Three 90 second rounds on the punching bag is what I do in my routine, so I begin punching the bag for ninety seconds. The first round is finished, and I begin the second one. Counting ninety seconds in my head is what I do, as I'm pummeling the punching bag. I finish, take a breather, then begin the last and final round on the punching bag. The third on the punching bag is finished-I begin the twenty push-ups. I finish the twenty push-ups, and every exercises in my routine is done. Looking at myself in the wall height mirror to my right I do. I see my reflection and on my forehead, sweat sparkles like pearls of dew. The single drops link up, making trails down my face like snail trails. I walk to my locker that's close by, unlock it then take out a towel, and I wipe my forehead impatiently with it. I close then lock my locker back after doing so. Back to the wall height mirror I look, and I see that there's no more sweat on my raisin-colored face. I sling the towel across my shoulder, and turn to go. I walk back out the see-through door, begin walking through everything I passed earlier after leaving the weight room, and while walking I stop to look at the large observation window-the large observation window shows what's going on in Exercise Room C which is the room I'm standing outside of right now.

Through the large observation window, I spot a Tae-Bo class in Exercise Room C. I see about eight women sweating in Lycra and sports bras kicking their legs out karate style to loud music. Thick is the female I'm looking at, and her ass is an apple-bottom. Her apple-bottom bounces as she moves in rhythm to the music while moving exactly the same way as her instructor that she's facing; every woman in that room I'm looking in is facing the exact same way except for one woman that is facing the group of women. I stare longingly at the female bodies until the music inside of Exercise Room C stops. I hear the music stop and see the females walk to a wall on the side of the room where their bags among other things are at-I see them walking to the stuff, as their instructor is talking. I assume to myself that the Tae-Bo class is over, and I see that I assumed right as a thick female and another woman she's talking to pass me. To her tall friend the thick woman says, "That's such a coincidence that you and Mrs. Rayfield chose to wear the same kick-ass fit on the same night. I think to myself: Mrs. Rayfield? At the tall woman's clothes I look, and I see that she's wearing a pink sports bra and black biker shorts. I take my eyes off of her as more of the class rushes out. A brunette passes me.

A blond and a short Oriental woman passes me as they're talking to each other. Another brunette passes me. Walking right behind the brunette is a sexy light-skinned Black woman. My eyes linger on her as she passes me, and I stop looking at her after staring for about ten seconds. When I turn around, I see a dark-skinned ponytailed Black woman wearing a pink sports bra and black biker shorts walking slowly while toweling the sweat off of her neck. The remark that the thick woman made goes through my mind, 'That's such a coincidence that you and Mrs. Rayfield chose to wear the same kick-ass fit on the same night', as I see that the dark-skinned ponytailed Black woman is also wearing a pink sports bra. I decide to approach her and see if she's the Mrs. Rayfield from Child Welfare that I talked to four days ago.

"Great workout," I say, as the dark-skinned ponytailed Black woman heads my way. The dark-skinned ponytailed Black woman says, "The best in Eddy. Looking to sign up?" Her voice sounds like the one I heard a few days ago. I say, "Maybe. First I thought I could ask you a question."

"Try Stacy up front. She can tell you the whole deal."

"I wasn't talking Tae-Bo," I say. "I want to know if your last name's Rayfield." The dark-skinned ponytailed Black woman just stares at me, then flaps her black ponytail off her shoulders to cool her neck.

"Yes. Why?" I look at Mrs. Rayfield with paternalism.

"You work with Child Welfare. I talked to you four days ago on the phone; about Joey." Mrs. Rayfield's eyes pierces into mine's.

"Marshall. Marshall Powers. So you're the young man who set into motion Joey's removal from his corruptible Mother."

"Where is he now?" I ask. Mrs. Rayfield says, "As of this moment, Joey is being provided substitute care in an institution. In recent years there have been a growing reluctance to place a child in one because of the conviction that institutionalization is detrimental to a young child's emotional well-being, but I felt that he needed to be in one. Butting heads with his Mother last Thursday afternoon made me feel that way." I ask, "You went to Frieda's house that afternoon after I called you?"

"Yes," Mrs. Rayfield says.

"I went there to investigate your complaint but after asking a few questions, the Mother became hostile. She threatened me with bodily harm which is when I then saw that your complaint was valid. I'm not empowered to remove the child without the parent's consent but I saw that Joey couldn't safely remain, so I petitioned a court the same day; the court ordered Joey's removal and he was took from her the very next day."

"I kind of feel bad," I say.

"Don't," Mrs. Rayfield says.

"You shouldn't feel that way-you've put a wrench in the Devil's plans, yeah, because-example: How many kids in this world are trained to be Bohemian? There are more White kids than Black kids who grow up to be headbangers, rock stars, or even alternative music artists. Influences!" Mrs. Rayfield slaps her open palm on a nearby wall. The flat crack, surprisingly loud, hangs in the air. Her palms sting I see-she looks at it's quick reddening with disfavor.

"I've heard that before Mrs. Rayfield," I reply, utterly relaxed.

"The reason's simple-our talent pool is so small that it's unlikely that any of us could be influences."

"But we've got to!" Again Mrs. Rayfield slaps the wall, but the scowl is reflexive.

"Utterly," I say, the ghost of a smile creasing my face. Mrs. Rayfield abruptly walks towards me. The dark-skinned ponytailed Black woman puts her hand on my cheek. Her fingers are extremely cold, but not quite as cold and professional as her manner.

"You did the right thing." Mrs. Rayfield takes her hand off of my cheek. She turns to go, starts walking, then turn around to look at me. "Oh, by the way, I do work out here every day at 1800. Stop by, I love would love to go a round with you in the ring," Mrs. Rayfield says, before returning to walk away. I smile to myself, and I too start to leave. I start walking through the weight room and pull up short. Just for a heartbeat.

The other exercisers in the weight room probably don't even notice. I doubt I falter longer than a few seconds. But in those seconds, eye contact's made. Standing about ten feet away, swiveling her torso from left to right while her hands are on her hips is that old White woman that went berserk in the waiting room at Sanskirt Hospital and Mrs. Winegardner is wearing grey legging along with a sleeveless blue shirt over her yellow sports bra. I take my eyes off her, then continue walking through the weight room to the outside towards my car.

After leaving Silver's Gym I decide to drive pass Frieda's house on this Monday night, before going home-it took me about twenty minutes to get to the trailer park she lives in. I drive into it before slowly riding over the several speed bumps at its entrance that lead to Frieda's trailer home that's in the back of this trailer park. As I'm slowly driving to it, I feel tightness in my muscles-I feel tightness in them since I just left Silver's Gym. This is a normal feeling for me since I exercise at Silver's Gym three times out the week, but I can feel it more than usual. My muscles are tighter than usual, my tendons are sore, and this feeling I have is pain. A function of the mind is pain's power; only my body feels pain. I can't eliminate the effects of Warren's death, or not do for him what I would want him to do for me. With the use of deadly force, I will punish his killer. Like my muscles can; my mind will never atrophy. I want Warren's killer dead: I can't let my dawg die in vain. Warren being dead isn't something I really care about, him being killed is what I care about. I wouldn't be ready to throw it all away if he died from sickness. Him dying from a sickness instead of another person's hand would have made me accept his death. Instead, I can't. He had to know that there would be retaliation.

What? He thought he was just gonna kill Warren and nothing would happen to him afterwards? I near Frieda's house, pull up to the curb on the other side of the street in front of it, and as I'm doing that I turn off my headlights. While I'm parked across the street from it, looking at Frieda's trailer home I do. I see that the frontroom light is on. Frieda's in there probably, but I know who ain't. Joey. Joey isn't in there anymore, and that's good. She was making him old before his time by letting him smoke. A child his age shouldn't be doing that. *"Don't be a pain!"*

What Anyanwu said to me earlier today at the Ice Cream Parlor is heard again, and I don't want to feel almost unbearable pain. I'm tougher than anybody that hurts me. Man for man I'm tougher than anybody that hurts me. Being ganged up on I'm accustomed to, but the dread of feeling almost unbearable pain makes me superhuman. I'll feel helpless if I'm not, as Jude called me, an automaton.

Being electrocuted after that nigga repeatedly blasted me at Blue Swallow Motel a few days ago felt like torture. The truth about torture is that the victim will always give in; it was only a matter of time before I told Jude that I'll sponsor Sequoia. Me becoming Sequoia is paradoxical because I was tortued before becoming it and tortured after becoming it. I know the reason why Jude walked out of that log cabin after I came to after being rescued-I know the reason why he said, 'I'll leave you alone with your thoughts,' right before walking out.

Jude stepped out of that room because he wants me to think about what might happen if I stop wearing Sequoia for good. He wants me to think about the bad luck that I'd go back to having-the torture of it. My baby-mamas do and say whatever they can to make me suffer. They know the many forms of torture. They are malicious and spiteful. Incredibly effective are their forms, but they're also surgically precise-they leave little damage. Why am I stuck on wearing Sequoia again? To do the job Jude said I have to? To deb myself from the earthly rewards I'll get? To get revenge on the nigga that killed Warren? Because of neural programming, I'm going to be tortured either way.

Backing down I'm not designed to do and that's why I'm stuck on wearing Sequoia again...and because I *want* to do the job gave to me, earn the earthly rewards, and kill the nigga that killed Warren. The most important reason, I'm being tortured because my programming won't let me help the enemy. The enemy that caused Warren to be a target for a marksman. That nigga sold his soul to the Devil, by killing Warren, but the retaliation that he's gonna get is a lagniappe from the buyer of it. He made his king-sized bed and now he must sleep in it. He'll sleep in it once his whereabouts become no longer unknown. I'll find out because I soldier-I serve as a soldier but I don't ever do the second verb definition of soldier: I don't pretend to work while doing nothing. I'll find him since he chose to be procrustean. Since he chose to be like that mythological Greek villain named Procrustes-Procrustes was a villain of Greek mythology that had his victims fit his bed by stretching them or cutting off their legs. Procrustes was a torturer that put his victims in pain not too different from the pain I'm feeling. A machine can't feel pain. I wouldn't be feeling pain if I really was one instead of just a person that functions like a machine. Sequoia is a Self-Aware Machine that is in my trunk right now.

A Self-Aware Machine is placed in the trunk of this grey Ford Taurus. And a Fully Realized Human is sitting in the driver's seat of the same car. Me. I'm a Fully Realized Human, because even though I mechanically do things, I know I'm organic. I'm derived from living things; machines aren't. Jude made the symbiosis between the Fully Realized Human and the Self-Aware Machine when he brought me and Sequoia together. I'm the most Fully Realized Human that Jude will ever meet probably because I know my limitations but I exceed them, or try to exceed them, every chance I get-I'm resisting the temptation to tell him that. I'll never tell him that-doing so will make him not believe me so he'll have to keep realizing it on his own and seeing my serendipity. I also can't never tell him that I'm not exactly sure why I'm the most Fully Realized Human because I *feel* (doesn't that prove my claim?) that doing so would be unwise. Very unwise. It would be that because I know my preeminence is tolerable to Jude only as long as he does not suspect my...humanity. I stop looking at the lighted window in Frieda's trailer home, put my car's gear into drive, then pull off. Out of this trailer park I start driving. I look at my car's radio display and see the time on its digital clock: 10:58 p.m.

As I'm driving, I think to myself that tonight's gonna be a early night-I'll be home in about twenty minutes. Going straight to sleep will be done once I get home. I slow down as I near the trailer park's entrance, stop, stare at the red traffic light, and wait for it to turn green; about half a minute passes before it does. Pulling out into the street while curving to the left is what my car does on this late Monday night. I've been going to Silver's Gym on Monday nights a long time now-not a Monday passes that I don't go. I'm dedicated to go going there; just like I'm dedicated to working. Tomorrow morning at 7:30 a.m. I'll be punching my social into the time clock. I'll be sleep by 11:30 p.m., and since my alarm clock's set to go off at 6:30 a.m., I'll get seven hours of sleep. That's rare. That's rare that I'll get that much. I usually get around three, four hours of sleep at night. Five at the most. Fifteen minutes later, I pull into my car garage. I lower the garage door behind me, get out of my car, then walk into my house.

I wipe sweat off my forehead with the back of my arm. It's 8:17 a.m. on this sunny Tuesday morning, and I'm again planting tree seedlings. Or at least about to. While I have on the tree backpack with a planting gun in my hand, I look to my left-this clearing I'm standing in is on the other side of a wall of trees that separate a dirt trail that leads campers to a lake. Fishing and skinny-dipping are two of the most common things campers do in it. As I'm looking at the trees, I see a vehicle driving towards the lake. I start walking towards the walls of trees, step through them, then emerge on the other side. Parked on land near the mooring of a small fishing boat is a SUV with faded red paint-Walt's vehicle. He can't be seen as I start walking towards it, but he comes into view when I get about five feet away from the SUV-I couldn't see Walt because he was leaning into his passenger's side door taking out a fishing pole and tacklebox. Walt lifts his head up from out of his car, sees me, and says, "Marshall," with his mouth so wide that it affords me a good view of his yellow and blackened teeth.

"What up Walt?" I ask, holding the planting gun and wearing the tree backpack. Walt grumbles while holding in one hand the tacklebox and the fishing pole under his armpit. "Hopefully my luck in catching more fish today." Walt takes his eyes off me, walks to the moored fishing boat, drops the fishing pole and tacklebox into it, then starts walking back towards me and the SUV. The sixty-six-year old man stares at me with eyes hardened by a innately merciless attitude, as he stretches his scraggly handlebar moustache that looks like it hasn't been trimmed for weeks. I ask Walt, "How many fish did you catch yesterday?" a split-second after he stops looking at me, turns, and looks down to open the left side passenger's back door of his SUV. Walt doesn't look up at me as he responds,

"Jeez I cry Marshall, look how busy I am." I look at Walt as he leans into his vehicle's back seat, leans back out with what looks like a waterskin in his hands, then closes the door back. Walt looks at me, and holds the drooping protuberant waterskin down by his stomach. "This is what I truly hate," Walt says as he hefts the waterskin.

"I loathe having to carry this bag of water next to my belly. What is man-a heat machine to keep water from freezing? The damn sloshing galls me, by God!" Walt turns and starts walking towards the moored fishing boat-as Walt was talking he struck me full in the face with a blast of halitosis strong enough to drop a Cannuvian Granite Ox. I only staggered, but then I was pretty far gone anyway.

I listen to the tire salesman tell me the cost of which one I'll need to replace my car's balding right rear tire. "I'll take that one," I say to him when he tells me. Before walking away the tire salesman nods. I turn my back to him, then continue pacing through this tire junkyard. I've been off from work for an hour and thirteen minutes now, it's 5:43 p.m., and I drove right here after I got off. While I'm pacing this tire junkyard, the cell phone in my pocket rings. I take it out, look at the caller, then answer it.

"What up Chester?" I answer.

"What up whodie," Chester says.

"What were you doing?" I say, "Replacing one of the balding tires; I'm at the tire junkyard."

"Which one you at?" Chester asks.

"This one over here on your side of town," I say. "Word?" Chester says. "That's good because a girl I know wants to meet you."

"What's her name?" I ask.

"She's on the line now," Chester says.

"Tell him your name."

"Hello Chester's friend," a girl's voice says, in an accent I can't peg.

"My name's Beatrix."

"Hello Beatrix," I say.

"Yeah, I met her friend on the chat line last night," Chester says.

"I was just talking to her and Wendy told me Beatrix was right there with her and wanted to know if I have a friend. I told her 'Yeah' and after she gave the phone to Beatrix, I called you on three way."

"I'm glad you did," I say.

"So Beatrix, how do you look?"

"How do I look?" Beatrix asks.

"Yeah," I say.

"I look like me," Beatrix says.

"I know that," I say, losing patience.

"Describe yourself to me."

"Ummm..." Beatrix begins to say. Chester says, "She's a snow bunny. Just like her friend Wendy."

"That's the one you met on the chatline last night?" I ask Chester.

"Yeah," Chester says.

"And Beatrix isn't just a regular snow bunny like Wendy. Tell him what you are Beatrix."

"Tell him my nationality?" Beatrix asks.

"Yeah," Chester says.

"I'm Dutch," Beatrix says.

"Have you ever been with a Dutch girl Chester's friend?"

"No," I say. "And you can call me Marshall instead of Chester's friend."

"Alright Marshall," Beatrix says.

"I'll start calling you that-hold on, Wendy wants to talk back to Chester." I hear rustling on the phone.

"Chester?" I hear Wendy say.

"Yeah," Chester says.

"So are you and Marshall gonna swing through tonight?" Wendy asks.

"You want to Marshall?" Chester asks me.

"What time Wendy?" I ask Wendy.

"Anytime before four," Wendy says.

"Beatrix's Mom is about to leave for work and she'll have the house to herself."

"Chester, do you know where she live?" I ask.

"Yeah," Chester says.

"You know the Waste-That-Little that you, me, and-" Chester pauses for a moment- "Warren went to last week?"

"Yeah," I say.

"Beatrix's house is somewhere in the neighborhood behind it," Chester says. Wendy says, "If you can come, we'll walk up to Waste-That-Little and meet you there."

"We're definitely coming," I say.

"I want to meet Beatrix. Does nine o'clock sounds good?"

"It does," Wendy says.

"Chester do you have any other friends?"

"Why?" Chester asks. Wendy says, "I ask because there are three of us here." A gleeful whoop comes out of Chester.

"There's three of you? I have another friend I can bring."

"Good," Wendy says. "She won't be a fifth-wheel."

CHAPTER 9

From the inside of my car Chester, Keith, and I all look at the three young girls huddled up at the pay phone near the entrance of Waste-That-Little; it's now 9:09 p.m. After leaving the tire junkyard about an hour ago, I started driving to Chester's aunt house to pick Chester up just as the sun was starting to set. When I got there I pulled my car up against the sidewalk curb in front of it, put my car in park, and took my foot off the brake. As soon as I did raindrops began to drizzle, hitting the windshield with every breath I took. The drizzling didn't last long because it stopped about ten minutes later when Chester finally walked out, after I called him and told him I was outside. I then started driving to Keith's Mom house, from Chester's aunt house with Chester in the passenger seat.

Chester used his cell phone to call Keith when I pulled up in front of Keith's Mom house while it was nighttime, and Keith didn't take as long as Chester to come out because he walked out of it less than a minute after I put my Ford Taurus into park. With Keith in the backseat of my car, I started driving. As I began driving to Waste-That-Little, Chester called Wendy. While he was talking to Wendy I got onto the highway then drove past the exit leading to Quartz

Road, right after Chester hung up with Wendy following him telling her we were on our way and to be waiting outside of Waste-That-Little with her two friends. Once driving past the exit leading to Quartz Road, I drove about half a mile before getting on Chief Street. Chief Street was drove down, and I pulled off of it here into Waste-That-Little's parking lot just a few seconds ago on this starry Tuesday night.

As I'm looking at the three young girls huddled up at the pay phone Chester says, "That's them." I smile inwardly as I look at them-one of them is Black and the other two are White. In some ways, I have never really grown up. Inwardly is how I also displayed the almost childlike glee over Chester telling me that a girl he knows wants to meet me. Maybe I handle my abilities so adroitly because of the ability to keep such close touch with the youthful enthusiasm that helps me bear. I bear an awesome responsibility for my children upon my shoulders-I shake off that weight, as easily as I can shake off a bedspread. Shaking off the tremendous weight is part of my duty and I'm busy performing it, moving through life with an almost reckless abandon. The way that a child, having just learned how to walk, will dash without fear or concept of personal consequences across a room, heedless of what can happen when an obstacle presents itself. I knew a nigga that was like a child.

A child, charging across this same room, whose knee was skinned very, very badly. By going to the house of one of these three young girls in my car, I'm also putting myself at risk of being charged with statutory rape. Concern with ever being charged with statutory rape has never been shown by this nigga in the passenger seat, and right now Chester's being talked to by the White girl I assume is Wendy. Wendy speaks to him as Beatrix tells me where to drive and turn while pointing her extended finger, Beatrix and her two friends are bunched up in the backseat with Keith, up front pass me towards the front windshield-Beatrix's sitting in the back in between me and Chester's seats.

As I'm driving to Beatrix's house, I start thinking about Judika. And why I'm not putting all my energy into trying to be with her. I want to be with her, and the effort I made yesterday shows that. I took her daughter to go get ice cream. I bought all those damn cookies I don't need. So why I am out here on a Tuesday night driving to a Dutch girl's house? A Dutch girl that's a different race from me? A Dutch girl that I know absolutely nothing about. Oh yeah, and a Dutch girl that's years younger than me. Beatrix isn't two years older than me like Judika is. I'm twenty-four to Judika's twenty-six, and I'm positive that Beatrix's just a schoolgirl that doesn't have a career like Judika does. That's what really attracts me to Judika: She has a career. A career as a teacher. I laughed a few days ago when we were on the phone, because she told me what Joey said a couple of weeks ago after she called on him.

"NBC, FOX, CBS, and Cartoon Network," is what she told me Joey said after she asked him, "What is 7 and 12 and 27 and 38?" during her math lesson he wasn't paying attention to. Judika told me that the lifestyle Joey was subjected to at home played a part in him being a class clown; her exact words were, "He's a class clown, but a smart class clown. She called him a smart class clown because of that other incident she also told me about. Judika told me that Joey scored a B-minus on a test she gave her entire class a day before Valentine's Day. Joey didn't like his test score so he brought her the next day a box of chocolates with a card on it and wrote on the card was a proclamation of love: "Be Mines".

Joey wrote that in hopes of flattering her into changing his test score; Judika told me she wrote, "Thanks, but it's still B-minus" on the back of the card then gave it back to Joey. Joey does sound like a class clown from the class behavior Judika has told me about him, and I laughed again when she told me a joke he asked her. Judika told me that she was teaching an english lesson when Joey raised his hand and asked her, "How do you know when you're in a Kentucky hotel?". Judika said she said, "I don't know" before Joey replied, "You know when you're in Kentucky hotel when you call the front desk, say 'I got to leak the sink' and the receptionist says gone ahead".

As I'm driving through the neighborhood behind Waste-That-Little, Beatrix tells me where to go. She points here and there before I enter a lane. The lane winds through a forest of pine, oak and pecan. At the end of it stands a house under construction. Even at this stage of completion I see that the structure will be contemporary and impressive. As I'm driving towards it Beatrix points to a house on the left of us that we're nearing and says, "There's my house right there". I look at it-Beatrix's house turns out to be a Georgian-style house that's nestled among others on picturesque Acorn Street-before pulling onto the driveway of her house. After I put my car into park then turn it off, we all get out.

"What time does your Mom get off work?" I ask Beatrix, giving her a once over. Her long yellow hair is hanging loose, over her shoulders, and her B-cup breasts are perky against the tight fit of a white t-shirt. When she was telling me how to get here, I still couldn't peg her spicy singsong accent as Dutch; the expression on this Dutch girl I'm looking at is perpetually quizzical, as though she doesn't ever quite understand what's going on around her.

"Four," Beatrix says, and holds up three fingers, her eyes drifting down to them. I also hold up three fingers.

"Four sounds great." While I'm holding up three fingers, I look at Keith and smile. Keith smiles back at me. Keith is sagging his black dickie shorts that almost reaches down to his ankles and I also see on him visible black boxers, a white tanktop, and a laserproof vest flapping loosely above the white tanktop-wearing the laserproof vest I own in an ensemble will never be done, and the other thing I'll never do is sell my lasergun. I'm no Annie Oakley with it, but at a distance of fifty feet and with a target the size of a soup plate, I can hold my own with the best.

"You have yourself a winner, Marshall," Keith says, eyeing the lean Black girl with medium length hair, a beauty mark on her right cheek, and a come-and-get-me smile. To Keith the lean Black girl says, "You can say that can again, if you can remember it." Keith directly looks at her.

"You know what they say: 'Birds of a feather, flock together'. Tell me, how do you spell puddle?"

I take my eyes off of Keith and look at the lean Black girl that's wearing a black baby-tee with the words Army Brat in gold lettering on it and under those words are the numbers 088586 that are also in gold lettering.

"It would be a blistering day in the Ice Age before I'd reveal my innermost secrets to one such as you," the lean Black girl says.

"Oh? And tell me," Keith asks, "What's your name?" I guess Keith says the first name that comes to his mind: "Plumbellina." The lean Black girl couldn't have reacted with more surprise if Keith unzipped his skin and stepped out of it.

"How did you know?" the lean Black girl asks after she catches her breath. Keith says, "I don't know. You just seemed like a Plumbellina." Beatrix quizzically looks at her Black friend then back at Keith.

"Her name's not Plumbellina; it's Dodonna." Dodonna gives her a look suggesting that she just betrayed her to the police.

"Thanks a lot, Beatrix."

"Why not???" Beatrix says.

I study Beatrix closely, but without impatience. In contrast, Beatrix's other companion stares at her as if she's about to burst into flames. Wendy takes her eyes off of Beatrix and looks at Chester. Wendy says, "So you're Chester," while scrutinizing him. Her scrutinization of Chester makes me do the same to her-Wendy's a lil fat White girl. The first thing I noticed about her is that she's carrying fifty pounds she doesn't need. The extra weight on her obviously didn't discourage her from wearing that brown shirt that says Brass Balls Saloon.

"So you're Wendy," Chester says uneasily. "Nice...to meet you."

"I know what you're thinkin'," Wendy says. "You're thinkin': 'She didn't sound fat on the phone'."

Chester doesn't respond to Wendy because he just looks at her, still grinning skeletally. Wendy pivots towards me. "What do you think?" That's an uncommonly frank question coming from her, infused with characteristic emotion. After a few seconds I say, "You have a bearlike physique."

"I'm in shape," Wendy jokes. "Round's a shape." The third thing I noticed about Wendy is her bright, confident demeanor. I know she couldn't give a damn. She has the body of a Braham, the mind of a hawk, and from what I seen so far the gentle soul of a butterfly. While Wendy takes her eyes off of me to look at Chester, I look up at the sky. I have never seen such stars as those in the velvety purple of the dark night. Gazing at their intensity, I feel instantly better. I feel instantly better about standing here in a Dutch girl's driveway instead of being with Judika over the phone or in person.

I lower my head, and look at the front of Beatrix's house again. Her house's a modern, Georgian-style, with a low hedge of evergreens running along the front. Beatrix sees me looking at the low hedge of evergreens and says, "My Dad is a fanatic about lawn maintence. He trims those almost every day and our lawn"-Beatrix points at the lawn I look at- "is clipped a perfect inch and a half above the ground, smooth as a carpet." I take my eyes off of the grass that's leveled like astroturf and look at Beatrix.

"Where's your Dad now?" Beatrix says, "Toon's in Vancouver."

"Why is he there?" I ask.

"Toon's a Chief Commissioner," Beatrix says, "and he's on assignment there. He told Mom that the olympics-bound daugther of an overbearing figure skating coach decided to quit the sport and fled to Vancouver, and the Mother followed her there. He said she followed her there with nothing but a passport and lasergun, before discovering the body of her dead daughter. The Mother insists that she didn't kill her daugther so Toon and the other detectives are investigating the young girl's death."

"Nothing stops a determined Mother's love," I say.

"You're right," Dodonna says, holding out her hand.

"It's"-she turns to Beatrix- "starting to rain again so we should go inside."

"It is, but this is a sissy rain," Beatrix says, also holding out her hand. Small raindrops continue dropping on me as I again sniff the air-the recent rain caused the air to smell like alfalfa gone bad-and it smells the same.

"Drizzling or not," Dodonna says, "I'm not gonna keep getting wet. I'm about to go in."

"To the house," Keith says. Dodonna half-smiles at Keith and says, "To the house. I'm so glad you didn't think I meant the middle of the river."

Chester, Wendy, me and Beatrix all look at the two of them take long strides to the front porch's awning. They make it to it and turn around to look at us, before we all do the same. Beatrix unlocks her front door, steps aside to let the others in it, then looks at me as I begin walking into her house last. I completely step into her house, walk further into the frontroom, then turn back to look at Beatrix as she's closing the door behind us. Beatrix takes her hand off of the doorknob and smiles at me.

"Hmmm," says Beatrix. "I'm still hungry. Let's go into the kitchen???"

I step aside and say while sweeping my arm, "After you," as I stand inches away from an ottoman in her frontroom. Beatrix walks past me, I follow her, and she chatters about every picture and every item of furniture she sees; as if she's never been *in* the house before. I look at Beatrix from behind as we're walking to the kitchen-she has a tiny, mythical Southern waist-and she seems normal enough by the time we reach the kitchen. We enter the kitchen, and Beatrix flips on a lightswitch in it. When the lights come on she points to a table pressed up against the wall.

"You can sit there," Beatrix says, pointing at the table with three chairs. I walk over to the table and sit down at one of its chairs. While sitting down, I look at Beatrix. Beatrix moves around the kitchen area opening metal cabinets that are painted to look like wood.

"I'm so hungry I can eat a tree!"-Beatrix turns to me- "You know???" Beatrix's actually squinting at me, and then her face relaxes a little, the white skin without a single blemish and the yellow hair resting on her shoulders, full but sleek. I don't respond as Beatrix waits for a response, and several seconds passes before she turns back around to open another metal cabinet. She takes a loaf of bread out of it, walks to the table I'm sitting at, and sits the loaf of bread on it.

"The veal Mom made yesterday," Beatrix says, smiling, "will go good with this bread." Beatrix turns away from me, and starts walking towards the refrigerator.

"Yes it will," says Beatrix to herself, walking towards it, hips swinging gracefully.

Beatrix takes out a large tupperware bowl, puts it in the nearby microwave, starts heating it up, and while its heating she opens the metal cabinet above it. Two plates is what she takes out of it, before walking to the table I'm sitting at and sitting them down on it. Beatrix sits the plates down, walks back to the microwave, and turns her back to it while waiting for the veal to finish heating. She puts her hands on the counter while looking at me.

"Are you attracted to me Marshall?" I decide to feed her ego.

"You're a gorgeous girl."

"I should be," Beatrix says.

"I've got an overnight case??? You know??? Just full of cosmetics that my Mom bought for me."

Just as Beatrix finishes talking, the microwave rings. Beatrix turns around and takes out the tupperware bowl with veal in it, closes the microwave door, then starts walking towards me and the table.

"God, this smells good, doesn't it?" says Beatrix.

"I didn't mean to read your mind, just happens." The tupperware bowl is sat down on the table in front of me, and Beatrix turns back around and walks to a cabinet by the refrigerator. She slides it out, takes out several eating utensils, and walks back to the table before sitting them down on it then sitting down herself. While sitting across from me Beatrix takes the top off of the tupperware bowl, picks up her fork, uses it to poke then pick up a piece of the veal then shakes it off of her fork onto her plate. Beatrix points at the tupperware bowl with her fork while looking at me.

"Help yourself."

I pick up the fork she sat down by the plate in front of me, and do exactly what she did. After putting the veal on my plate, I start cutting it with my fork. Once the veal is cut I look at Beatrix.

"I'm just glad you're here???" Beatrix says.

After saying that she jabs her fork through the piece of veal on her plate, picks it up, and stuffs it in her mouth and chews it lustily, her smooth apple cheeks furiously working without so much as a line or wrinkle or any real distortion. She really is a gorgeous girl.

"You could be anywhere," Beatrix says, as soon as she has swallowed a wad of chewed up meat big enough to catch in her windpipe and choke her to death. I say, "Other girls beat around the bush, play games, better experience has taught me not to let them get a word in edgewise-" "What's edgewise?"

"Sideways," I say.

"I got to get an education," says Beatrix, shaking her head. She sits the fork down, leans towards me, and sniffs.

"What's that cologne you're wearing?" "*Axe Deep Space* bodywash," I say.

"You think it's too late for me to ever be a truly educated person?"

"No," says I, "you're too smart to let a late start discourage you. Besides, you're already educated. You're just educated in a different way." Beatrix says, "Yeah, well, I didn't always want that myself. You know, I killed a man? I pushed him off of a fire escape in New Orleans and he fell four stories into an alley and cracked his head open."

"Why did you do that?" "He was trying to hurt me," Beatrix says.

"He shot me up with heroin and he was giving it to me and telling me that him and me were going to be lovers together. He was a goddamed pimp. I pushed him off of the fire escape." I ask, "Did anyone come after you?"

"No," says Beatrix, shaking her head. "I never told that story to anyone else."

"I won't either," I say.

"How many girls, do you think"-I start smiling- "had been turned on by this pimp?" Beatrix looks scornfully at me and nods.

"Lots of girls. Idiots."

"Why you call them idiots, Beatrix?" I ask.

"Why do I call them that?" Beatrix says, "I mean there's a difference between losing someone forever and having someone change genders. Most of the time, if I talk like this, you know, completely open-like, with no secrets, like really trying to get to know somebody??? You know??? I drive that person away."

Just as soon as she finishes talking, I look over Beatrix's shoulder. Dodonna is peeking her head in the kitchen from its entrance by the refrigerator. Beatrix sees me looking over her shoulder, turns around, and sees Dodonna.

"Get out of here!" Beatrix says firmly. Dodonna vanishes. Beatrix turns around, looks at me, smiles, then returns to eating her veal. We both finish the veal on our plates, get another, and continue eating. For a few minutes, we eat in silence. Suddenly Beatrix stares at the loaf of bread, slices of plain white bread. I don't consider bread like that fit for consumption. I only eat wheat bread, or rolls, or something correctly prepared to accompany a meal. Sliced bread! Sliced *white* bread! Beatrix picks up the loaf of bread, unties the bag, takes out the top slice, then puts the open loaf of bread back down on the table. I look at Beatrix as she mashes the bread in her hands together, then starts sopping up veal juice from out of the tupperware bowl. Pieces of the soggy bread are ate by her. Beatrix closes her eyes in a deliberate smile of satiation. She must be wearing some of the make-up her Mom bought her because her lashes are smoky and slightly violet, just like her lipstick, and glamorous and beautiful. She looks like a teenaged JonBenet Ramsey. Once she finishes the piece of bread, Beatrix opens her eyes and looks at me.

"I wish I had some chocolate," Beatrix says; her eyes says different; her eyes measures me as if for a casket.

"Why you say that?" I ask. "I just love chocolate," Beatrix says.

"I can't live for too long without chocolate. There was a time when I made chocolate sandwiches, you know? You know how to do that? You slap a couple of Hershey bars between white bread, and you put sliced bananas and sugar too, and I'm telling you, that's delicious."

"You're sure?" I say.

"Positive," Beatrix says.

Beatrix takes another slice of bread out of the bag, tears the middle out of it, and starts rolling the soft bread into a ball.

"Boy, I love it this way," Beatrix says.

"When I was little??? You know? I use to take a whole loaf, and roll it all into balls!"

"What about the crust?"

"Rolled it all into balls," Beatrix says, shaking her head with what she wants me to think is nostalgic wonder.

"Everything into balls."

"You're lying." I have a penchant for assertive statements.

"There's some other reason you're telling me that, and your ursiform friend meeting Chester on the chat line is part of it."

"There you go, showing off," says Beatrix, "but I know you don't mean any harm, you want to make the first move don't you? Did you know that if ursiform started with a *b*, I'd know what it meant?" I say, "Why you say that?"

"Because I'm up to the *b's* in my vocabulary studies," says Beatrix.

"I've been working on my education in several different ways, I'd like to know what you think about it. See, what I do is, I get a big-print dictionary??? You know??? The kind for old lady's with bad eyes??? And I cut out the *b* words, which gives me some familiarity with them right there, you know, cutting each one with the definition, and then I throw all the little balls of paper, oops, there we go again. Balls, more balls." Euphonious is how I look at Beatrix as she howls with laughter. When she stops I ask, "But what about all the *b* words, cut out, and rolled into balls?" Beatrix says, "Well, I put them in a hat, you know??? Just like names for a raffle."

"Yeah."

Ánd then I pick them out one at a time," Beatrix says.

"If it's some word nobody ever uses, you know, like Baedeker?? I just throw it away. But if it's a good word like bikini-'An atoll in the Marshall Islands'??? Well, I memorize it right on the spot."

"Oh, that sounds like a good method," I say.

"Guess you're more likely to remember words that you like." Beatrix says, "Fairly well, but really, I remember almost everything, you know?? Being as smart as I am?" Beatrix pops the bread ball into her mouth and starts pulverzing the frame of crust. Lecherously is how I smile at Beatrix.

"Even the meaning of Bacchanalia?"

"A drunken orgy," Beatrix says.

She nibbles on the crust ball.

CHAPTER 10

I park my Ford Taurus in my car garage and get out the car. I got off work about thirty minutes ago, and last night was risky. Being at the house of a seventeen-year-old girl while both of her parents were unaware that a twenty-four-year old was there made it that. Luckily Chester, Keith and me left from there before her Mom came home.

"Last night was risky," I say to myself, opening the door. Dark is the inside of my house, lit only by the blue digital clock on my microwave and the single, red, blinking diode on my answering machine. I walk over to my answering machine, hit the play button and start unbuttoning my Toad Island shirt. First message.

"It's Chamiqua. Give me a call."

Next message. "This is Judika. Call me when you get home. Will you do that? What Anyanwu?"

Third message. "What up Marshall. This Keith, and Chester's emaciated highway man looking self. We're feeling lucky and feel that we can pull some hos. We feel that we can pull some hos at that Beach Festival being held in Eddy today. You wanna go to it?"

* * * * * * *

"Damn," I say, pulling into the parking lot.

"Look at this parking lot. It's full. This mother is *full*."

I ride around the parking lot for a minute, but can't find a parking space. From his front seat Chester looks at me and his tinfoil covered teeth glints as he says, "Just keep riding around; someone will be leaving eventually." I aimlessly drive around the parking lot for a while, before I see a small sedan pulling out of its parking spot. While it's pulling out of its parking space, I sit in the driving lane. The small sedan backs out, drives away, and I pull into the parking space it was just in. I park, check my rearview mirror for one last look, and all three of us get out of my grey Ford Taurus.

Keith isn't wearing the laserproof vest he wore last night as he walks ahead of us, power-walking towards the beachwalk. Chester and I follow behind him, and we catch up with him as he steps onto the sidewalk in front of the stores along the beachfront. We start doing the usual sightseeing things tourists do. We start strolling along First Street. As we are, I look over to my far left-the ocean glistens in the late afternoon sunlight. I take my eyes off of the ocean, just as we pass a fat White girl wearing cut-off shorts walking with her friend.

"Daaaamn," Keith says, craning his neck to look back at the passing female.

"Big girl's letting it all hang out." Keith turns to Chester and leers.

"You know who that ho makes me think of?"

"I already know who you gonna say," Chester says.

"I'd rather have a fat bitch than a stuck-up bitch anyday." Keith nods his head as we're walking.

"Dodonna was that. That ho insulted me all kinds of ways last night."

I'm walking in between the two of them, so I look from the left to the right as they continue their conversation. While he's on the left side of me, Chester says, "I would have slapped the shit out of that ho the first time she insulted me."

"I wanted to," Keith says.

"I came this close-"-Keith holds up his fingers to indicate a one inch gap- "to slapping her when she asked me if I can walk and chew gum at the same time." Chester and I laugh and Chester says, "What did you tell her?" Keith scowls.

"I told her 'Let me get back to you on that'."

"That shirt she was wearing last night said 'Army Brat'," I begin, "so that sort of explains her attitude. I saw her as being off-hand, even rude, but that facial expression of vague astonishment she has goes good with your ugly mug."

"That police bitch don't think it's that, you think it's that. But you know???" says Keith, imitating Beatrix.

"Your opinion doesn't even matter???" Chester laughs.

"Why does that ho talk like that?" Keith asks me, with some tartness.

"I don't know why Beatrix talks like that," I say.

"I know why she talks like a slut; she told me her favorite actress is Vanessa Del Rio." Keith asks, "Who's Vanessa Del Rio?" I say, "She was a porno actress in the 20th century.'My favorite actress is Vanessa Del Rio' is what Beatrix told me; right after she told me the definition of bacchalnia. Beatrix also told me that if she could be any other race, she'd be Latin. She said she'd want to be Latin like Vanessa Del Rio, and do porn for at least twelve years like her."

"That ho really *is* off the chain," Chester says.

"Yeah," I say, "she is." I was reading an article about Beatrix's role model in some magazine a while ago and Vanessa Del Rio told the interviewer something I'll never forget. She dropped some real knowledge: 'Don't try to keep your kids from things, because they are going to make a beeline for it'." Keith extends both his arms.

"Bzzzzzz"-Keith stops imitating flying like a bee- "That is some real knowledge. Beatrix will have to apply that saying to the kid she's going to have if she doesn't slow down."- Keith leers at me- "Did Vanessa Del Rio do any drugs?"

"Yeah," I say, "In that article about her that person interviewing Vanessa asked her after they got on the subject of drugs, 'what did you do?'. Vanessa Del Rio's exact answer was 'Coke, quualudes, acid, everything'. She was put in jail once for having possession of coke and quualudes."

"Coke and quualudes?" Chester asks, unnessarily.

"Yeah," I say. I take my eyes off of Chester, look around at the Beach Festival goers, then at the sky on this nice Wednesday afternoon-the sky's a sparkling bowl of wondrously clear, cloudless blue. As we continue strolling, I look at Chester. Looking at him makes me think of how speechless he was last night when he first saw Wendy. On the outside, Wendy's far from being beautiful. She's not beautiful, at least not in the way society teaches us to admire. She's large and soft and round, her shapeless waist merges with her hips. Beatrix's waist don't merge with her hips, but Wendy has a nice personality. I look at Chester.

"Chester, what is it that Wendy said to you right before we left? She pulled you aside while me and Keith were talking to her friends." Chester says, "That fat ho said she wants to see me again and some other dumb shit. She said, what was it she said? Oh yeah, she leaned all close to me and said 'You don't have the eyes. The serious ones always have that look, like they're disconnected. Like they turned it off so long ago, they forgot how to turn it back on'. She told me that all the boys she dated in the past that had that look dumped her." Keith scoffs.

"You don't believe that shit I know. Who'll date her fat ass? I know I won't." Chester looks at me.

"If that ho only knew." Chester's brown eyes pierces into mines, and they remind me of Jude's look of detached vacuousness. Jude's expression is one I recognize from the streets, but the first thing about that is that Jude isn't a street person-Jude's eyes have that dazed, detached expression of a person more accustomed to dealing with machines than people. Chester says, "If I got to feel pain, then the whole city's gonna feel pain, I don't care who gets it."-Chester shudders and looks around then back at me- "Damn, that was a cold breeze. Someone must have opened a window. Anyway, I don't want nothing to do with Wendy; she has too much piggishness for me, and I'm gonna tell her that the next time she calls me." Keith proposes, "So if I fuck Wendy you won't get mad?""

No," Chester says.

All three of us step off of the sidewalk in front of a hotel, cross a short road leading into an alley, then step back onto a sidewalk in front of several store fronts. I look at the cloudless blue sky that is dotted by screeching white gulls searching above us. Looking at those gulls reminds me of that dream I had last week Wednesday night, early Thursday morning after leaving Frieda's party then going to sleep. That dream I had had me in it as a scoutmaster and an eagle above and behind me in the sky, just like those gulls are now. I was walking through Toad Island with my uniform on, and I was a Big Brother giving several kids a tour of it. When I turned to make sure no one left the Trail, I saw the dive bombing bird. It was a huge eagle, it folded its wings that were at least seven feet, that power-dived from at least six thousand feet towards Joey.

"Look out, Joey! Behind you!" is what I shouted to Joey.

I saw Joey turn to see the huge bird zooming towards him at it seemed 150 miles per hour, and it was the last thing that the seven-year-old would ever see. Cringing is what I did when the eagle struck Joey square in the face. Without stopping, it efficiently plucked out both his eyes and flew on. As I was blasting at the eagle with my lasergun, I woke up out of the dream. Another chunky White female wearing short shorts passes us and this time it's Chester that rubbernecks.

"Daaaamn, I'd love to hit that," Chester says, staring at the fat girls' butt that just passed us.

Chester looks back at us and Keith says, "What makes her different from Wendy? That ho had too much piggishness too."

"I know," Chester says, "but Wendy's throwing her pussy at me.

That ho that just passed us ain't. I probably can never get that"-Chester jerks his thumb backwards- "fat ho's pussy, but I always want what I can't have."-Chester pats the side of his do-rag underneath his hat- "I want waves...I brush my hair every night before I go to bed. I know that doesn't make sense. I know it gets messed up the instant I put my head down on the pillow. It's just a weird habit."

Trees are like habits. By infinitesimal degress is how a habit strengthens, just like a tree. And just like a tree, you can't see one grow, you can't see it thickening like a trunk, and you can't see it thickening its roots deeper and broader; a young habit can be plucked by thumb and forefinger, but ignore it a long time and you'll have to bring in lumberjacks to clear it out, but afterwards the roots will still cling desperately to life.

"I never discard a good habit. They tend to prolong your life," I say to Chester. I take my eyes off of Chester and Keith, me and him continue strolling through the beachwalk. We stroll into a densely covered area, and I'm stopped short.

"Mon chief," someone says. The accent is thick-foreign to this part of the world.

"Tell me you okay?" I turn in the direction of the voice and see two pairs of dark eyes, an odd but appropriate mixture of craziness and understanding. The two men I see are West Islanders, their long dreadlocks hanging over baggy coveralls. I speak to the bigger of the two West Islanders.

"What?"

"Ve give you this," the muscular West Islander says, handing me a flyer. I take it and look down at the picture on it that shows a White girl with long straight hair wearing a mink coat.

"What's this?" I say, looking down at it.

"That's our boss," the muscular West Islander says.

"Ve pass out album flyers for her; she's performing today." I look back down at the flyer and say, "Lilakoi," then look back up at them.

"You said she's performing today?"

"Yes," the muscular West Islander says. "And she's performing right now"-he points to a huge outside stage about 100 feet ahead of us to our left- "up there. Go check her out." Keith looks belligerently at the other West Islander. The West Islander looks at Keith.

"You okay, Mon?" Keith doesn't answer him and I say, "He's alright"-I then look at Chester and Keith- "Let's go see this Lilakoi."

I start slowly walking away from the two West Islanders and I pick up speed when Chester and Keith start following me. We start walking towards the outside stage ahead of us. As we near it, the hum of a crowd gets louder and louder. We continue walking down the sidewalk, reach the end of the building on our left, before we see on our left a large patch of grass that has on it mostly young people gathered to listen to iternant singers and punk bands. Into the crowd we walk, as I look at the female on the stage that is speaking. How she began the sentence isn't known but I catch the ending of it as she says, "....and they'll be there until the stink gets so bad they move to New Zealand."

Laughter erupts from out of the crowd, while I continue looking at the female on the stage. That White girl on the stage looks like she's about seventeen or eighteen, has long strawberry blond hair and is a knockout. From here I can see that she's wearing pink sandals and black leather pants paired with a small, sparkly, silvery halter top that ties around her neck and leaves her entire back bare. Her long strawberry blond hair is blown out straight, and both of her slender arms are adorned with rows of silver bangles. Since we're close to the stage I can see that her lips are done in pale pink, her face loaded on mascara, and that she rimmed her eyes in silvery pencil. A visitor from the future, or maybe a tv show, is what that White girl with the cheerleading body looks like she is. The laughter from the crowd finally dies down, and the White girl tosses her hair then starts talking again into the microphone in her hand.

"I'm not afraid to rain on my own parade," the White girl on the stage says. "This next record isn't therapy, but it's all sunshine from now on."

Another teenaged White girl on the side of me shouts, "Lilakoi!" Lilakoi looks at the girl, smiles, and runs her fingers through her hair while smiling at the girl. As if she's only talking to her Lilakoi says, "Perhaps you're familiar with our soon-to-be single, 'Lick Me Where I'm Pink?'" while looking at the girl on the side of me.

"Sing us a lil' bit!" the White girl shouts. Lilakoi beams, and she turns to her left to look at someone or something off stage. Lilakoi says, "Hit the boards, kid," and a second later music begins playing. I see Lilakoi toss her hair again and she beomes bouncy on the stage as she begins wailing, "Lick me where I'm pink! Pour yourself a drink! Don't wanna hear your problems, what am I, your fuckin shrink?!" I take my eyes off of Lilakoi, while she's singing to the loud music and moving from left to right on the stage, and look at Keith. Over Lilakoi's singing I ask Keith, "Would you hit that?" Keith smiles at me.

"Hell yeah I'd hit that. You see that bitch's lips?" I look back at Lilakoi, squint, then turn back to Keith.

"She has on pale pink lipstick but I can't see them that good." Keith says, "I can. She has a great mouth. I bet she can suck the chrome off a trailer hitch." I laugh, and look back at Lilakoi as she continues singing a verse of what sounds like a Norwegian Girl Guide song. Lilakoi wails: "I can't think of a person I'd rather have as a sister-in-law! Take your time when taking off my bra!" As soon as she finishes the last verse, Lilakoi looks directly at me. The girl beams her silent eyes at me. They blink moistfully, gracefully- and then, with a quick motion, she resumes singing while moving.

"Lilakoi, the salt shakers are full! Lilakoi, I need you to give the bus boy a hand because I have pull! I wrenched the M from that resturant's sign! I quit before they could fire me from where you dine!"

Lilakoi dreamily closes her eyes. Clearly she's suffering from the delusion that her music originates from some higher plane, rather than the tenth level of Hell she's really carving out. I see Lilakoi open her eyes, and slash her microphone in a figure-8 like a child with a sparkler.

CHAPTER 11

Later that night I walk into my house and see the red diode blinking on my answering machine. I walk over to it, press the PLAY button, and the message begins.

"Hello???" a very familiar voice says.

"Marshall this Beatrix. My Mom's off tonight so me, Wendy and Dodonna wanna know if we can hang out at your house. You still have my number right? Call me whenever you get home from-shut up, Dodonna. Dodonna just said 'Painting the town red', but I was gonna say from being Mr. Busybody. I want you to be that only some of the time; not all the time. Anyhow, call me when you get home." I hear a beep, signalling the end of the message. After the beep, I pick up my house phone. With it in my hand I start dialing Chester's number. His phone starts ringing, and Chester picks up on the third ring.

"What up whodie," Chester says.

"What up Chester," I say.

"I just made it back to my house, and listened to a message Beatrix left me. She wants to come here with Wendy. Get back ready because I'm gonna scoop you up before I pick them up."

"No, wait!" Chester exclaims.

"I told you and Keith earlier that I'm done with ho. I wouldn't touch her with a ten foot pole."

"You really don't want to holla at her no more?" I ask.

"Hell no," Chester says.

"I don't want a ho that looks like a refrigerator box."

"Alright," I say.

"I won't force you to keep her company."

"I know you won't," Chester says.

"Call Keith and see if he wanna keep her company while you and Beatrix kick it." I was gonna call Keith next anyway-Dodonna and Wendy will both be coming with Beatrix but I didn't tell Chester that.

"Alright," I say. Chester and I hang up with each other. Once hanging up with Chester, I dial Keith's number. Keith's phone starts ringing, and he too picks up on the third ring.

"What up Marshall?" Keith answers.

"What up Keith," I say.

"I just made it back to my house, and listened to a message Beatrix left me. She wants to come here with Wendy and Dodonna. Do you want to go with me to pick me them up?"

"Do I?" Keith exclaims.

"Hell yeah I wanna go with you to pick them up. Are you gonna pick me or Chester up first?"

"I already called Chester," I say, "and he said he don't wanna go." Keith hoots and says, "You and Beatrix seem to be locked in with each other, so I'll take two for the team." I smile.

"That's the spirit. I have to call Beatrix back then I have to take a shower first, but I'll be there to pick you up in about an hour. Alright."

"No prob," Keith says. Keith and I hang up with each other. Following me hanging up with Keith, I dial Beatrix's cell phone number. Beatrix picks up on the second ring.

"Shirley's Beauty Salon," a voice similar to Beatrix's says.

"Shirley's Beauty Salon?" I say.

"My bad, I must have the wrong number. I was trying to call this girl."

"Marshall!" the female voice says.

"I'm so sorry??? I always answer my phone with a made up name. To throw off my friends. It's me Beatrix."

"You shouldn't play on the phone," I say.

"I got your message about ten minutes ago Beatrix, and I'm calling you back."

"Goody," Beatrix says.

"So can me, Dodonna, and Wendy come over?"

"Absolutely," I say.

"I'll pick you up in about two hours."

"Double goody," Beatrix says.

"It's 6:13 p.m. right now so you'll pick us up at 8:13?"

"8:30," I say.

"I'll pick the three of you up again in the front of the Waste-That-Little at 8:30. Be waiting outside of it at that time. Alright?"

"Alright," Beatrix says.

Beatrix and I hang up with each other. Right after we do I walk directly to my bathroom, turn on my shower, take off my clothes, then get into the water. Soon I revert to the color of a normal raisin. I'm still a standout in crowds, according to what Judika told me, but at least now I'm a clean standout. A clean set of clothes is put on my clean body before I go to my car garage, get in my car, and start heading to pick up everybody. About two hours later, I return to my house. Keith, me, Beatrix and Beatrix's two friends all get out of my car. We walk into my house on this Wednesday night at 9:11 p.m. Before I turn on the lightswitch, the frontroom is dark. The light comes on, and I look at Beatrix. "Hey there, Marshall, I hope this doesn't hang you up, me being here," Beatrix says, speaking with a spicy, singsong accent.

"Listen, we can cut out of here any time you don't want us. We're no strangers to hitchhiking, I can tell you. We'll get to my house just fine. Hey, lookie, we're both wearing watches."-Beatrix raises her wrist to me and turns it sideways- "Mines a Peugeot"-Beatrix lowers her arm- "I bought it last week. Hey, can me and you go into your room now?" I say, "Yeah, sure, I'm glad to have you here." I look at Wendy and Dodonna standing next to her.

"I have cable and a whole lot of movies you two can watch, Keith"-I look at him standing beside me then back at the two young girls- "will keep you two company." With her hair falling to one side, Dodonna looks at me with the half-smile that irritated me before, captivating me.

"Wendy and I will watch tv," and Dodonna pauses, displaying her noted flair for the dramatic, before she concludes, "with Keith." Keith claps his hands and says, "What you girls wanna watch?" while leading them into my frontroom. As they're getting settled, Beatrix and I start walking to my bedroom.

"You live here by yourself?" Beatrix asks, walking behind me.

"Yeah," I say.

"My baby-mama used to live with me, up until about a month ago."

"I'm sorry to hear that???" Beatrix says, following me into my room that I just turned the lightswitch on in.

"You know what they say: 'One woman's trash is another woman's treasure'." I turn around and look at Beatrix sharply.

"Chamiqua didn't dump me; I dumped her."

"Oh," Beatrix says, before pausing for a few seconds.

"I think there's a reason why you agreed to me being here, and it doesn't have anything to do with"-she fumbles because she can't say the right words- "with me. With sex or hunger.

"It has to do with the fact that you're lonely and need companionship."

"Go on," I remark. My smile recovers its fierceness.

"Crazy or not, you're entertaining as hell."

"So you're not lonely and in need of companionship?" Beatrix asks slowly. Beatrix watches my face carefully after she talks, the way retarded people do. I choose my words cautiously.

"I am; but I'm not ready for another serious relationship."

"Small wonder," Beatrix says, "but you don't offend me." Beatrix stares hungrily at me, then takes my hand. She leads me to the bed, gently pushes me down on it, and looks at me while I'm laying down on it as she's standing up. Beatrix grabs the bottom of my shirt, says, "Let me help you take this off," right before she pulls it up over my face. She tosses my shirt on the floor and looks at me.

"My, you have a hairy chest. Your chest is that but it won't stop me from giving you a massage. Did you know that I once used to be a masseuse?"

"You did?" I ask.

"Yeah," Beatrix says.

"Toon didn't want to pay for my tuition though. Do you have any lotion?"

"Yeah," I say.

"Look"-I point at the dresser in the corner of the room-"on top of that dresser. There's some up there." Beatrix walks to it, picks up the lotion off the top of it, walks back to me with it in her hand, sits back on the bed next to me, then uncaps the lotion. She squirts a glob of it onto my naked chest, caps the top back, and puts the bottle of lotion onto the nightstand by my bed. "It's cold," I say to Beatrix, looking down at my chest that she covered thickly with lotion. Beatrix smiles and says, "Simmer down." Beatrix begins rubbing the lotion into my chest, and I look at her as she is. Since she's busy looking down rubbing lotion into my chest, the Dutch girl doesn't see the tiredness that just came over me. I close my eyes for just a second, head sagging. I jerk it upright and then fight a jaw-cracking yawn, reaching for the top of Beatrix's head....Just as I'm about to put my hand on it, we both hear a knock on my door. Beatrix and I look at it, before the door is slowly pushed open.

Walking into my bedroom is done by Beatrix's friend that resembles ursine: Wendy. Wendy looks at Beatrix, then the lotion on my chest-she smiles at me after seeing the lotion. "It looks like you want me to join the fun," Wendy says, as if she's been rehearsing saying that for hours. Wendy piggishly walks to the other side of my bed and gets on it. Beatrix resumes rubbing lotion into my chest, before she stops to let Wendy pick up where she left off. I don't protest as Wendy reaches to my chest, puts her hand on it, then continues spreading the lotion around. Piggish is how Wendy looks as she does, but getting head from her and Beatrix pops into my mind. I picture her and Beatrix's mouths going up and down my organ like a pogo stick. Tonight I want to be their child, and have them show me that it's not enough to just kiss your children and hug them. I'm sure that they already know that oral stimulation of the genitals of infants by the parents and relatives have resulted in some curious conditioned reflexes. I could write a book about that aspect of mid twenty-second century life.

"Rub harder," Beatrix says clinically, looking at Wendy rubbing my chest. I look at Beatrix.

"How far is the Netherlands from Moscow, Russia?" I ask.

"Not that far," Beatrix says.

"Why do you ask?"

"In Moscow," I start saying, "there's a school where they go to become world-class fellatrixes."

"A what?" Beatrix asks.

"Blow-job artists," I explain, right before looking at Wendy. From what I determined about them so far, Wendy is the complete opposite of Beatrix within herself. However, I didn't expect to have two rivals practically beside each another. (A plot device that, it auditions in my mind, could work in Lilakoi's songs).

I put my hand on this diseased tree, it's an old elm, and feel pity as I stroke it. Pity is felt because because it has been afflicted by Dutch elm disease: A fungus disease characterized by yellowing of the foliage, defoliation, and death.

Held in my other hand is the handle to a container of insecticide which I'm gonna spray on this elm to control the beetles on it-doing that helps limit the spread of the disease. I went to bed about 11:30 last night after taking them home. I drove Beatrix and her two friends to her house, then I drove Keith to his house. Me being sleepy played a part in why I took them home so early. I woke up when my alarm clock went off at 6:30 a.m. this morning, so I caught up on much needed sleep-about seven hours of sleep was had and that doesn't happen often.

After waking up, I drove here to work at Toad Island. It's now 10:06 a.m. on this gray, cloudy Thursday morning and I'm about to treat this elm that needs treatment. I saw that it needed treatment because the younger leaves on the upper part of the elm are starting to wilt-I think the lower branches will become infected later. Only a few days have passed since I discovered that this elm has Dutch elm disease, so it'll be a while before many of the leaves turn yellow and then brown, and they'll curl and drop off-some of the leaves remain attached to twigs. This elm was planted before I started working here at Toad Island, and that's one reason why it has Dutch elm disease-none of the elms I've planted here in my two years working at Toad Island will ever get Dutch elm disease because I've only planted disease-resistant elms, and that's the best way to control it. I don't know exactly how long this elm has had Dutch elm disease, but I do know that the disease is named that because it was first observed in the Netherlands in 1919. I stop stroking this tree, use the same hand to pick up the spray gun, and start spraying insecticide on the afflicted elm. I stop spraying it, and touch it once again. I feel the elm's thick, rough bark and wonder if I should feel a kinship with this old tree.

Putting my hand on this tree reminds me of that time when I was walking Walt to the carcass of a dead skunk I saw earlier before seeing him-I was walking him to it because Walt fly-fishes, and I saw that the carcass of it had many dipteran bait flying around it. While wearing the same short-sleeved grey Toad Island collared shirt and short black pants I'm wearing now, I led him through the woods among the smooth boles of the trees; some were silver, some dark as my skin, some speckled rufous, like me. I stroked each tree wonderingly as we were walking, and a sharp look is what I remember Walt shooting me; he shot me a sharp look but I decided to wait until he actually told me to stop. About half a minute before he shot me a sharp look, I stroked another tree. After I did, Walt asked me a question.

"You like trees?" is what Walt asked me that day and it seemed I amused him. It seemed like I amused him but I simply answered, "They inspire awe of course. But they also...clutter up the landscape." The way Walt looked when he said, "C...clutter?" almost made me laugh because of his expression. After he found what I said unbelievable I said, "Yes. I'm used to being able to see right to the edge, you know? To the horizon? Whereas anybody could be hiding behind trees."

After I said that Walt looked at me for a long time. He looked at me as if I said much more than I had said. He walked up to me, stopped right in front of my face, and stood nose to nose against me. While he was looking deep down into my eyes Walt said, "I am from the forest. I find hiding places very useful. I don't think there are enough of them here." After he said that Walt turned and continued walking the way we were going; I stood staring at him and then I sprinted after him, Walt's words echoing and reechoing in my head. *'I am from the forest. I find hiding places very useful. I am from the forest'.* Someday I might understand what he meant by that. Someday I might know why that is so important. Nine hours later, I am now putting my car into drive after Chester and his cousin got into the backseat of my car. Keith is sitting up front with me since I picked him up first. As I'm driving off from the front of Chester's aunt house, I look in my rearview mirror at Chester's cousin; I look at the young fourteen-year-old Black boy that is gangly, has nappy wicks in his hair, and wearing a piratical black patch over his eye.

"Aaaargh, ahoy matey," I say, looking in my rearview mirror at him.

"What's with the pirate patch, Dominic?" Dominic leans forward from his backseat towards my frontseat, looks at Keith looking at him, then looks at me. While smiling smugly at me Dominic says, "Those bitch-ass niggas jumped me a few nights ago."

"You were jumped?!" Keith exclaims, before eyeing Chester then looking back at Dominic.

"Chester didn't tell me you were jumped." Dominic looks back at Keith.

"He didn't find out until I told him last night; when I had to tell my Mom to take me to the hospital, so I could get this"-Dominic touches his eye patch- "put over my left eye that developed conjunctivitis." Keith asks, "Why didn't you tell him on the night, or at least the next day, that you was jumped?" Dominic looks back at Chester, I'm making a left turn as he is, and answers Keith while looking at his older cousin.

"I didn't want to give him more than he could handle," Dominic says.

"Those niggas jumped me around midnight at that block party on the same night that Warren was killed."- Dominic turns back to Keith- "I was caught slippin' walkin home, the party was only six blocks away, after midnight."

"Daaaamn," Keith says.

"So some niggas jumped you?"

"Yeah," Dominic says, "The scrawny one had a blackjack and he just stared at me like he was sizing me up. The other one said 'You think you can take me? Jump, motherfucker, jump!'." As I'm driving, I look at Dominic after he becomes silent; he is gingerly touching a bruise at the corner of his jaw. I take my eyes off of Dominic right before he starts talking again. Dominic says, "Luckily the bruise isn't the worst effect." I'm more worried about this conjuctivitis." Keith asks, "How long will the mucuous membrane lining the inner surface of your left eyelid be inflammed?" Dominic starts saying, "The doctor said-" When my cell phone rings, Dominic is interuppted from talking. As I'm driving I take my cell phone out of my pocket, look at it, and answer it.

"What up Mom," I answer, holding the cell phone with one hand and driving with the other. I listen to my Mom, before confirming.

"Yeah," I say. I'm on the way to his football game now. How long have you and Arthur been there?" Keith, Dominic, and Chester all look at me while I'm listening to my Mom.

"Alright," I say.

"I'm headed there now, and I'll be there in about twenty minutes."

My Mom tells me that she'll be looking for me and to drive safe, before the two of us get off the phone with each other.

"So who your lil brother's team playing again?" Chester asks, from the backseat.

"Forest High School," I say, turning on my blinker.

"The Governors are playing Forest. My lil brother's team is gonna beat Forest. I can feel it...in my nerves." While Dominic is still leaning in between the two front seats he looks at me and says, "I don't have to tell you not to try and live off your nerves, do I, podna?" I glance at the young, gangly boy again. The young, gangly boy that has clear skin; not even peach fuzz. I look at his one visible eye, and see that it should belong to somebody older. Much older. Like a hundred or so. It bores into me, as I look at him; as I look at the slim Black boy with wicks, a strong chin, and the air of an ambitious ferret; an ambitious ferret whose instinct for trouble is as searching as a particle sifter.

"No, you don't, little podna," I say.

I stop looking at Dominic, focus back on the road, and change the lane we're in-Dominic falls back from leaning in between the two front seats, and slouches in his backseat. As I'm driving, the sun continues setting. Right after I pull onto Chief Street, the sun completely sets-the sky is dark as I'm driving down it. Silent is the interior of my car for about five minutes while I'm driving, but that changes no more than a minute after I start driving down Chief Street. I hear a whoop, then see flashing blue lights appear in my rearview mirror. Beside me Keith says, "What they fuckin' with us for?" while he is turned around in his seat looking at the back window.

"I don't know," I say, still looking at my rearview mirror.

"But we're about to find out." I turn to my power window, lower it, and look at the driver door mirror. The policeman gets out of his cruiser, and starts walking towards my car while shining a powerful flashlight. "Shiiiit," Dominic says, also looking back at him.

"He looks like a nice cop. He ain't gonna write you a ticket for anything." While continuing to look at my driver's door mirror I say, "I hope a moving violation is the only reason why he pulled me over."

The policeman walks up to the side of the driver door, looks down at me, and says, "Sir, I noticed you were driving erratically." I become elated-a routine traffic stop! I answer, "I'm sorry. I'm sorry, I *was* driving erratically." The policeman frowns at me and says, "Is there a reason?"

"Yes, sir," I say.

"My cell phone rang in my pocket"-I take my cell phone out of my pocket- "and I just pulled it out to see who it was calling me. At that moment, I'm sure I began erratically driving."

"That's a neat phone you got there," the policeman allows.

"What kind is it?"

"It's an Android," I add.

"I'm sorry if we alarmed you."

"Mind taking a breathalyzer?"

"Not at all," I say.

"Because I definitely smell alcohol," the policeman says.

"Not on me," I say.

"You probably smell alcohol on one of my passengers." The policeman stares at me querously for many long seconds. He finally says, "Mind if I look inside?" I'd rather you didn't," I say. The policeman says, "Whatcha got in there?" "You'd never believe it," I say.

"I can call in a K-9 unit, Mr. Powers. If you want to do this the hard way."

"A K-9 for a law-abiding citizen?" I say.

"What's it gonna be sniffing for, prescription painkillers?" A second squad car brings a trained German shepherd called Clip by the officer. Chester, me, Keith and Dominic are ordered to stand back and observe. "Deidre was right about me," I mutter to my dawgs.

"I'm an asshole." Many minutes pass by-the panting German shepherd yaps and snaps and turns in circles, but it doesn't scratch at the locks. Following the German shepherd not sniffing anything, the K-9 officer looks at the policeman.

"The fuckhead is clean," the K-9 officer says to him. The policeman nods, and he says nothing as he writes me a ticket for improper lane changing. The policeman hands me the ticket and says, "You can pay by mail." I take the ticket, while smiling at him, and say, "I don't blame you for being suspicious." Keith scowls at the policeman and while the policeman is walking to his cruiser Keith says, "Make like a tree and split." After the policemen leave, we all get back into my grey Ford Taurus, and I continue driving to my lil brother's football game.

"What was that pig's name?" Keith asks me, none too quietly, as if he's making up a list of enemies and wants to include him.

"I don't know," I say, looking forward out the front windshield.

"But I do know I'm gonna pay this bitch if not tomorrow then Monday." Dominic leans forward in between the two front seats and says, "You know you have thirty days to pay it right?" I glance at Dominic then say, "I know, but I'd rather get it out the way." I make a left onto another street, drive down the street for a while, then get onto the same highway I drove on eight days ago; I get onto the same highway that I drove on while Chester, me and Warren were going to and from Frieda's house. I drive down it for a while, make a few turns before reaching Hancock High School, and once making it there I park in the parking lot belonging to Hancock Middle School right next to the football field. Chester, me, Keith, and Dominic all get out of my car and start walking towards Hancock High School's football field-under the night sky we start walking towards it as stars twinkle above us. About three minutes later, we reach the entrance to Hancock's football field that is blocked by a table with a woman sitting at it. The woman sitting down at the table smiles at us.

"Admission's five dollars. Two fifty for students."

I take out my wallet, pull out a five dollar bill, and say, "Here you go," while handing the bill to the woman. The woman takes it, puts the money in a jar on the tabletop, and rips off a ticket from a roll of them.

"Here's your ticket," the woman says, handing me the stub.

"Hold on to it so you can verify that you paid to get in if need be."

"Alright," I say, taking the ticket. I walk past her and the table, turn around, and look at my three dawgs also pay their way in. Once they do, we start walking into the actual football field.

"One of these teeny boppers want a thug," Keith says, looking from left to right at the large amount of people.

The large number of people we're intermingling in is mainly composed of students and their parents. All four of us walk underneath outside scaffolding, before entering the oval of Hancock High School's football field-the night sky is seen above us as we do. We start walking to the home side bleachers, walk up a set of steps leading up to them, and after getting to the top start walking across the front of the bleachers. Following behind me are Chester, Keith, and Dominic that are moving as if they themselves are followed by a suggestion of thunder, metallic and ominous; as if somebody and the crowd in this football stadium were after them. I don't need to turn around to see that their bodies are lean and hard, evidently due to their lives of hard work and as well as a lack of proper nourishment. While I'm leading them across the front of these bleachers I hear someone shout, "Marshall!" Towards the stands I look up but from who the shout came from I can't tell until, "Marshall!" is shouted again. I look at who shouted my name again and I see that it's Khadijah. Khadijah is a seventeen-year-old Black girl that has been inside my house before, and she has big breasts-her double D breasts are just a little bigger than the breasts on the Chicana standing up besides her, and I know that Khadijah's Mexican friend's name is Biannela. I smile at Khadijah, throw my hand up at her, then return to facing forward while walking across the front of the bleachers. About three seconds later I look back up in the stands, scanning the crowd for my Mom and stepdad. I spot them almost near the top bleacher and turn to my dawgs.

"My Mom's up there," I say, jerking my thumb to the area she's in.

"I'ma go up there and sit with her for a while."

"Alright," Chester says.

"Before you go Marshall," Keith says, "who was that Black bitch with the jugs that just called you?"

"Her name's Khadijah," I say.

"Why? You like her?"

"Hell yeah, I like her," Keith says.

"She has some"-Keith holds his hands out several inches from his chest and pretends cupping it- "airbags on her." Dominic readjusts his eye patch and looks at Keith, "Sorry, podna, I think you're not her type."

"He might be right," I say, now looking back at Keith.

"But I'll see what I can do after I finish sitting with my Mom." All three of them say, "Alright," and I turn around to start walking up the bleachers. While I'm walking up the bleachers, I look at the faces of the people I pass by. He has a fairly bland face, as if his greatest skill in life is blending into a crowd. She has a puerperal face-it carries a potentially dangerous combination of paranoia and eagerness. I take my eyes off of the woman with a puerperal face, and in the same motion continue walking up the bleachers. While walking up the bleachers, I make eye contact with my Mom. She is smiling at me and continues to do so when I make it to her and my youngest brother's Dad while they are both sitting down. I sit down next to my Mom.

"What up Mom?"

"Good evening baby," my heavyset Mom says, smiling at me.

"I'm glad you made it."

"Me too," Arthur says, sitting on the opposite side of my Mom.

"How was work today?" my Mom asks. I say, "I treated a dying tree today."

As soon as I finish answering a roar erupts from the bleachers. My Mom, me and Arthur all look down at the field dotted with people-the Governors has just stopped Forest from getting any yardage on a 3rd and 2. Once the roar dies down, my Mom looks back at me.

"Have you and Chamiqua made up with each other yet?" my Mom asks, a hint of grief on her face.

"No," I say.

"She's right for you," my Mom turns her head, pretending to look down at the football field.

"Your delinquent friends that came here with you ain't."

I stare silently at my Mom, and staring at her reminds me that she's a Black Christian woman that I used to live with in her trailer home about three years ago when I was on house arrest. Before going back to live with my Mom, I lived by myself in an apartment after Deidre left me. On that night I was took to jail, just Chester and I went to that restaurant where Khadijah's Mexican friend worked at as a waitress. Because of me being stupid and showing off that night, I went to jail. Chester and I sat down on barstools at that bar for a while, ordering drinks and food while talking to Biannela.

After being there for about an hour I decided it was time to go. I got up off of my barstool, walked to the door with

Chester following me, and walked out of that restaurant then drove off without paying the bill. That same Mexican bitch I was trying to impress gave the police my address; the police came to my house and arrested me. I didn't stay in jail for long, because the very next day I was gave bond. The bond I paid had a stipulation however: House arrest had to be on. House arrest was put on, I was escorted to a nearby office, and I sat down at the desk near that Black bald detective that put an ankle bracelet on my ankle. After securing the ankle bracelet on me, that detective and his partner drove me to my Mom's trailer-they drove me to my Mom's trailer which is where I lived at for a few months while I was on house arrest. By a stroke of luck, I was hired at a Wal-Mart while I was on house arrest. To be able to leave my Mom's trailer to go to work I had to have my work schedule wrote done on a form the police provided and have it signed by my counselor before the work week started, so he could enter into the monitor the times my ankle monitor tracker would show I'm no longer in the vicinity.

Accidentally writing that I needed to leave my house at 10:30 a.m. instead of 8:30 a.m. on that form my counselor signed caused me to be escorted out of that Wal-Mart while I was working on that Wednesday morning about two and a half years ago-that morning I left my Mom's trailer at 8:30 a.m. so I could be at work at my appointed time of 9:00 a.m., and on that other form I had 11:00 a.m. as my reported start time which is why I needed to leave the trailer at 10:30 a.m. so I could have thirty minutes to get to my job. Those same two detectives that drove me from the county jail with a ankle bracelet on were the same ones that escorted me out of Wal-Mart that Wednesday morning around 9:40

a.m.; being escorted out of my place of employment, both detectives flanked me like trees, was embarrassing. Many Wal-Mart shoppers stared at me, and I remember looking up and seeing a White man with a disarrayed shock of dark greying hair and a similarly greying thick handlebar moustache looking at me; he looked like a mad scientist. I stop looking at my Mom when I hear the announcer say over the loudspeaker, "Forest's punting team is now coming onto the field." I continue looking down at the field and see black helmets sporting big silver F's for Forest. While my Mom, Arthur, and me are looking down at the football field we hear the announcer say, "Forest's kicker has shown many highly accurate coffin corner kicks in tonight's game, so let's see if he can again kick the ball in a certain spot towards the Governors' visibly weaker receiving side. No doubt we'll be seeing every single player on the kicking team running towards a certain side somewhere around the Governors' ten yard line." Out the corner of my eye I see my Mom turn towards me and I turn towards her.

"Do you ever plan on settling down, Marshall?" my Mom asks.

"And I don't mean for play-play. I mean for good with a woman you'll spend the rest of your life with. You could have settled down with Roz, but you didn't. You could have with Deidre, but you also didn't. And now Chamiqua. You have a child with each and every one of those girls-a living soul that you and another human being brought into this world. I want you and Chamiqua to get back with each other, so the child you two have together can grow up in a household with a Father. If you two don't, don't introduce me to any new girls...unless she's a Christian woman and even then, I'll still be mad about you and Chamiqua separating." I stare at my Mom without saying anything, and I know why she said 'Christian woman'. My Mom's a Christian woman herself. I remember that night a few weeks after I was let off of house arrest but still living with my Mom in her trailer. On that night I had returned home late from that girl's apartment, Chester introduced the two of us to each other, to find my Mom waiting in the kitchen. My Mom took my hand wordlessly and led me out the front door. Where Oink Street meets the main road in front of her trailer neighborhood is where we traipsed about 1/3 of a mile to in the moonlight.

When we got to the main road, my Mom dropped to her knees and began to pray. Moans and wails that broke the peacefulness of the night was her praying that wasn't polite. I became further embarrassed and dumbfounded when my Mom crawled into the road and nuzzled her cheek to the grimy pavement. I was looking at her while she was on the ground when I said, "Ma, cut it out."

"Don't you see Him?" my Mom said, looking up at me.

"See who? You're gonna get runned over." My Mom replied, "Son, it's Jesus. Look there! Our Lord and Savior! Don't you see his face in the road?" I walked to the spot and peered at it intently.

"It's just an oil stain, Ma. Or maybe brake fluid."

"No! It's the face of Jesus Christ!" my Mom exclaimed. I replied, "Ok. I'm outta here." My Mom shouted, "Marshall!" as I began walking back to the trailer. Looking at her right now reminds me of the Road-Stain Jesus. I take my eyes off of my Mom and look at Arthur. While looking at him, I smile. I smile because the joke that everyone has heard-"You're so skinny you can hula hoop with a cheerio"-goes through my mind while looking at the very skinny middle aged Black man that gives my Mom happiness. My Mom married Arthur years ago, and he's alright with me because he makes her happy. Arthur stops looking down at the football game and looks back at me. I say, "What's the skinny Arthur?"

CHAPTER 12

Right after my younger brother's football game, miraculously won by the Governors, I drove all of my dawgs home. I am now driving back to my house on this cloudless Thursday night at 10:30 p.m. While I'm driving home, my cell phone rings. I keep one hand on the steering wheel of my moving car as I pull out my cell phone from out of my pocket, look at the number the call is coming from, then press the answer button on it before holding it to my ear.

"Jerome's Barber Shop," I answer.

"Ha-ha, very funny Marshall," Beatrix says.

"Hey, I'm just doing what was done to me," I say.

"What up Beatrix?"

"My excitement," Beatrix says.

"Where are you?" I switch lanes.

"I'm over here on the Northside; I just dropped Chester, his cousin, and Keith off. We all went to a football game."

"So you're over here by my house???" Beatrix asks.

"Yeah," I say, staring forward out the windshield.

"Goody," Beatrix says.

"You can come by here then??? I want you to come. My Mom's gone to work and I'm here by myself."

"Oh," I say.

"Has kids been coming to your house to get candy on this Halloween night?"

"Too much," Beatrix says.

"Trick-or-treaters have been constantly ringing my doorbell since seven o'clock." I say, "Well, another one's gonna be ringing your doorbell in-I say about ten minutes. Give me ten minutes to get your house. You there by yourself right? Dodonna and Wendy aren't with you?"

"No, they're not," Beatrix says.

"I'm here by myself."

"Great," I say.

"Give me about ten minutes to get there."

"Alright," Beatrix says. I hang up with Beatrix. Fifteen minutes later, I park in front of a house that's two houses down from the one that's directly across the street from Beatrix's. From the driver's seat of my parked car, I see two trick-or-treaters approach Beatrix's house. While they are walking up the driveway I get out of my car, walk to the back of my car, look from left to right to determine if I'm being watched, then open my trunk. I open my trunk, and quickly assemble onto my body the war drone known as Sequoia. I look down at my body, reduced to graceless androgyny by Sequoia's woodlike body and loglike helmet; I can feel the machinery attached to my body. I expressionlessly raise my arms in a wooden motion. I test one leg, then the other. I go on one toe.

My joints creak audibly. Towards Beatrix's house I start walking. I make it to the front door of her lawn just as she finishes dropping candy into that lil girl's, she's dressed up as a cowgirl, bag.

"Thank you!" the lil cowgirl with colonial clothing and a cowboy hat on says, while holding a trick-or-treat bag and plastic rifle.

"Thank you!" the other trick-or-treater says, dressed up as the tin man from *The Wizard of Oz*. They turn to begin walking away with their female chaperone, but Beatrix stops them. Beatrix says, "Wait!" and the two small trick-or-treaters and chaperone turn around. While looking at the lil cowgirl Beatrix says, "Show me what kind of aim Annie Oakley had." The lil girl says, "Okay," and gives her trick-or-treat bag to the adult with her. The only things she holds now is the plastic rifle. The lil girl raises the toy gun to her shoulder, sights along the barrel at a row of birds on a low tree branch, and makes noises as if she's firing at them. Beatrix claps her hands, the lil cowgirl takes her trick-or-treat bag back from her chaperone, and the two trick-or-treaters resume walking away with their chaperone.

While they are walking away, I look at the lil boy dressed up as the tin man. I nod. The look of that lil boy dressed up as the tin man feels wrong-the boy is being trained, it seems, to be a machine, not a person-but if that kid likes his costume, and his parents hadn't objected to him wearing it....Towards Beatrix I walk, as she is still standing at her open doorway. Beatrix turns, sees me approaching her, and says, "And who are you supposed to be?" I stop about five feet away from Beatrix and just stare at her. Many seconds pass as I do."

Well, who are you?" Beatrix asks again.

Again I just stare at her wordlessly. Beatrix says, "Ok. Since you wanna play games. I'll just leave you out here empty-handed???" Beatrix backs up and begins closing her door. As she is, I take off my helmet.

"Wait, Beatrix. It's me, Marshall."

Beatrix looks at my raisin-colored face that has hair which is braided tightly. "Marshall," Beatrix says, squinting at me. "Why are you in costume for the holiday, mental?" Instead of answering her I reply, "Halloween isn't what I'd call a holiday." Beatrix says, "Correct. It's a sacred day to those who pratice Wicca."

"Wicca?" I ask.

"Wiseness," Beatrix says.

"The religion of poor Christian womanhood. It's the oldest religion known to woman???"

"Never heard of it," I say flatly. Beatrix smiles at me, shakes her head while continuing to smile, and waves for me to come in. I walk into her house, and Beatrix looks at me as I start closing the door. When it closes completely Beatrix says, "I'm not gonna-as they say, beat around the bush??? I invited you over so me and you could get into our HotTubTideMachine-jacuzzi-together that's out back. Do you want to?" I say, "Sure." "Goody," Beatrix says, clapping her hands together.

"I'll be right back; let me change." Five minutes later, Beatrix returns wearing a bikini that shows off her criminally luscious body.

"Do you like?" Beatrix blurts, like a silly schoolgirl trying to ask the teacher if he thought the Sun is made of Gouda cheese.

"Beatrix," I say, noticing her outfit. "Would it be possible for me to get something like that you're wearing?" Beatrix has to stop and think about that, but when she does, her eyes light up.

"Toon has some swimming trousers," she says slowly.

"You can wear one of his'." Dashing back out is done by Beatrix, and she returns with a pair of blue swimming trunks with black stripes down the side. Beatrix holds them up to me, stretches them out, and says, "Will these do?" Twenty minutes later, Beatrix and I are sitting across from each other in the HotTubeTideMachine out back. We both are submerged up to our chests in it's warm water. "Toon bought this jacuzzi last week," Beatrix says. "This *HotTug*-that's the trademarked name of this-this *Hottug* was the first wood-fired hot tub back in the twentieth first century; and it was created by a Dutch designer named Frank de Druijn."

"Frank de Druijn," I repeat.

"I've never heard of him." We both become silent in the jacuzzi for a while as the moon's glow reflects onto the water's surface. Dirty thoughts go through my head as I look at Beatrix. Beatrix sits very still, her hands just trailing in the water.

"Do you want to know what I did last night after you brought me home?" I say, "No, what?"

"I watched a porno," Beatrix says.

"A porno titled *Voila*, and it was about this woman named Amy and a man named Tony; they were third cousins. They were third cousins to each other but that didn't stop Amy from jacking off Tony. She jacked off Tony using her feet." My eyebrows shoot up.

"She did?"

"Yeah," Beatrix says, loaded.

"Amy demonstrated her podiatry skills by using her feet to jack off her third cousin Tony." I feel one of Beatrix's feet come in contact with my groin and I begin to jump.

"He-hey!" I say, jumping.

"Let's just chill first."

"Whatever," Beatrix says sulkily, turning to Sequoia that I positioned to be standing up by the back porch's sliding glass door entrance. Sequoia is standing up by the sliding glass door entrance, and suffused over him is the only light that illuminates the back of Beatrix's house-the back porch light.

"What is that?" Beatrix says, looking at Sequoia.

"An infant city???" I follow Beatrix's gaze and reply, "If so, he's a good cause for urban renewal." Beatrix groans, and abruptly she swings around to face me again.

"We've got a problem." She says that but her tone isn't abrupt: She speaks laconically, as if all she wants is to engage me in conversation.

"For the last two days I've wanted you to give it to me, but you won't.

Why?" I alibi at Beatrix.

"You do know you're not eighteen yet right?" Beatrix sighs and says, "Oh, so that's it." Beatrix turns from me, picks up one of the goblets of wine off of the platter on the outrim of her *HotTug*, and starts sipping from the goblet. While holding the goblet Beatrix looks at Sequoia again. "Is your infant city man enough to give it to me?" I chuckle and say, "It doesn't have the tool to do that." Beatrix huffs, turns to me, says, "If you're unable to rise to the occassion, I have means to assist you," and picks up a goblet on the platter then holds it out to me. I take it and say, "It makes tall tree grow in forest?"

The work week is at an end, because I've just clocked out-I've just clocked out on this sunny Friday afternoon. Last night I went to Beatrix's house and got into her jacuzzi, but I don't plan on doing that again tonight. Or even right now. Right now I'm headed towards the Driver's License Ticket Office, so I can pay the improper lane changing ticket that I was gave last night; I'm not gonna even bother stopping at my house first so I can take off my work clothes. I'll go to the Driver License Ticket Office with my Toad Island uniform on. As I'm driving to it, I think about everything Jude said to me earlier this afternoon while I was inside that log cabin. Just for something to do, I made a detour to that log cabin while I was on the clock-Jude was in it of course.

"Marshall!" Jude said to me as I walked in.

"I'm glad you stopped by."

"Why is that?" I asked him.

"Well," Jude began, "I was just about to get pixilated, and you can join me."

"I certainly can," I said, walking towards Jude. I continued looking at Jude as he walked to the bar of real maple, slid open it's back cabinet, took out a bottle of Black Jack and two tumblers, put ice cubes in the two tumblers, uncorked the bottle of Black Jack, then pour it into both tumblers up to the rim. Jude held out one of the tumblers to me, and I took it. We toasted before Jude walked to one of the log cabin's windows. Jude stood at the window with the tumbler of Black Jack in one hand and the window cord in the other, pulling back the curtain. Weak afternoon sunlight streamed into the room. I looked at Jude as he held his tumbler of Black Jack up to the light, savoring its color and thickness. While he was looking at his tumbler

Jude said, "Bourbon County, Kentucky. It's where the name comes from. Did you know that, Marshall?"

"No, I didn't," I said, before taking a drink from my tumbler.

"Aged four years in charred oak barrels," Jude said.

"That's the system. I hate that they use barrels made of oak to age the Black Jack. That's the system however."-Jude looks at me- "Do you know how hard oak is to come by these days?" I took another drink, preferring the sipping to talking. I answered, "Pretty hard."

"Damn near impossible," Jude added, before taking a drink himself. "The stuff doesn't grow back fast, like pines or such. What are we gonna do for whisky when all the oat's gone?"

"Have you ever been to Moscow, Russia?" I asked Jude, ignoring his question at first.

"Not yet," Jude said.

"Oh," I said.

"Well, to answer your question: We'll drink vodka. It's not aged at all." Jude made his face even uglier by grimacing.

"Damn foreign drink. Though I guess everything is foreign up here." I raised the glass. "I'll drink to that." I put the tumbler to my lips, and started drinking while my head was thrown back. When I returned my head to an upright position, I saw Jude looking at me.

"So," Jude said, "how is Sequoia working out for you?"

"Alright," I said. "I wore Sequoia last night as a costume when I went to that girl's house."

"A girlfriend?" Jude asked.

"No," I said. "Beatrix's not a girlfriend, but I did like how she minced over to me with a lot of hip action and an effervescence greeting. Beatrix and cherry champagne-always bubbly."

"Oh-well, Sequoia can be used as a costume," Jude said.

"Several trick-or-treaters came to my house last night, and I liked some of the costumes I saw."

"What was the most interesting one you saw?" I asked. Jude said, "I'd say that little kid dressed as Pinocchio. He wore pants with suspenders and his pressed on wooden nose was about this"-Jude holds his free hand and the hand holding the tumbler of Black Jack out about a foot away from each other- "long. I gave him more candy than the others. And he said he'd save it for later. Ever hear of kids that age saving candy for later? What the hell's becoming of this world?" "You're asking the wrong person," I replied. Jude harrumphed, turned away while taking a drink from the tumbler, then looked back at me.

"So you said Sequoia is working out alright for you?" Jude asked. I nodded. Jude said, "In essence, you're no longer a human being. You're a *machina infernalis*-an infernal device."

"I am?" I asked Jude, eyebrow arched up.

"Do I need batteries yet?" Jude chuckled.

"Not if you don't want them." I casted my eyes over Jude's shirt and offered a supercilious smile.

"Tell me, Jude, is it necessary that I be the one to sponsor Sequoia?"

"That would depend on your definition of the word 'necessary'-but I feel it is," Jude answered. When I pull in the parking lot of the Driver's License Ticket Office near the beach, I stop thinking about my earlier conversation with Jude. As I'm approaching it I look at the front of the Driver's

License Ticket Office that has a glass window spanning the front of it, I can see inside of it, so I see the customers in it is only two people waiting in line. I park my grey Ford Taurus in true dickhead style, diagonally across two spaces-I should be in and out. The strategy behind doing that is that I can pull out quickly in my car if I have to. I get out of my car, close the driver's door, walk up to the front of the building, then walk into the Driver's License Ticket Office. The front glass door swings shut behind me and I proceed to the red velvet ropes, they're hooked onto movable silver posts, outlining the way towards the front counter. I walk alongside the red velvet ropes, before I approach the back of the next Driver's License Ticket Office customer in it. I stand behind the thin older White woman with a short bob hairstyle for a while, since the line doesn't move.

The line doesn't move because the woman standing at the only open front counter is debating with the clerk about a ticket she was gave. The thin older White woman in front of me and I listen to the woman at the counter, as she debates with the Driver's License Ticket Office clerk. While the woman says she contests the ticket gave to her, the thin older White woman with a short hairstyle turns around and looks at me.

"She's a piece of work, innit she?" the thin older White woman asks me, smiling. I smile back at the thin older White woman that appears to be in her late fifties and just nod.

"Not much of a talker, are you?" the thin fifty-something looking White woman says. I clear my throat.

"I can be a talker when I want to. If you don't mind me asking, what's your name ma'am?" The fifty-something looking White woman with hawklike features says, "Titicaca."

"Titicaca," I repeat.

"That's an uncommon name."

"It is," Titicaca responds.

"I was conceived fifty-eight years ago during the night when my parents were on vacation in Lake Titicaca, that lake in Bolivia Peru, which is why they chose to name me Titicaca. It's also an exotic name, innit it?"

"It is," I respond.

"What's your name young man?" Titicaca asks. Titicaca looks at me with her face that has a hawklike, patrician aspect and a wide, almost lipless mouth that conceals roughly-serrated edges of bone that supplant frailer teeth. I say, "Marshall." "Marshall," Titicaca says, before laughing.

"I had to marshal up some money so I could deb my tickets today; I have a lead foot and I do a poor job feeding parking meters." I begin saying, "That could suggest a certain disregard for rules....," before trailing off.

"My days disregarding rules are over," Titicaca says. "Besides, my daughter disregards rules enough for the both of us. If you don't mind me asking, why are *you* here at the Driver's License Ticket Office?" Titicaca looks me up and down, in a way that makes me think of a vulture eyeing something that is not quite dead. I say, "I'm about to pay an improper lane changing ticket I got last night." "Oh," Titicaca says. "I've never gotten an improper lane changing ticket. I went-" Titicaca is interrupted from finishing her sentence, when the clerk at the front counter says, "Next!" Titicaca looks at her and starts walking away, but suddenly turns back to me.

"I know I've just met you," Titicaca says.

"But I feel I must tell you this." Titicaca leans forward and quickly whispers in my ear, "Fight dirty, dear. It's your only hope." I look at Titicaca as she turns to walk away. I stand in the line by myself for about ten minutes before Titicaca finishes. She turns around and while passing looks at me and says, "Remember what I told you," as she is walking to the front door. I'm called to the front counter. Words are exchanged between the clerk and I, I pay the ticket, then I too walk out of the Driver's License Ticket Office. The Driver's License Ticket Office I just walked out of is in one of the many plazas that are situated two streets across from the beach, so I can smell and feel the breezy ocean air from where I'm standing-the climate under the roofed walkway is room temperature. Room temperature cools me as I look at the tangerine sun in the cloudless sky. I take my eyes off of the tangerine sun in the cloudless sky, and I look to my right towards the row of commercial beachfront properties nearest to the beach. A sidewalk traverses down across the front of the long line of commercial beachfront properties in front of me, and I walked on that same sidewalk two days ago-I walked on that same sidewalk when Keith, Chester, and I walked on it during the Beach Festival. Those West Islanders walked up behind us when we were walking on that same sidewalk two days ago. I thought of Yee after that West Islander said, "Mon Chief," to me because he had a foreign accent just like Yee. Yee is that Haitian my Mom married eighteen years ago, and Yee I know paid my Mom to marry him so he could stay in the United States. He wanted to be in the land of freedom instead of his hometown of Haiti. For him to be able to legally stay, Yee had to marry a

United States citzen. The United States citizen turned out to be my Mom that was a single Mother of two kids at the time. A identity card attesting the permanent resident status of an alien in the United States is what a green card is, and a green card is what Yee was gave after he married my Mom.

Exactly why my Mom agreed to marry a lil butt-ugly Haitian I don't know, but I do know that my Mom was debbed a lot of money for doing so; she was paid a lot of money for being oedipal...I get my why-the-hell-not attitude from my Mom. Yee and my Mom obviously aren't together anymore, but they were married to each other for over a year. They had to be. They had to be married to each other for a while to make the marriage look legit. Yee had everything together when he finally landed a job after marrying my Mom. He worked as a sanitation worker for about six months, before that incident which got him deported back to his hometown of Haiti. The incident involved a burgundy Jaguar XJ, a gay man, and four tons of raw garbage. According to what my Mom told me Yee told her, Yee borrowed one of his employer's trash trucks one night. He then drove to that restaurant where the gay man that's been flirting with him off and on was at while dining with his boyfriend. My Mom told me that Yee dumped a sour mound of garbage ten feet high onto the burgundy convertible while its top was down, destroying the perfectly splendid vehicle.

Right now I'm imaging virgin leather upholstery ripening under a ambrosial lode of spare ribs, crumpled wads of Kleenex, Black Jack bottles, leaky toothpaste tubs, orange rinds, eggshells, bacon grease, cottage cheese, cat litter, potato skins, coagulated gravy, chicken necks, coffee grounds, sanitary napkins, pizza crust, and fish heads. I wish I could have been there to see the grisly sight up close. A ghastly sight I saw that I wish I hadn't seen up close was when I saw that White man walking down the street that morning one minute, then falling down before crawling on the asphalt the next; he's OD'd or something. I looked at his dead body on the street that morning, before I peeled out of there. Either that man committed suicide by doing drugs all night, or accidentally did too much of whatever it was that he was doing. I'll never forget that morning after I just dropped Chester off after we were at that girl's house-I saw that junkie as I was driving home.

As far as I know, I was the only person that saw him staggering around like a zombie in the middle of the street. Others were probably looking at him from inside their houses, but I'm the only person that was looking at him from a car and from the street. I know I'll never OD'd on a drug. I'll never OD on any type of drug because I just drink. I don't smoke. I'm what they call a social smoker. If I go to a party or something and someone offers me something to smoke, I will. But as far as me just firing one up by myself I'll never do that. I can leave from here right now, go to a convenience store, buy a pack of cigarettes, and fire one up in my car but I won't do that. I'll also never go back to managing stockers at night. I was paid good and I had fun doing it, but I couldn't really have a night life while I was being a night manager. I remember that time when my younger brother, that Black male stocker, and that White woman stocker that looked Frieda all went to that bistro around 2 a.m. after we all got off of work. Now that I think about it, that Black male's stocker girlfriend looked like Judika.

Judika is a first grade teacher so I know she knows about the United States' worst school shooting that happened in the 21st century. Twenty elementary school kids and six adults that worked at that elementary were shot and killed on that day in the 21st century on December 16th, 2012 so she knows of it since she's an elementary teacher herself. An elementary teacher that teaches kids in the same age bracket as those whose lives were ended by another man that's in Hell right now. I know that that fucker's in Hell right now, engulfed in white-hot flames. If I'm sent to Hell, I'll torture that fucker myself. I'll torture, terroize that twenty-year-old man that killed all those innocent little kids at Sandyhook Elementary on December 16th, 2012. That twenty-year-old man was White, so he wasn't Haitian like Yee. I wonder why Yee's parents gave him such a Chinese sounding name. Yee was black as I don't know what so I know both of his parents, especially his Mom, had to be full Haitian. They gave their son a name that look and sound Chinese and I read it was Chinese authorities that seized 213 bear paws in that very old TIME magazine I read last week. That picture of all those severed bear paws, the grey palms of them were facing upwards, was appalling. It was appalling to see just the hands of many shaggy bear paws placed neatly in rows, and that caption by it said that the Chinese consider them a delicacy.

The Chinese consider bear paws a delicacy, but I know that there was nothing delicate about the Chinese' authorities sting to seize those particular bear paws which to them was contraband-they seized tat contraband from Russian smugglers in that area of China known as Inner Mongolia. Inner Mongolia isn't too far geographically from the Philippines, the place where Jude's race originates from. Jude saved my life when he shot that grizzly bear, so that's why I'm giving Sequoia my sponsorship. That grizzly bear would have mauled me if Jude didn't intervene. I owe him my life, and I'm sort of giving it to him through his machine. I'm still disgusted at seeing all those severed bear paws, but some of the bears whose paws they were probably deserved to die.

They probably mauled a person before like I almost was last week by that grizzly bear. I turn from looking across the street at the sidewalk I was walking on when I was approached by those two West Islanders, and start walking towards my car. I make it to my car, open the door and get into it, then put my hand on the inside door knob. I close my door, put my key into the ignition, start my car up, then crank my air conditioner up. Blowing wind blows onto me, since I've turned my air conditioner on high.

While my air conditioner is blowing, I turn on my radio. Several radio stations are flipped through, before I stop at the kind of station I listen to the most: Talk Radio. On the station I hear a radio personality asking a question to a child psychologist that responds solemnly. The female child psychologist then says that JonBenet Ramsey took flight when she started appearing in child beauty pageants. My ears perk up and I listen some more, pausing at the news-psychologists are worried about a sudden surge in infanticide-then flicking over to the sports station. I hear commentary of a high school football game that was played last night, but it's not the one I went to-it's not the one that was played by Hancock and Forest High School.

Football players wearing white pants with purple stripes down them, purple jerseys, and purple helmets with a picture of a governor down in a three point stance on it were steamrolled by that Forest player on the defense last night; my younger brother's team won but they were gave a run for their money all because of that Forest player that I saw make many bone-crunching tackles. I'm glad that my younger brother is on the Governor's defense and not offense, because that Forest player might have hurt my brother if he carried the ball. He might have hurt my brother, and then I would have had to hurt him or his older brother if he has one. I'm no stranger to fighting; I've been fighting all my life. I remember that fight I had back when I was in high school. I began beating that White boy up pretty good, before my ass was beat. I was beat up so bad that one of my eyelids became swollen. My Mom saw it when I got home, and what she put on it did help the swelling. On it my Mom put witch hazel. She put on it soothing alcoholic lotion made from witch hazel bark, and the swelling did go down quicker since she did.

There isn't any witch hazel bark in Toad Island. There isn't a single shrub of eastern North America bearing small yellow flowers in the fall found in Toad Island; I've been looking and haven't seen any. I wonder if Beatrix ever had witch hazel rubbed on her. She might have, since she's a witch herself. I know she is. She called Halloween 'A sacred day to those who pratice Wicca', and when I responded 'Wicca?' she said 'Wiseness'. Only a witch would believe that being in a religion that affirms the existence of magic is wise. Some lil kids dress up as magic users on Halloween, and that is why she said Halloween is 'A sacred day to those who pratice Wicca'. It's sacred to them because for one night their belief is glorified through innocent little children. I'm not 100% sure Beatrix might be a Christian because she said Wicca is 'The religion of poor Christian womanhood'. My Mom's a Christian and look what she did. She married a Haitian man from a country where voodoo originates from-voodoo is a religion that is derived from African polytheism and is practiced chiefly in Haiti. It's practiced chiefly there, and Yee was in Haiti all his life before he came to the United States, so I know he practiced voodooism. He practiced a religion different from my Mom's, but that didn't influence her to change her belief. It didn't influence her to change her belief, the same way she didn't influence him to change from an undercover witch doctor to a Christian. I'll never let Beatrix push witchcraft on me. It's a good thing that Beatrix is living right now in the 33rd century, and not back in the seventeenth century.

If she did, she would have been hunted. The word would have gotten out that she's a witch and a witch-hunt for her would have began-a searching out and persecution of persons accused of witchcraft would have began for her. Beatrix would have been tough to catch I know, but after being caught she would have burned at the stake. She would have died after feeling excruciating pain from fire. Fire was used to make excruciating pain for people also tortured on the Catherine Wheel. The Catherine Wheel was a type of torture in the medieval times that consisted of the victim being tied to a wheel that was sometimes set on fire-the Catherine Wheel, that instrument of execution is associated with Saint Catherine of Alexandria and that was probably the person that invented it.

The pain I feel pales in comparison to the pain excruciatingly felt by those tortured by the Catherine Wheel. It pales in comparison to it but the way I feel makes me want to feel the pain of it. I stop thinking, put my car gear into reverse, and I'm able to quickly fishtail from in front of the Driver's License Ticket Office since I'm parked diagonally across two spaces. Towards the stop sign facing the exit of this plaza I drive. I reach it, stop, and look to my right then to my left. I look to my right again, see no car coming, pull out, then start driving towards Third Street. Stopping at the stop sign in front of it I do.

After sitting for about ten seconds, I had to wait as a few cars passed by me, I pull out onto the street. I begin driving down Third Street on this sunny Friday afternoon. About half a minute passes as I'm looking around while driving, before I look to my left. Besides seeing cars zoom past me in the other two lanes which is for oncoming traffic going in the opposite direction, I see a plaza consisting of several stores. The lengthy parking lot in front of the plaza is sprinkled with parked cars I see, and the lanky figure of a Black man walking in the afternoon sunlight while wearing a backpack through the parking lot catches my eye. That looks like him. No, that can't be him. Only a glimpse of the lanky Black man is what I saw since I quickly pass by the plaza. I think that that was Luigi, so as soon as I get a chance, I'ma turn around. I near a traffic light, ease into the furthermost left lane, and wait for the traffic light to turn green. Once it does, I make a left turn to a road that isn't on the street which is what I pull back onto after turning into the road, making a U-Turn, then stopping at the stop sign before making a right back towards that plaza. I near the plaza, and make a right into its parking lot. Towards the spot where I saw that lanky Black man I drive.

About four seconds later I spot the back of him walking, and as I near him he turns woodenly to my approaching car then squints and mean-mugs me. Luigi! I thought he looked familiar when I looked at him from across the street. Luigi and I were tight like the fist on an afro pick logo, and it has been over two years since I've seen him or talked to him. I slowly pull up to the side of Luigi, as he clenches and unclenches his fists down at his sides while continuing to glaringly squint at my passenger door's that he can't see into since it's tinted. I stop, put my car into park, and use the button on my driver door to lower the passenger power window. As the window starts rolling down, Luigi bends down to look into my car. "Marshall!" Luigi shouts, seeing my face. "I thought I was got." I chuckle-that sounds like the old Luigi I knew. I give Luigi a once over and I see that his bushy hair puffs out from beneath a Washington Redskins' snap-back hat he's wearing with the brim facing me while it's tilted upwards. "Get in nigga. You're letting all my cold air out," I say, smiling. Luigi shrugs off the black backpack he's wearing, holds it in front of him, and drops down into my car.

As he partially turns to begin closing his passenger door, I give Luigi's apparel a once over. I see that Luigi is wearing a 10. Deep varsity jacket, slim-fit jeans, and Chuck Taylor grips along with the Washington Redskins' snap-back hat on his head. Luigi closes his door then looks at me. "Marshall, old pal,"-Luigi puts a hand to his heart- "I really thought I was got. You didn't have this car the last time I saw you." I say, "I sold the Cadillac and bought this Taurus.

What you been up to Luigi? It's been over two years since I've seen you."

"It's been two years since anybody here in Eddy has seen me," Luigi responds. "I got out of jail two days ago, and I've been staying at my girl's Mom house. You still live in Sailor's Port with Deidre?"

"No," I answer.

"Me and her aren't together anymore." "Halifax!" Luigi says.

"I'm sorry to hear that. Where do you live now?" "I live in a suburban neighborhood named Blacksmith's End," I say.

"I know where that's at," Luigi says. "I use to fuck a ho that stayed there. Blacksmith's End is about five minutes from here."

"It is," I say. "Me and my baby-mamma, you've never met Chamiqua, rented a three bedroom house out there. She lived with me for about a year there, but I kicked her out about three weeks ago."

"Why'd you kick her out?" Luigi asks. "That ho's a stripper," I begin, "and she wore a crotchless camisole on stage a few weeks ago. I told her that I was alright with her being a stripper as long as she didn't have sex for money. It got back to me that she let this nigga eat her out on the stage while he was tipping her." Luigi frowns. "Hos are two-faced. My girl"-Luigi points one of the stores in the plaza- "works at that surf shop there. She's working right now; that's where I was going."-Luigi turns back to me- "My girl never wears a mask and that's why I date her. She's one of those ride or die chicks."

"Was she riding with you while you was in jail?"

"She wasn't the whole time I was in jail," Luigi says.

"She started riding with me after I was in it for about a year. I think she feels guilty about not fucking with me right after I was sentenced, because she was the one who wanted me to stay with her at her house after I got out."

"Maybe," I say.

"She live alone?"

"No," Luigi says.

"She lives at her Mom's house with her Mom and lil brother. Living there's okay, but I can tell that her peeps don't really want me there." I turn away from Luigi, grab the tip of one of my braids, and roll it in between two of my fingers while I look out my window. I take my fingers off my braid tip and look back at Luigi.

"Come stay with me. You can sleep in either one of my two empty bedrooms. I'm sure that it'll be better, and you'll have more freedom, than staying with your girl's Mom." Luigi smiles at me and says, "Say no more I'm finna start crashing at your place."

"Alright," I say. "I'ma let you get back to walking to that"-I point to the surf shop- "store. Give me your girl's address, and I'll pick you and your stuff up later to-" "We can go to your house now," Luigi says.

"She doesn't get off until 9 and I was just going to it to chill with her until she got off."

"Alright," I say, putting my gear into drive. I put my foot on the gas, and start to slowly drive out of the parking lot. A left is made onto the main street, before I start back driving the direction I was before seeing Luigi. Luigi says, "So, where do you work at now?"-my peripheral vision sees Luigi nod at my clothes- "I see you have on a uniform."

Without taking my eyes off of the road I say, "I work at Toad Island; I just got off about an hour ago."

"Toad Island?" Luigi says.

"That national park across from Bikini Beach?" I say, "Yeah."

"What do you do there?" Luigi asks. I turn to Luigi and beam.

"I'm a forester there. I do all types of shit there-I manage and protect the woodland, supervise the campers in the recreational areas, direct the planning of new trees. I've been working there for two years now."

"So you're not a night manager anymore?" "No," I say, keeping my eyes on the road. "On my first day working at Toad Island, I put in my two week notice. Working eight hours out of the day there then going to the commissary that night was tiring, but I chose to do that. I could have put in my two week notice weeks before when I found out the day they wanted me to start. Keeping my night job until the day I actually started was playing it's safe."

"And being a real workaholic," Luigi adds. 'You've always been one. I remember when you were working at the commissary before I was sent to jail. Whenever a must-go to party or event went down, I'd tried to get you to take off so we could go to it. You'd always say 'I have to work tonight' or 'I don't want to take off'. You constantly work like you just got the job and you think you'll be fired if someone sees you taking a break. You were like that two years ago, and you're probably still like that." I near the end of the long street which presents me with a traffic light that is red. After stopping in front of the red traffic light, I turn to Luigi.

"Old habits die hard," I say, remembering the hair brushing habit Chester said he has while at the Beach Festival.

"You're right," Luigi says. "That's why I do things for no reason, and I'm afraid to dream." I say flatly, "We all have bad dreams." Luigi looks out his window while continuing to lean back in his seat. "I dream of machines," Luigi says safely.

"They're gears and metal, but they're people I know, and myself. Taking us apart is done by men and endlessly they put us together again. Whenever I have this dream, it happens all night." I continue looking at Luigi as he looks out the window of my stopped car. Luigi's voice starts trembling.

"When I wake up from the dream, I wonder: Were we built *for* something? Or were we only built so that people could take us apart? Am I a killer or hero?" Luigi turns to me and I say slowly, "The ghost in the machine."

Luigi says, "What?" I say, "This person I knew that's dead now told me about a nightmare he had. I wonder if shows really do leave a mental residue-ghost desires or memories. I think you have an unconscious, and it's trying to talk to you. Were we built to be took apart you ask, but why do you think that?" Luigi chest heaves and he says, "No reason. Forget I said it," before he looks at me earnestly.

"Please forget."

"Alright," I say. Luigi then sulkily says, "I've just told you all of that on the strength of a machine."

"Sometimes, dreams are all that separates us from the machines," I respond, right before I see the light turn green. I take my foot off of the brake, ease forward while curving to my left, and start driving on the different road.

"How's your Mom doing?" Luigi asks.

"She's doing alright," I say.

"That's good," Luigi says.

"I remember when I called your house one morning before you went to school-you were going to that community college that has a star as a mascot-and your Mom answered. I asked to speak to you and she said"-Luigi begins imitating my Mom's voice- "He has to go to school Luigi' and 'Don't be calling this early'."-Luigi returns to using his normal voice- "She told me not to be calling her house that early in the morning." "My Mom's caped," I say, looking forward while driving.

"She is," Luigi says.

"And I remember telling her that morning before I hung up that I was gonna kill myself. I told her that because me and the girl I was going out with at the time-Easter-were going through some problems."

"I remember you told me that," I say.

"My Mom told me that you told her you was going to kill yourself; she called you a con man." Luigi silently looks at me for a few long seconds before he admits, "Your Mom was right." I take a quick glance at Luigi.

"You're a con man; surely you understand the effect wishful thinking has on a target."

"Oh, it's very useful," Luigi grumbles.

"It also means that they're twice as dangerous when you finally pull the rug out from under them." I pass a WhiteTelephone Films on my left, before passing another surf shop that is right next to that video rental store. I drive for about ten more seconds, before making a right turn. I get onto the street, after making the right, and start driving towards my neighborhood. Five minutes later, Luigi and I arrive at my house.

CHAPTER 13

A pungent smell fills my nostrils as I begin pushing open my front door. Marijuana. My eyes see Luigi sitting on the couch looking dead at me with a joint in his hand. His face is serious, his eyes unwaveringly studying me as I partially turn to close the front door. When I turn completely back to facing Luigi he says, "You're just in time."

"I am?" I say, approaching him. I know what time it is-it was 7:42 p.m. on my clock radio I just looked at before getting out of my car-on this early Saturday night and I've been over at Chester's aunt house almost all day but I don't know what time Luigi is talking about.

"Yeah," Luigi says, holding the joint while tendrils of smoke drifts from its tip. "I just lit this fry-daddy up." The sofa to Luigi's left is what I plop down on, before I lean back and observe Luigi. A white wife beater, a gold Jesus piece chain, a silver Jesus piece chain, and a Chicago bulls wool cap are worn by him. Luigi's lanky lean body leans forward, and he uses his other hand to pick up a red plastic cup on the coffee table in front of us. After slugging back whatever it is in the red plastic cup, Luigi puts it back down on the coffee table and looks at me. "I'm higher than a motherfucker, Luigi says, gazing at me from under heavy-lidded eyes.

"Let me get high with you," I say, reaching out my fingers. Luigi grins and starts handing the joint to me.

"Lunch is served mon-sewer," Luigi says, while handing me the joint. I take the joint, raise it to my lips, and I take a toke. The weed smoke courses through my body, before I hand the joint back to Luigi.

"I almost killed myself, but God saved me," Luigi says, looking at the joint as he is taking it.

"You were saved," I say. Luigi says, "Yeah, yeah, that's obvious. This other stuff isn't. So listen," before taking a toke himself. He blows out a stream of smoke while handing it back to me. I take the joint and while I begin raising it to my lips Luigi says, "I've been drafted into the Lord's army. And you are bitter men." I take a deep lungful, let the smoke circulate through my lungs, and hand the joint back to Luigi.

"Why you say that?" I croak, handing Luigi the joint while blowing out smoke. Luigi takes it and says, "I can tell. Do you know what happened when God opened the seventh seal? Have you *read* Revelations?"

"No," I say. "Thought not," Luigi says, raising the joint to his lips.

"When the seventh seal was opened, seven angels appeared with seven trumpets. And when each one blew his boogie, a plague smote down on the earth."-Luigi takes a deep lungful then holds the joint out to me- "Here, take this shit it'll help you concentrate." I take the joint.

"First angel blew and hailed down blood on the earth," Luigi says.

"Second angel blew and a mountain of fire was cast into the sea. That's your volcanoes and shit." A new world begins opening in front of me. I know it might turn out to be a false world, but it's better than this shitty world I've been living in. Luigi continues, "And the third angel sounded, and there fell a great star from Heaven! Burning as if it were a lamp!" I take a pull of the joint, let the smoke and what Luigi just said marinate, and exclaim, "I'm the lamp!" Luigi nods. "And the name of the star is called Wormwood, and many men died because they were made bitter'. Are *you* bitter Marshall?"

"Nah," I lie, handing the joint to him.

"No. We're mellow," Luigi says, right before looking at the joint to take it.

"But now that Star Wormwood has blazed in the sky, bitter men will come. God has told me this, Marshall, and it's no bullshit. Check me out and you'll find I'm all about zero bullshit." Luigi takes another hit, then looks at me while I'm leaning forward with both of my elbows on my knees and hands touching while looking at him absently.

"Marshall?" Luigi says, and although he is close, his voice sounds to be coming from a galaxy far, far away.

"You okay?" I stop looking at him absently and say, "Yeah." "You had me worried there for a minute," Luigi says, putting down the nub that is burning his fingers.

"Let me ask you a question, Luigi," I say.

"I'm all ears," Luigi says. I continue leaning towards Luigi with my elbows on my knees when I say, "Jesus was born thousands of generations ago. Do we really know what *actually* happened at that time?" Luigi gives me a peculiar look then suggests:

"You and I-we can make a good guess, I'm sure. Everything fits too well into the scheme of things that always precede the following of a new religion. Christianity is a great education for children-" "Yes, indeed-" I say and in my drug induced state I can't help letting the words out of my mouth, "for children!" Luigi holds his palms up to me.

"Marshall, don't interrupt me; I wasn't finished."- Luigi lowers his palm- "As I was saying, Christianity is a great education for children and people find it impossible to accept the Bible as true because they cannot reconcile the miracles recorded in the Bible with the conclusion of modern science. Example-how is that an intelligent person can believe in the virgin birth? How could anyone believe that a virgin could have a baby? Like the nonbelievers, I too believe that it is *scientifically* impossible. I still believe in the virgin birth however, not just because the Bible says that it happened, but because I believe that the God of the Bible is able to make it happen-She is not bound by natural law. That may seem intellectually lazy, but it is the crux of the issue."

I smile at Luigi. "You ain't making no damn sense." Luigi jumps back as if I pulled a blaster on him.

"Okay then. Tell me if this makes sense. I see too much complexity and fine-tuning in the universe to doubt the existence of an intelligent and purposeful creator. Other struggle to reconcile an all-loving and all-powerful God with all the evil and suffering in our world; I don't-everything that happens is part of Her plan. They're the ones who are convinced that scientific methods are the best or only way to understand reality and determine truth. Their scientific methods makes it impossible to believe the stories in the Bible that bend or break natural laws: A virgin giving birth, a man walking on water, a person rising from the dead, a small amount of bread feeding thousands of people. Scientific methods gives us knowledge and measures some truth claims, but we can't assent that it is the *only* way we know truths. Certain truths can't in no way, shape, or form be tested scientifically and those are the ones we believe in as truths that we know in our hearts.

Some examples, without science we know; one, when we love someone; two, that a sunset is beautiful; three, that justice is better than injustice; and four, that Abraham Lincoln was the sixteenth president of the United States of America. How do we know that the sixteenth president of the United States was Abraham Lincoln? We know nothing about him from first hand experience or scientific inquiry. We've never met him. We didn't vote for him. We know because there's documentation-in books, letters, photos, and other historical records that tells us he was the sixteenth president. Because of the many reputable sources of the 1850's and 1860's, it would be ludicrous to deny that Lincoln was the sixteenth president of the United States. The record of Lincoln's presidency doesn't include claims of supernatural events as the Bible does-but, while it's *possible* that both were an elaborate hoax, it is highly *improbable*." I nod my head.

"You're right."

"I know I am," Luigi says, beginning to stand up. I look up at Luigi as his lanky frame stands up, pick up his red plastic cup from off of the coffee table, then look at me. "I bought Seagram's Gin some from that nearby liquor store earlier," Luigi says. "I'm about to get some more; my cup's empty." Luigi begins turning to walk to the kitchen, and I say, "Pour me some in a cup too."

"Alright," Luigi says, turning his neck to me while walking. Three minutes later, Luigi returns to the frontroom. While he was refilling his cup and getting me one, I turned on my big screen tv in my frontroom.

"What's this?" Luigi asks me, handing me a red plastic cup while looking at the tv. I take the red plastic cup.

"Some shit on the History Channel. I'm not watching it, I'm just flipping through channels." I point the remote in my hand at the tv, and change the channel.

"No, wait!" Luigi says, beginning to sit back down on the couch. "Turn it back." I turn the tv back to the History Channel, and the ruins of an ancient city is being shown on it. Luigi and I hear the unseen narrator on the screen say, "As the story goes, the Christian Lord rained down fire and burning sulfur from the sky on Sodom and Gomorrah." Luigi turns to me.

"Can you imagine rain being fire?" I return my head upright from throwing it back to take a gulp of the gin.

"Imagine what?" Luigi's smile stretches in his exasperation and he asks instead, "Have you heard of Lot?" while looking at me and gesturing to the big screen tv. I look at the big screen tv and say, "Sodom and Gomorrah. Lot's wife looked back and turned into a pillar of salt. You don't need to read the Bible to know that story." Luigi says, "Do you know that after his wife died, Lot's daugthers got him drunk and seduced him? They had two sons and both created nations." I widen my smile at Luigi.

"Unless they were called dead-beat daddys, I don't see what that has to do with me."

"One of the nations was Moab," Luigi says, holding the cup of gin.

223

"A woman from Moab married a Jew. His great-grandson was King David."

"So?" I say.

"What does that have to do with me?" Luigi beams at me.

"Jesus was a descendant of David. Had it not been for Lot's daughters, Jesus would not have been born. I use to be bitter; I've been down the road you're on. And since I have, I know what a bitter person is capable of. Evil. Lot's daughter's act of incest was evil-but, Jesus came from it. Righteous ends can come from evil means."

While I'm leaning forward looking at him with both of my elbows on my knees and holding the red plastic cup, both of my eyes bulge out at Luigi. I cock my head to the side a lil bit as I incredulously look at Luigi. "So righteous ends can come from evil means," I finally say, after about thirty seconds of silence.

"Yes," Luigi says.

"And I've told you that because from when I first saw you yesterday afternoon to today, I could tell that you have something on your chest that you need to get off. So, what is it that you have on your chest that you need to get off?" I look down at the red plastic cup held in both of my hands.

"There is something I need to tell you." I look up and stare into Luigi's eyes. After a few seconds, I begin telling him. "Last week Friday my dawg was killed," I begin, looking directly into Luigi's eyes. "He was killed at this hotel party that him, me and another nigga all went to together. After we got there, I stayed for about ten minutes, before leaving the two of them there; maybe he wouldn't have died if I stayed there but what happened happened. I left that hotel party at Blue Swallow Motel, was pulled over by the police while I was leaving it, and as I was driving away after the police let me go Chester called me. He called from his cell phone while he was in that motel room bathroom, and he told me that a nigga just shot Warren."

"Did you return to it?" Luigi says, before quickly saying, "My bad, I shouldn't have asked that. Of course you did." I smile at Luigi as if he's dumb then continue, "After Chester told me that I bust a U-Turn and returned to the motel room. When I got there, the nigga was already gone. He doesn't know it but he's a dead man walking."-I take a gulp from my red plastic cup then look back at Luigi- "I or none of my dawgs don't know exactly who he is; all we know is how he looks and Chester told me that the bitch whose party it was told him Warren's killer is that nigga named Treetop. Treetop's a walking dead man, because I'ma take him out the game when I find him." Luigi sits silent and still as a tree and stares into my eyes. After a stretch of silence Luigi says, "There are people so evil and capable of creating such misery that killing them is the only way they can be dealt with." "I'm not the only that thinks I see," I say. Luigi and I stare at each other in the frontroom of my house while we are both sitting down; Luigi starts to sip from his cup.

"I'm kind of shocked," Luigi begins, "that you just told me that."

"Why?" I say, my eyes narrowing in suspicion.

"Why are you shocked about it?" I definitely didn't like the sound of Luigi's tone.

"I'm shocked for two reasons," Luigi says.

"And those reasons are the way you were in the past; when we first met and before I was sent to jail. In the past you were downright secretive and hermetic. You didn't tell me nothing personal back then-the biggest bomb you dropped on me was that man sold you busted speakers for your car. I'm honored that you confided in me. I don't know the circumstances of why that nigga-Treetop-shot your friend, but I know what type of person you are. "You're no slimy type dude, so it's safe to say that you won't surround yourself by slimy type dudes, and your homeboy that was killed-what you said his name was?"

"Warren," I say. Luigi says," Your homeboy that was killed, Warren, wasn't slimy to provoke Treetop to kill him and be in the wrong. You've decided to end his life, and I'm riding with you 100%." As I'm looking at Luigi, a smile slowly crawls across my face. While I'm smiling at him I grip Luigi by the shoulder.

"You're a good man to ride with me, Luigi. I'm glad God brought us together." Luigi smiles back at me and says, "Let up a little, Marshall. That hurts." I let up a little, then let go completely. Luigi picks up another joint he has rolled off of the coffee table, while also picking up a lighter that's on it. The joint is put between his lips, he lights it, and he puts the lighter back down on the coffee table while smoke wisps out of the joint between his lips. I look at Luigi as he takes a long pull from it, before picking up the tv remote; he changes the channel. He flips through several channels, before stopping at a tv show that looks like it's a crime drama. While he is taking a second puff of the joint while looking at the big screen tv, Luigi and I see a policewoman talking to her partner while he's driving. "He wants, however, to add another dimension to his work-he wishes to become judge and jury as well as policeman," the policewoman says, looking at her partner inside the moving squad car. Luigi turns to me and says, "I hate crooked cops," while passing me the joint. "And informants who lick the ass of crooked cops." I take it, then take the first puff from it.

After taking the puff I calmly turn to Luigi and say, "What informant are you talking about, Luigi?" Luigi fixes me with a rampageous look. "Aries. That apostate' son of a bitch." Smoke rises from the joint held down in my hand.

"I've heard that name somewhere before. Oh yeah, Aries was that bassa Warren, Warren's cousin, and me saw on that night a few days before Warren died. You might be talking about the same one. How does he look?" Luigi says, "This Aries stays on the other side of town. Black dude. A Black dude that is a short guy with a little size on him, like he used to work out. Aries' always wearing a green jacket, dirty brown jeans, and a hat turned to the side of his head."

"That's him," I say, exhaling the second toke of weed smoke from my lungs.

"I saw him last week when I took Warren's cousin to that female bassa. Aries was talking to the guy she was with."

"That doesn't surprise me," Luigi says, taking the joint I'm handing to him.

"I know Aries good; I use to serve him. In his forty-one years, he has been through hell and back, and his near death experiences show it. He was once Eddy's pushman, but now he is no more than a junkie. That's why he moved to the other side of town. About a year before I was put in jail, Aries tried a dose of his own supply, and ever since then, he has been on the opposite side of the game, hooked on heroin and cocaine."-Luigi shakes his head- "He knew better." While Luigi is taking a puff of the joint I say, "Not at the time. That's the catch to it. The doubts always come later, and they're usually too late. Take yourself for instance, Luigi. When you had sex with that fifteen-year-old girl, did you have any doubts about it? Did you say to yourself, I am now going to commit statutory rape then if I have to lie say she told me she was 23?"

Luigi takes a second puff of the joint, holds the smoke in, and looks down at his hands for a long time without answering. Frustrated by Luigi's obstinacy, I try again.

"Doesn't God tell you that deceit and deception are sins?"

"Doesn't your law tell you not to kill?" Luigi counters.

"Yet criminals are executed. Context is everything, Marshall." Luigi starts passing me the joint; and I take it without saying anything. As I'm taking a toke from it, Luigi takes a drink out of his cup.

"Context is everything," Luigi repeats, putting his cup down, "which is why I'll start zapping *anybody* you tell me to, I'll spray those motherfuckers! Top to bottom, fore and aft!" I start passing the joint back to Luigi while saying, "I don't want a follower; I have enough of those. I want someone'll give orders right beside me. Is that clear?" Luigi takes the joint and while looking at me says, "Uh, extremely clear-pellucid, so to speak. Let me ask you something. How can I justify the expense involved?" No single word could have so electrified and infuriated as that one. I say, "*Justify?*" If Luigi had just confessed to murdering my kids, he couldn't have gotten a more incredulous reaction. "My bad," says Luigi, immediately switching to pedantic mode.

"I was raised on hearing my stepmom say that: 'How can I justify the expense involved?' So it's always there below the surface, but to me it's more like an atheist saying 'Oh my God' as a reflex."

I glare at Luigi for a few long seconds before I finally say, "Chance it." Luigi stares at me silently, turns to the tv then takes his first toke of the joint, and blows the smoke out before looking at me. "Niggas knew RG3 was gonna throw bullets," Luigi says, pushing into the world of sports metaphor.

"And they gonna say, 'Yo man, you should definitely try to work on handing the ball off'." Luigi raises the joint to his lips while delivering the weeded-out rationalization.

"I'ma throw bullets." I look at Luigi as he takes a long pull, exhales, then hands me the joint.

"Who's RG3?" I ask, taking the joint. Luigi says, "He was a Washington Redskins' quarterback in the 21st century."

"Oh," I say, before saying nothing else. Only the tv is heard in my smoke-filled frontroom as I take two tokes from the joint in my hand. The joint is handed back to Luigi. "The weed culture is like fuckin' graffiti, "Luigi says, explaining its cross-cultural appeal." You gotta be a part of the culture to really connect with it. Potheads and hippies, we flock...we're peaceful as hell. You don't hear about people getting zapped or people getting beat up because they was too high and turned into a weed monster."-Luigi pauses to take a toke, blows out smoke, then continues- "I've been smoking daily since going to Hancock High School. Since going to that diverse place where White kids had superior weed and played fucking hacky sack and shit."

"So you're geared more towards bong-ripping college kids than the streets?" I ask.

"I do not know-I smell both out as surely as any old wise defensive lineman on a Sunday afternoon," Luigi says absently. It is hard to tell who he is trying to insult, if anyone. Silence follow before Luigi continues, "Another diverse place I've been was Nova Scotia-I remember telling you before that my Dad was in the military. I split my childhood between time at my Mother's house in Chicago and stretches of adolescence in Wyoming, Nova Scotia-I was surprised when I found out I was going to Haifax-Russia, and Japan. All the places where my Dad was stationed-I lived at them with him and my stepmom. I credit those far-flung experiences as giving me a more expansive worldview-I had wild shit, squid and fucking dolphin and shark. I tried fucking fish eggs and threw up. I had fish eggs-real fucking fish eggs!" Luigi takes a long, deep, thoughtful toke from the joint. Whatever is in it causes the whites of his eyes to become dark and ruddy. He holds his breath for as long as he can as he continues.

"Have you ever had a taste for a really great egg sandwich?" I look at Luigi skeptically.

"No." Luigi exhales a long stream of smoke and says, "Oh, just asking," before handing me the joint. While I'm raising the joints to my lips Luigi gets up. He stretches his long body, his fingers almost reached to my ceiling, before turning to walk away. As he is walking towards the hallway leading to his room, I look at him. Luigi disappears completely, and I turn around then take another pull of the joint. A minute later, Luigi returns. I look at Luigi's bony body, I see his ribcage underneath the wife beater he's wearing, as he walks by to sit back down where he was at on the couch before getting up. As he cups his hands down near the coffee table, I look at the deck of cards in his hands.

"I bought these off of the canteen in jail," Luigi says, shuffling the cards.

"They call them 'Dead people cards' because the faces and information of homicide victims from unsolved murder cases are on them."

"Really?" I ask, beginning to hand the joint back to Luigi. Luigi shakes his head from left to right.

"That's all you." I say, "Alright," and lean back to my seat. While Luigi continues to shuffle the cards he looks at me and asks, "Do you play cards?" At first I don't answer. I'm holding the weed smoke in my chest, letting it marinate entirely in my lungs.

"My girl and I played a few games with these cards," Luigi explains in his mild way, "after I got out two days ago. I'm glad to be out of that hellhole."

"Are you out of the woods?" I ask, exhaling smoke. Luigi stops shuffling the cards to look at me questionably. He mutely shakes his head from left to right.

"I'm still in it. A little. But I have a map and a compass. Oh yeah, and a survival pack."

Obviously I've gave him some kind of permission to deal the cards. Luigi lets one fly towards me on the coffee table, drops one on the coffee table's surface in front of him, and says dolorously, "It's interesting how some games endure. For example-chess. Poker too-as a species, we've been playing practically forever. I also can't forget bridge. There are some gaming encyclopedias I've seen that don't mention whist-the game bridge comes from-but I use to play bridge as a teen with my stepmom.

She wasn't really good at it." I look up at my ceiling, blow out a stream of smoke, and look back at Luigi when I lower it. "Bridge and poker," Luigi says, still dealing out cards. "Only when you're playing games like that, life is pure. That's because they're closed systems. The cards, and the rules-I can't forget the ontological implications-are finite. Poker is truly a card game of course. It's a game of people. Your opponents are played with cards that are just a tool. That's why goody-goodys aren't good at it. Much closer to direct problem solving is bridge-the extrapolitan of discrete logical permutations. Observability, you can't ignore who your opponents are, but you win with your mind more than your guts." Luigi looks up at me.

"You can't win with your guts, Marshall. You have to use your mind." I take another pull of the joint. I don't say anything; I don't have anything to say. Temporarily I think about losing.

"There's a maxim in bridge," Luigi continues, returning back to dealing.

"If you need a certain card to be in a certain place, *assume* it is. If you need a particular distribution of the cards, *assume* it exists. As if you have the right to that assumption is how you should plan your strategy. Of course it doesn't always work. To be accurate, you can play for days without it working once. All that's beside the point. If your assumption is false you were going to fail anyway, and that's the point. You might as well count on that assumption, because that assumption represents the one thing you have to have in order to succeed. Without it, there's nothing you can do except shrug and go on to the next hand." My head is spinning from the smoke and thickness in my frontroom, smoking more seems to make the lightheadedness go away. Luigi is making a lot of sense. Pregnant is how Luigi sounds-it is highly malleable. For some reason he thinks I need to be told it; he presents it like it is important somehow. I've smoked the joint down to a roach, and I resist the impulse to slouch back on the sofa and close my eyes.

"So your advice"-I start saying to Luigi- "is to *assume* I will soon find Treetop. *Assume* I can get away scot-free after killing him." In response Luigi picks up the red plastic cup and raises it like a salute. Beaming as if he crossed paths with a deity, he says, "If you heard me say all that. there's hope for you yet."

CHAPTER 14

I wake up the next morning with a feeling that it is going to be a nice day. Yawning and stretching contentedly I do, before climbing out of my bed to get ready for work. To me the only downside to working at Toad Island is the schedule- every other Sunday has to be worked. Since I was off last Sunday, I have to work today. After taking a hot shower I go back into my bedroom, and put on my Toad Island uniform (the long black pants instead of the short ones are put on this time). Twenty minutes later, I start walking out of my house at 7:03 a.m. on the beautiful Sunday morning. At the end of the work day, I drive straight home. I park my car in the garage, turn it off and get out, then begin walking to the door leading from the car garage into my house.

My hand is placed on the doorknob, I turn it, push it open as I walk into my house, and as I'm walking into it I see Luigi sitting on my frontroom couch with both of his arms spread out on the couch's headrest. His arms are fully extended, as he looks at me.

"What's up Marshall?" Luigi says. I close the door behind me and look back at Luigi.

"What up Luigi." I walk into the frontroom where he's at, and look at what's showing on the tv.

"What you watching?" I ask, looking at the tv.

"Shit," Luigi says.

"On Sunday, hardly anything good comes on."-Luigi stares disgustedly at my tv while his arms are still stretched out on the couch's headrest- "I got up about three hours after you left for work this morning and I've been sitting here ever since." I turn to Luigi.

"I have many action movies you can watch." Luigi looks at me and says, "I looked through your collection and I've seen all of the ones you have."

"I'm sorry to hear that," I say, before turning back to the tv. "That looks like an infomercial."-I turn back to Luigi- "You know what would have kept you occupied?"

"What?" Luigi says.

"A video game system," I say, smiling.

"The mall doesn't close for another two hours, so let's go to it." Thirty minutes later, I pull my grey Ford Taurus into the mall's parking lot. Since it's a Sunday afternoon and nearing the mall's closing time, the parking lot isn't packed with cars; it isn't packed with cars like it usually is. Luigi and I walk through the parking lot, into the mall, then into one of the mall's two videogame stores. As we walk into it, we both look at a slovenly employee of the small videogame store that is standing behind the front counter's cash register.

"Let me know if y'all need help with anything," the hippy-looking employee says, greeting us. I say, "Alright," before nodding. Walking past a stand that has within it a small color tv to which a videogame system is hooked up is done by Luigi and I-two controllers attached to tubes that look like bellows jut out of the clear container that they are attached to, and the clear container surrounds the videogame system hooked up to the color tv. On our way here, I told Luigi that I was gonna buy a Playstation 2. A slip to purchase one is taken off of the wall by me, and for over ten minutes Luigi and I browse through the selection of Playstation 2 videogames than can be bought. After Luigi and I both choose one videogame, we walk up to the front counter. I hold out the three slips to the hippy-looking employee as he holds out his hand while looking at us approaching. He takes them, looks down, and says, "So you want a Playstation 2?"-the hippy looking employee transfers the slip below it to the top- "*Tekken 3*?"-he transfers the one below that one above it- "And *Madden 2004*?"

"Yeah," I say.

Five minutes later, Luigi and I begin walking out of that videogame store-a large plastic bag with the Playstation 2 and two videogames for it is in my hand as we are. Luigi looks at me.

"Let's go check out the new kicks; a lot of new ones have came out in two years."

"Let's go," I say, holding the large plastic bag. Towards one of the more popular shoe stores in the mall I start walking, and we make it to the shoe store less than a minute after Luigi expressed his desire to go into it. I follow behind Luigi as he walks through the shoe aisles, occasionally pulling out shoe boxes and looking at the shoes in it. While Luigi is looking into yet another shoebox he pulled out, I see a White girl who appears to be in her late teens walk past the aisle we're on-she looks down it as she is walking behind an older White woman who might be her Mom. "I like these," Luigi says, examing the shoes he pulled out. Luigi examines them for a while before I see that same White girl shyly along with mutely look down the aisle we're on, and this time she's by herself. Luigi doesn't see her since his back is turned to her, and I see that the White girl's eyes are focused on Luigi.

"Luigi, turn around," I say.

"That girl's looking at you." Luigi looks up at me, then turns around. I see him look at the girl, smile at her, then turn back to me. I say, "I'll go sit out front by the fountain while you talk to her."

"She wants me to talk to her," Luigi says, right before turning to look back at her. I take one last look at the White girl who appears to be in her late teens, before I turn to walk out of the shoe store. For about ten minutes I sit on the marble seating of the fountain placed in front of the shoe store, before Luigi walks out of it. I stand up as Luigi approaches me.

"My pimp hand's still strong," Luigi says, smiling.

"She asked for my number."

"You don't have a phone," I say. Luigi says, "I know. I gave her a fake number."

I went to the mall yesterday afternoon with Luigi after I got off of work, but I'm not going anywhere today; I just clocked out on this sunny Monday afternoon, and I'm headed home. Twenty minutes later, I walk into my house. I expectantly see Luigi sitting in the frontroom playing the Playstation 2 I bought yesterday. Luigi glances at me and says, "What's up Marshall," while holding out a game controller in his hand. "What up Luigi," I say, walking to my kitchen. I open one of the kitchen cabinets and take out a plastic bowl, before walking to the freezer. I open the freezer and take out the half gallon of rum raisin ice cream in it. With a spoon, I put scoops of the rum raisin ice cream into the bowl. After I'm finished, I walk out into the frontroom with the bowl of ice cream in my hand. I walk towards the other couch that Luigi isn't sitting on, and he looks up at me just as I start sitting down on it.

"How was your day?" Luigi asks me, holding the game controller in his hand.

"It was alright," I answer.

"I was well rested since I went to sleep early last night."-I turn to the big tv screen- "You're playing *Tekken 3* I see."

"Yeah," Luigi says, before turning back to the big tv screen, "I'm playing with my favorite character, Paul." While I'm raising a spoonful of the rum raisin ice cream to my mouth, I look at the big tv screen. I see fists being thrown at a small and petite girl by a tough-looking White man that is wearing biker clothing and outlandishly has an overly pointed high-top fade-it is so pointed that his blond high-top fade resembles an eraser on a pencil. High-top fades look more proper on Black males; Black males brought that hairstyle into existence. "I'm giving this bitch the business," Luigi says, pressing buttons on the game controller while bobbing and weaving. Loud onomatopoeia sounds come from the tv as I look at the big screen tv, and I see a move done by the fighter that I assume is Paul. When the female drops to the ground, I squint at her name by her power bar that just went down considerably.

"What's that girl's name?" I ask, squinting at it. "Zy-something."

Without taking his eyes off of the big screen tv Luigi says, "You pronounce her name Zy-yoo." She's a fighter from

China that does all types of acrobatic shit. Xiaoyu does acrobatic shit but none of it's"-Luigi animatedly jerks in his chair while pressing buttons- "helping her now. I'm beating the shit out of this ho." Another spoonful of the rum raisin ice cream is raised to my mouth, as I look at the brawl before my eyes. Paul, the fighter that Luigi is playing with, drills Xiaoyu with haymakers I see and the fight comes to an end when her power bar becomes depleted. Right after it did, Luigi turns to me.

"You wanna go mano-a-mano with me?" Luigi asks.

"Shiiit," I say, putting the bowl of ice cream down on the vulwood coffee table in front of me.

"You ain't said nothing but a word." I get up, walk towards the Playstaion 2 system that's on the floor in front of my big screen tv, bend down, and pick up the second controller. With the second controller in my hand, I walk back to my seat. After sitting back down I look at the big tv screen, and see that it is now on the fighter select menu; I press START.

"I unlocked all the hidden characters while you were at work," Luigi says, looking at the big tv screen and selecting Paul again. I scroll through the fighters, and stop at a woodsy-looking robot fighter. "Mokujin," I say, repeating the figther's name shown on the big tv screen.

"Yeah, it was one of the hidden fighters that I unlocked," Luigi says.

"It's an alright fighter that mimics the fighting style of other characters; the computer randomly selects the figthing style Mokujin will have at the beginning of each new fight." I stare long at Mokujin's image on my big tv screen-Mokujin and Sequoia look the same, akin to a humanlike log they both are.

"So, are you gonna select it?" Luigi asks, breaking into my reverie. I look at Luigi, and say, "Yeah," then turn back to the big tv screen. Mokujin is selected by me, and the stage where the fight between it and Paul will take place appears on the screen.

"You ready for this ass-whuppin?" I ask Luigi, as our two characters bounce in place before the cue to fight is said. Luigi looks at me. "Paul hands them out; he doesn't take them." We both turn back to my big tv screen when "Fight!" is said. Our two characters approach each other, and a melee begins. Fists, and metal orbs that serve as fists, are thrown. Kicks start flashing. Paul's biker vest realistically flutters as I slam him to the ground with a executed wrestling move; Luigi told me that the computer selected Mokujin to have the fighting style of a fighter named King, and that fightter with a lion head I saw earlier was King before telling me that King does wrestling moves.

As I'm being struck by combos from Paul, I start thinking about the damage Treetop did to Sequoia's computerized interface. Treetop made a wet Sequoia fry with a wet hissing sound by shooting it with a lasergun, the same one he used to kill Warren with, and that killed Sequoia's computerization which Jude fixed. Why Jude kept muttering that to himself while tinkering with Sequoia's innards I don't know. I don't know why Jude kept saying, 'There are dead computers being chased by dangling wires and tiny relay boards and transistors-electronic Furies perpetually tormenting a nonhuman brain', while fixing Sequoia. Paul unfortunately knocks Mokujin out, and pausing the game is what I do right after the second round starts. While the game is paused, I begin getting another spoonful of ice cream.

"Before it melts," I say to Luigi, bringing the spoon up to my mouth. After the ice cream is swallowed I unpause the game, continue our match, and I knock Luigi's Paul out. "Oh, glitch and double-glitch," says Luigi softly. We play *Tekken 3* for a long time, before I look towards my frontroom window and see that the sun is setting. I take my eyes off of the frontroom window and look at Luigi. "We've been playing this game for a while," I say. "Let's play the other one."

"You wanna play *Madden 2004* now?" Luigi asks.

"Yeah," I say.

"Alright," Luigi says, getting up off the couch. I look at Luigi as he walks towards the big tv screen, bend down towards the the Playstation 2 system in front of it, ejects it's tray that holds the game disc, take it out before putting it back into its case, then pick up the *Madden 2004* game box. Luigi takes out the game disc, places it on the tray that slid out the Playstation 2 for it to go back into the system, and walks back to his seat on the couch. About a minute later, the screen changes to the menu in which a NFL team can be selected-Luigi and I scroll through the teams to choose our selections.

We each stop at the teams we want to play with, and the menu box of them are left highlighted instead of us locking into the team by pressing START. On the big tv screen I see the helmet of the NFL team that Luigi leaves highlighted: The Washington Redskins. I take my eyes off of my big tv screen and look at Luigi. "Two days ago, you made a sports metaphor by using a quarterback for the Washington

Redskins. And five days ago-when I picked you up out of that parking lot-you were wearing a Washington Redskins snap-back hat. Why do you like the Redskins?" Luigi looks at me with a very serious face while saying, "My girl wasn't the only riding with me while I was in jail; her Mom was too. Who was it that accepted the calls everytime I called there? Her Mom. Who was it that brought my girl up to the prison every week so I could see her? Her Mom. Who was the only other person besides my girl that put money in my canteen account? Her Mom. Her Mom watched out for me, directed and harried me the way a kingbird does a hawk, or, the way a Mother does a child."

"That doesn't explain why you like the Redskins," I say.

"Yes it does," Luigi snaps.

"My girl's Mom favorite NFL team is the Washinton Redskins, so that's why I like them."

"I see," I say. Luigi takes his eyes off of me, looks at the big tv screen, then looks back at me.

"I see you're about to pick the Kansas City Chiefs. Why?" I too look at Luigi with seriousness.

"One of my distant relatives played for them way back in the 20th century. His name was Derrick Thomas. Derrick Thomas was a linebacker for them, and I paid a genealogist to simplify how we were related. He told me if I was alive when Derrick was that Derrick would have been my Mom's aunt son's son, my Mom's third cousin. Derrick Thomas died while he was employed by The Chiefs, and he died at the age of 33."

"He was 33?" Luigi asks.

"Yeah," I say.

"That's the same age Jesus died," Luigi says.

"I know," I say.

"He died on February 8th, 2000 when he was 33 from a car accident he was in on January 23rd, 2000" I take my eyes off of Luigi, stare at the red and white Kansas City Chiefs' helmet on the screen, then look back at Luigi. Luigi says, "So you're gonna pick Kansas City because one of its players are on your family tree?" I wonder who invented the term 'Family tree'? Whoever did invent it was privy to the nature of a tree that sprouts many branches and leaves on those branches. Untimely was Derrick Thomas' death, but the breaking off of that branch in my family tree enables an even stronger one to sprout in its place thousands of years later.

No one can deprogram me from believing that Sequoia's dendriform appearance really comes from me being related, albeit a little distantly, to Derrick Thomas. Sequoia has the appearance of wood and wood is combustible, but fires are put out by firefighters in a firestation ran by a Fire Chief. Sequoia just appears to be wood, but it is really metal-I never have to worry about feeling the heat of an open-hearth fire while I'm in it however. I know what I do have to worry about. Sequoia's weakness: Rain. Boats can become waterlogged, and so can Sequoia-I hate that. I hate that Sequoia can become waterlogged, have its circuitry saturated, then become susceptible to electricity. Those laserblasts that Treetop put into Sequoia short circuited the electronic currents coursing through it-they short circuited the electric currents, making me feel as if I was burned alive; maybe I shouldn't say burned alive.

Maybe I should just say burned. That would be more-accurate. It would be more accurate because even though

I'm alive I'm not like a normal human being. I'm alive like the automaton I am. Working all day, then coming home and instead of relaxing working in a different way. This different way that I'm working right now is bringing me dangerously close to being a couch potato. I don't want to be that. "Absolutely," I say, right before turning to the big tv screen and picking The Kansas City Chiefs, an explosive confirmation sound is heard when I do. I continue looking at the screen as Luigi picks the Washington Redskins to play with. As the screen is loading to go to another screen, Luigi looks at me.

"So Derrick Thomas was a linebacker for The Kansas City Chiefs," Luigi says.

"What number was he?" "58," I say, looking away from him and the tv while fiddling with one of my braid tips. I turn to the big tv screen when the football stadium that we'll be playing in appears on the screen: Arrowhead Stadium. Luigi says, "I don't care about you having homefield advantage, but I do care about the symbology of this game." I show Luigi a questioning look. "What symbology?" Luigi leans forward out of his seat, and with his right hand almost shaped into a karate chop he begins to wave it from left to right.

"The symbology of this game we're about to play," Luigi says, waving his hand from left to right.

"Think about it-Chiefs and Redskins are both titles and names of people. There are Fire Chiefs, and Indians whose skin tone resembles the color red-hence, the name Redskins. There are some redskin Indians who are burning in Hell where there is fire, and there are some Fire Chiefs burning in the fires of Hell which they can't extinguish like they did to the fires on Earth."-Luigi takes a dramatic pause- "You want to extinguish Treetop and just the fact that you're about to play with The Chiefs symbolizes that you're a Fire Chief-and an Indian Chief. And just the fact that I'm about to play you with the Redskins symbolizes that I'm an Indian who's following an Indian Chief." I look at Luigi for a long time before finally saying, "I do have chieftancy, but you think too much." Luigi shrugs, turns from me to look back at the big tv screen, and I do the same. We both look at the screen as several players from our teams face each other as the coin is tossed, the referee is about to determine who gets the ball first. Tails is what the side of the coin Luigi picked before the coin toss, and it landed on tails so he gets the ball first.

"Are you ready?" Luigi asks, looking at me right before my team kicks the ball off.

"I have to be," I respond.

The football soars through the air after I kick it, and the football game gets underway. Luigi and I start playing the game. For over an hour, we play against each other in *Madden 2004*. Right after we finish playing the third game which happened to be a tie-breaker, Luigi turns to me.

"I'm hungry," Luigi says.

"Are you hungry too?" I respond, "Yes."

"Good," Luigi says.

"Do you want to go get something to eat?"

"From where?" I ask.

"Woodenwhale's," Luigi says.

"I have a gift card for it."

I pull into Woodenwhale's parking lot, park my car, and I look at the time on my clock radio before Luigi and I get out of it-Luigi and I start walking towards the Woodenwhale's resturant at 8:44 p.m. on this cloudless Monday night. We make it to the door, and walk in; a Woodenwhale's hostess greets us seconds after we walk in.

"Welcome to Woodenwhales!" the bubbly White female hostess says.

"Table for two?!" The female hostess smiles winningly at us each in turn, but I don't trust smiles. I respond, "Yes. Give us a table with-"

"Our backs to the wall and an exit nearby," Luigi interrupts. Luigi is as good-or bad-as me when it comes to security measures.

"Sure thing" the female hostess says. "Follow me!" The bubbly hostess turns around, starts walking, and Luigi and I follow her. We are shown to a table that will have our backs to the wall after we sit down and does have an exit nearby.

"Decide on what to order," the hostess says, handing us each a Woodenwhale's menu, "and one of our waittresses will be with you in about five minutes to write down your choice."

"Excellent," Luigi says, holding the spreaded Woodenwhale's menu up in front of him. "Alright," I say, also looking at the Woodenwhale's menu. The hostess walks away, and Luigi and I look through the Woodenwhale's menus in silence. We look at them in silence, until overhearing the conversation of a White man seated in the booth behind ours. I look to my right to peripherally see the seated White couple and a waitress standing up in front of them. The portly White man is looking at the woman that I assume is his wife.

"That would be Her plan," the White man says while eyeing his wife, looking irritated. He then turns to the waitress and says, "Could you please see that my wife's entree is taken off our bill? The scrod was so freezer burned she couldn't eat it."

"What the hell," the White woman says. The White man jerks to his wife and snaps, "Hell has nothing to do with this, Desie." Right after he says that, our waitress comes.

"Are you two ready to order?" the Black waitress asks, looking at me and Luigi. "I am," Luigi says, pulling the Woodenwhale's gift card out of his pocket. "But before we order, can you check my card?" I look at Luigi as he hands the Black waitress his gift card. She takes it, then says, "Okay, I'll be right back," and starts walking away from the table. While she is gone, I look out of the nearby window. Cars zip down the road near this Woodenwhale's restaurant, and the black night sky that I look up at twinkles with stars. I stop looking out the nearby window when the waitress returns.

"I'm sorry sir," the Black waitress begins, handing Luigi back his Woodenwhale's gift card, "but your card has no money on it." Luigi takes the gift card and says, "It doesn't?" while looking at it dumbfoundingly. The Black waitress says, "Again I'm sorry, but it doesn't." Luigi turns to me.

"I thought there was money on it."

"Sure you did," I say, putting both of my hands on the table while getting to my feet.

"Let's go because I'm not gonna let you con me into footing the bill."

"I wasn't trying to con you into debbing the bill," Luigi says quickly, also getting to his feet then following behind me.

"You're the last person I'd...."

Driving home, Luigi breaks the long silence by turning to me and saying, "I've never told anyone this but I have an"- Luigi pauses and takes a deep breath- "Oedipus complex." I wait about five seconds before turning my head to Luigi. "A Oedipus complex? What's that?" Luigi says, "An Oedipus complex is the positive sexual feelings of a child toward the parent of the opposite sex and hostile or jealous feelings toward the parent of the same sex that may be a source of adult personality when unresolved."

"That only strengthens the opinion I have of you," I say, glancing forward before looking back at Luigi. "Why did you tell me that you have that?" Luigi says, "I want to you to see that I hold you in high esteem by telling you a secret of mines; a secret I've only told one other person- my ex-girlfriend, Easter-and now that you know, you're free to use it as you wish. You can use it as a trump card to make me dependent on you, you can cause a breach of trust by telling others my secret, you can hang it over my head every chance you get, you can- " I get the point," I interrupt. "How do I know you're not lying? You could be making up that mental disorder you have." Luigi remains slumped back in his seat as he moodily looks out his window of my moving car. He does that for about ten seconds, before looking back at me.

"I wish I were," Luigi says, "but I'm not."

"Okay then," I say vigorously.

"Tell me how you have Odisus, Odpus complex."

"Oedipus complex," Luigi corrects.

"Whatever," I say.

"You said Oedipus complex is the positive sexual feelings of a child toward the parent of the opposite sex.

Tell me, what was the sign that made your Mom aware of your mental disorder?" Luigi's right hand tightens on the door handle and he glares at me as though daring me to send a foe at him."

When I was a boy I used to peek between the crack in the door while Justine took her morning bath. At least I had until my Mother caught me and pinched my nose until it bled. Justine had a beautiful body, long and voluptuous like my girl's."

"Easter?" I ask.

"No," Luigi says.

"The girl I go out with now."

"I'll have to see her," I say, looking forward as I near my garage door as it is lifting. My grey Ford Taurus pulls into the car garage of my house, and I see it is 10:04 p.m. on this Monday night before I turn my car off.

I'm walking between the close crowding trees and the dry, crumbling grass and leaves underfoot. Small green birds, no larger than an infant's fist, dart in and out of the leaves. Those trees whisper among themselves like elderly ladies talking of the past softly with their heads close together in the warm, warm sun. It is now a few minutes past twelve o'clock on this Tuesday afternoon, and the work day is almost over. Almost over is my journey through this very woody area of Toad Island, since I'm nearing the end of it. I squint as I step into the blazing hot sun. This clearing leads to the large lake to be found in Toad Island-I start walking towards it. As I'm walking to it, I again see Walt's SUV; I see Walt's SUV with faded red paint parked near the mooring. Nearing it, I look out at the lake and see a fishing boat with a solitary occupant. I stop at the lee of a rocky outcrop, raise my left leg, and prop it onto one of the rocks while pulling up the fabric of my left pants leg. I lean forward with both of my elbows resting on my left leg, and a dramatic pose is held as I look out at the fishing boat. A minute passes. Then two. Then three. After I look out at the boat for around five minutes, it starts drifting towards me.

As it gets closer, I look at the fishing boat with a solitary occupant. Walt's greying goatee and similiarly greying shock of dark hair is seen up close when his boat stops at the other side of the rocky outcrop after gently bumping into it. "Marshall!" Walt says from within his boat.

"Get in!" As Walt looks up at me, squinting against the sun, which glares behind his head like a saint's halo, I can only make out the old geezer's blue and gray flannel shirt, dark handlebar moustache, and wide-brimmed hat. "No, no," I say, waving my hand from left to right.

"I'm on the clock; I was just watching you."

"Jeez I cry," Walt says.

"I want to show you what happened to a tree"-Walt turns and points across the lake, to where one far off tree stands apart from all the others, in solitary defiance- "over there."

"I can walk around and see it," I say, looking at to where he's pointing then looking back at him.

"If Walt doesn't come with you, you'll go alone, don't tell me you won't, goddammit." Like many kenotic people, he has the pretentious habit of occasionally speaking of himself by his own name.

"And what then? Walt will be to blame. And it'll take you longer to get over there if you walk all the way around."

"That's okay," I say.

"I'm a patient man."

"Patience is often an attitude that simply makes comfortable the inevitable," Walt says. I look out over the water and feel inside the broad emptiness I see there. Maybe the old man is right. Regardless, I will continue to look. I will dig if I have to. I will never give up. I feel chagrin while scrutinizing Walt.

"I can modify the inevitable." Walt replies, "But he who can modify his wants to suit the possibilities can live happily. He who desires the impossible cries because he can't soar like the birds-who cannot think or read."

"Why do you talk in aphroisms?" I ask.

"He who can't gain his end by worth, tries to gain it by words."

"That's what I'm talking about," I say.

"He who keeps what he has will never need to sell what he has not," Walt says.

"I'll sell what I don't have to get what I don't want," I say. Walt leans over the boat and spits in disgust.

"He who sells the ham must be content with snout meat and pig's feet. I really hope that you're not talking about a soul-a soul like the one I have."

"Where'd you find it? May I look there?" I ask.

"Found it at a finding place. And-"

"Yeah, yeah," I say.

"He who looks with the hawk's eye, finds what the hawk would find. He who looks with the eye of a clam, finds what the clam would find." Walt says, "Eye of a clam? My friend, I believe you've had too much sun. Anyone-"

"Yeah, He who gets too much sun, gets light from the darkness," I say. Walt says, "That's good. That's very good.

251

I'll have to remember that. You sure you don't want to ride with me?" I narrow my eyes at Walt as though he's just spouted blasphemy. For a few long seconds I look at him with narrowness before shrugging.

"Why the hell not?" Walt repeats, "Why the hell not?" and he shakes his head slowly, like a judge confirming a sentence. I climb down into Walt's fishing boat; I sit, albeit reluctantly. Out into the lake we start floating. We float lazily, above the broad emptiness, and I watch it all unwind beneath me like a rotting table of food in an old Dutch painting. I look at Walt as he paddles in the direction he's facing. "What kind of tree is it that you want me to see?" I ask, straddling the thwart while now looking away from Walt towards the other side of the lake that we're nearing. "A redwood?" Walt stops paddling, clears his throat, and in a grand tone says, "Redwood is a common name for a magnificent tree Though The Young Redwood Grows more like a weed than a tree. The tree I want to show you over there"-Walt points past me- "is a redwood. From what I've been told, last night a camper got up at midnight and ran over and started hacking it down, shoutin' that he hated it. Beat it up pretty good, too. Nobody in the camping park did a damned thing, except one guy yelled out: 'Give it a whack for me, I hate it too!'. That sounds funny but it's not, not really." I bleakly look at Walt. "How does the tree look?"

"I'll put it this way," Walt says.

"That redwood looks like a chewed-up pencil." I wince. Walt says, "That camper made it look like a chewed-up pencil, while standing among the redwood's needles that grow on its rough-barked branches before falling to the ground. The redwood's needles ages, yellows, and finally shake free of life. Those from the lowest limbs drop-hesitantly-to the ground, but the ones dying higher up, where gravity is feebler, are caught by the wind and dance to the exhaust grills, where they again become gravity's prey."

"I'm not a...tree surgeon," I say, trapping a *redwood needle* behind my teeth.

"But I'll see what I can do." Walt nods, and returns back to paddling.

I've been off from work for about two hours, and I'm sitting down in my frontroom-smoking a joint rolled by Luigi. While I'm taking a second pull from the joint, I continue recollecting in my mind what transpired this afternoon at work. That redwood Walt took me to did have many scratches in its bark: They were long, wide, and deep like those that bear left on other tree trunks I've seen. Walt stood beside me as I look at the marring of that tree. I frowned, turned to Walt, and looked at him. I looked at the old White man as he looked at the redwood while massaging his face as if he were trying to grow back his chin, his palms made a raw sound against the stubble of his beard. About five seconds passed before Walt stopped massaging his face, turned to me, and said, 'This reminds me of that crude joke about a nearsighted rabbi and a farsighted cheerleader'. I've never heard that joke and I don't know why the scarred redwood reminded him of it, but I didn't ask him to explain-I just looked at him instead, and chalked it up to the fey sentiments and intuition that comes with old age; Walt is sixty-six, looks fifty, moves like forty. He moves like he's forty and looks fifty, but he also looks and sounds two stages beyond grumpy. I exhale the toke, after holding the smoke in my lungs for about ten seconds, and hand it to Luigi.

Luigi takes the joint and starts raising it to his lips. He stops raising it, looks at me, and says, "It's quiet as fuck in here. Let's put on some music." I point to my stereo system inside of the entertainment center. "Gone ahead and turn it on." Luigi's rangy frame springs up off my couch, he walks to my entertainment center as smoke curls out of the joint smoldering in his hand, he opens the glass cabinet, and with one hand looks through the cds on the shelf. I see Luigi pick up the last cd he said out loud, and he opens the jewel case with two hands while the lit joint in his right hand is raised up away from it. He uses his left hand to pull out the cd, a finger on his left hand is used to turn on the cd player's power and eject the cd player's tray, and he places the Wiz Khalifa cd onto the tray before making it go back in. Once music from the first track of that cd starts blasting out of the speakers, Luigi picks up the cd player remote off of the shelf the cd player is on and he walks back to his seat on the couch. Luigi sits down, raises the joint to his lips again, and takes a deep toke. He takes a deep toke, holds the smoke in his lungs for about ten seconds, exhales a long stream of smoke, looks at me, raises the joint to his lips for a second toke before inhaling, and he looks at me while holding the smoke in.

"I can relate to Wiz Khalifa; him and I have a lot in common," Luigi croaks, talking over the music.

"There were many Luigis alive during the time he lived-Khalifa's music and image were similiarly created. I read somewhere that Khalifa rapped fast when he first came out. He rapped fast at first, but change to rapping slow around the time of his first major cd. He put a bit more muddled inflection in his thin voice"-Luigi blows out a long stream of smoke then hands me the joint which I take- "and started to stick to generic, crowd-pleasing subjects. Crowd-pleasing subjects such as"-Luigi points the joint in my hand- "marijuana, money, girls, and more marijuana. His rapping style was once east coast in it's aesthetic, but it became less so when he blew up. I read that Khalifa didn't dispute the fact that his content-marijuana, money, and girls-is redundant. He knew that his content was redundant. He didn't call it redundancy however-he called it consistency." Luigi looks away from me to the stereo system, aims the cd player remote in his hand at it, skips to another track, and looks at me as it starts playing.

"I like this song here," Luigi says, as the beat is playing.

"He talks about more of the same shit on it and Khalifa really was like the other consistent rappers of his time. Consistent rappers like Devin The Dude and Snoop Dogg. Devin The Dude talks about fucking, smoking weed and not having no money half the time. Snoop talks about gangbanging, smoking weed and pimping on hoes." Luigi reaches out to take the joint that I'm holding out to him. He takes the joint, takes a puff of it and croaks, "Pimping on hoes like I did on that White girl at that shoe store two days ago," before exhaling.

"I already have a girl so that's why I gave her a fake number." I lean all the way back on the couch until my back touches the headrest and I fold my arms accross my chest.

"What's your girl's name?"

"My girl's name is-"

Luigi begins saying, before the house phone rings. I get up and start walking towards my kitchen where the house phone is at. Before answering it I look at the caller ID on it, and I see that it is Chester. The phone rings a second time right before I answer it.

"What up Chester," I say, looking out into my frontroom at Luigi.

"What up whodie," Chester says.

"What were you doing?" "Nothin' really," I respond.

"Just chillin' with my dawg-you've never met him-and listening to music."

"Oh," Chester says. "I do hear music in the background. Is that Jay-Z?"

"No," I say. "That's another rapper from the 21st century named Wiz Khalifa."

"Good," Chester says.

"I'm glad you not listening to Jay-Z. I don't like that nigga. Warren's body can be viewed at his wake that begins at 7:30 tonight." I switch my house phone to my other ear, say, "Hold on," and while holding it there bustle pass my frontroom tv to the frontdoor. I open my frontdoor, pull it close as I step outside, look at the tangerine-colored sky that has a setting sun and clouds from rain is no longer pouring out of-it was raining about an hour ago-and then look down at the dust. The rain spattered the dust by my front lawn's grass lightly: The dust is the color of wine and tears.

"Where is Warren's wake gonna be at?" I ask, looking down at the dust. "Oarsman Funeral Home," Chester says.

"Alright," I say.

"It's almost seven-thirty so I'm about to get ready to go there. I'll be to your house in about an hour to pick you up, so be ready."

"I already am," Chester says.

"Me, Keith, and Dominic all are. We're just waiting on you to get here."

"Alright," I say again.

"I'll be there no later than 7:45; I'm about to get ready then start driving over there."

"We'll be here," Chester says. I turn around, open my front door, and walk back into my house. I close the door back and look at Luigi while walking further into the smoke-filled frontroom. Luigi looks at me as I'm heading towards the kitchen with the house phone pressed to my ear. Before he speaks to me, I see and hear him lower the volume on the stereo system that is still playing Wiz Khlaifa's music.

"Is that the nigga that took you to see that seventeen-year-old Dutch girl?" Luigi asks, while his face is balled up.

"Yeah," I say, lowering the phone a bit.

"This Chester." Luigi holds out his free hand towards me. "Let me speak to him." I raise the phone back to my ear and mouth and say, "Chester, my dawg wanna speak to you. His name's Luigi." I lower the phone from my ear, walk towards Luigi, then hand it over to him.

"What's up fool?" Luigi says, speaking into the phone while glaring down at the carpet. "You don't know me-I'm Marshall's friend named Luigi. I asked him to let me speak to you because a few days ago he told me that you introduced him to a seventeen-year-old girl recently. That's some foul shit. I had sex with a girl under eighteen and they put me in jail for two years-I just got done doing the bid. I've known Marshall for a while and I don't wanna see nothing bad happen to him." I look at Luigi as he places his hand holding the smoldering joint to his forehead while looking down and listening to something Chester's saying.

After a while Luigi returns back to talking when he raises his head right after saying, "I understand all that, but I'm telling you not to put Marshall in no shit. They'll hide him for messing with young girls. A young girl you've introduced him to." Luigi stops talking, and I again see him listening to something Chester's saying. Luigi's face slowly undergoes a transformation-first it becomes a grimace, then barbaric, and finally just plain ugly.

After he listens to Chester for about fifteen seconds Luigi explodes, "Listen here nigga! I don't care about that shit you're talking! All I'm saying is don't introduce Marshall to no more underage girls! If you do, you and I are gonna have problems! I'm through rapping!" Luigi jerks the phone from his ear, and holds it out for me to take back. I walk towards him, take the phone, then raise it to my ear. I say, "My bad Chester, I didn't know Luigi was gonna go off like that." "Tell that nigga he's barking up the wrong tree," Chester calmly says. "I will," I say, looking at Luigi staring at me.

"I'm gonna get off here so I can get ready; I'll be there in no later than an hour." I press the END button on my house phone, and look directly at Luigi. "So everything I said went in one ear and out the other?" Luigi says, lugbriously looking at me.

"You're still gonna go get him before the two of you go to an underaged girl's house?"

"No," I say.

"Chester didn't call me for that. Chester called me to see the dead body of our dawg that was killed. I'm about to go pick him up so we can go to Warren's wake."

CHAPTER 15

All four of us start walking away from my car towards Oarsman Funeral Home, looking down my glazed eyes glint like starlight from the wet pavement below. About ten seconds later, dressed in an all black Dior Homme Suit and London Fog hat with Gucci loafers, I step into Oarsman Funeral Home accompanied by Chester, Keith and Dominic. The funeral home we all step into was once a home but now is furnished the way no home ever was—our footsteps are deadened by unworn carpets of a very pale green. As invisible hands bonelessly trail up and down the keys of an electric organ, we stand out in the empty floor lobby of this funeral home. About a minute later, a light-skinned Black man wearing a solid black suit and a shorter Black man wearing a faded black suit walks out into the lobby we're in. I squint at the light-skinned Black man wearing a solid black suit as he approaches us and I think to myself: *He looks familiar*. It takes a while for me to remember where I saw him at, but when I do my eyes light up.

"I remember you," I say, hormonally looking at the avuncular-looking Black man with the solid black suit when he stops in front of us.

"Chester, me and Warren saw you in Waste-That-Little about a week and a half ago; your name's Terry."

"Welcome Marshall, I'm terribly sorry for your loss," says Terry, standing in front of that other Black man that looks like an old dawg of mines when I use to really run the streets. My old dawg and me no longer communicate with each other, so I don't know if he's also the co-worker at a funeral home.

"And the casket?" I ask.

Terry says, "Oh yes, it's right this way in Remembrance Parlor I," and he leads us to it. All four of us walk behind Terry and his assistant pass little silver half-tubes on the walls that shield a weak glow. We make it to Remembrance Parlor I, step into it, and I look around the little pink side room. I see that the colors of the walls are atonal half-colors, colors no one would live with, salmon and aqua and a violet like the violet that kills germs on toilet seats in gas stations. Terry ushers us through the little pink side room into the main room-on a few rows of chairs in front of the casket about six people sit, five of them women. Warren's Mom is the only person I recognize. Terry turns around to us.

"I'll leave you all on your own here. Come get us if assistance with anything is needed." Terry and his assistant walk past us, then out of Remembrance Parlor I. After they can no longer be seen all four of us turn back around, and start walking towards the casket. "This place gives me the creeps," Dominic says to me, and if that is the limit of the effects on him, I envy his thick skin. I feel like I had come to this mountaintop and can't breathe the thin air. We near the pearl white casket with gold and marble trim-once making it to the casket I take a deep breath and look down. Waxy-looking is Warren's face that familiarly has two fat braids hanging down on each side of his face. Chester, Keith, me and Dominic lugbriously stare at Warren-flat on his back, palms interlocked in funeral calm across his chest. We see that Warren is dressed in an all white linen B.B. shirt paired with white single pleated pants by Zanetti. While looking at Warren Chester says, "I can almost see the lightning crackling between you and that nigga's eyes." I look over at Chester. While I'm looking at Chester, Keith clears his throat fussily.

"Some people just get used to laserguns, with pratice," Keith says with gloomy relish, as if a preacher at the graveside of an unreformed drunkard.

"I never did. Guess I've been on both ends of them too many times." For about five minutes, all four of us look down into Warren's casket. We all are looking down into it until first Dominic walks away, then Keith, then Chester. I stand at Warren's casket alone, looking down into it.

"My God," I say after looking long and pensively at Warren's waxy-looking face. Part of me is fascinated, as always, by death. The rest of me wants to cry, "My God you really did die." A few seconds later, Warren's Mom steps up to the rim of the casket right beside me.

"Look at my baby. In a way, doesn't he look different to you?"

"No, it's just the make-up," I answer. I turn my head, pretending to look out the Remembrance Parlor I's main room window at the night street where cars are running. I look back at Warren's Mom, say, "S'cuze me," and turn around to begin walking towards Chester, Keith and Dominic. I make it to them and say, "You all ready to go?" They all nod their heads, and we begin walking out of Remembrance Parlor I. We walk out into the dimly lit hallway, and start walking down it-as we are I wonder to myself if the most recent additions to the roll of the dead have begun roasting in their metal lockers like chickens in a Dutch oven. We walk out into the front lobby and see Terry, standing up next to a podium he's looking down at. Terry looks up and sees us.

"Are you four young men leaving?"

"Yeah," I say. Terry walks away from the podium and approaches us.

"Then thank you for debbing your respects to the deceased. It is my sad duty to prepare Warren Douglass' body for God's acre. I didn't personally know the young man, but I do remember seeing him, you"-Terry looks at Chester- "and you"-Terry turns back to me- "at that Waste-That-Little recently. I remember making a comment and Warren laughed; his laugh could make a persimmon smile. I no longer believe that the momentum of a life headed in a worthwhile direction ends when the life does. His future will be invisible to me. But invisible is not the same as nonexistent." While I'm listening to Terry, I decide that he'd make a pretty good speaker for the dead. I just wish that I knew how much of his speech, the emotion Terry projects, is genuine, from Terry's heart, how much is merely the artifice of an actor, but I don't need to know that right now.

"Warren is dead as Adolf Hitler and-" Terry begins saying, interrupted by Oarman Funeral Home's front door being flung open. I look towards it and see a short Black guy with a little size on him and the short Black guy is wearing a green jacket, dirty brown jeans, and a hat turned to the side of his head. I instantly remember his name and where I saw him at-I wonder why running in here is being done by Aries, the bassa I saw that night while Warren and Warren's cousin were in my car.

"What's the meaning of this!?" Terry exclaims to Aries. Aries quickly shuts the door and turns back to Terry.

"I need help. That's what I always say, sometimes."

"You need help?" Terry asks.

"Yeah," Aries says, palms facing Terry while he's walking towards the avuncular-looking Black man.

"The cops are chasing me so I ducked in here. Where can I hide?"

"Nowhere you anti-social street bum," Terry growls.

"I'm not gonna harbor a fugitive." Aries reaches into his pocket and pulls out a wad of crumpled bills that are probably ones.

"Not even if I deb you?"

"No," Terry says forcefully. Aries shoves the money back in his pocket, and looks at us.

"What about you four? Can you guys help me?" Aries nods, looking among all four of us as if to guess who would attack him first.

"All for one, one for all. That's what I always say, sometimes." As soon as Aries stops talking, the door behind him bursts open. Aries snaps his head around, sees two uniformed police officers, and he starts running away from them. He zips pass me but his attempt to escape becomes futile seconds later when I see him tackled to the ground.

4:01 p.m. is the time it is on this sunny cloudless Wednesday afternoon-my work day will be over in less than thirty minutes. About a minute ago while walking through these woods I encountered a cloud of flying insects that didn't bite or sting but they were unpleasant to inhale. Me walking into a cloud of those types of flying insects is a sign. A sign that I'm not being harmless. A sign that me and Warren's hive-like clique aren't being harmless, but we are to his killer-Treetop-that is still breathing. From now on I'm gonna do nothing but focus on finding Treetop. When I do find him, it's over. I continue walking through these woods. I encounter more insects and they are different from the ones I came in contact with earlier, before I promised myself to find and kill Treetop.

The insects are more numerous here than they were back there, but they don't cause discomfort-the situation is analogous to a Medieval man trying to understand how and why a sophisticated machine works. I know a bit why a sophisticated machine like Sequioa works, and Sequioa's finishing resembles the bark of that tree trunk right there. Twined around that tree trunk just ahead are velvety-looking vines with huge pink flowers more than half a meter across. More than half a meter across was that steel baseball bat Treetop held in his hands last night in that dream I had. Chester, me, Keith, and Dominic surrounded him and Treetop looked nervous as he took mock swings at us as he turned in circles while we were closing in on him. We threw Treetop to the ground after we seized him, and the very bony twenty-something Black man screamed gutturally. He continued screaming that way as the four of us spread-eagled his thrashing arms and legs. I remember while Dominic was holding down his arm Dominic looked at me and asked, "Is this nigga an epileptic?" I responded,

"Why you wanna know?" and he said, "If he is we should jam wood between his teeth so he won't bite off his tongue".

Right after he said that Keith shrilled angrily while looking at him, "Fuck that shit! Get the tarantula and start tortuing this nigga!" I step over a log, and as soon as I step over it my cell phone rings. I pull my cell phone out of my pocket, look at it's screen to see who's calling, press TALK, then hold it to my ear.

"Who's this?" I ask, staring off into the woods.

"It's me Luigi, Marshall," Luigi says.

"What up Luigi?" I say.

"My chances at getting the job at this country club I'm about to go to," Luigi says. "I'm over here in Dumel Nequa at a payphone by a Marshalls, and I wanna know if you'll do me a favor."

"What?" I say. Luigi says, "Right now it's 4:06 and I know you're gonna be getting off in twenty four minutes-at 4:30-and my girl has to be to work at five. Can you stop by her house after you get off and take her to it?"

"Yeah," I say.

"Where do she live?" I stand quietly in the forest as I listen to Luigi tell me where his girlfriend lives at, and how to get to it. After he does I say, "Alright. I'll swing by there after work," then hang up.

Eddy Road is no longer on, when I make a left off of it into the neighborhood where Luigi said his girl lives. I drive pass it's front entrance that is divided by a median strip for those entering and leaving, make a quick left, then drive deeper down into the heart of this neighborhood. I look from left to right as I'm slowly driving, looking for the house number Luigi gave me. The house number Luigi gave me is spotted, I drive past it all the way to the cul-de-sac at the end of this narrow street, make a U-Turn, start driving back to it, and as I'm nearing the house I ease up to the curb in front of it. The sun shines brightly in the sky while I put my grey Ford Taurus into park in front of Luigi's girl house. I continue looking to my right, honk the car horn, and wait for Lilakoi to come out. Three days ago while Luigi and I were riding away from the mall, I asked what's his girl's name is and Luigi said, "Lilakoi".

After he did, I remembered Lilakoi as being the name of that pop singer at that Beach Festival Chester, me and Keith went to a week ago-we went to it last Wednesday afternoon. I asked Luigi if his girl is White, after he told me her name. Luigi responded, "Yes. She's also an aspiring singer, but right now she works at a surf shop, Lilakoi performed at the Beach Festival Eddy had a few days ago." I told Luigi that I went to it with two other people, and saw Lilakoi's performance. Luigi responded by smiling at me then saying, "Lilakoi has the body of a cheerleader with long legs." About a minute has passed since I honked my car horn, and no one still hasn't come out.

Since no one has come out, I honk my car horn a second time. Five seconds pass. Then ten seconds. Then twenty. As I'm beginning to honk my car horn a third time, I see the front door of Lilakoi's house begin to open. I lower my head from hovering in front of the steering wheel, while staring at the tall, stately, teenage White girl walking out of her house. Lilakoi walks out of her house, turns her back to me to close the front door then lock it, then starts walking down the sidewalk leading up to her house towards my car.

Long strides towards my car are done by the tall, stately teenage White girl, more properly like a figurehead on an old ship, with a B-cup bosom, flowing strawberry blond hair and slender arms. Lilakoi makes it to my car, puts her hand on the outside door knob of the passenger door, and opens it. She opens the door, before slowly lowering herself in the passenger seat.

"Afternoon, Lilakoi," I say formally, as Lilakoi is closing her car door. Lilakoi turns to me, and answers with a husky laugh. Huskiness goes into my ears, while I look at Lilakoi's version of a Bronx cheer. That's what it is because she is laughing at me instead of saying good afternoon back. About five seconds after she began to huskily laugh, Lilakoi stops and says, "Sorry for laughing, but Luigi said you look like Forrest Whitaker with braids."

"Do I?" I ask, before turning to put my car in drive.

"Not really," Lilakoi says. I pull off from the curb in front of Lilakoi's house, and I start driving out of this neighborhood. As I'm driving I look at Lilakoi as she says, "Can I smoke?"

"Gone ahead," I say, looking at the lippy White girl. I say lippy because she has lips that pout like a four-year-old's with a broken toy; I'm closely looking at her lips that Keith pointed out to me last week at the Beach Festival. Lilakoi reaches into her purse, pulls out a pack of *Salems*, extracts one of the cigarettes out of the box, then puts the box back in her purse. A lighter is taken out of her purse next. While Lilakoi is taking out her lighter, I make a right turn. A right turn is made, before I stop in front of the traffic light in front of this neighborhood that's across the street from a bar called Admiral Leaphorn's. Lilakoi puts the cigarette in between her pouty lips, uses one hand to light it, then puts the lighter back in her purse. A long drag is what she takes from it, and she begins exhaling the smoke as the traffic light turns green. I drive out onto the street while curving to my left, and I start driving down Eddy Road. I glance over at Lilakoi while driving.

"I'm riding with a celebrity in my car; I saw you perform last week at the Beach Festival." Lilakoi laughs her husky laugh again, while her eyes pierces into mines and she says, "I see myself as a bad singer, a lousy musician." I say, "Bad singer? Lousy musician? Those are dark words." Lilakoi says, "I'm a dark person," right before taking another puff from her cigarette. I say, "This from a woman whose look screams more Tinkerbell than Princess Of Darkness." Liakoi laughs again. "There was a bit of misrepresentation on my first album, of what kind of artist I am. I've always been dark; life kind of helped me to put that darkness into my music more.

My sophomore album, 'Randy Seance', which drops this coming May sulks in desolation-patches gothic organs and frail coos into a haunted house of songs. Songs that are melancholy and have somber appeal." I near the back of a slow driving Sentra, make a right into the other lane, then pass the vehicle. While continuing to look forward while driving I say, "'Lick Me Where I'm Pink' wasn't a dark song."

"I've got to have one or two air-popped songs on it," Lilakoi stresses. "Every song on my sophomore album can connect to other people or things that will live." I say, "That's good"-a few seconds of silence passes and I glance at Lilakoi- "When I saw you on that stage last week, what feelings were you feeling?" Lilakoi blows out another stream of smoke then looks at me.

"It's the Janis Joplin thing. You go onstage, make love to hundreds of people and then go to bed alone. I know I was gonna be lonely afterwards, but Luigi was released from jail the next day."

"I hope he gets the job he's applying to right now," I say, glancing at her while driving. "Before you started working at Sea Rainbow, where did you work?" "Places I don't miss," Lilakoi says, and stares at my car roof as if the highlights of her employment history are wrote there, a retail-and-fast-food version of the Sistine Chapel.

"Before Burlington's Coat Factory, I was at Old Navy, and before that I was at Pizza Hut, and before that was the Verizon Wireless on Avocado Street, and then I was at Belk-no, wait, that's wrong. I was at Victoria's Secret first, and Belk after that, and....". I make a left turn while I'm listening to Lilakoi. "Whitetelephone Films," Lilakoi says, "Pier 1 Imports, Ashley's Furniture, Burger King, Panda Express, Kaybee Toystores....". I say, "What about Marshalls? Luigi called me on a payphone by that store about a hour ago." Lilakoi takes a drag of her cigarette and lifts her chin as she blows out a cloud of smoke. "I've never worked there, but I want to." My foot is gently placed on the brake as I near a traffic light that is red. I stop at the light, and look at Lilakoi. Her hair, which hangs in a perfectly straight sheet of shimmering strawberry blond, is pulled back in a French knot-I suspect she lets it hang loose while she is off-duty.

"You've worked at many places." I say.

"What kind of music do you like?"

"All kinds," Lilakoi says. She licks her lips and tosses her hair. "My idol's Madonna. Except the whole yoga thing. I just can't get into that." Lilakoi takes another anxious drag of her cigarette. She looks similar to a fire-breathing dragon. While I'm looking at Lilakoi, the light turns green. I take my foot off of the brake pedal, and return to looking forward while driving. Ten minutes later, I pull into a parking space in front of Sea Rainbow. I turn to Lilakoi. "Sell a bikini for me." Lilakoi laughs her husky laugh, says, "I will," and she turns to start getting out of my car. Lilakoi gets out of my car, turns back around, and stoops down to look at me.

"One must suffer to be beautiful," Lilakoi intones, before backing up while closing the passenger door shut. I look at Lilakoi as she walks towards Sea Rainbow's entrance, and after she walks inside I reverse out of the parking spot then drive away.

"And then a giant robotic face looked forward behind the mountain range," Luigi says, looking at me while holding the game controller.

"The face stared down at the meadow with glowing yellow mechanical eyes. I felt like less than a mote in comparison with it. Like less than a molecule."

"Not less than a molecule," I say, also holding a game controller. "Yes, less than a molecule," Luigi says.

"Then the giant robot stood and stepped forward. It only took a couple of steps to reach the meadow, because it was over a kilometer high."

"That isn't a bad height for a party crasher," I say, before turning back to the tv screen and unpausing the game so the fight could resume. Three hours ago, I took Luigi's girlfriend to work. It is now 8:14 p.m., and Luigi and I are in my frontroom playing *Tekken 3*. At least we were until he started telling me about a dream he had last night.

"That dream I had last night was just about as weird," Luigi begins, moving from left to right while fighting with Paul, "as the one I had the night right before I got out. I was riding in a car my girlfriend was driving, and we had to stop when we neared the site of an accident involving a semi. Several of the cars were honking their horns, as if that would somehow solve all of the problems. Two females got out of their cars and gawked at the column of smoke and fire, while shading their eyes. As I looked at them I remember telling Lilakoi a prohecy: 'The trucker might have been overloaded and moving too fast, but at least he's getting a Viking funeral'." Mokujin knocks Paul out, Luigi stops talking, and he looks at me. "It looks like you'll be getting the Viking-" I start saying, before the house phone rings. "I'll get it." I put my controller down on the vulwood coffee table in front of me, get up off of the chair I'm sitting on, and start walking towards my kitchen towards the house phone. It rings a second time right before I glance at the caller ID and pick it up.

"What up Keith," I say.

"What up Marshall," Keith says.

"What were you doing?" I say, "Beating this nigga's ass in an old fighting game. Everything cool?"

"Yeah," Keith says listlessly.

"I was just calling to see if you were coping alright; calling to make sure looking at Warren's body didn't throw you for a loop."

"I'm coping alright," I say.

"Are you?" "I am and I ain't," Keith begins saying, "but I don't really like talking about my feelings."

271

"Me neither," I say. Keith says, "Say no more. I'ma get off here Marshall-I was just calling to see if you're alright...I'm glad you're not shell-shocked." A smile begins merging on my face. "Shell-shocked," I repeat, forming a smile.

"I'm not that Keith." Keith says, "Good. I'll holla at you later Marshall." Keith hangs up, and I do the same. I walk back to the frontroom, and Luigi takes his eyes off of the screen. "That wasn't the craddle robber I hope," Luigi says, looking at me. "It wasn't," I say, walking back to the chair I was sitting in then sitting down on it.

"That was my dawg, Keith. Let me ask you something Luigi. You call Chester a cradle robber-but, don't you think you're robbing the craddle yourself?" Luigi looks at me with surprise.

"No. Lilakoi is eighteen. She's been eighteen for over two months now." I say, "So that girl who fiendishly puffed on a cigarette, struck me as being wound far too tight, and appeared to teeter on the edge of snapping was underage when you first started talking to her?" Luigi takes a while to answer but when he does he says, "Yes. And that's why I don't want you to go down the same road I did. What do you have planned for tonight?"

"Nothing," I say.

"Good," Luigi says.

"You can get fucked up messing with young girls-I know this college hangout where girls in their 20's hang out at. Wanna go to it?"

CHAPTER 16

An hour later, Luigi and I start walking away from my car under the twinkling night sky: We enter the Pool Hall. The interior of this Pool Hall is dimly lit, and in it's dimness Luigi and I walk towards the Pool Hall employee looking at us while standing behind a lectern. Ten minutes later, Luigi starts racking up the pool balls as I stand near the pool table looking at him-my pool stick's butt rests on the ground while I hold it up out in front of me. Luigi finishes racking the balls, hooks the pyramid back onto the pool table's hook, picks up the pool chalk sitting on the pool table's edge, then grabs the pool stick he propped up against the pool table before racking the balls.

"I was a beast in Geometry," Luigi says, looking at me while chalking the tip of his pool stick. I raise my chin as I look at Luigi: "What's that s'pose to mean?" Luigi continues chalking his pool stick.

"It means I know all about lines, points, and angles; that's all pool is. When it comes time for me to bank a shot, I will." I say, "So what you're saying is, you think you're gonna beat me?"

"There ain't no think," Luigi says, putting the chalk back down on the pool table's edge. "I know I'm gonna beat you." I laugh.

"Don't get cocky; like you did that night we went to that sports bar with a dartboard." I have brawled with Luigi only once in my life (naturally, over a contested darts match) and he'd come out much the worse. Luigi says, "I'm not cocky; I'm confident," as he walks towards the other side of the pool table. He bends down, picks up the white cue ball out of the basket where balls drop, and he lines the white ball up facing the pyramid's apex.

"It's all on you," Luigi says, backing away from the pool table. "Go ahead and break." I just stare at Luigi for a few long seconds before speaking.

"You go first." Luigi switches the pool stick in his hand.

"You go first? Why you want me to go first?" Without moving I say, "The first shall be last, and the last shall be first." Luigi shrugs. "That's a true saying. But, I'll go first so you can make an effort to win-and that's all it'll be, an effort-after I break first." I look at Luigi as he walks around to face the apex of the ball pyramid, lean his long lanky body over, then slide the pool stick in his right hand back and forth on the back of his left hand. Luigi's eyes narrows as he sights the white cue ball with the tip of his pool stick, and seconds later he breaks the pyramid of balls. Clack! Clack! Clack! The many different colored balls disperse on the felt green surface of the pool table. Luigi sinks several balls. Luigi walks around to each of the baskets, pulls out then look at the ball, then after looking at each in turn he looks at me.

"I sunk four solid balls, so I'm solid," Luigi says while smiling, pumping his fist palm facing me up in the air. While also holding my pool stick I say, "Solid," as I also pump my fist palm facing him. Luigi and I begin playing the pool game, and about five minutes passes before I tell Luigi what I'm about to do. I finish my easy shot, sink the striped ball, and say, "I'll be right back. I'm about to buy a jug of beer." Luigi looks at me as I walk away; I return a few minutes later with a jug of beer in my hand and a glass already filled with beer in the other. "Your glass' waiting for you at the counter," I say, sitting the jug of beer down on the pool table's edge.

"I couldn't carry it."

"Alright," Luigi says, propping his pool stick up against the pool table. I look at Luigi as he goes to get his glass-Luigi returns with his glass in hand, and we resume playing the pool game. We resume playing the pool game while periodically taking swallows from our glasses. As we are playing it, two Black girls who appear to be in their early twenties approach the other pool table next to ours. Luigi gives me a knowing look, before he moves around our pool table to set up his next shot. Neither one of us say anything to the two Black girls, before we finish our game; I win by default since Luigi sunk the eight ball while two of his balls were still on the table.

"You lucked up," Luigi says, beginning to rack up the balls for another game. As he's racking up the balls, I pick up my glass of beer and take a swallow. While I'm lowering the glass from my mouth, I hear a voice behind me. "I like guys with braids," the voice says, before I turn around. I turn around, see the Black girl who spoke looking seductively at me, then smile at her.

"I like girls with apple-bottoms," I say, playfully craning my neck to the right to let her see I'm trying to get a good look at her butt. I stop playfully craning my neck, glance at her friend that is looking at me strangely, then back at the Black girl that spoke to me. The Black girl that I'm looking at is wearing weave and is short as well as fine-her hair is blond curls that would have been more fitting on a six-year-old beauty queen than on a college girl. The blond curls would have also been more fitting on a person with a watchful, foxy face. The Black girl smiles at me while holding her pool stick.

"What's your name?"

"M," I say. The Black girl squints at me.

"Em. Like Auntie Em in *The Wizard of Oz*?" I frown at her. Do I want to be associated with that woman? "It's just M," I say, giving her a shrug. "Oh," the Black girl says.

"I haven't seen you around. What's your major?" I think up the letter S then say, "Scatology." The Black girls nods as if she understands. I think to myself: Scatology is actually a major at this college. I also think: I'd have to check. "I'm poli-sci," the Black girl says.

"You said your major's political science?" Luigi asks, from the other side of the pool table. The Black girl looks at Luigi and says, "Yes." I look at her friend again, and she is still looking at me strangely. Luigi says, "So if I tell you the president we have now is a lameduck, would I be wrong?"

"Yes," the Black girl says.

"Why?" Luigi asks.

The Black girl looks at her friend that is now taking a sip out of her glass in her hand while looking at me then looks back at Luigi. The Black girl says, "You'll be wrong because a lameduck is an elected official continuing to hold office between an election and the inauguration of a successor. The leader we have now has already been inaugurated." Her friend adds while looking at me, "You're a lameduck."

"Madonna!" the Black girl wearing weave with blond curls exclaims.

"Don't be so rude!"

"It's okay," I say, holding out my hand to her then looking at Madonna.

"That's your opinion Madonna. Tell me this. We've just met-why you have such a strong opinion of me?" Madonna says, "My younger sister, Dodonna, took a picture of you with her camera phone-and, she told me everything. Lameducks fool around with underage girls."

"I've got to have a fistfight with that nigga Chester," Luigi says, looking at me while I'm driving. It is now 1:03 a.m. and ten minutes ago Luigi and I left the pool hall; Luigi's statement goes into my ears and I turn to him. I gaze deep into Luigi's eyes.

"A fistfight?" Before Luigi can respond, I divert my eyes to the flashing red and blue lights I see further up in front of us. I point ahead. Drawn up on the hard shoulder at the curve are two patrol cars, and a group of stern faced officers are photographing young kids with a polaroid. A pale youth that looks to be about twenty is being searched behind one of the cars. Down to his underwear is how the police have him. I see him offering no resistance, but one of the police officers holds his arm; evident enjoyment is on the face of another that is feeling in his crotch; the knapsack he was carrying is being searched by a third one. While Luigi and I look at it, I slowly pass the scene. When I pass it completely, Luigi turns around in his seat and continues looking at.

"The cops are the biggest gang there is," Luigi says, before turning all the way back around in his seat and I look at him. I hold my hatred like a shield before me. "I don't much like cops. They're professional thugs, turning a buck because they like hurting people better than they like not hurting them. And the stars on their black sleeves make it all legal." Behind Luigi's face that I'm looking at, I see pass his window blurring by within the darkness. Luigi says, "You sound just like Lilakoi; she said they're professional thugs too." I turn on my blinker, switch lanes, then look back at Luigi. I say, "I noticed when I was taking her to work that she didn't have any make-up on; she's proudly facing her appointment with Father time."

"I advised her not to wear any make-up," Luigi says.

"It did no good to advise Lilakoi to get some hobbies, change jobs, stop attending so many funerals, she rarely goes anywhere. Lilakoi thrives on misery. She's getting old before her time, and I'm not going to let her drag me down along with her." I lightly laugh.

"Lilakoi does groan and moan like she's been trapped at a funeral with no conclusion in sight." Luigi nods.

"That's a prophetic metaphor. A prophetic metaphor you'll experience yourself if the cops lock you up for messing with an underage girl, and force you to register as a sex offender when you get out. Having to register is a bad feeling-you didn't link up with nobody at the Pool Hall, so do you want to try your luck with some older woman tommorow night?" I look at Luigi.

"Where?" Luigi says,

"The bar where my girl's Mom works."

"Sure," I say.

I take my eyes off of Luigi, drive further into Blacksmith's End, make a few turns, and about a minute later I near my house. The visor above my head is reached to, and I press the button on the device clipped to it-towards my garage I continue slowly driving up to as the garage door is opening on this very early Friday morning.

It is now Friday afternoon, and the end of my work week is almost here. That's good because I need to get some much needed rest-I didn't go to sleep until about 1:30 last night after Luigi and I left that Pool Hall. Dense with foliage is this area of the forest I've been walking through for a while. Surely this forest must end somewhere. After I walk another thirty yards or so, it finally does end I see. I see up ahead an opening through the trees that will let me out into a clearing which I walk towards, before stepping past the things a child would color emerald-the green of the trees and green at the base of the trees is the green of crayons. Last time I walked to it, I approached Toad Island's largest lake from the other direction. But this time I'm over here instead of over there. I near the large lake, stand on one of its docks in its mooring, and look out at the solitary fishing boat in the lake; Walt is standing up in his boat while fly-fishing. I cup both of my hands over my mouth and shout, "Walt!" Walt turns, looks at me, and I wave one of my arms at him in a "Come here" gesture. Sitting down on a thwart in his boat

Walt does, before he starts rowing towards me. About half a minute later, Walt looks up at me from his fishing boat when he reaches the dock.

"Afternoon Walt," I say, looking down.

"Good afternoon-Friday afternoon, Marshall," Walt says.

"What may I do for you?" I clear my throat.

"You're an old-timer; many people you've known have died. When someone you know dies, how do you deal with the death?" Walt sits down in his boat then looks back up at me.

"I refuse to pretend to mourn. Mourning is little more than self-pity, and that isn't my style. I'm sixty-six, and I've seen deaths left and right, top and bottom, and the fact of it no longer scares me. I am resigned to it." I venture, "Maybe even hoping for it?" Walt scratches his scraggly handlebar moustache while squinting at me and I'm still trying to learn his way; the way he programmed himself to squint in place of smiling. After a few long seconds Walt says, "I'm in no hurry to get where I'm going."

"Me neither," I say, before deciding to tell him what happened. "Tonight will make exactly two weeks since my daw...friend was killed. I went to a funeral home the other night to look at his body."-I look down at the dock's planks-"I remember Warren rankin' on people and tellin' jokes." I look back up at Walt and he says, "Life's a joke, friend. Death's the punchline. Maybe someone will put your friend in a book." I arch my eyebrow up at Walt.

"Why you say that?" Walt says, "Death is but the last page in a remarkable book, for some it can even be the best part."

"I'll tell you what the best part's gonna be," I say.

"The best part's gonna be when Treetop is killed."

"Who's Treetop?" Walt asks. I say, "That's who killed Warren; he zapped him in the chest with a lasergun." Walt coughs suddenly, and his chest heaves. He coughs violently until he can expel the glob. Walt stops leaning over the boat, looks back at me, and says, "Ah, I'll beat this poison yet. Tell me something Marshall. I remember you telling me about a year ago-around the time we first met-that you went hunting and shot an antelope. Did you shoot that antelope in the chest?"

"Huh?" says I.

"No, it wasn't but fifty yards away, so I shot it through the head."

"That ruined the trophy didn't it?"

"Trophy?" I repeat.

"I don't understand. I didn't want a trophy, I wanted meat." Walt smiles beatific.

"So did I."

I walk back into my house at 7:48 p.m. with a white plastic grocery bag on this early Friday night-I return from the grocery store with a bag full of orange juice, milk, fresh fruit, and large Dutch *broodjes*, rolls filled with different kinds of cheese, meat, and fish. As I'm turning around from closing the door leading to the car garage, Luigi sitting on the couch watching tv turns around and greets me.

"You're back from the store," Luigi says, getting up then walking towards me.

"What did you get?" "Milk, orange juice, fruit," I begin saying, putting the white plastic grocery bag they're in down on the kitchen table, "and large Dutch *broodjes*."

"Dutch *broodjes?*" Luigi asks, looking at me while standing up near the kitchen table.

"What are those?" I pull the clear plastic container out holding the Dutch *broodjes.*

"They're rolls filled with different kinds of cheese, meat, and fish; they seem to be the Dutch version of chicken soup. You said you're getting a cold so I got these." I sit the container down on the kitchen table, open it, and Luigi reaches into it then takes a roll out.

"A Dutch *broodjes,*" Luigi says, looking at the roll he's holding up in front of him. "This should knock the cold I have right on out."-Luigi bites into the roll and looks at me while chewing- "Lilakoi's Mom starts her shift at Admiral Leaphorn's soon, so are you ready to go there and try your luck with some older women?" I say, "It's too early to go there now. We'll go there around ten, once the sun's down."

"That's a bet," Luigi says, walking away back into the frontroom while taking another bite of the Dutch *broodjes.*

Later that evening at 10:52 p.m., after I took a shower with *Axe Apollo Body Wash,* Luigi and I start walking through the dark parking lot towards Admiral Leaphorn's entrance. We reach the front door, I put my hand on its front door knob's handle, and pull it open. Also dimly lit is this not too crowded bar we walk into-I scan the sights in front of us. My eyes move across the bar floor, and they stop on a table to the back that has several people sitting at it; a small knot of rough-looking people lounge there, drinking, laughing, and trading stories of dubious orgins. I take my eyes off of them and look at the people at the table right next to it-the men slap each other's arm with exaggerated good humor that suggests they've been drinking for quite some time. My eyes are took off of them and I look at Luigi.

"Where do you want to sit?"

Luigi jerks his thumb to the bar and says over the country music that's playing, "Over there on the barstools." I nod, and start walking towards the actual bar. We walk past a few busy tables, a bunch of men clustered noisily around a jukebox in a corner, and as we near it I look at its tv-the tv over the bar is showing a martial arts movie. About ten bar stools line the front of the bar, only three of them on the other end to the left are beig sat on I see, Luigi and I sit down at; Luigi climbs onto his bar stool, and I do the same. A big, White, hairy barkeep is who I see when I glance to my right. I look at the barkeep, who is pouring out a drink for a tall Black girl and listening to her as she is probably telling a long tale of the last mark's perfidy.

I turn to Luigi as he is looking down at the bar to the far left end, where a familiar looking older White woman bartender is making small talk with her customer; I say small talk even though I can't hear their conversation because I saw the bartender spinning in a circle then laughing with her customer that already has a drink set in front of him. Luigi cups his hands over his mouth. "Titty!" The bartender turns and at first seems to make a face. But then she grabs a cocktail napkin and starts walking towards us. As she near us, I recognize her as being that older White woman that I saw last Friday at the Driver's License Ticket Office. The only thing that's different about her is the black and white bartender clothing she's wearing. She smiles at Luigi as she walks towards us, and she continues smiling at him when she stops in front of us.

"Luigi, my future son-in-law. What a surprise." Luigi puts his hand on my shoulder.

"I'd like you to meet a friend of mines," Luigi says loudly, looking at Titty. "Titty, this is Marshall."-Luigi stops looking at Titty and looks at me- "Marshall, that is Lilakoi's Mom-Titty." Luigi begins taking his hand off of my shoulder as I say,

"We've already met," to him. "We sure have; I remember you as that young man I saw last week at the DMV." Titty leans her elbows on the bar and looks at me while smiling with her closely cropped short dark hair and hawkish face. So she's Lilakoi's Mom. The woman Luigi calls Titty doesn't have a typical motherly face. She has deep, intelligent eyes and a nose almost jewellike in symmetry, a little too long for beauty on another woman, but on her part of the whole. I stop looking at Titty and look at Luigi.

"You call her Titty instead of Titicaca." Luigi shakes his head up and down.

"Yes; Titty sounds like her real name." I turn back to Titty. While still leaning over the bar she grins and pinches my cheek with fingers like mummified knotgrass.

"What can I get for you, Angelpants?"

"I'll take a glass of Black Jack," I say. Titty turns to Luigi and says, "What about you Son?" Luigi says, "Um," while looking down at the table. Titty continues smiling at him while he looks down, but as seconds passes she begins looking like she's ready for his answer. More than ever, she looks as ready as a hawk. Luigi looks up at her, and says, "Something strong. Something strong like Basil Hayden's Kentucky Straight Bourbon Whisky."

"Coming right up," Titty says, walking away. Three minutes later, Titty returns with our glasses. She gives me a large glass with Black Jack filled up to the brim, and she gives Luigi a large glass filled up with Basil Hayden's Kentucky Straight Bourbon Whisky filled up to the brim. Luigi and I begin picking up our glasses, while country music plays in the background. Titty looks at Luigi and says, "I have to help that barfly down there"-Titty points to a White trucker-looking woman down the bar to the far left- "but get my attention if you or Angelpants need anything."

"Alright," Luigi says, before Titty starts walking away. Luigi looks at Titty until she stops in front of the trucker-looking woman; he turns to me after taking his eyes off of her. "I could have gotten a job here," Luigi says, "but I didn't want it. I screamed when Titty offered to let me work in this bar as a bouncer. I made it clear to her that the only job I would accept in this Mickey Mouse bar is manager, and head manager at that, which meant that I would supervise her and everybody else."

"She didn't want that," Luigi says, looking at me while tilting his neck back to prepare drinking the Basil Hayden's Kentucky Straight Bourbon Whiskey. Luigi takes his eyes off of me, and begins throwing back a shot of his drink. I too begin drinking from my glass, and we both look around Admiral Leaphorn's while taking gulps from our drinks. Luigi says, "So last week Friday you bumped into Titty at the DMV, right before seeing me in that parking lot outside of Lilakoi's job at Sea Rainbow?"

"Yeah," I say tiredly and drink my liquor. I drink it gratefully. All too quickly, it is gone. About two more minutes passes while Luigi drinks from his glass while looking at the bar floor. I look at Luigi when he smacks after drinking the last of his liquor.

"Aaaah!" Luigi smacks, sitting his glass down. "That whiskey tasted like the liquid that rise to the top of a turned jar of sour cream, only more bitter. Outside of that it wasn't too bad, and it did quench my thirst almost immediately." As soon as Luigi finishes talking, Titty walks up. She walks up with a glass in her hand and sipping from it. Titty again leans her elbows on the bar while looking between Luigi and I as she is sipping her drink. "What is that you're drinking?" Luigi asks. "A mojito," Titty says.

"So tell me Son. How are things working out at Marshall's? You're not talking his ear off about the Roman Empire, the Trojan Horse and some David Copperfield shit I hope."

"No, I'm not," Luigi retorts, looking offended. "Now you tell me something, Titty. Lilakoi said this place is usually jumping on Friday nights, why isn't it crowded?" Titty saddens, and throws back a drink. "Well, the whole scene's turned to garbage now." Being a little drunk causes me to slur, "So a trail of garbage and refuse tags along this scene like a process server on a child-support case?" Titty justs looks at me for a few long seconds, then busts out laughing. "Yes, something like that, Marshall," Titty says to me, before turning back to Luigi.

"Like I was saying, the whole scene's turned to garbage now. Pity, cause eight, ten years ago Admiral Leaphorn's was really movin'. You'd get twenty, thirty regulars paying good each day, most getting drunk before they leave, and Admiral Leaphorn's was jammed at noon as it was at midnight, maybe more. My old boss was one who knew how to run things. Since he left it's all turned to nerf-feed." Titty raises the glass to her lips, closes her eyes, takes a drink, and while taking a drink from her glass I see her eyes dart open. Titty turns her head towards the front door; a almost birdlike movement-she looks pass my shoulders at it. I turn to see two mean-looking men and a meaner-looking woman walking into this bar. They all are mohawk-wearing, leather-clad, biker types.

"Not tonight," Titty says. She nods towards the mohawk-wearing woman and leans forward while we are looking at them to whisper confidentally to us,

"Lily and her two cronys have a reputation for fighting." I look at the three mohawk-wearing bikers as they walk towards a table then sit down at it; seconds later a Admiral Leaphorn's waittress approaches them. As the mohawk-wearing woman is talking to the waitress, Luigi and I turn back to Titty.

"Don't worry," Luigi says to Titty. "Marshall and I are here if anything pops off." "Nothing's going to pop off....I hope," Titty says, before raising her glass to take a sip from it. I ask Titty for a refill and Luigi does the same before she returns with our glasses. All three of us conversate with each other, people are walking throughout Admiral Leaphorn's as country music plays, while drinking from our glasses. Twenty minutes pass, Titty has been away from us for about a minute and I look at Luigi. I say, "You ready to go? Nobody here catches my eye." "Yeah," Luigi says, climbing unsteadily to his feet. Luigi and I begin moving to the front door, and as we are walking to it we start to pass the table that Lily and her two mohawk-wearing friends are sitting at. As I start passing the mohawk-wearing man sitting down closer to me looks up at me and sneers, "Tell me something boy. What's the title of that there movie"-he points towards the tv over the bar showing a martial arts movie- "that's playing?" I look away from him to the tv over the bar; a shirtless wiry Oriental man wearing black pants is punching a person. I turn back to the mohawked drunk. "I don't know." "Can't tell me?" persists the drunk. "Well, I'll tell you the title of it. *Drunken Monkey*. That there movie playing is *Drunken Monkey*, and you and your friend there"-the mohawked drunk nods at Luigi- "aren't drunken monkeys I hope. Can't have those on the road, causing good folks to be in car accidents and such."

I glance at Luigi, before I look back down at the mohawked drunk. I smile contemptuously at him, nod at his glass, and say, "What's that you're guzzling?" The mohawked drunk doesn't take his eyes off of me before he says, "Uncooked blue moon." Luigi says, "So you're guzzling uncooked blue moon, straight up. That's why your breath smells like a dirty drain." The mohawked drunk glares at Luigi, I look at Luigi, then back at the drunk and like Chester said 'I can almost see the lighting crackling between' their eyes. Luigi and the mohawked drunk's stare off last ten seconds. Then twenty seconds. When thirty seconds passes, my fists become clenched so tightly my fingernails cut into my palms. Without warning, the mohawked drunk springs up out of his chair to throw a punch at Luigi. His fist zooms towards Luigi's face, and Luigi sidesteps before the punch glances off the side of his head. Lily and the other mohawked man loudly push back their chairs as they too spring up from them-I reach for the leather vest worn by Luigi's attacker so I can grab him from the back; soon as I grab it tightly, I'm struck in the back. I turn around, see the mohawked female looking at me with both her fists raised in the air while one of her legs are raised, and before she can kick me again I quickly charge towards Lily to grip her.

She breaks away from the grip and lifts her knee with great zest and aplomb towards my stellar jewels. By moving to my left I barely avoid being kneed in the groin-I make a fist and put all my weight into a punch I aim at Lily's face; it connects and the ho crumples to the ground. Just as I turn to look at him, the other mohawked man barrels into me. Him and I fall to the ground, but I come out on top of him. I come down on top of the guy, bashing his face with a good forty pound weight advantage. Even at that, it takes a hell of a long time to whip the fight out of him. But when it goes, it goes all at once. Like turning off a light bulb. He slumps beneath me, blubbering through a bloody face. I quickly get up off the ground, turn, and see the mohawked man that started this fight limping out the front door. As I'm nearing the front door I look to my left, see Titty about ten feet away, and she shouts, "Don't follow him Marshall!"

"Where's Luigi?!" I say.

"He's okay!" Titty shouts.

"Don't follow Jim-he said he's going to get his lasergun! My bouncer will stop him from coming back in here with it!" I glower at her for a long second then say, "Fuck that!" right before I storm towards the door before shoving it open. Out into the brisk Friday night air I walk. I walk about five feet away from Admiral Leaphorn's entrance, then scan the parking lot. I see pick-ups and cars in this parking lot, but I don't see a sign of the mohawked man. I walk further out into the parking lot, and turn in a circle before stopping my eyes on my grey Ford Taurus. All of a sudden, a green laserblast whizzes past my face. I dive towards my car, and crouch down near its trunk. While I'm crouching down, I breathe heavily. Another blast is expected but none comes. None comes in a minute. Then two minutes. When three minutes comes, I reach into my pocket and take out my car keys. I use my car keys to unlock my trunk, I cautiously inch the trunk's door up just enough, raise myself to a sitting position, then start pulling Sequoia components out of my trunk.

While being watchful, I put on all the parts of Sequoia-my surroundings are looked at. When I'm completely encased in Sequoia, I stand to my feet. I push the trunk door closed, then I walk to where I was standing at when that laserblast whizzed my unhelmeted face. I scan all around me for about a second, before I feel a presence.

"Well, well, well, what do we have here?" Jim says, while creeping out into the light holding a lasergun.

"I watched you put that on boy. What is that? The Halloween costume you wore last week?" I look at Jim while standing motionlessly.

"What?" Jim says.

"You can't speak, bitch?" Again I don't say anything. "That's fine," Jim says, raising his lasergun at me.

"You don't have to say anything before I blast you." A few long seconds pass by as Jim steadily holds his lasergun at me. A green flash of light emerges from the barrel, and the green laserblast strikes Sequoia's wooden-looking torso. I just stumble backwards, wearing Sequoia is like having on a heavy duty laserproof vest, before I quickly rebound to charge towards Jim. Jim tries to sidestep me but I dive a meter to the right, leading with my shoulder. I am a free safety on my middle school football team again. My shoulder collides into Jim, and he topples to the ground. I come down on top of the dazed Jim, before I start smashing Jim in the face with Sequoia's hands that are silver metal orbs. I look at Jim's bloodied face and see that I kayoed him, before I take off the log-like helmet. I start climbing to my feet, but I quickly drop back down to introduce Jim's chin to my knee. After doing that, I really climb to my feet.

"This shit machine! This shit terminator!" I scream down at Jim, standing over him.

It is now 1:02 a.m. when I finally pull out of Admiral Leaphorn's parking lot, while Luigi is sitting in the passenger seat. After I bashed Jim's face in, I took off Sequoia then went back into the bar. Titty had two of her guys drag Lily and her other crony out of the bar, before they were laid out on the gravel besides that truck. After they all came to, the three of them drove off in their truck. As I'm stopped at the red traffic light in front of Admiral Leaphorn's, I look at Luigi; he is rubbing his head where the punk hit him.

"You know," Luigi says, "I have a bad headache from that punch."-Luigi turns to me while rubbing it- "What round is this?" I show a tender look at Luigi. "When you're knocked out, it doesn't matter what round it happens in." Luigi sadly shakes his head and turns away from me.

"Punks have to be taught object lessons if they ever expect to learn anything," Luigi says, rubbing his head while looking out his window. "That White dude was limping because I pretended that his shin was a soccer ball and that I wanted to kick it all the way downfield. I whacked him good." I ask, "Was that before or after you hit him with a Sunday punch?"

Luigi looks at me with fogginess on his face. I see that I'm gonna have to put it in plain English. I say, "A Sunday punch is anything capable of striking a fast hard blow to an opponent."

"Oh," Luigi says.

"I made him start limping after, after the knuckle express turned his nose to jelly." While I'm looking at Luigi, the traffic light I'm stopped in front of turns green. I turn on my right blinker, before I start to go; I begin curving to my right.

"Wait!" Luigi yelps.

"Let's go to Bikini Beach before we call it a night; that fight won't wreck my plans to find you an older woman."

"Alright," I say, curving my car to the left instead. My grey Ford Taurus starts gliding down almost lifeless Eddy Road on this dark early Saturday morning, and we arrive at the strip club about five minutes later. I park in the gravel parking lot outside of the strip club, Luigi and I get out of my car, walk to Bikini Beach's front entrance, are frisked by the bouncer, then walk into the strip club.

After we walk into Bikini Beach, I take my wallet out of my pants' pocket; a ten dollar bill is took out of it, before I hold it out to the Black woman at the entrance as I'm approaching her. Five minutes later, Luigi and I sit down at one of the round tables in front of the stage in the dark strip club. I look at the White woman on the stage working the pole as she looks out into the crowd; only a g-string is what the topless White woman is wearing. Luigi causes me to take my eyes off of her when he says, "That's who you should make it rain on; look at that White ho over there," while pointing to a topless waittress. At a nearby table, a round of beers are being served by a frizzy-haired redhead, wearing nothing but a tiny g-string and a smile. Only her flat ass is visible to me, but when she turns around I see her face. Frieda! "There we go," Luigi says, looking at her.

"I wanted you to see the knockers on that older woman. Her breasts are big, but she has a small ass. It looks like grits in a ziploc bag." The loud hip-hop music continues playing as I look at Frieda. She finishes serving her customers, looks up, and we make eye contact. Like Titty, at first she seems to make a face but she starts coming towards me. As she nears me, Luigi waves her towards us. Frieda looks at Luigi. She smiles at Luigi as she walks towards us, and she deliberately continues looking at him after she stops in front of us-she is trying her hardest I observe not to look at me. Luigi says to Frieda, "I hear you're quite an attraction around here."- Luigi's eyes descend to the g-string she's wearing- "What happened to the fig leaf?"

"I don't wear fig leaves," Frieda says, smile plastered on her face.

"What about your kids?" Luigi says.

"You have any kids?"

"Yes," Frieda says.

"I have a son."

"Where is he?"

Frieda wheels towards me with the smile still on her face.

"Oh, I don't know. Maybe he's livin' out in the woods like an animal, reading girlie magazines or some shit like that."

I'm woke up by my buzzing alarm clock-I got into my bed about 3:45 this morning, after Luigi and I left Bikini Beach. My head is still laying on the pillow when I throw my hand out and bring it down upon the button, on the alarm clock, that will stop the buzzing sound. For about five minutes, I stare at the revolving fan blades while laying on my back before I decide to finally get up. Unlighted is my bedroom-only a few rays of the sun filter through my bedroom's curtain windows. I glance at the time on my clock one more time, see that it is 2:37 p.m., before walking into my bedroom's bathroom. Into the bathroom I walk-I switch on the bathroom lightswitch.

At my reflection in the huge bathroom mirror I look, before seeing a swarthy twenty four year old male with braided hair. My eyes are took off of myself, I take my toothbrush out of the toothbrush holder, pick up the tube of toothpaste laying on the counter sink, uncap the toothpaste, then squeeze a bit of it onto my toothbrush's bristles.

After squeezing a dollop of the toothpaste on my toothbrush, I recap the toothpaste then sit it back down on the bathroom sink. I start brushing my teeth. Three minutes later, I turn on the faucet to wet my toothbrush. It becomes wet, I put the toothbrush back in my mouth to slurp up the water off of it, I put my toothbrush under the running faucet to collect more water, the wet toothbrush's bristles are raised to my mouth again, water is again slurped off of it, and repeat the process several times. I completely finish brushing my teeth, sit the toothpaste back in the toothbrush holder, lean my neck down near the running faucet, quickly slurp up a mouthful of water, turn off the faucet while raising my head back up, and with the mouthful of water I throw my neck back to start gurgling. I stop gargling the water then quickly lean forward to spit the toothpaste in the sink; next I begin walking out of the bathroom while turning off its lightswitch.

Out through my bedroom into the hall I walk. From the hall I walk to my kitchen on this early Saturday afternoon; this early Saturday afternoon following the bar fight I was in at the place called Admiral Leaphorn's the night before. Into the kitchen I walk. I fix myself lunch-the leftover cajun rice and fried chicken in Tupperware bowls from the dinner I cooked a few days ago is took out of the refrigerator, before both together being dumped on a plate that I put in the microwave. My lunch is heated up for two minutes, I take out the plate, put ketchup on two fried chicken legs, take a spoon out of my kitchen drawer, then walk into my frontroom holding it. I sit down on my frontroom couch with it in my hand. In the quietness of my frontroom, I eat from the plate. I finish my lunch, put the spoon back on the plate, then while it is on the coffee table in front of me I push it away. Leaning back on the couch I'm sitting on is done, before I stretch out on it.

While I'm supine, I look at *The Other Side of Suffering* by John Ramsey. I pick it up and decide to read a chapter of the book. I read a few pages of it, before my telephone rings. I make the page I'm on dog-eared, close it, lean over towards the coffee table while I'm laying down, and sit the book down on my vulwood coffee table. The house phone rings a second time as I'm walking towards it. I look at the caller ID, recognize Lilakoi's cell phone number, then pick up the phone before it can ring again.

"What up Lilakoi," I answer.

"Much, I'm having a major melt down," Lilakoi says.

"Why?" I ask. "Cause I just lost my boyfriend, and I'm freaking out like it's the beginning of the end."

"What do you mean 'lost'?" I ask, attempting to sound interested. "Luigi's been arrested again-he was arrested this morning while on his way to that job interview in Dumel Nequa. When they took him downtown and allowed him to use the phone, he called me." I immediately start thinking about all Luigi told me very early this morning as we were headed back here from Bikini Beach. Luigi told me that he had a job interview to go to in about eight hours at eleven, and since I'm probably too tired to not worry about getting up and taking him to it. Getting up at nine and catching the N3 to Dumel Nequa is what Luigi told me he was gonna do.

"What happened?" I ask, really wondering what did.

"Why was he arrested?"

"One of his ex-girlfriends set him up," Lilakoi wails. "Luigi told me while he was sitting on the bus stop, he saw the car belonging to his ex-girlfriend Easter pass by. He said seconds later this girl standing by the bus stop cell phone rings. Luigi told me she answered it, looked dead at him, then walked a few feet away from out of hearing range. 'He asked me if I got a man and if not do I want one right before showing me his dick' is what Luigi told me that girl told the police she flagged down about five minutes after hanging up her cell phone. These predatory bitches caused my boo to be locked up!"

"What they charged him with?" I ask sympathetically.

"His *third* sexual harassment charge," Lilakoi says pointedly.

"When Luigi moved out to go over there, I use to hope that he'd get arrested. It would serve him right. But now

I'm filled with mixed emotions. Anger-because of Luigi dissing my Mom. Guilt-because Luigi just started getting his life back on track by going to a promising job interview. And sadness-because there is absolutely nothing I can do for Luigi."

"You can bond him out," I offer.

"No I can't!" Lilakoi exclaims, flustered.

"Luigi's a sexual offender and this is his third sexual harassment charge. The judge's gonna throw the book at him. Luigi's not getting out no time soon." I feel a lump in my throat, imagining the disappointment and heartache Lilakoi must also be feeling. Not even two weeks ago, Warren died on me. Now, it's like Luigi died on me. It's like he died on me, because if what Lilakoi says is true, he's not getting out of the system no time soon. First Warren left, and now Luigi left. Why do the good die young? "My Mom told me about the fight that you and him were in last-" Lilakoi begins saying, before my phone beeps. I take the phone from my ear, see it's Chester's number, then lift the phone back to my ear. I say, "Lilakoi, I have a important call on the other end."

"Whatever," Lilakoi says, before hanging up. When she hangs up, I click the dial tone over to answer the incoming call.

"What up Chester," I answer.

"What up whodie," Chester says.

"What were you doing?" I say, "Getting some bad news. The carpet-munching girlfriend of the nigga I've been letting stay with me-the one that argued with you over the phone-just told me he was arrested this morning."

"Play with fire and you're gonna get burned," Chester says.

"Are you still talking to her?"

"No," I say, "I just got off the phone with her." Chester says, "Good. So that means you're about to be on your way to pick us up; you told me earlier this week that we'll go to The Mall and Splashdown today. Remember?"

Treetop trudged into the holding cell. Before his eyes he saw young and old men, men who were also just recently arrested. As he was walking further into the room the cell door loudly shut behind him. Clanging is what it did while the police officer jiggled the door handle to make sure the cell door was locked into place. Trudging past a Black man who he knew to be a dope addict is what Treetop did before reaching the urinal placed in the back of the holding cell. With his back turned to the seven other men in that cell, they were all gazing at the tall Black guy, he began urinating into it. He urinated for a long, long time, holding the urge to urinate earlier in the backseat of that police car was finally able to be relieved.

"They got me fucked up!"

Treetop shouted after he finished, turning around then looking at the Black man he knew. "I got a sales charge because of an undercover. I thought that cracker wearing all those gold chains was a smoker-I sold vice a bag of weed and now I'm here in this fuck shit!" The Black man he was talking to just nodded, not really sure what Treetop wanted him to say to his explanation of why he was there. Treetop began prancing in that squalid holding cell, his too-tall construction body ambling back and forth pass the other unfortunates in there with him, their eyes glued onto the Black man who appears to be in his very early twenties to them.

Wanting to kick himself in the ass is what Treetop wanted to do as he paced back and forth in that holding cell composed of only steel and concrete, nothing in it could catch on fire except the clothes of its occupants, and he wanted to do that because he wasn't successfully cautious enough after seeing others hit with a sales charge from being greedy-him selling to someone he didn't know resulted into him taking a trip to the place where hardheads are. He's been there twice before; the first offense was related to the possession of a weapon; the second offense came from assaulting a crackhead, with a mountain bike, who owed him ten dollars. He beat the crackhead half to death with that mountain bike and was sentenced to a one-to-three year term.

A year Treetop did, time was easy for him, because he knew that he was lucky to get only a slap on the wrist. Because of all the things that he did, he also knew that he should have been in prison for life. His first offense stemmed from the weapon he used to commit murder: His laser version of a .45 was on him when he was caught with it in a project hall. Treetop was spared from forever languishing in the system the first time he was sentenced, loudly gasping in the courtroom is what he did when the judge sentenced him to a one-to-three year term. He did a year in the county jail when he was seventeen, before getting out it at the age of eighteen. An eighteen-year-old Treetop went right back to the streets. How long will this glow last? Who am I gonna have to make an example out of? And, best of all, what possessed that eighteen-year-old ho to start sucking my dick while I'm driving? Those are three questions Treetop asked himself not too long after he got out of jail. Still, Treetop took precautions even though he felt like he couldn't be touched.

He never took females to his house. He sought out independent girls, who he could have sex with at their house. Sex with those types of girls were always either had at their house or a hotel. Paying for a hotel room he didn't mind. The amount of money he spent on hotel rooms was to him a necessary expense, especially since having sex at a hotel instead of his house made him less paranoid. He could count on one hand the number of people he invited to his house. That small number included his Mom who sometimes went to his house to volunteeringly clean, mop the bathroom and kitchen floor. She began cleaning Treetop's bathroom after commenting that it was filthy. It was. However, he felt that it shouldn't matter since he was the only person that lives there, Treetop contributed to his bathroom returning back to being dirty. By selling drugs, Treetop paid his monthly rent. He only sold to people he knew and the ones they introduced him to. He made a serve out of his car one day, sitting in the passenger seat was his baby-mama, to a White boy one of his associates referred him to. Meeting the White boy by his neighborhood's public park is what Treetop did while his baby-mama was in the car, before selling him twenty five dollars worth of weed. Treetop bought his ounces from a connect introduced to him from a young Black girl he was having sex with. Following him learning that her White friend's name was Allison, he had sex with her even though she was underaged.

"Stop pacing Treetop and sit down," the Black man who Treetop knew finally said.

"You're making me think of those panthers in the menagerie." Treetop stopped and looked at him.

"I don't want to." The Black man gave Treetop a hard look.

"You'll do what it takes. Otherwise you can add vandalism, breaking and entering, and malicious mayhem to your list of charges."

"Shut the fuck up Slim," snarled Treetop, who permits no one to disrespect him. On him he has on an auburn football jersey, and a temper to match.

"Shut the fuck up and leave me alone."

"No one's gonna leave you alone," Slim said in a children-must-not-disbehave voice. "Especially not me." Treetop continues, "I don't feel like talking." While he's sitting down Slim says, "And I don't feel like listening," as he is looking at Treetop's moving body.

"But I am." Treetop remained pacing while looking down at the ground as he said, "There's nothing to talk about. I sold to an undercover. They busted me. I'm here. End of story."

"If it was only that simple...." Slim says wisely. "Do you know why you're here?" Treetop stopped and looked at Slim. "I just told your fuck-ass why." Slim said, "No, you told me *how* you got here, but you didn't tell me *why* you got here. Do you know why you're here?" Treetop said, "No, I don't. But I'm sure your freebassin' ass gonna tell me." Slim said, "I do freebase, and I'll be the first one to tell you or"-Slim looked around at the other six men in the holding cell-" anybody else that I do. "-Slim turned back to Treetop -" I'm not ashamed that I do. What I'm ashamed of is when young Black men like you are put here because Satan, not

God, wants you here-and that's why you're here; Satan put you here." Treetop glared at Slim.

"How in the fuck you know he put me here?" It could have been God that got me flipped." Slim chuckled. "Come on now Treetop. You and I both know that you can't flood the streets while you're in here-Satan knows that too. You've offended him somehow, so he figured he'd offend you by having you put here. You remember what you said to me a while ago? When I asked you why do you sell drugs?"

"I forgot," Treetop said. Slim said, "You said 'I'm just doing my job'. If you were just doing your job earlier today, then why are you here? Why isn't every person that's just doing their job in here with you? I'll tell you why. They don't know any better, but you...you work it. You justify anything by calling it duty. Just lump it all together, good and bad, and call it duty so you won't have to think about it. Covers a lot of territory, doesn't it, Treetop?"

"Depends on the work shift," Treetop said coldly. "Tell me, Slim, you're a civilized junkie; you obviously lack the gumption to murder anybody outright. Do you believe in karma?"

"Oh, yes," Slim said. "I've never simply killed someone, but I experience karma too-the punishment isn't as bad. For those who believe in an afterlife-and I am one of those-the person is still who he or she was in life, and if too harshly judged in life receives recompense, or if too lighty judged in life, receives punishment."

"So you're basically saying on the sly that I'm going to Hell?" Treetop asked. "You're not going to the moon," Slim said. Treetop scoffs, and starts pacing the holding cell again. Looking at him is done by all of the other criminals in it. "The moon," Treetop repeats, pacing. "If I didn't believe that if we took every drug off the planet and put them on the moon, that a Black man from the hood would build a spaceship within a few months to get there, I would have stopped. Now my reason has changed, I'm just gonna start robbin' niggas."

"I killed a nigga that tried to rob me!" the young bald-headed Black man sitting next to Slim said. Treetop spun around to face the Black man, and looked at him with bulging eyes. "What's that s'pose to mean, nigga?" Treetop tightly said. The Black man said, "It means you already know what time it is if you try to rob me." "Yeah, time to take all your shit," Treetop snarled, "while I hold in your face the big ass four-five I bought from Money Tree on Chief Street." The Black man makes a disbelieving sound. "You're lying through your teeth. I know you have a record-felons can't buy laserguns from pawnshops." Treetop said, "I had a bitch buy it for me dumb-ass nigga."

"What's her name?" the Black man asked. "I- " Treetop puts his hand to his mouth in absurdly childlike fashion. "I didn't ask." "You didn't ask her because there ain't one," the Black man said. Treetop sneered at the Black man. "I tell you what, walk your happy-ass down Chief Street one night when I'm out, and see if I don't run up on you. Then try to buck the jack so I can make you fall to the ground like one of Paul Bunyan's trees." As soon as Treetop finished talking, the sound of the holding cell's door being opened went into all of their ears. Treetop turned to the cell door. He saw a short Black guy with a little size on him. The short Black guy with a little size on him looked at the police officer as he closed the cell door, before looking at Slim. "Aries!" Slim said.

"I'm glad you're here. Tell Treetop here"-Slim pointed at the tall skinny Black man-" which is worse, to die having lived or to live having died." Aries looked at Treetop and walked towards him. He walked towards him, stood motionlessly and silently in front of him, while thinking about what he was going to say.

"Death hastens those who hasten death," Aries finally said.

"That's what I always say, sometimes."

Into the parking space I park, and we all get out of my car on this late Saturday afternoon as the sun is setting-Chester, me, Keith, and Dominic. Towards the mall we start walking. One of the many doors at its entrance is opened by me before we all step into the mall. We walk past people as we near the middle of the mall where there's a flow of traffic coming from shoppers, window shoppers, and those just strolling through it like us. I look over at Dominic that's no longer wearing the eyepatch then down at what covers his feet: Teva sandals and blue socks. "Why did you say you're wearing your sister's sandals again?" I ask, looking back up at him while we are all walking. Chester answers for him, "Dominic's wearing them because he's young and arrogant. He thinks his shit smells like roses." Keith snickers and leans towards Dominic. "You sure you want to take that, podna?"

"Hell naw, I ain't gonna take that," Dominic says, looking at Chester.

"At least I don't sit in a car for hours talking with Dallas while passing blunt after blunt. Telling stories that go from you willing to die for a person to how much you want that person dead." Keith and I laugh. "That was a low blow Dominic," Chester says.

"Hey, I can't help it if you're a lil tall," Dominic says. We take our eyes from off of each other, and continue walking through the mall. Five minutes later, we approach a sunglass cart store in the middle of the walkway. "Let's look at the shades," Dominic says, walking towards the sunglass cart. The cashier of the sunglass cart is sitting down at it on a stool, and I look at her odd attire-baggy sweatpants and an orange mesh University Of Florida football jersey. While we are all circled around it looking at the hooked sunglasses, I look at Dominic put on a pair of enormous black-out shades. "Let's go," Dominic says, looking at me while wearing the enormous black-out shades. "That ho"-he cranes his neck to look around- "ain't looking." I shake my head from left to right while grinning then begin walking away-Dominic follows me.

As we are walking away, Keith and Chester sees us. They walk from the other side of the sunglass cart and follow us. When we get about fifty feet away from the sunglass cart, Dominic takes the enormous black-out shades he didn't deb for off and holds them down in front of him while walking. He then sweeps back his wicks with his right hand, holds the shades back out in front of him again with both hands, then puts them on. Dominic steps out in front of us, and looks at us while walking backwards. "How you niggas like my shades?" Dominic asks, beaming at us.

CHAPTER 17

We enter the plaza and all visible places around the structure are filled with people. *Filled.* There doesn't seem to be room to breathe further ahead. Thirty minutes ago, all four of us left the mall when it closed. We left the mall, and it was 9:07 p.m. when I started driving here to The Splashdown on this crepuscular Saturday night. We made it here, got out of my car, and started walking towards the inside of The Splashdown that could be heard long before it was seen. My ears hear a busy sort of beehive sound, mingled with the lighter noises of a carnival. Chester, me, Keith, and Dominic walk further ahead while we are in the open-air section of The Splashdown. If an angry, stormy ocean could talk, it would sound like this crowd we merge into.

"I've never seen so many people in one place before," Dominic says, looking all around him while his eyes are hidden beneath the enormous black-out shades. While also walking and looking around, Chester says, "Looks like a million sugar ants around a giant honeycomb," then coughs. Chester coughed, a horrible, rattling whine. He used to be a rangy man at one time, but that was in a past he could never recover. He is a cornfield scarecrow now. I take my eyes off of Chester, look at the outside stage ahead of us, then to my right at Keith. "Who's supposed to be performi-", I start saying to Keith, before seeing past him a tall twiggy Black man walk by. The tall twiggy Black man walks past Keith, while looking dead at me with eyes that appear on the verge of pinging out. It takes me just a second to recognize Treetop.

A few seconds after I do, Treetop takes off of me his eyes that seemed to peel my mind open like a child peeling fruit, sucking it dry then discarding the husk; he takes them off of me and continues walking. Chester, Keith, and Dominic all look at me.

"Why did that nigga look at you like that?" Dominic asks. Chester says, "That's the nigga that killed Warren," to Dominic then looks back at me.

"What you wanna do?"

"You already know," I say calmly, with a voice that's low and measured. I take my eyes off of Chester, look at Treetop's back, and say, "I must follow him," as I'm starting to walk. Chester, Keith, and Dominic follow behind me. My eyes are zeroed in on Treetop's back while I say, "A child cannot go through the forest alone; he will come to some harm."

I look at Treetop's car parked in front of the Carpool gas station, while I'm sitting behind the steering wheel of my car that's parked in the parking lot of the strip club that's across the street from Carpool. Dark is the interior of my car that Chester, me, Keith, and Dominic is sitting in-Chester is sitting to the left of me in the passenger seat. While still looking forward, Chester says, "Surprised you didn't zap him right there in The Splashdown."

As I'm looking at the car across the street, I respond, "There were too many people there, some of them no doubt influential. I couldn't risk any of them getting hit by a stray laserblast." While looking across the street as he leans forward through our two front seats Keith adds, "You did the right thing by not blasting that nigga there, and following him to this Carpool gas station he stopped at." I turn to Keith, briefly look at him, then look back at Dominic. "You okay Dominic? You're quiet back there, you haven't said nothing since we've left The Splashdown." Dominic just looks at me for many long seconds. I begin to turn back around, but stop when I see him starting to speak.

"Push back and they respect you; act soft and they push harder," Dominic finally says, while looking at me with the enormous black-out shades.

"I can't act soft then," I say, right before turning back around. I look across the street, never taking my eyes off Carpool's front entrance. Ten seconds pass. Then twenty. After thirty seconds pass, I see Treetop walking out of the store. As he is I quickly slip the ski mask in my lap over my head, grip with my left hand the lasergun in my lap, then put my right hand on the door handle.

"Showtime," I say, opening my car door then jumping out. I push my car door close, switch the lasergun to my right hand, then dash to the street I must cross. I stand on the sidewalk, look from left to right, and see that I have a second or two to cross before more cars start to zoom past. Sprinting across the street is what I do, before reaching the other side's sidewalk. I dash onto it, run up under Carpool's lighted canopy that shields people from being rained upon, then from behind I near the driver's side door of Treetop's car that he just got into. As I'm sneaking up to it, Treetop begins lowering his window. I reach the window as I'm hoisting my lasergun upwards, and Treetop's eyes widen impossibly when he sees the barrel of my lasergun pointed at his head that I won't waste time squeezing a shot at.

"Take this fucker," I say, pulling the trigger. An intensely bright ray beam cuts through the fluorescent lighting and strikes Treetop in the side of the head, passing through with a weird corona of light that lights up his eyes with a deadly glow. The scream Treetop makes is deafening: a amalagam of a human scream of agony and the squealing of a pig going to slaugther, but with its volume stepped up five-fold. I wince at the hideous sound, but keep firing at Treetop. The first shot sears the side of his head. The second punches a smoking hole through his chest, the third hits his thigh, and the fourth shot seemingly hits his wrist. I stop firing, look at Treetop's jaw that has dropped slack as pink-tinged smoke pours from his nostrils and mouth, then start running like a bat out of hell back to my car.

I'm woke up out of my sleep by the sound of my doorbell ringing-Judika's here. Twenty five minutes ago, I talked to her on the phone and she asked me if she could come over. I agreed, before getting off the phone with her. Instead of me getting up to get ready, I drifted back to sleep. I drifted back to sleep on this late Sunday afternoon, because I didn't go to sleep until 2 a.m. early this morning-like a skunk in a strong wind, it's all coming back to me. I'm not one of life's natural born killers. For all the times I fantasized about killing Treetop, from that night at Blue Swallow Motel right up to last night at Carpool, I wondered if I could actually aim a lasergun at him in cold blood and pull the trigger.

Treetop deserved it. I took his life. I crawl out of my bed, light shimmers into my dimly lit bedroom through the window curtains, and start heading to the front door; a yellow t-shirt and short black pants is what I'm wearing as I do. My front doorbell rings a second time, while I'm walking down the hallway. Five seconds later, I reach the front door and open it. Before me I see the most beautiful Nubian woman I've ever seen. Judika smiles at me before I see that she's wearing a bikini-top with Aztec designing on it, a fishnet cardigan with yellow fringing, a skirt with Aztec designing and in her hand she's holding a yellow purse. "Judika, hi," I say, smiling. "Come in."

While I'm backing up to let her through, I look down at her feet. I see her red painted toenails since she's wearing sandals. Judika walks completely inside, I close my front door, then I look at her. Judika smiles sheepishly at me and says, "I'm just gonna come out and say it. Here goes. Whenever I think about you-I mean, about you separate from me-I feel like dying."

"Why? I'm nobody to die over." I chuckle. Judika walks towards me while saying, "Marshall, I'm in no mood for flippant answers," and she stops right in front of me. I give her my little boy look.

"Didn't your Mom ever warn you about people like me?"

"She did, but I really want to be with you," Judika says, like a woman accustomed to speaking to those both below and above her station. I smile at Judika, put my hand on her cheek, and start stroking it. About ten seconds later I finally build up the confidence to kiss her. I kiss her, not a short kiss of friendship but a long, searching lover's kiss. I embrace her, she embrace me, and we go around in circles as I lead her to my bedroom. Inside of my bedroom we claw at each's other's clothes until we're both naked-hopping into my king-sized bed is what we do next. We make love for a long time. After we finish making love, beads of sweat gleam like a glycerin on my forehead, I look at Judika as she's sitting up in my bed-her back is propped up against the headboard and so is mines. Sitting upright next to me, Judika says, "I'm glad that I put on a touch of perfume, something with spice but lacking any sweetness whatsoever." I nod, my expression fascinated. "Leatherwood. A scent few women can carry off."

"So I've heard." Her frown like a prosecutor's. "When's the last time you had sex?" Judika sniffs; the sharp scent of her pine-smelling perfume wafts. "That doesn't matter," I say tangentially, or so I think," because your face is one that I could stand to look at for a very long time." I stare once again into her eyes-it is like peering down a vortex. The vortex in her eyes reveals to me a level I can't help but suspect she conceals from most other acquaintes, a level possessing a modicum of vulnerability and uncertainty, not to mention a need to find someone she could trust. For some reason, I divine, she has selected me for the job. "Is that so?" Judika says, fluffing the pillow. I say, "That's so."

"You have a few skeletons in your closet," says Judika.

It's a flat statement, neither accusatory or questioning, like a clerk court reading a charge.

"But I want to save you-a big, hairy chested hero has saved me and I'm going to save him. That's why I want us to work side by side, and you teach me how to see the flow in things, the way you do. Eddy's a growing town, and we can grow with it. We can live as though we were in Eden: Me, you, and Anyanwu." I frame Judika's face between my hands. "You're terrific, you know that?"

"Does that mean that I don't have to worry about you with those mysterious Eastern women?" I pretend to ponder it.

"Do you know how to belly dance?" Judika socks me in the arm. "That would be a sight to see, with the belly I'm going to have soon."

EPILOGUE

Yesterday around this time, Judika and I were holding on to each other, in my king-sized bed, after we made love that filmed our naked bodies with sweat. The sweat on each of our bodies was the aftermath of afternoon delight, and we were in that half world between satiation and sleep. While we were in that half world between satiation and sleep yesterday, Judika told me that Anyanwu was having a play today. She said that she'd like for me to come to it, and I told her I would. So here I am standing with Judika at the foot of the stage inside of the auditorium at Eddy Elementary School. When Judika looks up at the stage, I pull an earpiece from my pocket. The *Bluetooth* is the earpiece that I pull out of my pocket, and it is talked on like a cellphone as it is clipped to my ear-it looks like an earring with a chip on it. I clip the *Bluetooth* to my left ear. Judika looks back at me.

"Marshall, should I be aware of some sort of lifestyle change?" I crack a weak smile at Judika-she is dressed in a simple, sleeveless brown dress and a pair of gold hoop earrings that does wonders against her slender ebony look. Anyanwu's play is a semiformal occassion, although Judika looked nearly as good in those zebra printed shorts that I saw her wearing when she came back to my house on the first day that I met her.

"This right here is a *Bluetooth*"-I point to the ear it's clipped on-"and I have to call the day care again to see if Chamiqua picked up Jumanji yet."

"Oooh," Judika coos.

"After you get off of it, can I use it? I wanna call my Dad." I look skeptically at Judika.

"Why you wanna call him?" Judika says, oddly reluctantly,

"My Dad needs a little helping out. The last woman he was with cuckold, and ever since they've divorced, I've been doing the things that the woman he's with now should be doing. She's a junkie who doesn't like to clean and she'd rather buy dope than what's needed; I have to call my Dad and see if he needs me to bring some toiletries." I control my brows. That was the first time I've heard Judika say one word about either of her parents.

"Why are you buying them toiletries?" I ask.

"You know those funky people don't use them." A smiling Judika socks me in the arm.

"You don't even know what a toiletry is."

"Yes I do," I say.

"A toiletry is any article, as soap, cologne, or a comb used in dressing or completing one's toilet."

"I'm impressed," Judika says sarcastically.

"You should be," I say, looking around the back of her.

"So, you clean for your Dad?"

"Yes," Judika says.

"And I wear those yellow latex gloves with an unusual grain while I'm scrubbing their toilet." Judika holds both hands out above her stomach, palms down, as is she's imagining those gloves on her own hands.

"They're really *immaculate* gloves." Right when Judika finishes talking, the lights in the not-so crowded auditorium dims. I say not-so crowded but there is a lot of people here-the auditorium is so large that no student concert or play could filt it, which gives productions a melancholy air of failure. That's the last thing I want this play to be. I don't want it to be a failure, since Judika's daugther is in it. I remember Anyanwu telling me about this play she was gonna be in while riding with me to that Ice Cream Parlor; the one we went to about two weeks ago. Anyanwu seemed excited as she told me the rehearsals she had, her co-actors, and the plot of the play. I told Anyanwu that I'd have to come to her play and see it, and Anyanwu must have told her Mom that I said that.

"The play is about to begin," Judika says, looking at me in the dim light.

"What's the name of it again?" I ask.

"*The Frogs*," Judika says.

"It's a comedy wrote by a Greek playwright named Aristophanes, and it was first performed in January 405 B.C."

"I let out a low whistle." We're in the thirty third century so that was over thirty three thousand years ago. What is this play-*The Frogs*-about?" Judika looks towards the stage then back at me.

"Anyanwu doesn't make an appearance in the play until the end, so we can miss this part while I explain to you what it's about. The plot of the play is a parody of two traditional myths. One tells how Hercules, in the last of his twelve labors, brought up Cerebus-the guardian dog of the Greek underworld, Hades-from the lower world and along the way freed Thesus."

"I've heard of him," I say. "He was mentioned in that book I had to read in college; Thesus was that hero in Greek mythology who killed a minotaur and conquered the Amazons."

"You're right," Judika says. "He was also the legendary founder of united Athens. The other tells how the Greek god of wine and ectacsy-Dionysus-rescued his Mother from the land of the dead." Judika stops talking, and looks at me with futurity on her face.

"Are those really the two myths that this play is based on?" I ask, smiling.

"Because those two myths weirdly relate to us; I'm the Hercules that brought up the dog from the underworld and also freed that hero from it-and you're the Mother that was rescued from the land of the dead by the Greek god of wine and ecstasy: You drunk so much yesterday that I thought I was having sex with a alky." Judika lightly nudges me.

"Marshall! Of course those really are the two myths this play is based on." "Just checking," I say.

"In Eddy Elementary's version of *The Frogs*," Judika continues, "Dionysus descends to the underworld to resurrect a writer of tragedy plays. He goes down to the underworld to resurrect Euripides, after Hercules gives him advice to do so; Hercules is played by one of my students; Dionysus is played by a fourth grader, and Euripides is played by a kid I taught last year."

Judika looks vicariously at me-"Will you let me teach you?"

"Do you think I could stop you," I reply quickly. Judika smiles.

"That's no answer," she says, "even if it's true. Anyway, Euripides has recently died in the play and Hercules is going to the underworld to raise him from the dead. When he gets there he must cross a marsh that borders the underworld, and while crossing it the god of stength hears a chorus of frogs. He hears a chorus of frogs repeatedly croaking 'Brekekekex, ke-ex, ke-ex'. That scene in the play"-Judika looks at the stage then back at me-" is coming up soon, and it illustrates why the play is named *The Frogs*. When Dionysus enters the land of the dead, he witnesses a contest in poetry between the older playwright Aeschylus and Euripides; Euripides challenged the older playwright's claim to the throne in Plato's court. In a sense, the debate between the two of them is the earliest extensive passage of literary criticism since the writer of *The Frogs*-Aristophanes-satires the pomposity of Aeschylus' style and triviality of Euripides'. Aeschylus' style is pompous and Euripides' is trivial, but Dionysus makes his choice of who to resurrect on purely ethical grounds-in the end, he chooses Aeschylus to return to life so that his moral teaching may revive and regenerate the failing society of Athens." I frown at Judika.

"Thanks, you just gave away the end of the play." Judika says,

"I'm sorry, it's just that when I get to talking it's hard for me to stop." I look at the stage.

"When does Anyanwu's part begins?" Judika says, "Here she comes right now." I squint and see three kid-sized trees waddling onto the stage. The kid-sized trees each have a hole cut in the trunk of them, and inside of the holes I see the face of a kid-two of the faces that I see are Black and the other one is White. While still looking at the stage I ask Judika,

"Which one's Anyanwu?"

"The tree in the middle," Judika says, pointing at it. I look at the tree in between the two other trees and see it along with the other two stop, after all three of them get into a position on the stage where I can clearly see their faces poking out of the holes cut out in the trunk of their tree costumes-I look at the face poking out of the trunk of the middle tree, and see Anyanwu's cute brown face.

"What are their tree costumes made out of?" I ask Judika, looking at the stage. "Papier-mache," Judika says.

"I helped make their tree costumes." I glance at the other trees on each side of Anyanwu. Just like Anyanwu's, their costumes are three-pronged. I guess they slipped the papier-mache tree costumes over their heads, encasing their arms into two green pom-pom looking "leaves"-I see the faces in their tree's trunk hole and above them is a green head of "leaves" in a full evenly rounded shape. Looking at the sizes of the trees causes me to think of infant trees, and the young Dutch girl's remark when she referred to Sequoia as a infant city, cities are also made up of lots of metal, begins to make some kind of sense. Less than a minute after Anyanwu appeared on the stage, I turn to Judika. I say,

"Let me take a wild guess. Anyanwu's dressed up as that tree."-I nod at her on the stage- "So she doesn't have any lines in this scene." Judika nods.

"Or the entire play." "Fudge," I say, sweeping my right arm and snapping my right hand fingers at the same time. Judika laughs lightly.

"That's what I said after finding out she didn't-but I'm not the casting or play director so I couldn't have changed it. That's okay because my baby's going to be something better than an actress." I wait for Judika to say what. Five seconds pass. Then ten. When fifteen seconds passes without her telling me, I see that I'm gonna have to ask.

"What's she's going to be" I ask.

"An engineer," Judika says. "She told you she wanted to be that?" I ask. "Not exactly," Judika says.

"The other day, she asked me what an engineer is. I hope from her asking me what an engineer is that she wants to be one."

"Maybe," I say.

"What did you tell her?"

"I told her," Judika explains, "that an engineer is a person who designs and builds machines. It's impossible for us to imagine an age without robots-but every machine in the world had to be invented at one time or the other." I say,

"You're right," then look back at the stage. I see Anyanwu, and the two other trees flanking her, still standing in one place. Minutes pass by as Judika and I watch the play. While we are watching the play unfolding before our eyes, I glance at Anyanwu. She is doing a good job playing as a tree-I see no movement from her. I wonder if she's sweating and starting to feel uncomfortable in the papier-mache armor she's wearing; standing in one place for somebody her age might be tiring. I look at the two kids on each side of Anyanwu-they'd be tiring now, too. That is the trouble with armor. The protection it provides comes at too high of a cost. Most of the cost I'll have to deb has to do with Sequoia, and my fear that even if I do fight against evil,

I'd still be wearing a being conceived outside of thy divine grace. Maybe it's best for all concerned, but if I really cared what was best I wouldn't be here in the first place.

Judika says, "I was reading that book on your coffee table yesterday-*The Other Side Of Suffering*-and there was a picture of a very young JonBenet Ramsey being embraced by her older brother, Burke. To me, he looked to be about four-years-old in that picture of him holding on to his little sister who was wearing diapers and a 101 Dalmations pajama set. Her father wrote that Burke and her were close and 'She could climb trees like any boy in the neighborhood'."

"I remember reading that," I say. Judika says,

"I just thought I'd bring that up." We both turn back to the stage, and see the three little kids wearing tree costumes wobbling off of the stage.

"Judika, are those shittah trees?" I whisper, almost afraid that any sound from my throat would be tantamount to a curse.

"No, they're not those trees found in the Bible," Judika says promisingly.

"They're not based on no kind actually-we just made regular looking trees." Judika takes her eyes off of me, looks at the stage, and I do the same. We silently watch the play, and about fifteen minutes later it ends when all the children cast members of *The Frogs* walk onto the stage-the children on the stage all take a bow, and seconds later the auditorium lights come on.

"Here comes Anyanwu!" Judika says, following her daugther with a gaze. I look to where Judika is looking and I see dashing towards us the six-year-old Black girl with a helmet in her hands. Judika kneels down and holds her arms out. "You did great Anyanwu!" Anyanwu runs into Judika's arms. Judika embraces her and gives her a kiss on the side of her head. After she does that, Anyanwu is released.

"What you got there?" Judika says, beginning to stand up.

"Andy's knight helmet!" Anyanwu says.

"She gave it to me backstage!" I look down at Anyanwu and say,

"Andy was wearing that knight helmet during the play. That's a nice looking stage prop." A smiling Anyanwu looks up at me.

"I'll tell her you said so. Mrs. Denslow said we're getting pizza, all kinds of soda, and- "-the girl gives a strangely adult shrug-" potato chips, I'm about to go get some!" Anyanwu hands Judika the knight helmet with a neck flare and dashes away. Judika smiles at Anyanwu's retreating back, then looks at me more seriously.

"When my Dad had his act together and took care of his kids, we made model gliders together. Two things were required to get them to fly. First we had to give them a running start. Then we had to let them go."-Judika looks at me with lugbriousness-

"Learning just when to let go was the hardest part." I take Judika in my arms and feel not merely content, but supernally happy.

"I believe she'll soar high Judika." After we are embraced for about ten seconds, Judika starts to pull away. While I'm releasing her, I reach for the knight helmet with a neck flare in her hands. She hands it over to me, I put it on, and she smiles at me.

"Okay," Judika says, "but I don't want her to soar too high."

"Don't worry, I'll make sure she won't." I fold my arms over my broad chest and punctuate my resolution with an abrupt nod which causes the eyeslit visor to fall. I look comical, but steadfast.